Mary Balogh is [illegible] hor. A former teacher, she grew up in Wales and now lives in Canada.

Also by Mary Balogh

Mistress Couplet:

No Man's Mistress
More than a Mistress

The Secret Mistress (prequel to the Mistress Couplet)

Huxtables Series:

First Comes Marriage
Then Comes Seduction
At Last Comes Love
Seducing an Angel
A Secret Affair

Simply Quartet:

Simply Unforgettable
Simply Love
Simply Magic
Simply Perfect

Bedwyn Series:

One Night for Love
A Summer to Remember
Slightly Married
Slightly Wicked
Slightly Scandalous
Slightly Tempted
Slightly Sinful
Slightly Dangerous

The Proposal

Mary Balogh

piatkus

PIATKUS

First published in the US in 2012 by Delacorte Press
an imprint of the Random House Publishing Group,
a division of Random House, Inc., New York, USA
First published in Great Britain in 2012 as a paperback original by Piatkus
Published by arrangement with the Bantam Dell Publishing Group
Reprinted 2012

A CIP catalogue record for this book
is available from the British Library.

ISBN 978-0-7499-5603-5

Printed and bound by CPI Group (UK) Ltd, Croydon, CR0 4YY

Papers used by Piatkus are from well-managed forests
and other responsible sources.

MIX
Paper from
responsible sources
FSC® C104740

Piatkus
An imprint of
Little, Brown Book Group
100 Victoria Embankment
London EC4Y 0DY

An Hachette UK Company
www.hachette.co.uk

www.piatkus.co.uk

Prologue

The Survivors' Club

The weather could have been better. Low clouds scudded across the sky, blown along by a brisk wind, and rain that had been threatening all day had started to fall. The sea was rough and metal gray. A chill dampness penetrated even to the interior of the carriage, making its sole occupant glad of his heavy greatcoat.

His spirits were not to be dampened, however, even though he would have preferred sunshine. He was on his way to Penderris Hall in Cornwall, country seat of George Crabbe, Duke of Stanbrook. His Grace was one of the six people he loved most in the world, a strange admission, perhaps, when five of those people were men. They were the six people he *trusted* most in the world, then, though *trust* seemed too impersonal a word and there was nothing impersonal about his feelings for these friends. They were all going to be at Penderris for the next three weeks or so.

They were a group of survivors of the Napoleonic Wars, five of them former military officers who had been incapacitated by various wounds and sent home to England to recuperate. All of them had come to the attention of the Duke of Stanbrook, who had borne them off to Penderris Hall for treatment, rest, and convalescence. The duke had been past the age of fighting in the wars himself, but his only son had not been. He had both fought and died in the Peninsula during the early years of the campaign there. The seventh member of the club was the widow of a surveillance officer who had been captured by the enemy in the Peninsula and died under torture, which had been conducted at least partially in her presence. The duke was a distant cousin of hers and had taken her in after her return to England.

They had formed a close bond, the seven of them, during the lengthy period of their healing and convalescence. And because for various reasons they would all bear the mark of their wounds and war experiences for the rest of their lives, they had agreed that when the time came for them to return to their own separate lives beyond the safe confines of Penderris, they would return for a few weeks each year in order to relax and renew their friendship, to discuss their progress, and to offer one another support in any difficulty that might have arisen.

They were all survivors and strong enough to live independent lives. But they were also all permanently scarred in one way or another, and they did not have to hide that fact when they were together.

One of their number had once dubbed them the Survivors' Club, and the name had stuck, even if only among themselves.

Hugo Emes, Lord Trentham, peered as best he could through the rain that was now pelting against the carriage window. He could see the edge of the high cliffs not too far distant and the sea beyond them, a line of foam-flecked gray darker than the sky. He was on Penderris land already. He would be at the house within minutes.

Leaving here three years ago had been one of the hardest things any of them had ever done. Hugo would have been happy to spend the rest of his life here. But of course, life was forever changing and it had been time to leave.

And now it was time for change again . . .

But he would not think of that yet.

This was the third reunion, though Hugo had been forced to miss last year's. He had not seen any of these friends for two years, then.

The carriage drew to a halt at the foot of the steps leading up to the massive front doors of Penderris Hall and rocked for a few moments on its springs. Hugo wondered if any of the others had arrived yet. He felt like a child arriving for a party, he thought in some disgust, all eager anticipation and nervously fluttering stomach.

The doors of the house opened and the duke himself stepped between them. He proceeded down the steps despite the rain and reached the foot of them as the coachman opened the carriage door and Hugo vaulted out without waiting for the steps to be put down.

"George," he said.

He was not the sort of man who normally hugged other people or even touched them unnecessarily. But it might very well have been he who initiated the tight hug in which they were both soon enveloped.

"Goodness me," the duke said, loosening his hold after a few moments and taking a step back in order to look Hugo over. "You have not shrunk in two years, Hugo, have you? In either height or breadth. You are one of the few people who can make me feel small. Come inside out of the rain and I shall check my ribs to discover how many you have crushed."

He was not the first to arrive, Hugo saw as soon as they were inside the great hall. Flavian was there to greet him—Flavian Arnott, Viscount Ponsonby. And Ralph was there too—Ralph Stockwood, Earl of Berwick.

"Hugo," Flavian said, raising a quizzing glass to his eye and affecting bored languor. "You big ugly bear. It is surprisingly g-good to see you."

"Flavian, you slight, beautiful boy," Hugo said, striding toward him, his boot heels ringing on the tiled floor, "it is good to see *you,* and I am not even surprised about it."

They wrapped their arms about each other and slapped each other's back.

"Hugo," Ralph said, "it feels like just yesterday that we saw you last. You look the same as ever. Even your hair still looks like a freshly shorn sheep."

"And that scar across your face still makes you look like someone I would not want to meet in a dark alley, Ralph," Hugo said as the two of them came together and hugged. "Are the others not here yet?"

But even as he spoke he could see over Ralph's shoulder that Imogen was coming downstairs—Imogen Hayes, Lady Barclay.

"Hugo," she said as she hurried toward him, both hands extended. "Oh, Hugo."

She was tall and slender and graceful. Her dark blond hair was dressed in a chignon at the back of her head, but the very severity of the style merely emphasized the perfect beauty of her rather long, Nordic face with its high cheekbones, wide, generous mouth, and large blue-green eyes. It also emphasized the almost marble impassivity of that face. *That* had not changed from two years ago.

"Imogen." He squeezed her hands and then drew her into a close embrace. He breathed in the familiar scent of her. He kissed one of her cheeks and looked down at her.

She raised one hand and traced a line between his eyebrows with the tip of her forefinger.

"You still frown," she said.

"He still *scowls,*" Ralph said. "Dash it, but we missed you last year, Hugo. Flavian had no one to call ugly. He tried it on me once, but I persuaded him not to repeat the experiment."

"He had me mortally t-terrified, Hugo," Flavian said. "I wished you were here to hide behind. I hid behind Imogen instead."

"To answer your earlier question, Hugo," the duke said, clapping a hand on his shoulder, "you are the last to arrive and we have been all impatience. Ben would have come down to greet you, but it would have taken him rather too long to get down the stairs only to have to go up them again almost immediately. Vincent stayed in the drawing room with him. Come on up. You can go to your room later."

"I ordered the tea tray as soon as Vincent heard your carriage approaching," Imogen said, "but doubtless I will be the only one drinking from the pot. It is what I get for allying myself with a horde of barbarians."

"Actually," Hugo said, "a cup of hot tea sounds like just the thing, Imogen. I hope you have ordered better weather for tomorrow and the next few weeks, George."

"It is only March," the duke pointed out as they made their way upstairs. "But if you insist, Hugo, sunshine it will be for the rest of your stay here. Some people *look* rugged but are mere hothouse plants in reality."

Sir Benedict Harper was on his feet when they entered the drawing room. He was leaning on his canes, but his full weight was not on them. And he actually walked toward Hugo. So much for those experts who had called him fool for refusing to have his crushed legs amputated after his horse had been shot from under him. He had sworn he would walk again, and he was doing just that, after a fashion.

"Hugo," he said, "you are a sight for sore eyes. Have you doubled in size, or is it just the effect of the greatcoat?"

"He is a sight to *cause* sore eyes, certainly," Flavian said with a sigh. "And no one told Hugo that multiple capes on a greatcoat were designed for the benefit of those underendowed in the shoulder department."

"Ben," Hugo said and caught the other man carefully in his arms. "On your feet, are you? You have to be the most stubborn man I have ever known."

"I believe you could give me some stiff competition," Ben said.

Hugo turned to the seventh member of the Survivors' Club and the youngest. He was standing close to the window, his fair curls as overlong and unruly as ever, his face as open and good-humored, even angelic. He was smiling now.

"Vince," Hugo said as he advanced across the room.

Vincent Hunt, Lord Darleigh, looked directly at him with eyes as large and blue as Hugo remembered them—lady-killer eyes, Flavian had once called them in order to draw a laugh out of the boy. Hugo always found his accurate gaze a little disconcerting.

For Vincent was blind.

"Hugo," he said as he was caught up in a hug. "How good it is to hear your voice again. And to have you back with us this year. If you had been here last year, you would not have allowed everyone else to make fun of my violin playing, would you? Well, everyone except Imogen, anyway."

There was a collective groan from behind them.

"You play the violin?" Hugo asked.

"I do, and of course you would not have allowed the ridicule," Vincent said, grinning. "They tell me you look like a large and fierce warrior, Hugo, but if you do, then you are a fraud, for I can always hear the gentleness beneath the gruffness of your voice. You shall listen to me play this year, and you will not laugh."

"He may well weep, Vince," Ralph said.

"I have been known to have that effect upon my listeners," Vincent said, laughing.

Hugo removed his coat and tossed it over the back of a chair before sitting down with everyone else. They all drank tea despite the duke's offer of something stronger.

"We were very sorry not to see you last year, Hugo," he said after they had chatted for a while. "We were even sorrier about the reason for your absence."

"I was all ready to come here," Hugo said, "when word of my father's heart seizure reached me. So I was prepared to leave almost immediately, and I arrived before he died. I was even able to speak with him. I ought to have done it sooner. There was no real need of the near estrangement between us, even though I broke his heart after I insisted that he purchase a commission for me, when all my life he had expected that I would follow him into the family business. He loved me to the end, you know. I suppose I will always be thankful that I arrived in time to tell him that I loved him too, though it might have seemed that words came cheap."

Imogen, who was seated beside him on a love seat, patted his hand.

"He would have understood," she said. "People *do* understand the language of the heart, you know, even if the head does not always comprehend it."

They all looked at her for a silent moment, including Vincent.

"He left a small fortune to Fiona, my stepmother," Hugo said, "and a large dowry to Constance, my half sister. But he left the bulk of his vast business and trading empire to me. I am indecently wealthy."

He frowned. The wealth sometimes felt like something of a millstone about his neck. But the obligation it had brought with it was worse.

"Poor, poor Hugo," Flavian said, pulling a linen handkerchief from a pocket and dabbing his eyes with it. "My heart bleeds for you."

"He expected me to take over the running of the businesses," Hugo said. "Not that he demanded it. He just *expected* that it was what I would want, and his face glowed with pleasure at the prospect even though he was dying. And he spoke of my passing it all on to *my* son when the time comes."

Imogen patted his hand again and poured him another cup of tea.

"The thing is," Hugo said, "that I have been happy with my quiet life in the country. I was happy in my cottage for two years, and I have been happy at Crosslands Park for the past year—though, of course, it was bought with some of my newfound wealth. I have been able to excuse my procrastination by telling myself that this is a year of mourning and it would be unseemly to rush into action as though all I ever wanted was his fortune. But the anniversary of his death is tomorrow. I have no further excuse."

"We have always told you, Hugo," Vincent said, "that being a recluse is not really suited to your nature."

"More specifically," Ben said, "we have compared you to an unexploded firecracker, Hugo, just waiting for a spark to ignite it."

Hugo sighed.

"I like my life as it is," he said.

"So the fact that you were given your title as a reward for extraordinary valor is to mean nothing after all?" Ralph asked. "You are planning to return to your middle-class roots, Hugo?"

Hugo frowned again.

"I never left them," he said. "I have never *wanted* to be a member of the upper classes. I would despise them all collectively, as my father always did, if it were not for the six of you. Purchasing Crosslands might have seemed a bit pretentious, but I wanted my own little bit of the country in which to be at peace. That's all."

"And it will always be there for you," the duke said. "It will be a quiet retreat when the press of business is getting you down."

"It's the *son* part that is getting me down now," Hugo said. "He would have to be legitimate, wouldn't he? I would have to have a *wife* in order to produce him. That's what is facing me after I leave here. I have decided. I have to find a wife. Perish the thought. Pardon me, Imogen. I have nothing whatsoever against women. I just don't really want one permanently in my life. Or in my home."

"You are not looking for romance or romantic love, then, Hugo?" Flavian asked. "That is very wise of you, old chap. Love is the very d-devil and to be avoided as one would the plague."

The lady to whom Flavian had been betrothed when he went to war had broken off their engagement when she found herself unable to cope with the wounds he brought home from the Peninsula. Within two months she had married someone else, a man he had once considered his best friend.

"Do you have anyone in mind, Hugo?" the duke asked.

"Not really." Hugo sighed. "I have an army of female cousins and aunts who would be only too delighted to present me with a parade of possibilities if I were to say the word, even though I have neglected them all shamefully for years. But I would feel out of control from the first moment. I would hate that. Actually, I was hoping someone here would have some advice for me. On how to go about finding a wife, that is."

That silenced them all.

"It is actually quite simple, Hugo," Ralph said at last. "You approach the first reasonably personable woman you see, tell her that you are a lord and indecently wealthy to boot, and ask her if she would fancy marrying you. Then you stand back and watch her trip all over her tongue in her eagerness to say yes."

The others laughed.

"It is that easy, is it?" Hugo said. "What a huge relief. I shall go down onto the beach tomorrow, then, weather permitting, and wait for reasonably personable women to hove by. My problem will be solved even before I leave Penderris."

"Oh, not *women,* Hugo," Ben said. "Not *plural.* They will be fighting over you, and there is much to fight over, even apart from your title and wealth. Go down to the beach and find *one* woman. We will make it easy for you and stay away from there all day. For me, of course, that will be simple, since I do not have a decent pair of legs with which to get down there anyway."

"Now that we have your future satisfactorily settled, Hugo," the duke said, getting to his feet, "we will allow you to go to your room to freshen up and change and perhaps rest before dinner. We will, however, discuss the matter more seriously during the coming days. Perhaps we will even be able to suggest some practical course of action. In the meanwhile, let me just say how very splendid it is to have the Survivors' Club all together again this year. I have longed for this moment."

Hugo gathered up his greatcoat and left the room with the duke, feeling all the seductive comfort and pleasure of being back at Penderris in company with the six people who meant most to him in the world.

Even the rain pattering against the windowpanes only served to add a feeling of coziness.

Chapter 1

Gwendoline Grayson, Lady Muir, hunched her shoulders and drew her cloak more snugly about her. It was a brisk, blustery March day, made chillier by the fact that she was standing down at the fishing harbor below the village where she was staying. It was low tide, and a number of fishing boats lay half keeled over on the wet sand, waiting for the water to return and float them upright again.

She should go back to the house. She had been out for longer than an hour, and part of her longed for the warmth of a fire and the comfort of a steaming cup of tea. Unfortunately, though, Vera Parkinson's home was not hers, only the house where she was staying for a month. And she and Vera had just quarreled—or at least, Vera had quarreled with *her* and upset her. She was not ready to go back yet. She would rather endure the elements.

She could not walk to her left. A jutting headland barred her way. To the right, though, a pebbled beach beneath high cliffs stretched into the distance. It would be several hours yet before the tide came up high enough to cover it.

Gwen usually avoided walking down by the water, even though she lived close to the sea herself at the dower house of Newbury Abbey in Dorsetshire. She found beaches too vast, cliffs too threatening, the sea too elemental. She preferred a smaller, more ordered world, over which she could exert some semblance of control—a carefully cultivated flower garden, for example.

But today she needed to be away from Vera for a while longer, and from the village and country lanes where she might run into

Vera's neighbors and feel obliged to engage in cheerful conversation. She needed to be alone, and the pebbled beach was deserted for as far into the distance as she could see before it curved inland. She stepped down onto it.

She realized after a very short distance, however, why no one else was walking here. For though most of the pebbles were ancient and had been worn smooth and rounded by thousands of tides, a significant number of them were of more recent date, and they were larger, rougher, more jagged. Walking across them was not easy and would not have been even if she had had two sound legs. As it was, her right leg had never healed properly from a break eight years ago, when she had been thrown from her horse. She walked with a habitual limp even on level ground.

She did not turn back, though. She trudged stubbornly onward, careful where she set her feet. She was not in any great hurry to get anywhere, after all.

This had really been the most horrid day of a horrid fortnight. She had come for a month-long visit, entirely from impulse, when Vera had written to inform her of the sad passing a couple of months earlier of her husband, who had been ailing for several years. Vera had added the complaint that no one in either Mr. Parkinson's family or her own was paying any attention whatsoever to her suffering despite the fact that she was almost prostrate with grief and exhaustion after nursing him for so long. She was missing him dreadfully. Would Gwen care to come?

They had been friends of a sort for a brief few months during the whirlwind of their come-out Season in London and had exchanged infrequent letters after Vera's marriage to Mr. Parkinson, a younger brother of Sir Roger Parkinson, and Gwen's to Viscount Muir. Vera had written a long letter of sympathy after Vernon's death, and had invited Gwen to come and stay with her and Mr. Parkinson for as long as she wished since Vera was neglected by almost everyone, including Mr. Parkinson himself, and would welcome her company. Gwen had declined the invitation then, but she had responded to Vera's plea on this occasion despite a few misgivings. She knew what grief and exhaustion and loneliness after the death of a spouse felt like.

It was a decision she had regretted almost from the first day. Vera, as her letters had suggested, was a moaner and whiner, and while Gwen tried to make allowances for the fact that she had tended a sick husband for a few years and had just lost him, she soon came to the conclusion that the years since their come-out had soured Vera and made her permanently disagreeable. Most of her neighbors avoided her whenever possible. Her only friends were a group of ladies who much resembled her in character. Sitting and listening to their conversation felt very like being sucked into a black hole and deprived of enough air to breathe, Gwen had been finding. They knew only how to see what was wrong in their lives and in the world and never what was right.

And that was precisely what *she* was doing now when thinking of them, Gwen realized with a mental shake of the head. Negativity could be frighteningly contagious.

Even before this morning she had been wishing that she had not committed herself to such a long visit. Two weeks would have been quite sufficient—she would actually be going home by now. But she had agreed to a month, and a month it would have to be. This morning, however, her stoicism had been put to the test.

She had received a letter from her mother, who lived at the dower house with her, and in it her mother had recounted a few amusing anecdotes involving Sylvie and Leo, Neville and Lily's elder children—Neville, Earl of Kilbourne, was Gwen's brother and lived at Newbury Abbey itself. Gwen read that part of the letter aloud to Vera at the breakfast table in the hope of coaxing a smile or a chuckle from her. Instead, she had found herself at the receiving end of a petulant tirade, the basic thrust of which was that it was very easy for Gwen to laugh at and make light of her suffering when Gwen's husband had died years ago and left her very comfortably well off, and when she had had a brother and mother both willing and eager to receive her back into the family fold, and when her sensibilities did not run very deep anyway. It was easy to be callous and cruel when she had married for money and status instead of love. Everyone had *known* that truth about her during the spring of their come-out, just as everyone had known that she, Vera, had married beneath her because she and Mr. Parkinson had loved each other to distraction and nothing else had mattered.

Gwen had stared mutely back at her friend when she finally fell silent apart from some wrenching sobs into her handkerchief. She dared not open her mouth. She might have given the tirade right back and thereby have reduced herself to the level of Vera's own spitefulness. She would not be drawn into an unseemly scrap. But she almost vibrated with anger. And she was deeply hurt.

"I am going out for a walk, Vera," she had said at last, getting to her feet and pushing back her chair. "When I return, you may inform me whether you wish me to remain here for another two weeks, as planned, or whether you would prefer that I return to Newbury without further delay."

She would have to go by post or the public stagecoach. It would take the best part of a week for Neville's carriage to come for her, after she wrote to inform him that she needed it earlier than planned.

Vera had wept harder and begged her not to be cruel, but Gwen had come out anyway.

She would be perfectly happy, she thought now, if she *never* returned to Vera's house. What a dreadful mistake it had been to come, and for a whole month, on the strength of a very brief and long-ago acquaintance.

Eventually she rounded the headland she had seen from the harbor and discovered that the beach, wider here, stretched onward, seemingly to infinity, and that in the near distance the stones gave way to sand, which would be far easier to walk along. However, she must not go *too* far. Although the tide was still out, she could see that it was definitely on the way in, and in some very flat places it could rush in far faster than one anticipated. She had lived close to the sea long enough to know that. Besides, she could not stay away from Vera's forever, though she wished she could. She must return soon.

Close by there was a gap in the cliffs, and it looked possible to get up onto the headland high above if one was willing to climb a steep slope of pebbles and then a slightly more gradual slope of scrubby grass. If she could just get up there, she would be able to walk back to the village along the top instead of having to pick her way back across these very tricky stones.

Her weak leg was aching a bit, she realized. She had been foolish to come so far.

She stood still for a moment and looked out to the still-distant line of the incoming tide. And she was hit suddenly and quite unexpectedly, not by a wave of water, but by a tidal wave of loneliness, one that washed over her and deprived her of both breath and the will to resist.

Loneliness?

She never thought of herself as lonely. She had lived through a tumultuous marriage but, once the rawness of her grief over Vernon's death had receded, she had settled in to a life of peace and contentment with her family. She had never felt any urge to remarry, though she was not a cynic about marriage. Her brother was happily married. So was Lauren, her cousin by marriage who felt really more like a sister, since they had grown up together at Newbury Abbey. Gwen, however, was perfectly contented to remain a widow and to define herself as a daughter, a sister, a sister-in-law, a cousin, an aunt. She had numerous other relatives too, and friends. She was comfortable at the dower house, which was just a short walk from the abbey, where she was always welcome. She paid frequent visits to Lauren and Kit in Hampshire, and occasional ones to other relatives. She usually spent a month or two of the spring in London to enjoy part of the Season.

She always considered that she lived a blessed life.

So where had this sudden loneliness come from? And such a tidal wave of it that her knees felt weak and it seemed as though she had been robbed of breath. Why could she feel the rawness of tears in her throat?

Loneliness?

She was not lonely, only depressed at being stuck here with Vera. And hurt at what Vera had said about her and her lack of sensibilities. She was feeling sorry for herself, that was all. She *never* felt sorry for herself. Well, almost never. And when she did, then she quickly did something about it. Life was too short to be moped away. There was always much over which to rejoice.

But *loneliness*. How long had it been lying in wait for her, just waiting to pounce? Was her life really as empty as it seemed at this moment of almost frightening insight? As empty as this vast, bleak beach?

Ah, she *hated* beaches.

Gwen gave her head another mental shake and looked, first back the way she had come, and then up the beach to the steep path between the cliffs. Which should she take? She hesitated for a few moments and then decided upon the climb. It did not look quite steep enough to be dangerous, and once up it, she would surely be able to find an easy route back to the village.

The stones on the slope were no easier underfoot than those on the beach had been; in fact, they were more treacherous, for they shifted and slid beneath her feet as she climbed higher. By the time she was halfway up, she wished she had stayed on the beach, but it would be as difficult now to go back down as it was to continue upward. And she could see the grassy part of the slope not too far distant. She climbed doggedly onward.

And then disaster struck.

Her right foot pressed downward upon a sturdy looking stone, but it was loosely packed against those below it and her foot slid sharply downward until she landed rather painfully on her knee, while her hands spread to steady herself against the slope. For the fraction of a moment she felt only relief that she had saved herself from tumbling to the beach below. And then she felt the sharp, stabbing pain in her ankle.

Gingerly she raised herself to her left foot and tried to set the right foot down beside it. But she was engulfed in pain as soon as she tried to put some weight upon it—and even when she did not, for that matter. She exhaled a loud "Ohh!" of distress and turned carefully about so that she could sit on the stones, facing downward toward the beach. The slope looked far steeper from up here. Oh, she had been very foolish to try the climb.

She raised her knees, planted her left foot as firmly as she could, and grasped her right ankle in both hands. She tried rotating the foot slowly, her forehead coming to rest on her raised knee as she did so. It was a momentary sprain, she told herself, and would be fine in a moment. There was no need to panic.

But even without setting the foot down again, she knew she was deceiving herself. It was a bad sprain. Perhaps worse. She could not possibly walk.

And so panic came despite her effort to remain calm. However was she going to get back to the village? And no one knew where she was. The beach below her and the headland above were both deserted.

She drew a few steadying breaths. There was no point whatsoever in going to pieces. She would manage. Of course she would. She had no choice, did she?

It was at that moment that a voice spoke—a male voice from close by. It was not even raised.

"In my considered opinion," the voice said, "that ankle is either badly sprained or actually broken. Either way it would be very unwise to try putting any weight on it."

Gwen's head jerked up, and she looked about her to locate the source of the voice. To her right a man rose into sight partway up the steep cliff face beside the slope. He climbed down onto the pebbles and strode across them toward her as if there were no danger whatsoever of slipping.

He was a great giant of a man with broad shoulders and chest and powerful thighs. His five-caped greatcoat gave the impression of even greater bulk. He looked quite menacingly large, in fact. He wore no hat. His brown hair was cropped close to his head. His features were strong and harsh, his eyes dark and fierce, his mouth a straight, severe line, his jaw hard set. And his expression did nothing to soften his looks. He was frowning—or scowling, perhaps.

His gloveless hands were huge.

Terror engulfed Gwen and made her almost forget her pain for a moment.

He must be the Duke of Stanbrook. She must have strayed onto his land, even though Vera had warned her to give both him and his estate a wide berth. According to Vera, he was a cruel monster, who had pushed his wife to her death over a high cliff on his estate a number of years ago and then claimed that she had jumped. *What kind of woman would* jump *to her death in such a horrifying way,* Vera had asked rhetorically. *Especially when she was a* duchess *and had everything in the world she could possibly need.*

The kind of woman, Gwen had thought at the time, though she had not said so aloud, *who had just lost her only child to a bullet in Portugal,* for that was precisely what had happened a short while before the duchess's demise. But Vera, along with the neighborhood ladies with whom she consorted, chose to believe the more titillating murder theory despite the fact that none of them, when pressed, could offer up any evidence whatsoever to corroborate it.

But though Gwen had been skeptical about the story when she heard it, she was not so sure now. He *looked* like a man who could be both ruthless and cruel. Even murderous.

And she had trespassed on his land. His very *deserted* land.

She was also helpless to run away.

Hugo had gone alone down to the sandy beach below Penderris after breakfast, the rain having stopped during the night. He had been teased about it. Flavian had told him to be sure to bring his future bride back to the house so that they could all meet her and decide if they approved his choice.

They had all made merry at his expense.

Hugo had informed Flavian where he could go and how he could get there, though he had been immediately obliged to apologize as he had used a soldier's language in Imogen's hearing.

The beach had always been his favorite part of the estate. In the early days of his stay here, the sea had often soothed him when nothing else could. And more often than not he had come down here alone, even then. Despite the closeness and camaraderie that had developed among the seven members of the Survivors' Club while they were all healing and convalescing, they had never lived in one another's pockets. On the contrary, most of their demons had had to be faced and exorcised alone, and still did. One of the main attractions of Penderris had always been that it offered more than enough space to accommodate them all.

He had recovered from his own particular wounds—as far as he could ever recover, that was.

If it came to counting blessings, he would need the fingers of both hands at the very least. He had survived his war experiences. He had been awarded the promotion to major he had craved, as well as the unexpected bonus of his title as a result of the success of his final mission. Last year he had inherited a vast fortune and a hugely profitable business. He had family—uncles and aunts and cousins who loved him, though he had largely ignored them for many years. More important, there was Constance, his nineteen-year-old half sister, who adored him, though she had been a mere infant when he went off to war. He had a home of his own in the country, which provided him with all the privacy and peace he could possibly ask for. He had his six fellow members of the Survivors' Club, who had sometimes seemed closer to him than his own heart. He enjoyed robust good health, perhaps even perfect health. The list could go on.

But each time he made the mental list of his blessings, it became like a two-edged sword. Why had *he* been so fortunate when so many others had died? More important, had his ruthless ambition, which had brought personal success and rewards that were far in excess of what he had expected, actually *caused* a number of those deaths? Lieutenant Carstairs would say yes without hesitation.

There were no reasonably personable women strolling along the beach, or any *un*personable ones either, for that matter. He would have to invent a few for the amusement of his friends when he returned to the house, though, and a few stories surrounding his encounters with them. Perhaps he would even add a mermaid or two. He was in no hurry to get back, however, even though it was a chilly day made worse by a rather raw wind.

When he had returned to the pebbled part of the beach and to the foot of the ancient collapse in the cliff face that gave access to the headland and the park of Penderris above, Hugo stood for a few moments and gazed out to sea while the wind whipped at his short hair and turned the tips of his ears numb. He was not wearing a hat. There was really no point when he would have been chasing it along the sand more than he would have been wearing it.

He found himself thinking about his father. It was inevitable really, he supposed, when today was the first anniversary of his death.

Guilt came with the thoughts. He had worshipped his father as a lad and had followed him everywhere, even to work, especially after his mother's death of some woman's trouble when he was seven—the exact nature of the ailment had never been explained to him. His father had described him affectionately as his right-hand little chap and the heir apparent. Others had described him as his father's shadow. But then had come his father's second marriage, and Hugo, thirteen years old and at an awkward stage of adolescence, had developed a chip on his shoulder as large as a boulder. He had still been young enough to be shocked that his father could even *think* of replacing his mother, who had been so central to their lives and happiness that she was simply irreplaceable. He had grown restless and rebellious and determined to establish his own identity and independence.

Looking back now, he could see that his father had not loved him less—or dishonored the memory of Hugo's mother—just because he had married a pretty, demanding young wife and soon had a new daughter upon whom to dote. But growing young boys cannot always see their world rationally. Further evidence of that was the fact that he, Hugo, had adored Constance from the moment of her birth when he might have been expected to hate or resent her.

It was a stage of his life, fairly typical of boys his age, that he might well have outgrown with a minimum of harm to all concerned if there had not been something else to tip the balance. But there had been that something else, and the balance had been tipped irretrievably when he was not even quite eighteen.

And he had decided quite abruptly that he would be a soldier. Nothing would dissuade him, even the argument that he did not have the character for such a rough life. If anything, that argument only made him the more stubborn and the more determined to succeed. His father, disappointed and saddened, had finally purchased a commission in an infantry regiment for his only son, but it was to be the one and only purchase. He had made that clear. Hugo was on his own after that. He would have to earn his promotions, not have them bought by his wealthy father, as most other officers did. Hugo's father had always rather despised the upper classes, for whom privilege and idleness often went hand in hand.

Hugo had proceeded to earn those promotions. He had actually *liked* the fact that he was on his own. He had pursued his chosen career with energy and determination and enthusiasm and a driving ambition to reach the very top. He would have reached it too, if his greatest triumph had not been followed within a month by his greatest humiliation and he had not ended up here at Penderris.

His father had loved him steadfastly through it all. But Hugo had turned his back upon him, almost as if his father had been to blame for all his woes. Or perhaps it was shame that made him do it. Or perhaps it was the sheer impossibility of going back home.

And how had his father repaid him for his neglect? He had left almost everything to him, that was what, when he might conceivably have left it all to Fiona or to Constance. He trusted his son to keep his businesses going and to pass them on to a son of his own when the time came. He had trusted him too to see to it that Constance had a bright, secure future. He must have understood that she might have no such thing if she was left to her mother's sole care. He had made Hugo her guardian.

Now his year of mourning, his excuse for inactivity thus far, was over.

He stopped when he was halfway up the slope. He still was not ready to return to the house. He turned off the slope and climbed a short way up the cliff beside it until he reached a flat, rocky ledge he had discovered years ago. It was sheltered from most winds, and even though it cut off any view of the sandy stretch of beach farther west, it still allowed him to see the cliff face opposite and the pebbled beach and the sea below. It was a starkly barren prospect, but it was not without a certain beauty of its own. Two seagulls flew across his line of vision, crying out some piece of intelligence to each other.

He would relax here for a while before seeking out the company of his friends.

He scooped up some small pebbles from the ledge beside him and tossed one in a high arc to the beach below. He heard it land and saw it bounce once. But his fingers stilled around the second stone as a flutter of color caught the edge of his vision.

The cliff on the other side of the pebbled slope curved outward toward the sea. Full tide reached it sooner than it did the cliff on which he sat. There was a way around the base of the jutting cliff to the village a mile or so away, but it could be a treacherous route if one was not aware of the approaching tide.

Someone walked that stretch of pebbled beach now—a woman wearing a red cloak. She had just appeared around the headland, though she was still some distance off. Her bonneted head was down. She appeared to be concentrating upon her footing. She stopped and looked out to sea. It was still some way out and was no imminent danger to her. If she had strolled from the village, however, she really ought to be turning back soon. The only other way back was up over the headland, but that would involve her in trespassing on Penderris land.

She turned her head to look at the steep pebbled slope to the top as though she had read his thoughts. She did not see him, fortunately. He was in the shade, and he sat very still. He did not want to be seen. He willed her to turn back the way she had come.

She did not turn back, however. Instead, she came in the direction of the slope and then began to trudge upward, her cloak and the brim of her bonnet flapping in the wind. She looked small. She looked young. It was impossible to tell *how* young, though, since he could not see her face. For the same reason there was no knowing if she was comely or ugly or simply plain.

His friends would tease him for a week if they ever found out about this, Hugo thought. He had a mental image of himself jumping down from his perch, striding purposefully toward her across the stones, informing her that he was both titled and enormously wealthy, and asking her if she fancied marrying him.

Though it was not a particularly amusing thought, he had to quell an urge to chuckle and give away his presence.

He stayed very still and hoped that even yet she would turn back. He resented having his solitude threatened by a stranger and a trespasser. He could not remember its happening before. Not many people from outside the estate came this way. The Duke of Stanbrook was feared by many in this part of the country. The inevitable rumor had blossomed after the death of the duchess that he had actually pushed her over the cliff from which she had jumped. Such stories did not die easily despite lack of any evidence. Even those who did not actually fear him seemed wary of him. And his contained, austere manner did not help allay suspicion.

Perhaps the woman in red was a stranger to these parts. Perhaps she did not realize she was climbing directly into the dragon's lair.

Hugo wondered why she was alone in such a desolate setting.

The loose pebbles gave under her feet as she climbed. It was never an easy ascent, as he knew from experience. And then, just when it seemed she would go safely past and not see him at all, her right foot dislodged a small avalanche of stones and slid down sharply after them. She landed awkwardly on her knee and both hands, her right leg stretched out behind her. For a moment he had a glimpse of slim bare leg between the top of her half boot and the hem of her cloak.

He heard a gasp of pain.

He waited. He really did not want to have to reveal his presence. It soon became apparent, however, that she had done some serious damage to her foot or ankle and that she was not going to be able to pick herself up and go on her way. She *was* young, he could see. And she was small and slender. Beneath the brim of her bonnet, blond tendrils of hair were blowing in the wind. He still had not seen her face.

It would be churlish to remain silent.

"In my considered opinion," he said, "that ankle is either badly sprained or actually broken. Either way it would be very unwise to try putting any weight on it."

Her head jerked up as he climbed down onto the pebbles and made his way toward her. Her eyes widened in what looked like fear rather than relief that help was at hand. They were large blue eyes in a face of exquisite beauty even though she was no girl. He guessed her age to be close to his own thirty-three.

He was irritated. He hated it when people were afraid of him. People often were. Even some men. But especially women.

It might have occurred to him that a scowling countenance was not best designed to inspire confidence, especially in a lonely, desolate setting like this. It did not, however.

He scowled down at her from his great height.

Chapter 2

❦

"Oh!" she cried. "Who are you? Are you the Duke of Stanbrook?"

She *was* a stranger to this part of the country, then.

"Trentham," he said. "You walked over from the village?"

"Yes. I thought I would walk back across the headland," she said. "The pebbles are far larger and more difficult to walk on than I expected."

She was unmistakably a lady. Her clothes were well cut and looked expensive. She spoke with a cultured accent. There was a general indefinable air of good breeding in her manner.

He would not hold it against her.

"I had better take a look at that ankle," he said.

"Oh, no." She recoiled in horror. "That will be quite unnecessary, thank you, Mr. Trentham. It is my weak ankle. It will be fine in a moment and I shall be on my way again."

Ladies and their sense of dignity! And their denial of unpleasant reality.

"I will take a look anyway." He went down on his haunches and held out one large hand. She looked at it, leaned back on her hands, bit her lip, and gave no further argument.

He rested her boot on his hand and felt her ankle with the other hand, careful not to cause her undue pain. He did not think it was broken, though he was reluctant to remove her half boot for a more thorough examination. The boot was providing some support if there really was a break. Her ankle was already swelling, though. *Some* damage had been done. She was not going to be walking back to the village or anywhere else today, not even with the assistance of an arm to lean upon.

More was the pity.

She was still biting her lip when he looked up at her. Her face was ashen and taut with pain—and perhaps embarrassment. He had bared her leg almost to the knee. There was a ragged hole in her silk stocking there, he could see, and her knee was grazed and even slightly bleeding. He reached into the pocket of his greatcoat, where he had put a clean linen handkerchief this morning. He shook it out, folded it three times across the bias, and wrapped it about her knee before securing it with a firm knot below the kneecap. Then he lowered her cloak and stood up.

There were splashes of color high on her cheekbones.

Why the devil, he thought as he gazed down at her, had she not stayed down on the beach where she belonged? Or taken more care as she climbed the slope? But one thing was clear. He could not simply leave her here.

"You are going to have to come to Penderris," he said none too graciously. "A physician ought to look at that ankle as soon as possible and clean and bandage your knee properly. I am not a physician."

"Oh, no," she cried in dismay. "Not Penderris. Is it even close? I did not realize. I was advised to give it a wide berth. Do you know the Duke of Stanbrook?"

"I am a guest at his home," he said curtly. "Now, we can do this the hard way, ma'am. I can hoist you to one foot and support you about the waist while you hop along at my side. But I warn you it is some distance to the house. Or we can do it the easy way, and I will simply carry you."

"Oh, no!" she cried again, more forcefully this time and half shrank away from him. "I weigh a ton. Besides . . ."

"I doubt it, ma'am," he said. "I believe I am quite capable of carrying you without dropping you or doing permanent damage to my back."

He bent over her, wrapped one arm about her shoulders while he slid the other beneath her knees, and straightened up with her. She freed one arm hastily from her cloak and flung it about his neck. But it was quickly obvious that she was startled and alarmed—and then very indignant.

He had, of course, offered her a choice but had not waited for her to make it. But really there had been no choice. Only a daft woman would have chosen to hop along at his side merely to preserve a bit of feminine dignity.

He strode upward with her as best he could while allowing for the give of the pebbles.

"Do you always," she asked him, her voice breathless and coldly haughty, "do exactly as you please, Mr. Trentham, even when you appear to be offering an option to your victims?"

Victims?

"Besides," she continued without giving him a chance to answer her question, "I would have chosen *neither* option, sir. I would prefer to make my own way home on my own two feet."

"That would be downright silly," he said, not even trying to hide the scorn he was feeling. "Your ankle is in a bad way."

She smelled good. It was not the sort of perfume that all too many women splashed all over themselves, the sort that assaulted one's nasal passages and throat and set one to sneezing and coughing. He suspected that it was a very expensive fragrance. It clung enticingly about her person but did not invade his own. Her dress was a pale mushroom color and appeared to be made of finest wool. *Expensive* wool. This was no impoverished lady.

Just a careless and silly one.

And were not ladies supposed to be trailed by maids and assorted chaperons wherever they went? Where was *her* entourage? He might have been saved from personal involvement if she had been properly accompanied.

"That ankle is *always* troublesome," she said. "I am accustomed to it. I habitually limp. I fell from a horse and broke it a number of years ago, and it was not set properly. I really must ask you to put me down and allow me to go on my way."

"It is badly swollen," he said. "If you have come from the village, you have a mile to go to get back there. How long do you estimate it would take you to hop or crawl that distance?"

"I believe," she said, her voice cool and disdainful, "that is my concern, Mr. Trentham, not yours. But you are the type of man who must always be right, I perceive, while other people must always be wrong—at least in your estimation."

Well, good Lord! Did she think he was *enjoying* playing Sir Galahad?

They were still on the upward slope, though they had left the pebbles behind and were on the firmer ground of coarse, scrubby grass. He stopped abruptly, set her down on her feet, and took one step away from her. He clasped his hands behind his back and looked steadily at her with an expression that had used to wither soldiers in their tracks.

He was actually going to enjoy this.

"Thank you," she said with chilly hauteur—though she had the grace to look suddenly apologetic. "I thank you for coming to my assistance, sir. You could easily have avoided doing so. I had not seen you, as you must have realized. I am Lady Muir."

Ah, *definitely* a lady. She probably expected him to bow and scrape and tug on his forelock.

She took one step back from him—and collapsed in an undignified heap on the ground.

He stood looking down at her and pursed his lips. She would not like *that* loss to her dignity.

She rose to her knees, set her hands flat on the ground, and . . . *laughed*. It was a merry sound of pure amusement, though it did end in a little hiccup of pain.

"Mr. Trentham," she said, "you have my permission to say 'I told you so.' "

"I told you so," he said—one must not disoblige a lady. "And it is *Lord* Trentham."

Silly of him to insist upon that detail, perhaps, but she irritated him.

She turned to sit on the ground. It was probably still damp from yesterday's rain, he thought. Serve her right. He gazed down at her with hard eyes and set jaw.

She sighed as she looked up at him. Her face had turned pale again. He would wager that that ankle was throbbing like a thousand devils. Maybe five thousand after her attempt to put weight on it.

"You gave me a choice a short while ago," she said, all the haughtiness gone from her voice, though a trace of her laughter remained. "And since I am not a silly woman, or at least do not wish to appear silly, I choose the second. *If* the option is still open to me, that is. You would be quite within your rights to withdraw it now, but I would be much obliged if you would carry me to Penderris, *Lord* Trentham, even though I find the thought of imposing my presence there deeply distressing. Perhaps you would be good enough to lend me a carriage when we get there so that I do not even have to enter the—"

He bent and scooped her up again. As humble pie went, she had eaten a fair portion.

He strode onward in the direction of the house. He did not try to make conversation. He could only imagine the sort of reception he was going to get, and the sort of teasing he was going to have to endure for the rest of his stay at Penderris.

"You are or have been a military gentleman, Lord Trentham," she said, breaking the silence a couple of minutes later. "I *am* right, am I not?"

"What makes you say so?" he asked without looking down at her.

"You have the bearing of an officer," she said, "and the hard-jawed, intense-eyed look of a man accustomed to command."

He looked down briefly at her. He did not reply to her words.

"Oh, this is going to be horribly embarrassing," she said a couple of minutes later as they approached the house.

"But better, I daresay," he said curtly, "than lying out on the slope above the beach, exposed to the elements and waiting for the seagulls to come and peck out your eyes."

Uncharitably, he wished that that was precisely where she was, though he would not wish the eye-pecking gulls on her.

"Oh," she said with a grimace. "When you put it that way, I must confess you are right."

"I sometimes am," he said.

Lord! Today's grand joke had been that he was to go down onto the beach to find a personable woman to marry. And here he was, right on cue, carrying a genuine *lady* back with him. A damnably pretty one too.

Perhaps she was not single, though. Indeed, she almost certainly was not. She had introduced herself as Lady Muir. That suggested that somewhere, perhaps in the village a mile away, there was a Lord Muir. Which fact would not save him from the teasing. It would merely enhance it, in fact. He would be accused of the most naïve form of miscalculation.

It was going to take him a long time to live this one down.

Gwen would have been experiencing surely the worst embarrassment of her life if her mind had not been more preoccupied with pain. She felt embarrassed nevertheless.

Not only was she being taken to a strange house owned by a man of some notoriety who was not expecting her, but also she was being carried by a large, morose stranger who had done nothing to hide the fact that he despised her. And the trouble was that she could hardly blame him. She had behaved badly. She had made an idiot of herself.

She was pressed against all that muscled strength she had observed as he approached her across the pebbles, and he felt really quite disturbingly masculine. She could feel his body heat through his heavy clothing and her own. She could smell his cologne or his shaving soap, a faint, enticing, distinctively male scent. She could hear him breathing, though he was not panting from his exertions. Indeed, he made her feel as though she weighed nothing at all.

Her ankle was throbbing very badly indeed. There was no use in continuing to pretend that she would be able to walk back to Vera's once she had shaken off the first twinges of pain.

Oh, dear, he really *was* a morose man. And a silent one. He had not even confirmed or denied being a military officer. And he had nothing else to offer by way of conversation, though to be fair, he probably needed all his breath to carry her.

Goodness, she would have nightmares about this for a long time to come.

He was making his way straight for the front doors of Penderris Hall, which looked like a very grand mansion indeed. He was, as she might have expected, totally ignoring her plea to be taken directly to the carriage house so that she might avoid the house altogether. She just hoped the duke was not going to be close by when she was carried inside. Perhaps one of his minions would summon a carriage to convey her back to Vera's. Even a gig would do.

Lord Trentham climbed a short flight of steps and turned sideways in order to thump his elbow against one of the doors. It was opened almost immediately by a sober-looking man in black who resembled all butlers the world over. He stood aside without comment as Lord Trentham carried her into a large square hall tiled in black and white.

"We have a wounded soldier here, Lambert," Lord Trentham said without any trace of humor in his voice. "I am going to carry her up to the drawing room."

"Oh, no, please—"

"Shall I send for Dr. Jones, my lord?" the butler asked.

But before Lord Trentham could answer or Gwen voice a further protest, someone else arrived on the scene, a tall, slender, blond, extremely handsome gentleman with mocking green eyes and one elevated eyebrow. *The Duke of Stanbrook,* Gwen thought with a sinking heart. She could scarcely have imagined a scene more lowering than this if she had tried.

"Hugo, my dear chap," the gentleman said, his voice a lazy drawl, "however did you do it? You are a marvel. You found the lady on the beach, did you, and swept her literally off her feet with your charm, not to mention your title and fortune? This makes for a very affecting scene, I must say. If I were an artist, I would be d-dashing for my canvas and brushes in order to record it for the delight of your descendants to the third and fourth generation."

He had lowered his eyebrow and lifted a quizzing glass to his eye as he spoke.

Gwen glared at him. She spoke with as much chilly dignity as she could muster.

"I twisted my ankle," she explained, "and Lord Trentham was obliging enough to carry me here. I do not intend to impose upon your hospitality any longer than necessary, Your Grace. All I ask is the loan of some conveyance to take me back to the village, where I am staying. You *are* the Duke of Stanbrook, I presume?"

The blond gentleman lowered his glass and raised one eyebrow again.

"You elevate me in rank, ma'am," he said. "I am flattered. I am not, alas, Stanbrook. I daresay Lambert will call out a gig for you if you insist, however, though Hugo looks eager to impress you with his superior strength by d-dashing upstairs with you in his arms and arriving in the drawing room without any noticeable shortness of breath."

"It is a good thing you are *not* me, Flavian," another, older gentleman said as he approached from the back of the hall. "You appear not to know the first thing about hospitality. Ma'am, I fully agree with both Hugo and my good butler. You must be taken up to the drawing room to rest your foot on a sofa while I send for the doctor to assess the damage. I am Stanbrook, by the way, and entirely at your service. You must tell me whom I may summon to offer you some comfort. Your husband, perhaps?"

Oh, dear, this was getting worse and worse. If there were just a dark hole in the middle of the hall, Gwen thought, she would be happy to have Lord Trentham drop her into it. The duke was much as she had originally pictured him—tall, slender, and elegant, with handsome, finely chiseled features and dark hair silvering at the temples. His manner was courtly, yet his gray eyes were contrastingly cold and his voice chilly. He spoke of hospitality but made her feel like the worst kind of intruder.

"I am the widow of the late Viscount Muir," Gwen told the duke. "I am a guest in the home of Mrs. Parkinson in the village."

"Ah," the duke said. "She lost her husband recently, I recall, after he had suffered a lingering illness. But off you go on your way upstairs, Hugo. I will hope to have the pleasure of some conversation with you later, Lady Muir, after your ankle has been tended to."

He made it sound as if it would be anything but a pleasure. Or perhaps her extreme discomfort was causing her to do him an injustice. He *was* offering hospitality and the services of a physician, after all.

How could one sprained ankle cause such pain? Or perhaps it was broken.

Lord Trentham turned to stride toward a broad staircase that wound upward in an elegant curve. She could hear the Duke of Stanbrook giving orders for both the doctor and Vera to be sent for without further delay. The gentleman with the quizzing glass, the one who spoke with an affected sigh in his voice and a slight stammer, appeared to be offering to perform the errand himself.

The drawing room was empty. That was one mercy, at least. It was a large, square room with wine-colored brocaded walls hung with portraits in heavy gilded frames, and an ornately sculpted marble fireplace directly opposite the door. The coved ceiling was painted with scenes from mythology, the frieze beneath it heavily gilded. The furnishings were both elegant and sumptuous. Long windows looked out upon lawns enclosed by hedges, but they nevertheless afforded a distant view of cliffs and the sea beyond. A fire crackled in the hearth, and the warmth of the room prevented the outdoors from looking too starkly bleak.

Gwen took in room and view at a glance and felt all the humiliation of being an uninvited—and unwelcome—guest in such a home. But for the moment at least there seemed no point in making a fuss and demanding yet again the loan of a carriage to take her back to Vera's.

Lord Trentham lowered her to a brocaded sofa and reached for a cushion to put under her injured ankle.

"Oh," she cried, "my boots are going to get the sofa *dirty*."

That would be the very last straw.

But he would not let her swing her legs to the floor. Neither would he allow her to bend forward to remove her own boots. He insisted upon doing it for her. Not that he uttered a word of command, but it was difficult to bat aside such large hands and such massive arms or to prevail against such deaf ears.

He *had* done her a kindness, she admitted grudgingly, but did he have to be so unpleasant about it?

He undid the laces of her left boot and removed it without any trouble at all before placing it on the floor. He went far more slowly with the other boot. Gwen untied the ribbons of her bonnet, pulled it off her head, and dropped it over the side of the sofa so that she could rest her head back against the cushioned arm. She closed her eyes—and then pressed her head back harder and clenched her eyes more tightly as she was engulfed in a fresh wave of agony. He had surprisingly gentle hands, but it was not easy for him to ease off her boot, and once it *was* off, there was nothing left to support her foot or hold it firm against the swelling. She felt him lift it onto the cushion.

But pain sometimes dulled sensibility, she thought a few moments later as she felt his hands reach under her skirt, first to remove the handkerchief he had wrapped about her knee earlier, and then to roll down her torn stocking and ease it off over her foot.

Warm fingers probed the swelling.

"I do not believe anything is broken," Lord Trentham said. "But I cannot be certain. You must keep your foot where it is until the doctor comes. The cut to your knee is superficial and will heal in a few days."

She opened her eyes and was acutely aware of her bare foot and a length of bare leg elevated on the cushion. Lord Trentham was standing upright, his hands clasped at his back, his booted feet slightly apart—a military man at ease. His dark eyes were gazing very directly back into hers, and his jaw was set hard.

He resented her being here, she thought. Well, she had tried very hard *not* to be. She resented being resented.

"Most women," he said, "do not bear pain well. You do."

He was insulting her sex but complimenting her personally. Was she supposed to simper with gratitude?

"You forget, Lord Trentham," she said, "that it is women who bear children. It is generally agreed that the pain of childbed is the worst pain there is."

"You have children of your own?" he asked.

"No." She closed her eyes again and for no apparent reason continued—on a subject she almost never spoke of, even to those nearest and dearest to her. "I lost the only one I conceived. It happened after I was thrown from my horse and broke my leg."

"What were you doing riding a horse when you were with child?" he asked.

It was a good question, even if it *was* an impudent one too.

"Jumping hedges," she said, "including one neither Vernon—my husband—nor I had ever jumped before. His horse cleared it. Mine did not and I was tossed off."

There was a short silence. Why *on earth* had she told him all that?

"Did your husband know you were with child?" he asked.

It was an unpardonably intimate question. But she had started this.

"Of course," she said. "I was almost six months into my confinement."

And now he would think all sorts of uncomplimentary things about Vernon without understanding at all. It was unfair of her to have said so much when she was certainly not prepared to launch into lengthy explanations. She seemed to have done nothing but show herself in a bad light since she first set eyes upon him and cringed in fear. Yes, she really had. She had *cringed.*

"This was a child you *wanted*?" he asked.

Her eyes snapped open and she glared at him, speechless. What sort of question was *that*?

His eyes were hard. Accusing. Condemning.

But what did she expect? She had made both herself and Vernon seem unpardonably reckless and irresponsible.

It was time to change the subject.

"Is the blond gentleman downstairs a guest at Penderris too?" she asked. "Have I imposed upon a house party?"

"He is Viscount Ponsonby," he said. "There are six guests here, apart from Stanbrook himself. We gather here for a few weeks each year. Stanbrook opened his home to us for several years during and after the wars while we recuperated from various wounds."

Gwen gazed at him. There was no outer sign of any wound that might have incapacitated Lord Trentham for that long. But she had been right about him. He *was* a military man.

"You were or are all officers?" she asked.

"Were," he said. "Five of us in the recent wars, Stanbrook in previous ones. His son fought and died in the Napoleonic Wars."

Ah, yes. Shortly before the duchess leapt from the cliff top to her death.

"And the seventh person?" she asked.

"A woman," he said, "widow of a surveillance officer who was tortured to death after being captured. She was present when he was finally shot."

"Oh," Gwen said, grimacing.

Now she felt worse than ever. This was far more terrible than imposing upon a simple house party. And her own sprained ankle seemed embarrassingly trivial in comparison with what the duke and his six guests must have endured.

Lord Trentham had picked up a shawl from the back of a nearby chair and came closer to spread it over Gwen's injured leg. At the same moment the drawing doors opened again and a woman came inside carrying a tea tray. She was a lady, not a maid. She was tall and very straight in posture. Her dark blond hair was pulled back in a chignon, but the simplicity, even severity, of the style emphasized the perfect bone structure of her oval face with its finely sculpted cheekbones, straight nose, and blue-green eyes fringed with lashes a shade darker than her hair. Her mouth was wide and generous. She was beautiful, despite the fact that her face looked as though it were sculpted of marble. It looked not only as though she never smiled but as if she were incapable of doing so even if she wished. Her eyes were large and very calm, almost unnaturally so.

She came toward the sofa and would have set the tray down on the table beside Gwen if Lord Trentham had not taken it from her hands first.

"I'll see to that, Imogen," he said.

"George guessed that you would consider it quite improper to be in a room alone with a strange gentleman, Lady Muir," the lady said, "even if he *did* rescue you and carry you back to the house. I have been designated as your chaperon."

Her voice was cool rather than cold.

"This is Imogen, Lady Barclay," Lord Trentham said, "who never seems to consider it improper to stay at Penderris with six gentlemen and no chaperon."

"I would entrust my life to any of the six or all of them combined," Lady Barclay said, inclining her head courteously to Gwen. "Indeed, I have already done so. You are looking embarrassed. You need not. How did you hurt your ankle?"

She poured three cups of tea as Gwen described what had happened. This, then, she thought, was the lady who had been with her husband when his torturers had killed him. Gwen had an inkling of the torments she must have lived through every minute of every day since. She must forever be asking herself if there was anything she might have done to prevent such a disaster. Just as Gwen forever asked it of *herself* with regard to Vernon's death.

"I feel very foolish," she said in conclusion.

"Of course you do," Lady Barclay said. "But it could have happened to any of us, you know. We are always up and down to the beach, and that slope is quite treacherous enough even without the shifting stones."

Gwen glanced at Lord Trentham, who was silently sipping his tea, his dark eyes resting on her.

He was, she thought in some surprise and with a little shiver of awareness, a terribly attractive man. He ought not to be. He was too large to be either elegant or graceful. His hair was too short to soften the harshness of his features or the hard line of his jaw. His mouth was too straight and hard-set to be sensuous. His eyes were too dark and too penetrating to make a woman want to fall into them. There was nothing to suggest charm or humor or any warmth of personality.

And yet . . .

And yet there was an aura about him of almost overpowering physicality. Of masculinity.

It would be an absolutely wonderful *experience,* she thought, *to go to bed with him.*

It was a thought that shocked her to the roots of her being. In the seven years since Vernon's death she had shrunk away from the merest thought of another courtship and marriage. And she had never in her life thought of any man in any other connection.

Did this unexpected and rather ridiculous attraction have anything to do with the equally unexpected wave of loneliness she had felt down on the beach just before she met him?

She made conversation with Lady Barclay while these strange thoughts buzzed about in her head. But really it was difficult to concentrate fully upon either words or thought. Pain, as she remembered now from the time when she broke her leg, could never confine itself to the injured part of one's body but throbbed instead all through it until one did not know quite what to do with oneself.

Lord Trentham got to his feet as soon as she had finished her cup of tea, took an unused linen napkin off the tea tray, and crossed to a sideboard, where he must have found a jug of cold water among the liquor decanters. He came back with a wet napkin from which most of the water had been squeezed, spread it over Gwen's forehead, and held it in place there with one hand. She rested the back of her head against the cushion again and closed her eyes.

The coolness, even the pressure of his hand, felt very good.

Where was the insensitive brute she had judged him to be?

"I have been hoping to distract her with conversation," Lady Barclay said. "She is as pale as a ghost, poor thing. But she has uttered not a moan of complaint. She has my admiration."

"Jones is certainly dragging his feet," Lord Trentham said.

"He will come as soon as he is able," Lady Barclay said. "He always does, Hugo. And there is no better doctor in the world."

"Lady Muir has suffered a previous injury to the same leg," Lord Trentham said. "I daresay it hurts like a thousand devils."

They were talking of her as if she were not there to speak for herself, Gwen thought. But for the moment she did not care. For the moment she was distancing herself as far from the pain as she could get.

And there was warmth in their voices, she noticed. As if they were fond of each other. Almost as if they were genuinely concerned for her.

Even so, she *wished* the physician would come soon so that she could ask the Duke of Stanbrook again for a carriage to take her to Vera's.

Oh, how she hated to be beholden to anyone.

Chapter 3

When Flavian returned with the doctor, he brought Mrs. Parkinson too. It was that lady who hurried into the drawing room first. She curtsied low to Imogen and Hugo and assured them that His Grace was kindness itself, that *they* were kindness itself, that she would be grateful to Lord Ponsonby for the rest of her days for bringing her word of her dearest friend's accident so promptly and insisting upon bringing her here in His Grace's carriage despite the fact that she would have been happy to walk ten times the distance if it had been necessary.

"I would walk five—nay, even ten—miles for dear Lady Muir's sake," she assured them, "even if it *was* careless of her to wander onto His Grace's land when I had specifically warned her to be careful to avoid giving offense to such an illustrious peer of the realm. His Grace would have been quite justified if he had chosen to refuse her admittance to Penderris, though I daresay he hesitated to do so when he learned she is *Lady* Muir. I suppose it is *that* fact I have to thank for my invitation to ride in the carriage, for such a distinction has never been offered me before, you know, despite the fact that Mr. Parkinson was the younger brother of Sir Roger Parkinson and was fourth in line to the title himself after his brother's three sons."

It was only after she had delivered herself of this remarkable speech, looking from Hugo to Imogen as she did so, that the lady turned toward her friend, her hands clasped to her bosom.

Hugo and Imogen exchanged a poker-faced glance in which

volumes were spoken. Flavian had come to stand silently just inside the door, looking openly bored.

"Gwen!" Mrs. Parkinson cried. "Oh, my poor dear Gwen, *what* have you done to yourself? I was beside myself with worry when you did not return from your walk within the hour. I feared the worst and blamed myself most bitterly for having felt too low in spirits to accompany you. What would I have done if you had met with a fatal accident? What would I have said to the Earl of Kilbourne, your dear brother? It was really too, too naughty of you to cause me such panic. All of which I felt, of course, because I love you so dearly."

"I twisted my ankle, that is all, Vera," Lady Muir explained. "But unfortunately, it is impossible for me to walk, at least for the present. I hope not to have to impose upon the duke's hospitality for much longer, however. I trust he will be kind enough to allow the carriage to return to the village with the two of us once the doctor has looked at my ankle and bound it up."

Mrs. Parkinson regarded her friend with open horror and uttered a slight shriek as she clasped her hands even more tightly to her bosom.

"You must not even *think* of being removed," she said. "Oh, my poor Gwen, you will do your leg irreparable damage if you attempt anything so reckless. You already have that unfortunate limp from a previous accident, and I daresay it has deterred other gentlemen from paying you court since dear Lord Muir's passing. You simply must not risk becoming entirely lame. His Grace, I am assured, will join me in urging you to remain here until your ankle is quite healed. You must not worry that I will neglect you. I shall walk over daily to bear you company. You are my dearest friend in the world, after all. I am sure this lady and this gentleman as well as Viscount Ponsonby will also urge you to stay."

She smiled graciously in turn upon Imogen and Hugo, and Flavian, sounding even more bored than he habitually did, introduced them.

Mrs. Parkinson was probably close to Lady Muir in age, Hugo guessed, though time had dealt less kindly with her. Whereas Lady Muir was still beautiful even though she was probably past the age of thirty, any claim to good looks Mrs. Parkinson might once have had was long past. She also carried too much weight upon her frame, and most of it had settled quite unbecomingly beneath her chin and about her bosom and hips. Her brown hair had lost any youthful luster it might once have had.

Lady Muir opened her mouth to speak. She was clearly dismayed at the suggestion that she remain at Penderris. She was prevented from expressing her sentiments, however, when the door opened again to admit George and Dr. Jones, the physician he had enticed from London years ago when he opened his home to the six of them, and others whose stay had been of shorter duration. The doctor had remained ever since to tend the poor who could not pay his fee, as well as the richer folk who could.

"Here is Dr. Jones, Lady Muir," George said. "He is the most skilled of physicians, I do assure you. You may feel confident in entrusting yourself to his care. Imogen, would you be so good as to remain here with Lady Muir? The rest of us will withdraw to the library. Mrs. Parkinson, may I offer you tea and cakes there? It was good of you to come with Flavian and the doctor at such short notice."

"It is I who ought to remain with Lady Muir," Mrs. Parkinson said, nevertheless allowing herself to be ushered toward the door. "However, my nerves are stretched thin, Your Grace, after tending my poor dear husband for so long. Dr. Jones will tell you that they have come very near to breaking altogether since his passing. I do not know *how* I am going to be able to give dear Lady Muir the care she is going to need in my home, though I am more than eager, as you may imagine, to have her removed there. I feel responsible for what has happened. If I had been with her, as I would have been if I had not been feeling so low in spirits this morning, then I would have kept her a decent distance from

Penderris. I am vexed that she trespassed, though I suppose it was more careless than deliberate on her part."

George had closed the drawing room doors by this point and was making his way downstairs with Mrs. Parkinson on his arm. Hugo and Flavian were following along behind them.

"It will be my pleasure to have Lady Muir remain here, ma'am, until she can walk again," George said. "And the doctor has already confirmed that you are worn down after your devoted attention to your husband during his long illness."

"That is very obliging of him, I am sure," Mrs. Parkinson said. "I shall come every day to visit Lady Muir, of course."

"I am delighted to hear it ma'am," George said, nodding to a footman to open the library doors. "My carriage will be at your disposal."

Flavian and Hugo exchanged glances, and the former cocked one eyebrow. *Shall we sneak off while we may?* the look seemed to ask.

Hugo pursed his lips. It was tempting. But he followed George and his guest into the library, and Flavian shrugged and came behind him.

"I *do* regret this imposition upon your hospitality, Your Grace," Mrs. Parkinson assured George. "But it is not in my nature to abandon a friend when she is in need. And so I will accept your kind offer of a carriage each day even though I would be delighted to *walk* here. I will be absolutely no bother to you or your guests while I *am* here. It is *Lady Muir* I will be visiting. I shall certainly not expect tea each day."

A maid had just come into the room and was setting down a tray on the large oak desk by the window.

It was hardly surprising, Hugo thought, that Mrs. Parkinson cultivated the friendship of Lady Muir. She was, after all, the widow of a lord and the sister of an earl, and Mrs. Parkinson was obsequious to a fault. It was less clear why Lady Muir was *her* friend. She had struck Hugo as being decidedly haughty and high in the instep. He had not warmed to her despite her undeniable beauty. Though she *had* laughed at her own predicament after she demanded to be set down and he obliged her. And then she had asked to be carried after all. *But* she had once lost her unborn child through the incredible recklessness of her own behavior and the carelessness of her husband's. She was the sort of upper-class woman he most despised. She seemed totally wrapped up in self. And yet she was Mrs. Parkinson's friend. Perhaps she enjoyed being worshipped and adored.

Poor George was being left to bear all the burden of conversation alone since he, Hugo, was standing in morose silence wishing that he had not stopped earlier to climb to that ledge on the cliff but had come straight back to the house. And Flavian was over by one of the bookshelves, leafing through a book and looking disdainful. Flavian always portrayed disdain exceedingly well. He never even needed to speak a word.

This was grossly unfair to George.

"You have known Lady Muir for a long time, Mrs. Parkinson?" Hugo asked.

"Oh, my lord," she said, setting down her teacup and saucer in order to clasp her hands to her bosom again, "we have known each other *forever*. We made our come-out together in London when we were mere girls, you know. We made our curtsy to the queen on the very same day and danced at each other's come-out ball afterward. People were good enough to call us the two most dazzlingly pretty young ladies on the marriage mart that year, though I daresay they were merely being kind to me. Though I did have more than my fair share of beaux, it is true. More than Gwen, in fact, though I suppose that was in part due to the fact that she took one look at Lord Muir and decided that his title and fortune were worth setting her cap at. I might have married a marquess or a viscount myself had I chosen, or any one of a number of barons. But I fell deeply in love with Mr. Parkinson and never regretted for a single moment relinquishing the dazzling life I might have had with a titled gentleman and ten thousand or more a year. There is nothing more important in life than romantic love, even when its object is the mere younger brother of a baronet."

How had Muir died, Hugo wondered, having allowed his mind to wander. He did not ask.

The doctor was being shown into the room, and he confirmed Hugo's suspicion that his patient's ankle was severely sprained though not apparently broken or fractured. Nevertheless, it was imperative that she rest her leg and put absolutely no weight upon it for at least a week.

The Survivors' Club was going to have to expand to admit one more member, it seemed, even if just temporarily. George had allowed Mrs. Parkinson to win her point and give herself the opportunity to insinuate her company upon them for some days to come. Lady Muir was staying.

Mrs. Parkinson was the only one among them who looked gratified at the verdict, even though at the same time she dabbed a handkerchief to her eyes and heaved a soulful sigh.

It would have been better, Hugo thought, if he had not gone down onto the beach at all today. Last evening's joke ought to have been warning enough. God sometimes enjoyed getting in on a joke and giving it his own peculiar twist.

The new sprain had been aggravated by the old break, which in its turn had been poorly set. He would dearly like to have a word with the physician who had set it, Dr. Jones said with some severity after he had explained the situation to Gwen. He ordered her not to put her foot to the ground for at least a week but rather to keep it elevated at all times, not even on a low stool but whenever possible on a level with her heart.

It would have been a gloomy enough pronouncement under any circumstances. Even at home, the prospect of remaining inactive for so long would have been irksome. And at Vera's, another week without any escape from the company of her hostess and her friends would have been rather like being sentenced to a stay in Purgatory. Nevertheless, even that would have seemed like Paradise in comparison with the reality she faced. She was going to have to spend a week—*at least* a week—at Penderris Hall as a guest of the Duke of Stanbrook. She was being forced to impose herself upon a reunion of men—and one woman—who had spent long months together here recovering from wounds sustained during the wars. They were surely a closely bonded group. The last thing any of them would want was the forced presence of an outsider, a stranger to them all, who was nursing nothing more lethal than a hurt ankle.

Oh, this was the stuff of nightmares.

She was humiliated and in pain and homesick—*dreadfully* homesick. But most of all she was angry. She was angry at herself for continuing along the beach after discovering how difficult a terrain it was to walk upon, and for choosing to climb that treacherous slope. She had a weak ankle. She *knew* her limitations and was usually quite sensible about the sort of exercise she undertook.

Most of all, though, she was angry—quite furious, in fact—at Vera. What true lady would suddenly close her home to the very friend she had begged to come and keep her company in her grief and loneliness, just because that friend had suffered a slight accident? Should her reaction not have been quite the opposite? But Vera had been patently, embarrassingly self-serving in her unwillingness to allow Gwen to be conveyed to her house. Much as she had railed against the Duke of Stanbrook before today, she had obviously been thrilled beyond words at being offered a chance to come here to Penderris today, and in his crested carriage, no less, for all the other inhabitants of the village to witness. She had seen the chance to extend the thrill and become a daily visitor here for the next week or so and had proceeded to grasp it, without any consideration whatsoever for Gwen's feelings.

Gwen nursed her humiliation and pain and anger while she reclined upon the bed in the guest room that had been assigned to her. Lord Trentham had carried her up here and deposited her on the bed and left her almost without a word. He *had* asked if he could fetch her anything, but both his face and his voice had been without expression and it was clear he did not expect her to say yes.

Oh, she must *not* give in to the temptation to shift all the blame for her discomfort onto the occupants of Penderris Hall. They had taken her in and been remarkably kind to her. Lord Trentham had carried her all the way up from the beach, or very close to it. And his hands had been surprisingly gentle when he removed her boot. He had brought her that cool cloth and pressed it to her forehead just when the pain had been threatening to get beyond her control.

She must *not* dislike him.

She just wished he did not make her feel like a spoiled, pampered, petulant schoolgirl.

A maid distracted her after a while. She brought more tea and the news that a portmanteau of her ladyship's belongings had been brought over from the village and was now in the dressing room adjoining the bedchamber.

The same maid helped her wash and change into a gown more suitable for evening. She brushed out Gwen's hair and restyled it. And then she left the room and Gwen wondered what would happen next. She hoped desperately that she could remain in her room, that the maid would bring up a tray at dinnertime.

Her hopes were soon to be dashed, however.

A knock on her door was preceded by the appearance of Lord Trentham, looking large and actually rather splendid in a well-fitting tailed evening coat and other evening attire. He was also glowering. No, that was unfair. His face in repose rather naturally glowered, Gwen thought. He had the look of a fierce warrior. He looked as though the niceties of civilized living were unimportant to him.

"You are ready to come downstairs?" he asked

"Oh," she said. "I would *really* prefer to stay here, Lord Trentham, and be no bother to anyone. If it is not too much trouble, perhaps you would ask for a tray to be sent up?"

She smiled at him.

"I believe it *would* be too much trouble, ma'am," he said. "I have been sent to bring you down."

Gwen's cheeks grew hot. How very mortifying! And what a vastly unmannerly answer. Could he not have phrased it differently? He might have told her that her company would be no bother to anyone. He might even have gone as far as to say that the duke and his guests were looking *forward* to her joining them.

He might have *smiled.*

He strode toward the bed, bent over her, and scooped her up.

Gwen set one arm about his neck and looked into his face even though it was disturbingly close. *She* could retain her manners even if he could not.

"What do you all do during your reunions?" she asked politely. "Reminisce about the wars?"

"That would be daft," he said.

Was he always so rude? Or was it just that he resented her and could not even be civil to her? But he could have carried her to the village instead of bringing her here. Obviously he was such a strong giant that her weight was no object to him.

"You studiously avoid all mention of the wars, then?" she asked as he made his way downstairs with her.

"We suffered in this place," he told her. "We healed here. We bared our souls to each other here. Leaving here was one of the hardest things we had had to do in a long while, perhaps in our whole lives. But it was necessary if our lives were ever to have meaning again. Once a year, though, we return to make ourselves whole once more, or to bolster ourselves with the illusion that we are whole."

It was a lengthy speech for Lord Trentham. But he did not look at her as he spoke. His voice sounded fierce and resentful. It put her in the wrong again. It implied that she was a soft and pampered lady who could not possibly understand the sort of suffering he and his friends here had endured. Or the fact that that suffering never quite came to an end, that the sufferer was forever scarred by it.

She *did* understand.

When wounds healed, everything should be mended. The person concerned should be whole again. That seemed to make good sense. But *she* had not been mended when her leg knit together after being broken. Her leg had been poorly set. She would not have been whole even if her leg had healed perfectly, though. She had also lost her unborn child as a result of the fall. It might even be said that she had *killed* her child. And Vernon had never been the same after it had happened, though that did beg the question—*the same as what*?

When one had once suffered a great hurt, there was always a weakness afterward, a vulnerability where there had been wholeness and strength before—and innocence.

Oh, she *did* understand.

Lord Trentham carried her into the drawing room and set her down on the same sofa as before. But this time the room was not empty. There were, in fact, six other people present apart from the two of them. The Duke of Stanbrook was one, Lady Barclay another, Viscount Ponsonby a third. Gwen wondered fleetingly what *his* wounds had been. He looked dazzlingly handsome and physically perfect, just as Lord Trentham looked *large* and physically perfect.

It was obvious what was wrong with one of the other gentlemen. He hauled himself to his feet when Gwen came into the room, using two canes strapped to his arms. His legs looked unnaturally twisted between the canes, and it appeared as though he was supporting much of his weight on his arms.

"Lady Muir," the duke said from his position before the hearth, "I appreciate your making the effort to join us. I fully understand that it must have *been* an effort. I am delighted to have you as a guest in my home, though I regret the circumstances. I look forward to becoming better acquainted with you during the coming week. You will not hesitate, I hope, to ask for anything you may need."

"Thank you, Your Grace," she said, flushing. "You are very kind."

His words were courtesy itself, though his manner was stiff, distant, austere. But at least he *was* courteous. Unlike Lord Trentham, he was clearly a gentleman from head to toe. An extremely elegant gentleman too.

"You have met Imogen, Lady Barclay, and Flavian, Viscount Ponsonby," he continued, crossing the room to pour a glass of wine, which he brought across to her. "Allow me to introduce Sir Benedict Harper."

He indicated the man with the twisted legs. He was tall and slim, with a thin face and angular features that had once perhaps been purely handsome. Now they gave evidence of prolonged suffering and pain.

"Lady Muir."

"Sir Benedict." Gwen inclined her head to him.

"And Ralph, Earl of Berwick," the duke said, indicating a good-looking young man if one ignored the scar that slashed across one side of his face. He nodded to her but neither spoke nor smiled.

Another dour man.

"My lord," she said.

"And Vincent, Lord Darleigh," His Grace said.

He was a slight young man with curly fair hair. He had an open, cheerful, smiling face, and the largest, loveliest blue eyes Gwen had ever seen. Now *there* was a man destined to break young hearts, she thought. There was no sign of any injury he might have sustained either to body or soul. And he was so very young. If he really had been an officer during the wars, he must have been a mere boy . . .

He seemed out of place in this group. He looked too young and carefree to have suffered greatly.

"My lord," Gwen said.

"You have the voice of a beautiful woman, Lady Muir," he said, "and I am told you have the looks to match. It is a pleasure to make your acquaintance. Imogen says that you are horribly embarrassed to be here, but you need not be. We sent Hugo down onto the beach today to find you. He has a well-earned reputation for never failing in any mission set him, and this was no exception. He fetched a rare beauty."

Gwen was feeling a jolt of shock that had nothing to do with his last words. Indeed, for a few moments she did not even fully comprehend what they were. She had suddenly realized that despite the loveliness of his eyes and the fact that he appeared to be gazing directly at her, *Lord Darleigh was blind.*

Perhaps his was the worst injury of all, she thought. She could imagine little worse than losing one's sight. Yet he smiled and was purely charming. Did his smile extend all the way inside himself, though? There was something slightly disturbing about his cheerful demeanor now that she understood the devastation the wars had wreaked upon his life.

"If Hugo had fetched a gargoyle, Vincent," the Earl of Berwick said, "it would have made no difference to you, would it?"

"Ah," Lord Darleigh said, turning his eyes with great accuracy in the direction of the earl and smiling sweetly, "it would not matter to me, Ralph, would it, provided she had the soul of an angel."

"A hit indeed, Ralph," Viscount Ponsonby said.

And that was when Gwen heard the echo of what Viscount Darleigh had said to her—*We sent Hugo down onto the beach today to find you . . . He fetched a rare beauty.*

"Lord Trentham came to *find* me?" she asked. "But how did he know I would be there? I did not plan that walk ahead of time."

"You would do well, Vincent," Lord Trentham said, "to tie your tongue in a knot."

"Too late," Viscount Ponsonby said. "Your secret must out, Hugo. Lady Muir, for a number of reasons, all of which seem sound to Hugo, he has decided to take a bride this year. His only p-problem is selection. He is arguably the finest soldier the British armies have produced in the last twenty years. He is not, alas, equally renowned as an accomplished l-lover and wooer of the fair sex. When he explained his situation to us last evening and added, wise man, that he was not in search of any grand love affair, he was advised to look about him for a personable female, explain to her that he is a lord and really quite f-fabulously wealthy, and then suggest that she marry him. He agreed that he would go down to the beach today and find such a woman. And here you are."

If her cheeks grew any hotter, Gwen thought, they would surely burst into flame. And all her earlier embarrassment and anger had returned with interest. She looked at Lord Trentham, who was standing stiff and erect like a soldier at ease, but *not* at ease, and her chin lifted and her eyes sparked.

"Perhaps, then, Lord Trentham," she said, "you would care to inform me of your stature and wealth now, in the presence of your friends. *And* make me your offer of marriage."

He looked directly at her and said nothing. He was not really given the chance.

"Ma'am," Lord Darleigh said, his blue eyes on hers again, though now they looked as troubled as his voice sounded. "I spoke to make everyone *laugh*. It was not until the words were out of my mouth that I realized how unpardonably embarrassing they were to you. We were, of course, all *joking* last evening, and it was pure chance that you were on the beach and hurt yourself and that Hugo happened to be there to offer you assistance. I beg you to forgive me and to forgive *Hugo*. He is blameless in your embarrassment. The fault is all mine."

Gwen transferred her gaze to him. And she laughed.

"I beg your pardon," she said. "I can quite see the funny side of the coincidence."

She was not sure she spoke the truth.

"Thank you, ma'am." The young lord sounded relieved.

"It is time *that* particular topic of conversation was put to rest," Sir Benedict said. "Where is your home, Lady Muir? When you are not staying with . . . Mrs. Parkinson, is it?"

"I live at Newbury Abbey in Dorsetshire," Gwen said. "Or rather, my home is the dower house in the park. I live there with my mother. My brother and his family live at the abbey—the Earl of Kilbourne, that is."

"I knew him slightly in the Peninsula," Lord Trentham said, "though he had a viscount's title then. He was shipped home, if I remember correctly, after his scouting party was ambushed in the mountains of Portugal, leaving him close to death. He made a full recovery, then?"

"He is well," Gwen said.

"It was Kilbourne's wife, was it not," the duke asked, "who turned out to be the long-lost daughter of the Duke of Portfrey?"

"Yes," Gwen said. "Lily, my sister-in-law."

"Portfrey and I were close friends in the long-ago days of our youth," the Duke of Stanbrook said.

"He is married to my aunt," she said. "Those family relationships are a little complicated, to say the least."

The duke nodded.

"Lady Muir," he said, "it will be best for you, I believe, if we excuse you from sitting at the dining room table with us. Although I could provide a stool for your foot, it would not be adequate. The good doctor was quite adamant in his instruction that you keep your foot *elevated* for the next week. You will, therefore, dine in here. I do hope that will not be too inconvenient for you. We will not desert you entirely, however. Hugo has been appointed to bear you company. I can assure you that he will *not* assail your ears with tales of his wealth or with suggestions that you marry him in order to secure a part of it for yourself."

Her smile was austere.

"I daresay I will never live down that faux pas," Lord Darleigh said ruefully.

The duke offered his arm to Lady Barclay and led her from the room. The others followed. Sir Benedict Harper, Gwen noticed, did not use his canes as crutches even though they looked sturdy enough to bear his weight. Rather, he walked slowly and with painstaking care, using them for balance.

The silence in the drawing room after the door had closed behind the diners seemed almost unbearably loud.

Chapter 4

It had *not* been his fault, Gwen thought, that joke and the coincidence of her being on the beach today of all days. It just *felt* as if it were his fault. She resented him anyway. She had just been horribly embarrassed.

And Lord Trentham looked as if he resented her. Probably because *he* had just been horribly embarrassed.

His eyes were on the door as though he could still see his fellow guests through its panels and longed to be on the other side with them. She wished quite fervently that he was there too.

"Will Sir Benedict ever walk without his canes?" she asked for something to say.

He pursed his lips, and for a moment she thought he would not answer.

"The whole world beyond these walls," he said eventually, still watching the door, "would say a resounding no. The whole world called him fool for refusing to have the legs amputated and then for not accepting reality and resigning himself to living the rest of his life in bed or at least in a chair. There are six of us within this house who would wager a fortune apiece on him. He swears he will dance one day, and the only thing we wonder about is who his partner will be."

Oh dear, she thought after another short silence, this was going to be an uphill battle.

"Do you often see people down on the beach?" she asked.

He turned to look at her.

"Never," he said. "In all the times I have been down there, I have never encountered another soul who was not also from this house. Until today."

There was a suggestion of reproach in his voice.

"Then I suppose," she said, "it seemed a safe thing to say to your friends, who were teasing you. That you would find a woman to whom to propose marriage down on the beach, I mean."

"Yes," he agreed. "It did."

She smiled at him, and then laughed softly. He looked back, no answering amusement in his face.

"It all really *is* funny," she said. "Except that now you will doubtless be teased endlessly. And I am confined here for at least a week with a sprained ankle. *And,*" she added when he still did not smile, "you and I will probably be horribly embarrassed in each other's company until I finally leave here."

"If I could throttle young Darleigh," he said, "without actually committing murder, I would."

Gwen laughed again.

And silence descended once more.

"Lord Trentham," she said, "you really do not need to bear me company here, you know. You came to Penderris to enjoy the companionship of the Duke of Stanbrook and your fellow guests. I daresay your suffering together here for so long established a special bond among you, and I have now intruded upon that intimacy. Everyone has been most kind and courteous to me, but I am quite determined to be as little of a nuisance while I must remain here as I possibly can be. Please feel free to join the others in the dining room."

He still stood looking down at her, his hands clasped behind his back.

"You would have me thwart the will of my host, then?" he asked her. "I will not do it, ma'am. I will remain here."

Lord Trentham. *He could be anything from a baron on up to a marquess,* Gwen thought, though she had never heard of him before today. And if what Viscount Ponsonby had said was correct, he was also extremely wealthy. Yet he did not have the manners of a thick plank.

She inclined her head to him and resolved not to utter another word before *he* did, though she would thereby be lowering her manners to the level of his. So be it.

But before the silence could become uncomfortable again, the door opened to admit two servants, who proceeded to move a table closer to the sofa and set it for one diner. Before those servants had time to leave the room, two others entered bearing laden trays. One was set across Gwen's lap while the other was carried to the table, where the various dishes were set out for Lord Trentham's dinner.

The servants left as silently as they had come. Gwen looked down at her soup and picked up her spoon as Lord Trentham took his place at the table.

"I beg your pardon," Lord Trentham said, "for the embarrassment a seemingly harmless joke has caused you, Lady Muir. It is one thing to be teased by friends. It is another to be humiliated by strangers."

She looked at him in surprise.

"I daresay," she said, "I will survive the ordeal."

He returned her look, saw that she was smiling, and nodded curtly before addressing himself to his dinner.

The Duke of Stanbrook had an excellent chef, Gwen thought, if the oxtail soup was anything to judge by.

"You are in search of a wife, Lord Trentham?" she said. "Do you have any particular lady in mind?"

"No," he said. "But I want someone of my own sort. A practical, capable woman."

She looked up at him. *Someone of my own sort.*

"I was not born a gentleman," he explained. "My title was awarded to me during the wars, as a result of something I did. My father was probably one of the wealthiest men in England. He was a very successful businessman. But he was not a gentleman, and he had no desire to be one. He had no social ambitions for his children either. He despised the upper classes as idle wastrels, if the truth were told. He wanted us to fit in where we belonged. I have not always honored his wishes, but in that particular one I concur with him. It would suit me best to find a wife of my own class."

Much had been explained, Gwen thought.

"What did you do?" she asked as she pushed back her empty soup bowl and drew forward her plate of roast beef and vegetables.

He looked back at her, his eyebrows raised.

"It must have been something extraordinary," she said, "if the reward was a title."

He shrugged.

"I led a Forlorn Hope," he said.

"A *Forlorn Hope*?" Her knife and fork remained suspended above her plate. "And you survived it?"

"As you see," he said.

She gazed at him in wonder and admiration. A Forlorn Hope was almost always suicidal and almost always a failure. He could not have failed if he had been so rewarded. And good heavens, he was not even a gentleman. There were not many officers who were not.

"I do not talk about it," he said, cutting into his meat. "Ever."

Gwen continued to stare for a few moments before resuming her meal. Were the memories so painful, then, that they were not even tempered by the reward? Was it there that he had been so horribly wounded that he had spent a long time here recovering his health?

But his title, she realized, sat uneasily upon his shoulders.

"How long have you been widowed?" he asked her in what, she guessed, was a determined effort to change the subject.

"Seven years," she said.

"You have never wished to marry again?" he asked.

"Never," she said—and thought of that strange, crashing loneliness she had felt down on the beach.

"You loved him, then?" he asked.

"Yes." It was true. Despite everything, she had loved Vernon. "Yes, I loved him."

"How did he die?" he asked.

A gentleman would not have asked such a question.

"He fell," she told him, "over the balustrade of the gallery above the marble hall in our home. He landed on his head and died instantly."

Too late it occurred to her that she might have answered with some truth, as he had done a short while ago—*I do not talk about it. Ever.*

He swallowed the food that was in his mouth. But she knew what he was about to ask even before he spoke again.

"How long was this," he asked, "after you fell off your horse and lost your unborn child?"

Well, she was committed now.

"A year," she said. "A little less."

"You had a marriage unusually punctuated with violence," he said.

Her answer had not needed comment. Or, rather, not such a comment. She set her knife and fork down across her half-empty plate with a little clatter.

"You are impertinent, Lord Trentham," she said.

Oh, but this was her own fault. His very first question had been impertinent. She ought to have told him so then.

"I am," he said. "It is not how a gentleman behaves, is it? Or a man who is not a gentleman when he is talking to a *lady*. I have never freed myself of the habit, when I wish to know something, of simply asking. It is not always the polite thing to do, I have learned."

She finished the food on her plate, moved the plate to the back of the tray, and drew forward her pudding dish. She picked up her wineglass and sipped from it. She set it down and sighed.

"My closest family members," she said, "have always chosen to believe quite steadfastly that Vernon and I had a blissful love relationship that was blighted by accident and tragedy. Other people are notably silent upon the subject of my marriage and my husband's death, but I can often almost *hear* them thinking and assuming that it was a marriage filled with violence and abuse."

"And was it?" he asked.

She closed her eyes briefly.

"Sometimes," she said, "life is too complicated for there to be a simple answer to a simple question. I did indeed love him, and he loved me. Often our love *was* blissful. But . . . Well, sometimes it seemed to me that Vernon was two different people. Often—most of the time, in fact—he was cheerful and charming and witty and intelligent and affectionate and a whole host of other things that made him very dear to me. But occasionally, although he remained in many ways much the same, there was something almost . . . oh, *desperate* about his high spirits. And I always felt at such times that there was the finest of fine lines between happiness and despair, and he trod that line. The trouble was that he never came out of it on the side of happiness. He always tumbled the other way. And then for days, occasionally even for a few weeks, he was plunged into the blackest of black moods and nothing I could say or do would pull him free—until one day, without any warning at all, he would be back to his usual self. I learned to recognize the moment when his mood was turning to the over-exuberant. I learned to dread such moments because there was no coaxing him back from the brink. Though for the last year his moods hovered most of the time between black and blacker. And you are the *only* person, Lord Trentham, to whom I have spoken of such things. I have no idea why I have broken my silence with a near stranger."

She was partly horrified, partly relieved that she had revealed so much to a man she did not even particularly like. Though there was much, of course, that she had *not* said.

"It is this place," he said. "It has been the scene of much unburdening over the years, some of it all but unspeakable and all but unthinkable. There is trust in this house. We all trust one another here, and no one has ever betrayed that trust. Did you go on that mad ride when Lord Muir was in one of his excitable moods?"

"At that time in my marriage," she said, "I still clung to the belief that I could avert his black moods by humoring his wild whims. He wanted me to ride with him that day and brushed aside all my protests. And so I went, and I followed wherever he led. I was terrified that he would hurt himself. What I thought I could do to keep him from harm just by *being* with him I do not know."

"But it was not he who was hurt," he said.

Except that in many ways he had been hurt as badly as she. And neither of them had been hurt as badly as their child.

"No." Her eyes were shut tight again. Her spoon was clutched, forgotten, in one hand.

"But it *was* he who got hurt on the night he died," he said.

She opened her eyes and turned her head to look coldly at him. What *was* he? Her inquisitor?

"That is *enough,*" she said. "He did not abuse me, Lord Trentham. He never raised a hand or voice to me or belittled me or lashed out at me with words. I believe he was ill, even if there is no name for his illness. He was not mad. He did not belong in an asylum. Neither did he belong on a sickbed. But he was ill nevertheless. That is hard for anyone to comprehend who did not live with him constantly, day and night, as I did. But it is true. I loved him. I had promised to love him in sickness and in health until death parted us, and I *did* love him to the end. But it was not easy, for all that. After his death I grieved deeply for him. I was also weary of marriage to the marrow of my bones. That one marriage brought me great joy, but it also brought almost more misery than I could bear. I wanted peace afterward. I wanted it for the rest of my life. I have had it now for seven years and am perfectly content to remain as I am."

"No man could change your mind?" he asked.

Even just yesterday she would have said no without any hesitation at all. Even this morning she had been in denial of the essential emptiness and loneliness of her life. Or perhaps that brief moment on the beach had been instigated by nothing more serious than her quarrel with Vera and the bleakness of her surroundings.

"He would have to be the perfect man," she said, "and there is really no such thing as perfection, is there? He would have to be an even-tempered, cheerful, comfortable companion who has known no great trouble in his life. He would have to offer a relationship that promised peace and stability and . . . Oh, and simplicity with no excessive highs and lows."

Yes, she thought, surprised, *such a marriage would be pleasant.* But she doubted there was a man perfect for her needs. And even if there was one who *seemed* perfect and who wished to marry her, how would she know for sure what he was like until after she had married him and lived with him and it was too late to change her mind?

And how could she ever be worthy of happiness?

"No passion?" he asked her. "He would not have to be good in bed?"

Her head snapped around in his direction. She felt her eyes grow wide with shock and her cheeks flame with heat.

"You really *are* a plain-spoken man, Lord Trentham," she said, "or else an extraordinarily impertinent one. Pleasure in the marriage bed need not involve *passion,* as you put it. It can be simply shared comfort. *If* I were looking for a husband, I would be happy with the shared comfort. And if *you* are looking for a wife who is practical and capable, passion cannot count a great deal with you either, can it?"

She was feeling horridly discomposed and had spoken quite indiscreetly.

"A woman can be practical and capable *and* lusty too," he said. "She would have to be lusty if I were to marry her. I am going to have to give up other women when I wed. It would not be seemly to seek my pleasure outside my marriage bed, would it?

It would not be fair to my wife or a good example to my children. And *there* is middle-class morality for you, Lady Muir. I am lusty but believe in marital fidelity."

She set her spoon down on her plate, careful this time not to let it clatter. And then she spread her hands over her face and laughed into them. Could he possibly have just said what she knew very well he *had* said?

"I am really quite, quite sure," she said, "that this has been the strangest day of my life, Lord Trentham. And now it has culminated in a short lecture on lust and middle-class morality."

"Well," he said, pushing back his chair and getting to his feet, "that is what you get when you sprain your ankle within sight of a man who is not a gentleman, ma'am. I will remove that tray from across your lap and set it down on the table here with my dishes. You *have* finished eating, have you?"

"I have," she said while he suited action to words and then turned back to look down at her.

"Why the devil," he asked her, "were you staying with Mrs. Parkinson? Why are you her friend?"

She raised her eyebrows at both the blasphemy and the questions.

"She lost her husband lately," she said, "and was feeling unhappy and lonely. I know both feelings. I knew her long ago and have corresponded with her from time to time ever since. I was free to come and so I came."

"You realize, I suppose," he said, "that she feels nothing whatsoever for *you,* but only for your title and your close connection with the Earl of Kilbourne. And that she will come here daily only because it is Penderris Hall, home of the Duke of Stanbrook."

"Lord Trentham," she said, "Vera Parkinson's loneliness is very real. If I have helped alleviate it in some small degree during the past two weeks, then I am satisfied."

"The trouble with the upper classes," he said, "is that they rarely speak the truth. The woman is a horror."

Oh, dear. Gwen feared she would hug that last sentence to herself with glee for a long time to come.

"Sometimes, Lord Trentham," she said, "tempering the truth with tact and kindness is called good manners."

"You use them even when you scold," he said.

"I try."

She wished he would sit down again. Even if she were also standing he would tower over her. As it was, he looked like a veritable giant. Perhaps the enemy against whom he had led the Forlorn Hope had taken one look at him and fled. It would not surprise her.

"You are not by any manner of means the sort of woman I am in search of as a wife," he said, "and I am in a totally different universe from the husband you hope to find. But I feel a powerful urge to kiss you, for all that."

What?

But the trouble was that his outrageous words aroused such a surging of raw desire to all the relevant parts of her body that she was left gaping and breathless. And despite his massive size and his cropped hair and his dour, fierce countenance, and his lack of gentlemanly manners, she *still* found him overpoweringly attractive.

"I suppose," he said, "I ought to restrain myself. But there *was* the coincidence of that meeting on the beach, you see."

She closed her mouth and mastered her breathing. She was not going to let him get away with such impertinence, was she?

"Yes," she heard herself say as she gazed into his eyes far above her own, "there was that. And there is a school of thought, I have heard, that claims there is no such thing as coincidence."

Was he really going to kiss her? Was she going to *allow* it? She had not gone unkissed for seven years. She had allowed a few restrained embraces from various gentlemen of her acquaintance. But never from any to whom she had felt any greater attraction than liking. And none from any real physical desire—not on her part, anyway.

For a few moments she thought he would not kiss her after all. There was no unbending of his stiff posture and no softening of his expression. But then he leaned forward and downward, and she lifted her hands to set on his shoulders. Oh, goodness, they were broad and solid. But she knew that. He had carried her . . .

He touched his lips to hers.

And she was engulfed in a sudden heat of desire.

She expected that he would crush her in his arms and press his mouth hard against hers. She expected to have to ward off a hot outpouring of ardor.

Instead, he spread his hands lightly on either side of her waist, his thumbs beneath her bosom but not pushing up against it. And his lips brushed softly over hers, tasting her, teasing her. She moved her hands in to cup the sides of his great neck. She could feel his breath against her cheek. She could smell that faint soap or cologne scent she had noticed earlier—something enticingly masculine.

The heat of her desire cooled. But what replaced it was almost worse. For it was not a mindless embrace. She was very aware of *him*. And she was very aware that, despite all appearances, there was gentleness in him. She had felt it in the touch of his hands on her ankle, of course, but she had ignored it then. It had seemed to be contrary to all else she had observed of him.

He lifted his head and looked steadily into her eyes. Oh, goodness, his were no less fierce than they usually were. She gazed right back and raised her eyebrows.

"I suppose," he said, "if I were a gentleman, I would now be offering abject apologies."

"But you gave me advance warning," she said, "and I did not say no. Shall we agree, Lord Trentham, that this has been a *very* strange day for both of us, but that now it is almost over? Tomorrow we will put all this behind us and return to more decorous behavior."

He stood upright and clasped his hands behind him. She was beginning to recognize it as a familiar pose.

"That seems sensible," he said.

Fortunately, there was no time to say more. A tap on the door was followed by the appearance of two servants come to clear the table and take away the trays. And within moments of the door closing behind them, it opened again to admit the duke and his other guests returning from the dining room.

Lady Barclay and Lord Darleigh came to sit close to Gwen and engaged her in conversation while Lord Trentham moved away to play cards with three of the other gentlemen.

If she were to awake now, Gwen thought, she would surely judge the dream of today to be the most bizarre she had ever dreamed. But alas, the events, beginning with the arrival of her mother's letter this morning, had been just *too* bizarre not to have been real. And was it possible to dream of taste? Somehow she could still taste Lord Trentham on her lips, though he had eaten the same food and drunk the same wine as she.

Chapter 5

The members of the Survivors' Club stayed up long after Hugo had carried Lady Muir up to her bed. It was their custom to relax during the day, sometimes together or in smaller groups, often alone, but to sit up together deep into the night, talking upon the more serious matters that concerned them.

This night was no exception. It began with apologies from Vincent and teasing from everyone else. Vincent was teased about his loose tongue, Hugo about the happy progress of his search for a wife. They both took it in good part. There was no other way to take it, of course, that would not draw worse.

But finally they all grew more pensive. George had been having a recurrence of the old dream in which he thought of *just* the right thing to say to dissuade his wife from jumping over the cliff at the precise moment when she did jump. He had been waking up in a cold sweat, crying out and reaching for her. Ralph had met the sister of one of his three dead best friends at a soiree in London at Christmastime, and she had lit up with delight at seeing him and with eagerness to talk about her brother with someone who had been close to him. And Ralph had been close. The four of them had been virtually inseparable all through school and had ridden off to war together at the age of eighteen. He had watched the other three being blown to pieces just a fraction of a moment before he had almost but not quite followed them into the hereafter. He had left Miss Courtney's side to fetch her a glass of lemonade. He had fully *intended* to take it to her. Instead, he had walked right out of the house and left London the next morning. He had offered no explanation, no apology, and had not seen her since.

By the following morning, Hugo was feeling horribly embarrassed about the previous evening. Most specifically about that kiss. He had no explanation for it. He was not a ladies' man. He had always had a healthy sex life, it was true, though not so much in the past few years, first because of his illness and more recently because he was *Lord Trentham—that* millstone about his neck—and it somehow did not seem right to be dashing off to brothels whenever the mood took him. Besides, he lived in the country, far away from any such temptation. He could not remember kissing any respectable woman since he was sixteen and had found himself hiding in the same broom closet as one of his cousin's school friends during a game of hide-and-seek at the cousin's birthday party.

He had never, *ever* kissed a *lady*. Or felt any burning desire to do so.

He did not even particularly like Lady Muir. He had judged her to be an irresponsible, frivolous, arrogant, bored, spoiled aristocrat, albeit a beautiful one. Of course, the story she had told of her husband had added some depth to her character. She had undoubtedly suffered a difficult marriage, with which she had coped as best she was able. And she did, he admitted grudgingly, have a sense of humor and an infectious laugh.

All of which was no explanation at all for his sudden urge to kiss her after he had removed her dinner tray from her lap. Or an excuse for giving in to that urge.

And why, in the name of all that was wonderful, had she allowed it? He had done nothing to ingratiate himself with her. On the contrary, he had been downright surly. He had a tendency to be that way with the upper classes, members of the Survivors' Club excepted. He had not been well received by his fellow officers in the military. The majority of them had treated him with disdain and condescension, a few with open hostility for his daring to break into their ranks just because his father could afford to purchase his commission. Their ladies had ignored him entirely, just as they ignored their servants. All of which had not particularly bothered Hugo. He had wanted to be an officer, not a member of any social club. He had wanted to distinguish himself on the battlefield, and he had done that.

But last night he had kissed a *lady*. For no reason at all except that she had set her hands over her flushed face and laughed helplessly after he talked about giving up whores when he married. And there had still been laughter in her voice when she had spoken—*I am really quite, quite sure, that this has been the strangest day of my life, Lord Trentham. And now it has culminated in a short lecture on lust and middle-class morality.*

Yes, that was what had made him want to kiss her.

He wished to God he had kept his wishes on a tighter rein.

He was going to have to avoid her as much as he possibly could for the rest of her stay here. It was going to be dashed awkward coming face to face with her again.

It was a resolve he kept until after luncheon. He spent the morning, while it rained outside, in the conservatory with Imogen. While she watered the plants and did magical things to them that made them look fresher and altogether more attractive, he read the letter from his half sister that had arrived with the morning post. Constance wrote to him at least twice a week. She was nineteen years old and basically a lively, pretty girl who was ready and eager for beaux and marriage. But her mother was a selfish, possessive woman who had used her delicate health and ailments real or imagined to manipulate those around her for as long as Hugo had known her. She kept her daughter a virtual prisoner at the house, always at her beck and call. Constance rarely went out except to run brief and specific errands. She had no friends, no social life, no beaux. Not that she complained openly to Hugo. Her letters were invariably cheerful—and almost empty of any real content because she really had nothing to say.

It was Hugo's duty to set that all right. A duty impelled by love. And by the fact that he was her guardian. And by a promise to his father that he would secure a happy future for her as far as he was able.

She was one of the main reasons for his decision to marry. He did not have the slightest idea how to launch her onto middle-class society on his own or how to steer suitably eligible middle-class men in her direction. If he married . . . No, *when* he married, his wife would know how to introduce her sister-in-law to the sort of men who could offer her security and happiness for the rest of her life.

There was, of course, his other reason for deciding to marry. He was not a natural celibate, and his need for sex—regular, lusty sex—had been asserting itself all too painfully for the past while and warring against his contrasting inclination toward privacy and independence.

He had decided when he left Penderris three years ago that above all else he wanted a life of peace. He had sold out of the army and settled in a small country cottage in Hampshire. He had supported himself by growing a kitchen garden and keeping a few chickens and doing odd jobs for his neighbors. He was big and strong, after all. His services had been much in demand, especially among the elderly. He had kept quiet about his title.

He had been happy. Well, contented, anyway, despite all the warnings from his six friends here that he resembled an unexploded firecracker and was surely going to burst back to life again at some time in the future, perhaps when he least expected it.

Last year, after his father's death, he had purchased Crosslands Park not far from the cottage and set up on a slightly grander scale there. Somehow word of his title had leaked out. He had proceeded to grow a somewhat larger garden and cultivate a few crops, to keep a few more chickens, and to add a few sheep and cows. He had hired a steward, who had in his turn hired some laborers to help with the farm work. Hugo had continued to do much of it himself, though. Idleness did not suit him. He still did odd jobs for his neighbors too, though he steadfastly refused to accept payment. His park was undeveloped, his house partly shut up since he used only three rooms with any regularity. He had a very small staff.

But he had been happy there for a year. Contented, anyway. His life was unexciting. It lacked challenge. It lacked any close companionship even though he remained on good terms with his neighbors. It was the life he wanted.

And now he was going to change everything by marrying—because really he had no choice.

The letter lay long forgotten in his lap. Imogen was still in the conservatory. She sat on one of the window ledges, her legs drawn up before her, a book propped against them. She was reading.

She felt his eyes on her and looked up, closing the book as she did so.

"It is time for luncheon," she said. "Shall we go in?"

He got to his feet and offered his hand.

Lady Muir, he learned in the dining room, was in the morning room, George having judged it a more cozy place for her during the daytime. A footman had carried her down, and George himself and Ralph had taken breakfast in there with her. She had asked for paper and pen and ink afterward in order to write to her brother. Mrs. Parkinson was with her now and had been for the past few hours.

"Poor Lady Muir," Flavian said. "One feels almost inclined to rush to her rescue like a knight in bright armor. But one might f-find oneself being coaxed into escorting her friend home, and the prospect is enough to make any knight turn tail and run and bedamned to chivalry."

"It is all taken care of," George assured him. "Before the lady arrived, I suggested to Lady Muir that in her weakened condition she might perhaps wish to rest this afternoon instead of facing the exertions of a prolonged visit. She understood me perfectly and agreed that yes, indeed, she expected to need a sleep after luncheon. My carriage will be at the door in forty-five minutes."

The clouds had moved off and the sun was shining an hour

later when Hugo was standing out on the terrace, trying to decide whether to take a long walk along the headland or to be more lazy and stroll in the nearer park. He decided upon the lazy alternative and spent an hour wandering alone about the park. It was not at all elaborately designed, but even so there were flower gardens and shady walks and tree-dotted lawns and a summerhouse in a dip that sheltered it from any wind blowing off the sea. The small structure offered a view along a tree-lined alley to a stone statue at the far end.

It all made Hugo think with some dissatisfaction about his own park at Crosslands. It was large and square and barren, and he had no idea how to make it attractive. One could not just stick alleys and arbors and wilderness walks any old where. And the house rather resembled a large barn from which all the animals had fled. It *could* be lovely. He had sensed that when he had decided to buy it.

But whereas he could appreciate beauty and effective design when he saw them, there was no creative corner of his mind in which original designs would pop to life. He needed to hire someone to plan it all for him, he supposed. There were such people, and he had the money with which to employ their services.

He wandered back to the house after an hour or so.

Was Lady Muir really sleeping, he wondered as he let himself in at the front door. Or had she simply been glad to avail herself of the excuse with which George had presented her to get rid of her tiresome friend? If she was alone in the morning room and *not* sleeping, of course, George would surely have arranged that someone bear her company. He was good at such niceties of hospitality.

Hugo did not need to go near her. And he certainly did not want to. He would be very happy never to see her again. It was difficult to explain, then, why he paused outside the morning room door and leaned his ear closer to it.

Silence.

She was either upstairs, resting, or she was in there, sleeping.

Either way, he was quite free to proceed on his way to the library, where he planned to write to Constance and to William Richardson, the very capable manager of his father's businesses, now his own.

His hand went to the handle of the door instead. He turned it as silently as he could and pushed the door ajar.

She was there. She was lying on a chaise longue, which had been turned so that she would have a view out through the window to the flower garden beyond. It already sported a few spring flowers and a whole lot of green shoots and buds, unlike Hugo's flower garden at Crosslands, of which he had been very proud last summer. He had planted all summer flowers and had had a glorious show of blooms for a few months and then . . . nothing. And they had all, he had learned later, been annuals and would not bloom again this summer.

He had much to learn. He had grown up in London and had then gone off to fight wars.

Either she had not heard the door open or she was asleep. It was impossible to tell which from where he stood. He stepped inside, shut the door as quietly as he had opened it, and walked around the chaise until he could look down at her.

She was asleep.

He frowned.

Her face looked pale and drawn.

He should leave before she awoke.

Gwen had nodded off to sleep, lulled by the blissful silence after Vera left and by the dose of medicine the Duke of Stanbrook had coaxed her into taking when he had discerned from the paleness of her face that she was in more pain than she could easily endure.

She had not seen Lord Trentham all morning. It was a great relief, for she had awoken remembering his kiss and had found the memory hard to shake. Why ever had he *wanted* to kiss her, since he had given no indication that he either liked her or was attracted to her? And why on earth had she consented to the kiss?

She certainly could not claim that he had stolen it before she could protest.

Neither could she claim that it had been an unpleasant experience.

It most decidedly had not been.

And that fact was perhaps the most disturbing of all.

She had endured Vera's visit for several hours before the duke himself came to the room, as promised, and very courteously yet very firmly escorted her out to his waiting carriage after assuring her that he would send it for her again tomorrow morning.

Vera had been quite vocally put out at being left alone with Gwen throughout her visit. When their luncheon had been brought to the morning room, delicious though it was, she had protested at the discourtesy of His Grace's not having invited her to join the rest of his guests at the dining room table. She was chagrined at the arrangements that had been made for her return home—and its early hour. She had assured His Grace on her arrival, she had told Gwen, that she would be happy to walk home and save him the trouble of calling out his carriage again if one of the gentlemen would only be kind enough to escort her at least part of the way. He had ignored her generous offer.

But what could one expect of a man who had killed his own wife?

How she *hoped,* Gwen thought as she drifted off to sleep, that Neville would not delay in sending the carriage for her once he received her letter. She had assured him that she was quite well enough to travel.

Would she see Lord Trentham today? It was perhaps too much to expect that she would not, but she did hope that he would keep his distance and that the duke would not appoint him to take dinner with her again this evening. She had embarrassed herself enough with regard to him yesterday to last her for the next lifetime or two.

He was the last person she thought of as she fell asleep. And he was the first person she saw when she woke up again some indeterminate time later. He was standing a short distance from the chaise longue upon which she lay, his booted feet slightly apart, his hands clasped behind his back, frowning. He looked very much like a military officer even though he was dressed in a form-fitting coat of green superfine and buff-colored pantaloons with highly polished Hessian boots. He was frowning down at her. His habitual expression, it seemed.

She felt at a huge disadvantage, stretched out for sleep as she was.

"Most people," he said, "snore when they sleep on their back."

Trust him to say something totally unexpected.

Gwen raised her eyebrows. "And I do not?"

"Not on this occasion," he said, "though you do sleep with your mouth partway open."

"Oh."

How dare he stand there watching her while she slept. There was something uncomfortably intimate about it.

"How is your ankle today?" he asked.

"I thought it would be better, but annoyingly it is not," she said. "It is *only* a sprained ankle, after all. I feel embarrassed at all the fuss it is causing. You need not feel obliged to keep talking about it or asking me about it. *Or* to continue keeping me company."

Or watching me while I sleep.

"You ought to have some fresh air," he said. "Your face is pale. It is fashionable for ladies to look pale, I gather, though I doubt any wish to look pasty."

Wonderful! He had just informed her that she looked pasty.

"It is a chilly day," he said, "but the wind has gone down and the sun is shining, and you may enjoy sitting in the flower garden for a while. I'll fetch your cloak if you wish to go."

All she had to do was say no. He would surely go away and stay away.

"How would I get out there?" she asked instead and then could have bitten out her tongue since the answer was obvious.

"You could crawl on your hands and knees," he said, "if you wished to be as stubborn as you were yesterday. Or you could send for a burly footman—I believe one of them carried you down this morning. Or I could carry you if you trust me not to become overfamiliar again."

Gwen felt herself blushing.

"I hope," she said, "you have not been blaming yourself for last evening, Lord Trentham. We were equally to blame for that kiss, if *blame* is the right word. Why should we *not* have kissed, after all, if we both wished to do so? Neither of us is married or betrothed to someone else."

She had the feeling that her attempt at nonchalance was failing miserably.

"I may take it, then," he said, "that you do not wish to crawl out on your hands and knees?"

"You may," she said.

No more was said about the burly footman.

He turned and strode from the room without another word, presumably to go and fetch her cloak.

That had been nicely done of her, Gwen thought with considerable irony.

But the prospect of some fresh air was not to be resisted.

And the prospect of Lord Trentham's company?

Chapter 6

It *was* chilly. But the sun was shining, and they were surrounded by primroses and crocuses and even a few daffodils. It had not occurred to Gwen before now to wonder why so many spring flowers were varying shades of yellow. Was it nature's way of adding a little sunshine to the season that came after the dreariness of winter but before the brightness of summer?

"This is so very lovely," she said, breathing in the fresh, slightly salty air. "Spring is my favorite season."

She drew her red cloak more snugly about her as Lord Trentham set her down along a wooden seat beneath the window of the morning room. He took the two cushions she had carried out at his suggestion, placed one at her back to protect it from the wooden arm, and slid the other carefully beneath her right ankle. He spread the blanket he had brought with him over her legs.

"Why?" he asked as he straightened up.

"I prefer a daffodil to a rose," she said. "And spring is full of newness and hope."

He sat down on the pedestal of a stone urn close by and draped his arms over his spread knees. It was a relaxed, casual pose, but his eyes were intent on hers.

"What do you wish for your life that would be new?" he asked her. "What are your hopes for the future?"

"I see, Lord Trentham," she said, "that I must choose my words with care when I am in your company. You take everything I say literally."

"Why say something," he asked her, "if your words mean nothing?"

It was a fair enough question.

"Oh, very well," she said. "Let me think."

Her first thought was that she was not sorry he had come to the morning room and suggested bringing her out here for some air. If she were perfectly honest with herself, she would have to admit that she had been disappointed when it was a footman who had appeared in her room this morning to carry her downstairs. And she had been disappointed that Lord Trentham had not sought her out all morning. And yet she had also hoped to avoid him for the rest of her stay here. He was right about words that meant nothing, even if the words were only in one's head.

"I do not *want* anything new," she said. "And my hope is that I can remain contented and at peace."

He continued to look at her as though his eyes could pierce through hers to her very soul. And she realized that though she *thought* she spoke the truth, she was really not perfectly sure about it.

"Have you noticed," she asked him, "how standing still can sometimes be no different from moving backward? For the whole world moves on and leaves one behind."

Oh, dear. It was the house, he had said last evening, that inspired such confidences.

"You have been left behind?" he asked.

"I was the first of my generation in our family to marry," she said. "I was the first, and indeed the only one, to be widowed. Now my brother is married, and Lauren, my cousin and dearest friend. All my other cousins are married too. They all have growing families and have moved, it seems, into another phase of their lives that is closed to me. It is not that they are not kind and welcoming. They are. They are all forever inviting me to stay, and their desire for my company is perfectly genuine. I *know* that. I still have remarkably close friendships with Lauren, with Lily—my sister-in-law—and with my cousins. And I live with my mother, whom I love very dearly. I am very well blessed."

The assertion sounded hollow to her ears.

"A seven-year mourning period for a husband is an exceedingly long one," he said, "especially when a woman is young. How old *are* you?"

Trust Lord Trentham to ask the unaskable.

"I am thirty-two," she said. "It is possible to live a perfectly satisfying existence without remarrying."

"Not if you want to have children without incurring scandal," he said. "You would be wise not to delay too much longer if you do."

She raised her eyebrows. Was there no end to his impertinence? And yet, what would undoubtedly be impertinence in any other man she knew was *not* in his case. Not really. He was just a blunt, direct man, who spoke his mind.

"I am not sure I can *have* children," she said. "The physician who tended me when I miscarried said I could not."

"Was he the man who set your broken leg?" he asked.

"Yes."

"And you never sought a second opinion?"

She shook her head.

"It does not matter, anyway," she said. "I have nieces and nephews. I am fond of them and they of me."

It *did* matter, though, and only now at this moment did she realize how much it did. Such was the power of denial. What *was* it about this house? Or this man.

"It sounds to me," he said, "as though that physician was a quack of the worst sort. He left you with a permanent limp and at the same time destroyed all your hope of bearing a child just after you had lost one—without ever suggesting that you consult a doctor with more knowledge and experience of such matters than he."

"Some things," she said, "are best not known for sure, Lord Trentham."

He lowered his eyes from hers at last. He looked at the ground and with the toe of one large booted foot he smoothed out the gravel of the path.

What made him so attractive? Perhaps it was his size. For although he was unusually large, there was nothing clumsy about him. Every part of him was in perfect proportion to every other. Even his cropped hair, which should lessen any claim to good looks he might possess, suited the shape of his head and the harshness of his features. His hands could be gentle. So could his lips . . .

"What do you do?" she asked him. "When you are not here, that is. You are no longer an officer, are you?"

"I live in peace," he said, looking back up at her. "Like you. And contentment. I bought a manor and estate last year after my father died, and I live there alone. I have sheep and cows and chickens, a small farm, a vegetable garden, a flower garden. I work at it all. I get my hands dirty. I get soil under my fingernails. My neighbors are puzzled, for I am *Lord Trentham*. My family is puzzled, for I am now the owner of a vast import/export business and enormously wealthy. I could live with great consequence in London. I grew up as the son of a wealthy man, though I was always expected to work hard in preparation for the day when I would take over from my father. I insisted instead that he purchase a commission for me in an infantry regiment and I worked hard at my chosen career. I distinguished myself. Then I left. And now I live in peace. And contentment."

There was something indefinable about his tone. Defiant? Angry? Defensive? She wondered if he was happy. Happiness and contentment were not the same thing, were they?

"And marriage will complete your contentment?" she asked him.

He pursed his lips.

"I was not made for a life without sex," he said.

She had asked for that one. She tried not to blush.

"I disappointed my father," he said. "I followed him like a

shadow when I was a boy. He adored me, and I worshipped him. He assumed, *I* assumed that I would follow in his footsteps into the business and take over from him when he wished to retire. Then there came that inevitable point in my life when I wanted to be myself. Yet all I could see ahead of me was becoming more and more like my father. I loved him, but I did not want to *be* him. I grew restless and unhappy. I also grew big and strong—a legacy from my mother's side of the family. I needed to *do* something. Something physical. I daresay I might have sown some relatively harmless wild oats before returning to the fold if it had not been for . . . Well, I did not take that route. Instead, I broke my father's heart by going away and staying away. He loved me and was proud of me to the end, but his heart was broken anyway. When he was dying, I told him that I would take over the reins of his business enterprises and that I would, if it was at all in my power, pass them on to *my* son. Then, after he died, I went home to my little cottage and bought Crosslands, which was nearby and just happened to be for sale, and proceeded to live as I had for the two years previous except on a somewhat grander scale. To myself I called it my year of mourning. But that year is up, and I cannot in all conscience procrastinate any longer. And I am not getting any younger. I am thirty-three."

He looked up, as did Gwen, as a group of seagulls flew by, calling raucously to one another.

"I have a half sister," he said when they had passed from sight. "Constance. She lives in London with her mother, my stepmother. She needs someone to take her out and about. She needs friends and beaux. She needs and wants a husband. But her mother is a virtual invalid and is unwilling to let her go. I have a responsibility to my sister. I am her guardian. But what can I do for her while I remain single? I need a wife."

The arm of the seat was digging into Gwen's back despite the cushion. She squirmed into a different position, and Lord Trentham jumped to his feet to plump up the cushion and reposition it behind her.

"Are you ready to go back in?" he asked.

"No," she said. "Not unless you are."

He did not answer her. He went to sit back down on the stone pedestal.

Why had he become a virtual recluse? Everything in his life would lead one to expect him to be just the opposite.

"Was it during the Forlorn Hope you led that you sustained the injuries that brought you here?" she asked.

His gaze was so burning and so steady that she almost leaned sideways against the back of the seat in order to put more distance between them. He did not talk about that attack, he had told her yesterday—*ever.*

And why did she want to know? She was not usually inquisitive to the point of intrusiveness.

"I sustained not a scratch during that Forlorn Hope," he said. "Nor in any other battle I fought. If you were to examine me from head to toe, you would never guess that I had been a soldier for almost ten years. Or you would guess that I was the sort of officer who cowered in a tent and gave orders without ever coming out to risk intercepting an errant bullet."

His life had been as charmed as the Duke of Wellington's, then. It was said that Wellington had often ridden recklessly within range of enemy guns despite all the efforts of his aides to keep him out of harm's way.

"Then why—" Gwen began.

"—was I here?" he said, interrupting her. "Oh, I had wounds right enough, Lady Muir. They were just not visible ones. I went out of my head. Which is not actually an accurate description of my particular form of madness, for if I *had* been out of my head, all would have been well. The fact that I was still *in* it was the problem. I could not get out. I wanted to kill everyone around me, especially those who were most kind to me. I hated everyone, most of all myself. I wanted to kill *myself.* I believe I started to talk in nothing lower than a bellow, and every second or third word was foul even by the standards of a soldier's vocabulary. It infuriated me that I soon ran out of words strong enough to get the hate out of me."

He looked down at the ground between his feet again. Gwen could see only the top of his head.

"They sent me home in a straitjacket," he said. "If there is anything more calculated to increase fury above the boiling point, I do not know what it is, and I do not *want* to know. They did not want to send me to Bedlam, though, even if that was where they thought I belonged. They were too embarrassed since I was sort of famous and had just been promoted and feted and given my title by the king—or by the prince regent, actually, since the king was himself mad. Ironical, that. I would not go home to my father. Someone knew the Duke of Stanbrook and what he was doing here for a few other officers. And he met me and brought me here—without the straitjacket. He took the risk. I don't think I ever *would* have killed anyone else but myself, but he was not to know that. He asked me not to kill myself—*asked,* not told. His wife had done that, he told me, and it was in a sense the ultimate act of selfishness since it left behind untold and endless suffering for those who had witnessed it and been unable to do anything to prevent it. And so I remained alive. It was the least I could do to atone."

"To atone for what?" she asked softly. For some reason she had the blanket he had spread over her legs bunched against her bosom, held there with both hands.

He looked up with blank eyes, as though he had forgotten that she was there. Then awareness returned.

"I had killed close to three hundred men," he said. "Three hundred of my *own* men."

"Killed?" she asked.

"Killed, *got* killed," he said. "It is all the same. I was responsible for their deaths."

"Tell me," she said, her voice still soft.

He returned his eyes to the ground. She heard him inhale deeply and exhale slowly.

"It is not for a woman's ears," he said. But he continued anyway. "I led my men up an almost sheer slope into the guns. It was certain death. We got stopped in our tracks when we were halfway up. Half of us were dead, the other half discouraged. Success seemed impossible. My lieutenant wanted me to give the order to retreat. No one would ever blame us. Going on was pointless suicide. But it was what we had all volunteered for, and I was determined to go on and die in the attempt rather than return defeated. I gave the order to advance and did not look back to see if anyone followed me. And we succeeded. Although there were almost none of us left, we had made the breach that enabled the rest of the forces to swarm in past us. Of the eighteen survivors, I was the only one unhurt. And a few more died afterward. But I did not care. I had accepted the mission and I had completed it successfully. I was showered with accolades and rewards. Only me. Oh, and my lieutenant won his captaincy. All the other men, living and dead, meant nothing. They were cannon fodder. Unimportant in life, instantly forgotten in death. I did not care. I was on a cloud of glory."

He scuffed the gravel he had smoothed out earlier.

"And why should I not be?" he asked. "It was a Forlorn Hope. All those men were volunteers. All of them expected to die. I did myself, because I led from the front."

Gwen licked her lips. She did not know what to say.

"Two days before I went out of my head," he said, looking up at her with eyes that were quite frighteningly bleak, "I went to see two of the men. One was my lieutenant, newly promoted. He had massive internal injuries and was not expected to live. He had great difficulty breathing. He managed nevertheless to collect enough phlegm in his mouth to spit at me. The other had had both legs amputated and was unquestionably going to die though he was taking his time about it. I knew it. He knew it. He grasped my hand and . . . *kissed* it. He thanked me for thinking of him and coming to see him. He said it made him a proud man. He said he would die a happy man. And other daft things like that. I wanted to bend down and kiss his forehead, but I was afraid of what the other people milling about would think or say to one another afterward. I merely squeezed his hand instead and told him I would be back next day. I *did* go, but he had died half an hour before I arrived."

He gazed at Gwen.

"And now you know my shame," he said. "I went from great hero to gibbering idiot within a month. Are your questions all answered?"

There was a hardness in his eyes, a harshness in his voice.

Gwen swallowed.

"Feeling guilt when one has clearly done wrong," she said, "is natural and even desirable. One can perhaps say or do something to put right the wrong. Feeling guilt when there has been *no* clear wrong is altogether more poisonous. And of course, Lord Trentham, you did not do wrong. You did *right*. There is no use in my laboring that point, however, is there? Countless other people must have told you the same thing. Your friends here must have said it. It does not help, though, does it?"

His eyes searched hers, and she lowered them while she busied her hands with restoring order to the blanket.

"I feel for you," she said. "But your breakdown was shameful only when looked at from the perspective of tough, ruthless masculinity. One does not expect a military commander to care for the men under him. The fact that you *did* care—that you *do* care—makes you far more admirable in my eyes."

"Not many battles would be won, Lady Muir," he said, "if commanders placed the safety and well-being of their men ahead of victory over the enemy."

"No," she agreed. "I suppose not. But you did not do that, did you? You did your duty. Only afterward did you allow yourself to grieve."

"You would turn my very cowardice into heroism," he said.

"Cowardice?" she said. "Hardly that. How many commanders lead their men to certain death from the front? And then visit their horribly wounded men, especially those who will surely die? And even those who hate and resent them?"

"I brought you out here," he said, "to enjoy the fresh air and the flowers."

"And I have done both," she said. "I feel considerably better. Even my ankle is not aching nearly as much as it was earlier. Or perhaps the effects of the pain medicine the Duke of Stanbrook suggested I take have not worn off yet. The air is lovely today even with the nip in it. I am reminded of home."

"Newbury Abbey?" he said.

She nodded.

"It is as close to the sea as Penderris Hall is," she said. "There is a private beach below the abbey with towering cliffs behind it. It is very similar to here. It is surprising, though, that I was walking down by the sea yesterday. I do not often go down onto the beach at home."

"You do not like sand in your shoes?" he asked.

"Well, there is that too," she said. "But also I find the sea too vast. It frightens me a little, though I am not sure why. It is not really the fear of drowning in it. I think it is more that the sea is a reminder of how little control we have over our lives no matter how carefully we try to plan and order them. Everything changes in ways we least expect, and everything is frighteningly vast. We are so small."

"That fact can actually be comforting at times," he said. "When we lash out at ourselves for having lost control, we are reminded that we never can be in total control, that all life asks of us is to do our best to cope with what is handed to us. It is easier said than done, of course. Indeed, it is often impossible to do. But I always find a stroll on the beach reassuring."

She smiled at him and was surprised to discover that she actually rather liked him. At least she understood him better than she had yesterday.

"The fresh air has brought color to your cheeks," he said.

"And to my nose as well, no doubt," she said.

"I was playing the gentleman," he said, "and avoiding any mention of that. I have been trying hard not even to *look* at it."

The joke surprised and delighted her. She lifted one hand to cover her nose and laughed.

He got to his feet and closed the distance between them. He took the blanket, which was still in an untidy heap across her waist, and spread it over her legs again before straightening up and looking down at her. He clasped his hands behind his back. Gwen reached for something to say and failed.

"I am not a gentleman, as you know," he said after a beat of silence. "I have never wanted to be one. When I must mingle with the upper classes, they may accept me or reject me as they will. I am not offended at being considered inferior. I know that I am not. Only different."

Gwen tipped her head to one side.

"What point are you making, Lord Trentham?" she asked.

"That I do not feel inferior to *you,*" he said, "though I am indeed very different. I have no ambition to court you or marry you and thus propel myself imperceptibly upward on the social scale."

Yesterday's irritation with him returned full force.

"I am glad for your sake," she said, "since you would be bound for certain disappointment."

"But I do find myself quite irresistibly attracted to you," he said.

"Irresistibly?"

"I *will* resist if I must," he said. "With one word from you I will resist."

Gwen opened her mouth and closed it again. How had they got to this point? Just a few moments ago he had been baring his soul to her. But perhaps that was the explanation. Perhaps the emotion he had been feeling then needed to be translated into something else, something softer and more familiar.

"Resist *what*?" she asked, frowning.

"I would like to kiss you again," he said, "at the very least."

She asked the question that ought to have remained unasked. "And at the very most?"

"I would like to bed you," he said.

Their eyes locked and Gwen felt a rush of desire that fairly robbed her of breath. Good heavens, she ought to be smacking his face—except that it was far above the reach of her arm. Anyway, she *had* asked and he had answered. Suddenly it felt more like July than early March in the garden.

"Gwendoline," he said. "Is that your name?"

She looked at him in surprise. But Vera had used her name yesterday in his hearing, of course.

"Everyone calls me Gwen," she told him.

"Gwendoline," he said. "Why shorten a name that is perfectly beautiful in its entirety?"

No one had ever called her by her full name. It sounded strange on his lips. Intimate. She ought to object quite firmly to such overfamiliarity.

He was Hugo. The name suited him.

He sat down beside her suddenly, and she scooted over to the inside of the seat to make room for him. He turned sideways and rested one hand on the back of the seat.

Was he going to—? Was she going to—?

He lowered his head and kissed her. Openmouthed. Her own mouth opened reflexively, and there was sudden heat between them. His tongue pressed hard into her mouth, and one of his arms came about her back while the other spread over the back of her head. Her hands, trapped inside her cloak, pressed against his broad, very solid chest.

It was not a brief embrace, as last night's kiss had been. But it gentled, and after a while his lips roamed over her face, up over her temples, down to her ear, where she could feel his breath, his tongue, his teeth nipping the lobe. He kissed his way along her jaw and back up to her mouth.

I would like to bed you.

Oh, no. This was too much. And that was the understatement

of the year. She pressed her hands against his chest, and he raised his head. She found herself gazing very deeply into those very dark, very intense eyes.

He was a little frightening. At least, he *ought* to be.

She drew breath to speak.

"You are both in grave danger of missing your tea," a cheerful voice said, making them jump apart, "and it looks as if George's chef has outdone himself with his cakes today—or so I have been informed. I have not tasted them yet. I elected to postpone the delight and come out here to summon you. Ralph saw from the morning room window when he went to fetch Lady Muir that you were both out here."

Lord Darleigh, looking directly at them in that extraordinary way he had even though he could not actually see them, smiled sweetly.

"Thank you, Vincent," Lord Trentham said. "We will be there in a moment."

He got to his feet and folded the blanket over his arm while Gwen gathered up the two cushions. And then he stooped to scoop her up. He did not look at her, and she did not quite look at him. They did not speak as he carried her inside, following behind Lord Darleigh.

That had been very unwise, she thought. Another grand understatement. *And* indiscreet. The Earl of Berwick had seen them through the window. *What* exactly had he seen?

Lord Trentham carried her into the drawing room, where everyone greeted her politely and no one cast knowing glances at either her or Lord Trentham.

Chapter 7

Hugo was more than usually silent and withdrawn for the rest of the day. And he found himself quite unfairly resenting the presence of Lady Muir. Without her, he would be relaxing with his friends, talking, laughing, teasing and being teased, playing cards, reading, sitting in companionable silence—whatever moved them, in fact. Activities at Penderris were rarely planned.

Everyone else seemed to be enjoying Lady Muir's company. No one else appeared to resent her. Perhaps that was because she was a *lady* and was a part of their world. She joined in the conversation with apparent ease, yet without in any way trying to dominate it. She could talk on virtually any topic. She could listen and laugh and make just the right comments and ask just the right questions. She liked them all, it seemed, and they had grown to like her. She was the perfect lady.

Or perhaps it was because none of the others had kissed her—twice.

Ben was appointed to take dinner with her. Both he and she seemed happy with the arrangement. Not long after dinner she suggested retiring to her room.

"You are in pain, Lady Muir?" George asked.

"Hardly at all when I keep still," she said. "But you are a club. I daresay the evenings are the time when you most enjoy being together for companionship and conversation. I will withdraw."

She was sensitive too. And tactful. More evidence of the perfect lady.

"There is really no need," George said.

"A sprained ankle qualifies as a war wound," Ben said, "and a club stagnates if it never increases its membership. We will expand to include you, Lady Muir, at least for this year. Consider yourself an honorary member."

She laughed.

"Thank you," she said. "I am honored. Actually, I *am* in some discomfort even if it does not quite amount to pain. I shall be more comfortable lying on my bed."

"I shall summon a footman, then," George said, but Hugo was already on his feet.

"No need," he said. "I shall carry Lady Muir upstairs."

He resented her most because she disturbed him. He did not dislike her, as he had yesterday. But she was of an alien world. She was beautiful and elegant and well dressed and self-possessed and charming. She was everything a lady ought to be. And she attracted him, a fact that annoyed him. He had always been able to look at ladies, even sometimes to appreciate their looks and allure, without ever desiring them. One ought not to desire alien species, no matter how beautiful they were.

Was he totally daft?

He had even told her this afternoon—alas, there was no possibility that his memory was playing tricks on him—that he would like to bed her.

He wondered if he ought to apologize. But an apology would only bring that scene in the garden alive again. It was perhaps best forgotten or at least left to lie dormant.

Besides, how could one apologize for kissing a woman *twice*? Once might be explained away as an impulsive accident. Twice suggested definite intent or a serious lack of control.

His foot was on the top stair before either of them spoke.

"You have been very silent tonight, Lord Trentham," she said.

"At the moment I need all my breath to carry you," he told her.

He paused outside her room while she turned the handle of the door. He stepped inside with her and set her down on the bed.

He propped a few of the many pillows behind her back and positioned one beneath her right foot. He straightened up and clasped his hands behind his back. Someone had already lit the candles, he realized.

He would love to turn on his heel and leave the room without another word or a backward glance, but he would make himself look like an idiot or an unmannerly clod if he did so.

"Thank you," she said. And in the next breath, "I am sorry."

He raised his eyebrows.

"*You* are sorry?"

"It must be a coveted treat to return here each year," she said. "But you have been uncomfortable this evening, and I can only conclude that I am the cause. I have written to my brother and asked him to send the carriage as soon as possible, but it will be a few days before it arrives to take me home. In the meanwhile, I shall try to stay out of your way. Any serious involvement between us is out of the question for all sorts of reasons—it is out of the question for *both* of us. And I have never been one for meaningless flirtation or dalliance. My guess is that you have not either."

"You came up early tonight because of *me*?" he asked her.

"You are a member of a group," she said. "I came up because of the *group*. And I really am a little tired. Sitting around all day makes me sleepy."

Any serious involvement between us is out of the question for all sorts of reasons.

Only one reason came to mind. She was of the aristocracy; he was of a lower class despite his title. It was the *only* reason. She was being dishonest with herself. But it was a huge reason. On *both* their parts, as she had said. He needed a wife who would pull cabbages from the kitchen garden with him, and help feed those lambs that could not suck from their mothers, and shoo chickens and their squawking and flapping wings out of the way in order to retrieve their eggs. He needed someone who knew the social world of the middle classes so that a husband could be found for Constance.

He bowed stiffly. Words were clearly superfluous.

"Good night, ma'am," he said and left the room without waiting for her reply.

He thought he heard a sigh as he closed the door.

It was mostly Vincent's turn that night.

He had woken up in a fit of panic in the morning and had been fighting it all day. Such episodes were growing less frequent, he reported, but when they *did* happen, they were every bit as intense as they had ever been.

When Vincent first came to Penderris, he had still been more than half deaf as well as totally blind—a result of a cannon exploding close enough to have propelled him all the way back to England in a million pieces. By some miracle he had escaped both dismemberment and death. He had still been something of a wild thing, whom only George had been able to calm. George had often taken the boy right into his arms and held him close, sometimes for hours at a time, crooning to him like a baby until he slept. Vincent had been seventeen at the time.

The deafness had cleared, but the blindness had not and never would. Vincent had given up hope fairly early and had adjusted his life to the new condition with remarkable determination and resilience. But hope, pushed deep inside rather than banished completely, surfaced occasionally when his defenses were low, usually while he slept. And he would awake expecting to see, be terrified when he discovered he could not, and then be catapulted down to the depths of a dark hell when he realized that he never would.

"It robs me of breath," he said, "and I think I am going to die from lack of air. Part of my mind tells me to stop fighting, to accept death as a merciful gift. But the instinct to survive is more powerful than any other and I breathe again."

"And what a good thing that is," George said. "Despite all that might be said to the contrary, this life is worth living to the final breath with which nature endows us."

The rather heavy silence that succeeded his words testified to the fact that it was not always an easy philosophy to adopt.

"I can picture some things and some people quite clearly in my head," Vincent said. "But I cannot with others. This morning it struck me—for only about the five thousandth time—that I have never seen any of your faces, that I never will. Yet every time I have such a thought, it is as raw as it was the first time I thought it."

"In the case of Hugo's ugly countenance," Flavian said, "that is a signal mercy, Vincent. *We* have to look at it every day. And in the case of *my* face . . . Well, if you were to see it, you would despair, for you will never look so handsome yourself."

Vincent laughed, and all of them smiled.

Hugo noticed Flavian blinking away tears.

Imogen patted Vincent's hand.

"Tell me, Hugo," Vincent said, "were you *kissing* Lady Muir when I came to fetch you in for tea? I could hear no conversation as I approached the flower garden though Ralph had assured me you were both out there. He probably sent me deliberately so that the lady would not be embarrassed at what I might see."

"If you think I am going to answer *that* question," Hugo said, "you must have cuckoos in your head."

"Which is all the answer I need," Vincent said, waggling his eyebrows.

"And my lips are sealed," Ralph said. "I will neither confirm nor deny what I saw through the morning room window, though I *will* say that I was shaken to the core."

"Imogen," George said, "will you cater to our collective male laziness and pour the tea?"

The Duke of Stanbrook produced a pair of crutches for Gwen the following morning, explaining that they had been needed when his house was a hospital but had lain untouched and forgotten for several years since. He had had them tested for safety, he assured her. He measured them for length and had a few inches sawn off them. He had them sanded and polished. Then Gwen was able to move around to a limited degree.

"You must promise me, though, Lady Muir," he said, "not to bring the wrath of Dr. Jones down upon my head. You must not dash about the house and up and down stairs for eighteen hours out of every twenty-four. You must continue to rest your foot and keep it elevated most of the time. But at least now you can move about a room and even from room to room without having to wait for someone to carry you."

"Oh, thank you," she said. "You cannot know how much this means to me."

She took a turn about the morning room, getting used to the crutches, before reclining on the chaise longue again.

She felt a great deal less confined for the rest of the day, though she did not move about a great deal. Vera spent most of the morning with her, as she had the day before, and stayed until after luncheon.

Her friends, she reported happily, quite hated her for being on intimate visiting terms with the Duke of Stanbrook. His crested carriage had been seen to stop outside her house a number of times. Their jealousy would surely cause them to cut her acquaintance if they did not find it more to their advantage to bask in her reflected glory and boast to their less privileged neighbors of being her friends. She also complained of the fact that His Grace did not see fit to send anyone in the carriage to bear her company and that again today she was not invited to take luncheon in the dining room with the duke and his guests.

"I daresay, Vera," Gwen told her, "the duke is touched by your devotion and considers that you would find it offensive to be taken away from me when I cannot sit in the dining room with you."

She wondered why she bothered to try to soothe ruffled feathers that never stayed smooth for long.

"Of course you are right," Vera said grudgingly. "I *would* be offended if His Grace parted me from you for a mere meal when I have given up a large part of my day just to offer you the comfort of my company. But he might at least give me the opportunity to refuse his invitation. I am surprised that his chef serves only three courses for luncheon. At least, he serves only three here in the morning room. I daresay they enjoy a larger number of courses in the dining room."

"But the food is plentiful and delicious," Gwen said.

Vera's visits were a severe trial to her.

After the Duke of Stanbrook had borne her friend off to his waiting carriage, Gwen felt a little agitated. What if Lord Trentham came again as he had yesterday? The weather was just as lovely. She could not *bear* to find herself tête-à-tête with him again. She had no business being attracted to him, or he to her. She had no business allowing him to kiss her, and he had no business asking it of her.

If he came again this afternoon, she thought, she could pretend to be asleep and to *remain* asleep. He would have no choice but to go away. But she was not sleepy today.

She was saved anyway from having to practice such subterfuge. There was a tap on the door not long after Vera left, and it opened to reveal Viscount Ponsonby.

"I am on my way to the l-library," he said in his languid voice and with his slight stammer. "Everyone else is off enjoying the sunshine, but I have such a stack of unanswered letters that I am in grave danger of being buried under it or lost behind it or some such dire thing. I must, alas, set pen to p-paper. It occurred to me that you may wish to try out your new crutches and come to select a book."

"I would be more than delighted," she said, and he stood in the doorway watching while she hoisted herself onto her crutches and moved toward him.

Her ankle was still swollen and sore to the touch. There was still no possibility of getting on a shoe or putting any weight on it. It was somewhat less painful today, however. And the cut on her knee was now no more than a scab.

Lord Ponsonby walked beside her to the library and turned a sofa that was by the fireplace so that light from the window would fall on it.

"You may remain here and read or w-watch me labor," he said, "or you may return to the morning room after choosing a book. Or you may run up and down stairs, for that matter. I am not your jailer. If you need a volume from a high shelf, d-do let me know."

And he retreated behind the large oak desk that stood near the window.

Gwen wondered about his stammer. It was the only imperfection she could detect in his person. Perhaps he too had come through war physically unscathed but had gone out of his head, as Lord Trentham had phrased it. She had not thought a great deal before this week about the mental strain of being a military man. And yet it showed a lamentable lack of imagination on her part that she had not.

She read for a while, and then Lady Barclay found her and invited her to the conservatory to see the plants. There were some long wicker seats there, she explained, on which Lady Muir could rest her foot. They sat there and talked for a whole hour. Later, they went for tea in the drawing room.

It was Lady Barclay who dined with her that evening.

She wanted to broach the subject of Lady Barclay's loss and assure her that she understood, that she too had lost a husband under violent, horrifying circumstances, that she too felt guilty over his death and doubted she would ever free herself of the feeling. And perhaps it was more than just a feeling. Perhaps she really *was* guilty.

But she said nothing. There was nothing in Lady Barclay's manner to suggest that she would welcome such intimacy. Anyway, Gwen never talked about the events surrounding Vernon's death or the fall that had caused it. She suspected she never would.

She never even *thought* about those events. Yet in some ways she never thought of anything else.

Later in the evening, she admitted when asked that she played the pianoforte, though not with any particular flair or talent. It did not matter. She was persuaded to cross the drawing room on her crutches in order to sit at the instrument and play, rusty fingers and all. Fortunately, she acquitted herself tolerably well. And then she was persuaded to remain there in order to accompany Lord Darleigh as he played his violin. She moved to the harp with him afterward while he explained to her how he was learning to identify all the many strings without seeing them.

"And his *next* trick, Lady Muir," the Earl of Berwick said, "is to *play* the strings once he has identified them."

"Heaven defend us," Lord Ponsonby added. "Vincent was far less d-dangerous when he had his sight and the only weapons at his disposal were a sword and a giant cannon. He is threatening to start *embroidering,* Lady Muir. Lord knows where his needle will end up. And we have all heard horror stories about silken bonds."

Gwen laughed with them all, including Lord Darleigh himself.

When she withdrew to her room soon after, she was not allowed to climb the stairs with her crutches. A footman was summoned to carry her up.

Lord Trentham did not offer.

She had not seen him all day. She had scarcely heard his voice all evening.

She hated the idea that she had very possibly ruined his stay at Penderris. She could only hope that Neville would not delay in sending the carriage once he had received her letter.

She felt depressed after she had been left alone in her room. She was not tired. It was still quite early. She was also rather restless. The crutches had given her a taste of freedom but not the real thing. She *wished* she could look forward to a long early morning walk or, better yet, a brisk ride.

She did not feel like reading.

Oh dear, Lord Trentham was so dreadfully *attractive*. She had been aware of him with every nerve ending in her body all evening. If she was being strictly honest with herself, she would be forced to admit that she had chosen her favorite apricot evening gown with him in mind. She had played the pianoforte aware only of him in the small audience. She had looked everywhere in the room except at him. Her conversation had seemed too bright, too trivial because she had known he was listening. Her laughter had seemed too loud and too forced. It was so unlike her to be self-conscious when in company.

She had hated every moment of an evening that on the surface had been very pleasant indeed. She had behaved like a very young girl dealing with her first infatuation—her first very *foolish* infatuation.

She could not possibly be infatuated with Lord Trentham. A few kisses and a physical attraction did not equate love or even being *in* love. Good heavens, she was supposed to be a mature woman.

She had rarely spent a more uncomfortable evening in her life.

And even now, alone in her own room, she was not immune—at least to the physical attraction.

What would *it be like,* she found herself wondering, *to go to bed with him?*

She shook off the thought and reached for the book she had taken from the library. Perhaps she would feel more like reading once she started.

If only Neville's carriage could appear, like some miracle, tomorrow. Early.

She felt suddenly almost ill with homesickness.

Chapter 8

The last two days had been sunny and springlike in all but temperature. Today that deficiency had more than corrected itself. The sky was a clear blue, the sun shone, the air was warm, and—that rarest of all weather phenomena at the coast—there was almost no wind.

It felt more like summer than spring.

Hugo stood alone outside the front doors, undecided what he would do for the afternoon. George, Ralph, and Flavian had gone riding. He had decided not to accompany them. Although he could ride, of course, it was not something he did for pleasure. Imogen and Vincent had gone for a stroll in the park. For no specific reason, Hugo had declined the invitation to join them. Ben was in the old schoolroom upstairs, a space George had set aside for him for the punishing exercises to which he subjected his body several times a week.

Ben had assured George that he would look in upon Lady Muir when he was finished and make sure she was not left alone for too long after the departure of her friend.

Hugo had agreed to see Mrs. Parkinson on her way in George's carriage, and that was what he had just done. She had looked archly up at him and simpered and commented that any lady fortunate to have *him* beside her in a carriage would never feel nervous—not about the hazards of the road at least, she had added. Hugo had not taken the hint to play the gallant and accompany her to the village. He had drawn her attention instead to the burly coachman up on the box and assured her that he had never heard of any highwaymen being active in this part of the country.

What he really ought to do, he thought now, since he had almost deliberately isolated himself for the afternoon, was go down onto the beach, his favorite old haunt. The tide was on the way in. He loved to be close to the water, and he liked being alone.

He had not looked at Lady Muir just now when he had stepped into the morning room to escort her friend to the carriage. He had merely inclined his head vaguely in her direction.

It was really quite disconcerting how much two reasonably chaste kisses could discompose a man. And probably a woman too. She had not spoken to him before he escorted her friend from the room, and though he had not looked at her, he was almost certain that she had not looked at him either.

Ach, this was ridiculous. They were behaving like two gauche schoolchildren.

He turned and stalked back into the house. He tapped on the morning room door, opened it, and stepped inside without waiting for an invitation. She was standing at the window, propped on her crutches, gazing out. At least, he assumed she had been gazing out. She was now looking at him over her shoulder, her eyebrows raised.

"Vera has gone?" she asked him.

"She has." He took a few steps closer to her. "How is your ankle?"

"The swelling has gone down considerably today," she said, "and it is far less painful than it was. Even so, I cannot set the foot to the ground and would probably be unwise even to try. Dr. Jones was very specific in his instructions. I am annoyed with myself for allowing the accident to happen, and I am annoyed with myself for being so impatient to heal. I am annoyed with myself for being in a cross mood."

She smiled suddenly.

"It is a lovely day," he said.

"As I see." She looked back out through the window. "I have

been standing here trying to decide whether I will take my book and sit in the flower garden for a while. I can walk that far unassisted."

"When the tide is coming in," he said, "it cuts one part of the long beach off from the rest and makes a secluded, picturesque cove out of it. I have been there often when I simply want to sit and think or dream, or sometimes when I want to swim. It is a couple of miles along the coast but is still a part of George's land. It is quite private. I thought I might go over there this afternoon."

Actually he had not given a thought to the cove until he started to speak to her.

"It can be approached by gig," he added, "and the cliff is not high there. The sands are quite easy to reach. Would you care to come with me?"

She maneuvered the crutches and turned to face him. She was just a little thing, he thought. He doubted the top of her head reached his shoulder. She was going to say no, he thought, half in relief. What the devil had prompted him to make such an offer anyway?

"Oh, I *would,*" she said softly.

"In half an hour?" he suggested. "You will need to go upstairs to get ready, I daresay."

"I can go up alone," she said. "I have my crutches."

But he strode forward, relieved her of them, and swung her up into his arms before striding off in the direction of the stairs. He waited for a tirade that did not come. Though she did sigh.

He went back for her half an hour later, after informing Ben that he was taking her out for a drive and gathering the things they would need to take with them—a blanket for her to sit on, cushions for her back and her foot, and, as an afterthought, a large towel. He had also gone to the stables and carriage house and hitched a horse to the gig and brought it around to the front doors.

This, he thought, was *not* a good idea. But he was committed now. And he could not feel quite as sorry as he knew he ought. It was a lovely day. A man needed company when the sun shone and there was warmth in the air. Not that he had ever before entertained such a daft thought. Why would a sunny day make a man feel lonelier than he felt on a cloudy day?

He carried Lady Muir back downstairs and settled her in the gig before taking his place beside her. He gathered the ribbons in his hands and gave the horse the signal to start.

Spring was her favorite season, she had told him two days ago, full of newness and hope. Somehow today he could understand what she meant.

It was one of those perfect days in early spring that felt more like summer except for a certain indefinable quality of light that proclaimed an earlier season. And the green of the grass and leaves still held all the freshness of a new year.

It was the kind of day to make one rejoice just to be alive.

And it was the kind of day on which one could wish for nothing better than to be driving out in the air with an attractive man beside one. For some reason she could not quite fathom, and despite the nuisance of her sore ankle, Gwen felt ten years younger this afternoon than she had felt in a long while.

She ought *not* to be feeling any such thing. But, on the other hand, why not? She was a widow and owed allegiance to no man. Lord Trentham was unmarried and, at present at least, unattached. Why should they *not* spend the afternoon in each other's company? Whom were they likely to harm?

There was nothing wrong with a little romance.

If she had brought a parasol with her, she would have twirled it exuberantly above her head. Instead, she played a sprightly tune on an invisible keyboard across her thighs before clasping her hands more quietly in her lap.

The gig proceeded a short way along the driveway in the direction of the village, but then it looped back behind the house along a narrower lane, which then ran parallel to the cliffs, in the opposite direction from the village. There was a patchwork quilt of brown, yellow, and green fields and meadows on the one side, the cultivated park of Penderris on the other. The sea, several shades deeper blue than the sky, was visible beyond the park. The air was fragrant with the smells of new vegetation and turned soil and the salty tang of the sea.

And with the faint musky odor of Lord Trentham's soap or cologne.

It was impossible to keep her shoulder and arm from brushing against his on the narrow seat of the gig, Gwen discovered. It was impossible not to be aware at every moment of his powerful thighs alongside hers, encased in tight pantaloons, and of his large hands plying the ribbons.

He was wearing a tall hat today. It hid most of his hair and shaded his eyes. He looked less fierce, less military. He looked more attractive than ever.

Her physical response to his presence was a little unnerving since she had never really experienced it with any other man. Not even with Vernon. She had thought him gorgeously handsome and wondrously charming when they had first met, and she had tumbled very quickly and willingly into love with him. She had liked his kisses before they married, and she had often enjoyed the marriage bed after.

But she had never felt like *this* with Vernon or anyone else.

Breathless.

Filled with an exuberant energy.

Aware of every small detail with her senses. Aware that *he* was aware, though neither of them spoke during the journey. At first, she could not think of anything to talk about. Then she realized that she did not really need to talk at all and that the silence between them did not matter. It was not uncomfortable.

After a mile or two the lane sloped downward, and almost at the bottom of a long hill they turned onto an even narrower track in the direction of the sea. Soon even the track disappeared, and the gig bounced over coarse grass to the edge of the low cliff.

Lord Trentham got out to unhitch the horse and tether it to a sturdy bush nearby. He allowed it enough room to graze while they were gone.

He draped a blanket over his arm and handed her some cushions, as he had done when he took her into the garden two days ago, and he lifted her out and carried her down to the cove below along a narrow zigzagging path, across a gentle slope of pebbles, and onto flat golden sand. Long outcroppings of rock stretched out to the sea on either side of the small beach. It was indeed a private little haven.

"The coastline constantly surprises, does it not?" she said, breaking the long silence at last. "There are long, breathtakingly lovely stretches of beach. And sometimes there are little pieces of paradise, like this. And they are equally beautiful."

He did not answer. Had she expected him to?

He carried her in the direction of a large rock planted firmly in the middle of the little beach. He took her around to the sea side of it and set her down on one foot, her back against the rock, while he spread the blanket over the sand. He took the cushions from her arms and tossed them down before helping her to sit on the blanket. He propped one cushion behind her back, plumped one beneath her right ankle, and folded the other beneath her knee. He frowned the whole while, as though his task required great concentration.

Was he regretting this? Had his invitation been impulsive?

"Thank you," she said, smiling at him. "You make an excellent nursemaid."

He looked briefly into her eyes before standing up and gazing out to sea.

There was not a breath of wind down here, she noticed. And the rock attracted the heat of the sun. It felt more than ever like a summer day. She undid the fastenings of her cloak and pushed it back over her shoulders. She was wearing just a muslin dress beneath it, but the air felt pleasantly warm against her bare arms.

Lord Trentham hesitated for a few moments and then sat down beside her, his back against the rock, one leg stretched out in front of him, the other bent at the knee, his booted foot flat on the blanket, one arm draped over his knee. His shoulder was a careful few inches away from her own, but she could feel his body heat anyway.

"You play well," he said abruptly.

For a moment she did not understand what he was talking about.

"The pianoforte?" She turned her head to look at him. His hat had tipped forward slightly on his head. It almost hid his eyes and made him look inexplicably gorgeous. "Thank you. I am competent, I believe, but I have no real talent. And I am *not* angling for further compliments. I have heard talented pianists and know I could practice ten hours a day for ten years and not come close to matching them."

"I suppose," he said, "you are competent in everything you do. Ladies generally are, are they not?"

"The implication being that we are competent in much but truly accomplished in little and talented in even less?" She laughed. "You are undoubtedly right in nine cases out of ten, Lord Trentham. But better that than be utterly helpless and useless in everything except perhaps in looking decorative."

"Hmm," he said.

She waited for him to be the next to speak.

"What do you do for *fun*?" he asked.

"For *fun*?" That was a strange word to use to a grown woman. "I do all the usual things. I visit family members and play with their children. I attend dinners and teas and garden parties and social evenings. I dance. I walk and ride. I—"

"You *ride*?" he asked. "After the accident you had?"

"Oh," she said, "I did not for a long while after. But I had always enjoyed riding, and not doing so cut me off from much interaction with my peers and much personal pleasure. Besides, I hate not doing something simply because I do not have the courage. Eventually I forced myself back into the saddle, and more recently I have even forced myself to encourage my mount to a pace faster than a crawl. One of these days I shall actually allow it to *gallop*. Fear must be challenged, I have found. It is a powerful beast if it is allowed the mastery."

He was gazing with half-closed eyes at the incoming water. The sun was glinting off its surface.

"What do *you* do for fun?" she asked.

He thought about it for a while.

"I feed lambs and calves when their mothers cannot," he said. "I work in the fields of my farm and particularly in the vegetable garden behind the house. I watch and somehow participate in all the miracles of life, both animal and vegetable. Have you ever smoothed bare soil over seeds and doubted you would ever see them again? And then a few days later you see thin, frail shoots pushing above the soil and wonder if they will ever have the strength and endurance to survive. And before you know it, you have a sturdy carrot or a potato the size of my fist or a cabbage that needs two hands to hold."

She laughed again.

"And that is *fun*?" she asked.

He turned his head and their eyes met. His looked very dark beneath the brim of his hat.

"Yes," he said. "Nurturing life instead of taking it is fun. It makes a man feel good here." He patted a lightly closed fist against the left breast of his coat.

He was titled. He was very wealthy. Yet he worked on his own farms and toiled in his own vegetable garden. Because he enjoyed doing so. Also because it offered him some absolution for having spent his years as an officer killing men and allowing his own men to be killed.

He was not the hard, cold ex-military officer she had taken him for when they first met. He was . . . a man.

It was a thought that made her shiver slightly, though not from cold.

"How are you going to go about finding a wife?" she asked him.

He pursed his lips and looked away again.

"The man who manages my father's business empire," he said, "or *mine,* I ought to say, has a daughter. I met her when I went to London for my father's funeral. She is very lovely, very well schooled in all the skills a woman would need to be the wife of a wealthy, successful businessman, very willing—as are her mother and father—and very young."

"She sounds ideal," Gwen said.

"And frightened to death of me," he added.

"How old *is* she?" she asked.

"Nineteen."

"Did you do anything to make her less frightened?" she asked. "Did you, for example, *smile* at her? Or at least not *frown*? Or *scowl*?"

He turned his eyes on her again.

"*She* was courting *me,*" he said. "Her *parents* were courting me. Why should I do the smiling?"

Gwen laughed softly.

"Poor girl," she said. "Will you marry her?"

"Probably not," he said. "Undoubtedly not, in fact. She would not be lusty enough for me. And my own lust would cool in a hurry if she were to cringe away from me in bed."

Oh! He was deliberately trying to shock her. Gwen could see it in the hardness of his eyes. He thought she was mocking him.

"Then she will have had a happy escape," she said, "even if she does not realize it. You need someone older, someone not easily intimidated, someone who will not cringe from your lovemaking."

She looked deliberately back into his eyes as she spoke, even though it took a great deal of effort. She had *no* experience in this type of talk.

"I have relatives in London," he told her. "Prosperous ones. Success in business seems to run in the family, though no one was quite as good at it as my father. They will be happy enough, I daresay, to introduce me to eligible women of my own sort."

"Your own sort being middle-class women who may possibly derive fun out of getting soil beneath their fingernails," she said.

"In my experience, Lady Muir," he said, his eyes narrowing again, "middle-class women can be every bit as fastidious as ladies. Often more so, because for reasons I find hard to understand many of them aspire to *be* ladies. I have no plan to put my wife to work after I marry her—not work in the fields or barn, anyway. Not unless she chooses to involve herself. I once commanded men. I have no wish now to command women."

Ah. This was not turning into the relaxing, perhaps slightly romantic afternoon she had anticipated.

"I have offended you," she said. "I am sorry. There will be any number of eligible women only too eager to be introduced to you, Lord Trentham. You are titled and wealthy, and you have a hero's reputation. You will be considered a great prize. And some women may not even be daunted if you scowl at them."

"*You* are clearly not daunted," he said.

"No," she said, "but you are not courting me, are you?"

The words seemed to hang in the air between them. Gwen was very aware of the sound of the incoming tide, of the crying of gulls far overhead, of the intense gaze of his eyes. Of the heat of the sun.

"No," he said, and he got abruptly to his feet and leaned back against the rock, his arms crossing over his chest. "No, I am not courting you, Lady Muir."

He only wanted to bed her.

And she wanted to bed him. Everything in her eyes and the tense lines of her body told him that though she would surely deny it, even to herself, if he were to confront her with the fact.

Which he was not about to do.

He had *some* sense of self-preservation.

Bringing her here had been a ghastly mistake. He had known it from the first moment, even before he had carried her from the morning room to get ready for the outing.

For someone who had some sense of self-preservation, he appeared to have even more of a tendency toward self-destruction.

A puzzling contradiction.

She did not break the silence. He *could* not. He could not think of a mortal thing to say. And then he thought of one thing he could at least *do*. And that thought gave him something to say.

"I am going for a swim," he said.

"What?" She turned her head sharply and looked up at him. She looked startled, and then her face lit up with laughter. "You would freeze. It is *March*."

Nevertheless.

He pushed away from the rock and tossed his hat down onto the blanket.

"Besides," she said, "you did not bring a change of clothes."

"I will not be wearing clothes into the sea," he told her.

That arrested the smile on her face—and brought flaming color to her cheeks. But she laughed again as he lifted his right foot to haul off his Hessian boot.

"Oh," she said, "you would not dare. No, ignore that, if you please. You certainly would not be able to resist a dare, would you? No self-respecting man of my acquaintance ever would. Remove your boots and stockings, then, and paddle at the edge of the water. I shall sit here and gaze enviously at you."

But after removing his boots and stockings, he shrugged out of his coat—not an easy thing to do without the help of his valet. His waistcoat came next, and she licked her lips and looked slightly alarmed.

He unknotted his neckcloth and flung it down onto the pile of garments that was beginning to accumulate. He dragged his shirt free of the waistband of his pantaloons and pulled it off over his head.

The air was perhaps not quite as warm as it had felt when he was fully clothed, but he was heated from within. Anyway, it was too late to change his mind now.

"Oh, Lord Trentham." She was laughing again. "Do spare my blushes."

He hesitated for a moment. But he would look an utter idiot if he merely wet his feet after all this. And soggy pantaloons would be horribly uncomfortable during the return journey to the house in the gig.

He really had no choice.

He peeled off his pantaloons and was left standing only in his drawers. He would *not* withdraw those, he decided somewhat reluctantly, even though he had only ever swum naked before.

He strode down the beach without looking at her.

The water on his feet and then about his ankles and knees and thighs felt as if it had just flowed from beneath the ice cap at the North Pole. It took his breath away even before he was fully immersed. But there was one consolation. It would be the perfect antidote to an unwilling and quite inappropriate ardor.

He dived under a wave, thought he was dead of shock, discovered he was not, and swam outward until he was beyond the foam of the breakers. Then he swam with powerful overarm strokes parallel to the beach until he could feel his arms and legs again and his breath steadied and the water felt merely cold. He turned and swam back the way he had come.

He tried to remember how long it was since he had had a woman. Since he could not come up with a satisfactory answer, it was obviously far too long.

Chapter 9

Gwen completely forgot about her ankle for a while. She sat with her knees drawn up, her arms wrapped about them, her feet flat on the blanket.

Her heart felt like a separate being inside her bosom, thumping to get out. She could not seem to calm it down or steady her breathing. And despite the short sleeves of her dress, it still felt more like July than March.

She had never seen a man naked, or even naked with the exception of his drawers. It was an odd fact, perhaps, when she had been married for a number of years. But Vernon had been very particular about respectability. During the day he had not liked her to see him even in as little as his shirtsleeves. At night he had come to her in a nightshirt and dressing gown.

Oh, she had seen Neville and her cousins in their drawers when they swam during childhood summers, she supposed, just as they had seen her in her shift. But they had all been just children at the time.

She was undeniably shocked that Lord Trentham would unclothe himself right in front of her. It was . . . well, it was *barbaric*. No gentleman would have removed so much as his coat without asking her permission first—and most would not even have asked simply because it would not be seemly.

But her shock owed less to prudish outrage, she had to admit as she watched him swim, than it did to reaction at the sight of his almost naked body. It was perfection itself. It was nothing short of magnificent, in fact. She had nothing with which to compare it, it was true, no one with whom to compare him. But she did not think any man *could* compare. His shoulders were wide, his chest broad. His hips were slim, his legs long and powerful. When he stood still, he looked like a finely sculpted god—not that she had ever seen such a sculpture. When he moved, he fairly rippled with muscle and looked like a warrior god sprung to vibrant life.

Could she be blamed for finding him knee-weakeningly, heart-poundingly attractive? For finding it difficult to breathe normally? For forgetting something as mundane as a sore ankle?

Could she be blamed for wanting a repetition of his kisses? For wanting, in fact, far more than just kisses? For feeling something as raw and unladylike as . . . lust?

It was a good thing, perhaps, that he had gone for a swim, that he was using up energy she knew he had wanted to use on *her*, that his absence gave her time to get both her body and her emotions under control. In fact, there was no *perhaps* about it. It was undoubtedly a good thing.

But how could she bring herself under control when he swam with such ease and grace and power, when even at this distance she could see the powerful muscles of his arms and shoulders and legs, the water and the sunlight causing his flesh to gleam as if it were oiled? She could look away, of course. But how could she do that when within a few days she would be gone from Penderris and would never see him again?

She gripped her legs more tightly and felt the raw ache of unshed tears in her throat and up behind her nose. And she also felt the *dull* ache of an abused ankle. She gave it her full attention and stretched her leg out again. She repositioned the cushions carefully beneath her knee and foot. She did not look toward the sea or, more specifically, to the almost naked man swimming in it.

It would serve him right if his extremities froze and fell off.

He was deliberately flaunting himself before her. A peacock used the gorgeous colors and extravagant size of its plumage to attract the female. *He* used his almost naked body.

Had he stripped and dashed for the water to cool off? Or had he done it to send her temperature soaring in the opposite direction?

Gwen leaned her head back against the rock behind her, felt the obstruction of her bonnet, and pulled impatiently at the ribbons so that she could toss it aside. She set her head back again and closed her eyes. The sunlight was bright. The insides of her eyelids were orange.

It did not matter why he was swimming. *He* did not matter. Not really. Or at least her *feelings* for him did not matter. They were here to relax, to take advantage of an unusually lovely day in beautiful surroundings.

But you are not courting me, are you? she had said to him. It had not really been a question, but he had answered it anyway. *No, I am not courting you, Lady Muir.* And somehow it was the question and the answer that had sparked everything that had followed. And she had started it. It was her fault, then.

She was thirty-two years old. She had had beaux when she first made her come-out and then a husband. She had had a lengthy widowhood interspersed with more beaux. She was not without experience. She was no innocent, naïve girl. But suddenly she *felt* like one, for there had been nothing in her experience to help her understand the sheer lust that she and Lord Trentham felt for each other. How *could* she understand it when he was not at all the sort of man who could be expected to attract her, either as a flirt or as a possible husband? This, she supposed, this new, unexpected feeling, was what led people to have affairs.

She ought to hurry back to the safety of the house before he came out of the water, she thought—until she opened her eyes and remembered that she was a few miles from the house and that she still could not put weight on her right foot. She had not even brought her crutches. Besides, it was too late. He was swimming toward the beach, and then he was standing up and wading toward the shallow water and out onto the beach.

Water streamed down his body and droplets glistened in the

sunlight as he approached. His short hair was plastered to his head. His drawers clung to him like a second skin. Gwen did not even try to avert her eyes.

He bent and picked up the towel he had brought with him and dried his chest and shoulders and arms with it—and then his face. He looked down at her. His swim had done nothing to lighten his mood, it seemed. He was frowning, even perhaps scowling.

"You said you would watch me with envy," he said.

Had she said that?

"Oh, what are you *doing*?" she cried suddenly.

He was leaning over her and scooping her up into his arms. His skin was cold and smelled of salt and maleness. It was very . . . bare. She could feel the wetness of his drawers against her side before he hoisted her higher. She wrapped both arms about his neck.

"No."

But he was striding down the beach again, and the tide was higher now than it had been when he first went in. It must be almost on the turn.

"Why come to a beach," he said, "if one is merely going to sit and observe? One might as well stay at home and read."

"Oh, please," she begged as he waded into the water and she could feel a few splashes of it, cold against her bare arms. "*Please,* Lord Trentham, don't drop me in. I have no change of clothes. And it must be like the arctic."

"It is," he said.

She was clinging more tightly then and pressing her face to his neck and laughing helplessly.

"I may *sound* amused," she said, "but I am *not.* Please. Oh, *please,* Hugo."

He was holding her higher still in his arms, she realized. And he was holding her tightly. A trick? To lull her into a false sense of security?

"I am not going to drop you," he said, his voice low against her ear. "I would not be so cruel. But there is nothing like being out here, seeing the light create many colors and shades on the water, and listening to it and smelling it."

He turned right about with her as she raised her head, and then spun about twice more as she lifted her head and laughed with the sheer exuberance of it. It was cooler out here, though not really cold—though perhaps his body heat had something to do with that. She had never really liked the water. But they seemed to be in a vast and shimmering liquid world, which was sheer beauty and no threat at all. She felt perfectly safe in the warm, strong arms of a man who would not drop her—who would never drop her.

She had called him *Hugo,* she realized. Oh, dear, had he noticed?

"Gwendoline," he said as he stopped spinning.

He had noticed.

Her eyes met his, just inches from her own. But she could not bear the intensity she saw there. She dipped her head to rest against his neck again and closed her eyes. Would she remember the poignant wonder of this moment for all the rest of her life? Or was it a foolish fancy to imagine that she would?

She rather thought this might be more than just physical attraction. What she was feeling was not *just* lust, though it was undoubtedly that too. There was also . . . Oh, dear. Why were there never words to describe feelings adequately? Perhaps she was falling in love with him, whatever *that* meant. But she would not think of it now. She would work it out some other time.

He sighed then, deeply and audibly.

"I expected to despise you," he said. "Or at the very least to be irritated by you."

She opened her mouth to reply and shut it again. She did not want to begin any conversation. She wanted simply to enjoy. She raised her head and set her temple against his cheek. They gazed across the water together, and she knew that she *would* remember. Always and ever.

After a few minutes he turned without a word and waded out of the sea with her and up the sand to the blanket, where he set her down. He peeled off his wet drawers, picked up the towel, and dried himself off again without turning his back.

Gwen would not look away. Or perhaps she *could* not. She was not even shocked.

"You may say no," he said, looking down at her as he dropped the towel. "It would be best to say it now if you must, though. But you may say it at any time before I enter your body. I will not force myself upon you."

Ah, always the man of plain speech.

Gwen was holding her breath, she realized. Had it come to this, then?

Foolish question.

She knew many women who were of the opinion that widows were to be envied provided they had the means with which to live independently—as Gwen did. Widows were free to take lovers as long as they were discreet about it. In some circles they were almost expected to do so, in fact.

Gwen had never even been tempted.

Until now.

Who would know?

She would know. And Hugo would know.

Who would be hurt?

She might be. He almost certainly would not. No one else would. She had no husband, no fiancé, no steady beau. He had no wife.

She would be sorry afterward. She would be sorry either way. If she said no, she would forever wonder what it would have been like and would forever regret that she had not found out. If she did *not* say no, she would forever be plagued with guilt.

Perhaps.

Perhaps not.

The thoughts tumbled through her mind in a confused jumble.

"I am not saying no," she said. "I *will* not say no. I am not a tease."

And thus were decisions of great moment made, she thought. Impulsively, without due consideration. From the heart rather than from the head. From impulse rather than from a lifetime of experience and morality.

He came down beside her and moved the cushion at her back so that it lay flat and she could set her head on it. He tossed aside her cloak and the two cushions beneath her right leg. He slid large, blunt fingers into her hair and tilted her face up and kissed her openmouthed. His tongue pressed deep and withdrew again.

He knelt beside her and drew her dress off her shoulders and down over her breasts, which were lifted into prominence by her stays.

He looked at her while she resisted the foolish urge to cover herself with her hands. But he did it for her when he spread a hand over one of her breasts and lowered his head to the other. She spread her fingers wide over the blanket on either side of her as he took her nipple into his mouth and suckled her, rubbing his tongue over the tip as he did so. With his thumb and forefinger he rolled the nipple of the other breast, squeezing almost but not quite to the point of pain.

An almost unbearably raw ache spread upward to her throat and downward through her womb to settle between her thighs. She lifted her hands and set one over his wrist, the other against the back of his head. His hair was damp and warm.

He kissed her again then, his tongue simulating the nuptial act with long, deep strokes into her mouth.

He was, she realized over the next several minutes, ten times, perhaps a hundred times, more experienced than she. She knew only kisses of the lips and the act itself.

He did not unclothe her fully, but his hands found their way unerringly beneath her clothes to unlace her stays and find places that gave him pleasure and were sweet agony to her. They were large, blunt-fingered hands whose gentleness she had discovered before. But they were more than just gentle. There was erotic seductiveness in them. They could and did play her like a musical instrument—and not just with competence, she thought with wry humor, but with sheer talent too.

And finally, when her body hummed with desire and need almost to the point of pain, he used one of those hands on the heart of her. It found her beneath the muslin of her dress and the silk of her shift, and his fingers made skilled love to her, parting, stroking, teasing, even scratching. One finger slid long and rigid inside her and she clenched muscles about it and both heard and felt her own wetness. The finger was removed and replaced with two, and then they were removed and replaced with three. They played inside her as she tried to capture them with her muscles, driving her to near madness. She clutched his shoulders and kneaded them with her fingers. At the same time the pad of his thumb was doing something that she did not consciously feel but to which she reacted by shattering about his fingers and hand, crying out as she did so.

He was right over her then, blocking the sunlight, his knees pushing her legs wide, his weight on his forearms, his eyes gazing intently down into hers.

"We can be satisfied with that if you wish," he said, his voice harsh. "It is still not too late to say no."

Some semblance of her virtue would remain intact.

"I will not say no," she told him.

And she felt him against the sensitive area he had just been caressing, finding her, positioning himself, and then pressing hard and firm into her until he was deeply imbedded.

She had inhaled slowly, she realized, and was holding her breath. He was indeed large. But he was not hurting her. Quite the contrary. He had made very sure that she was wet enough to receive him without discomfort. She exhaled, relaxed, and then clenched her inner muscles about him.

She was glad. Oh, she was glad. She would *never* be sorry.

He had waited for her, she realized. He was still gazing down into her eyes, though his had lost some of their usual intensity and were heavy lidded and naked with desire. But he would wait no longer. He had given her exquisite pleasure even before entering. Now it was his turn. And he took it. He lowered his head until his forehead touched her shoulder, and worked her with deep, swift, powerful strokes, half his weight on her, the other half still supported on his forearms. She could hear the raggedness of his breathing.

She lifted her legs from the blanket and twined them about his thighs. She felt a momentary twinge in her right ankle but ignored it. She tilted her pelvis so that he could come deeper still. And she listened to the wet sucking of his withdrawals and felt the deep, satisfying penetration of his thrusts. Although she knew this was not primarily for her—he was deep in the throes of his own physical need—she felt again the heightened sensation of renewed passion and pressed against him, matching his rhythm with the clenching and unclenching of her muscles, moving her hips in a rhythmic circular motion.

She had no real experience. Ah, incredibly she had almost none. She mated with him out of pure instinct.

But she certainly had not done anything to dampen his ardor. He worked her with undiminished power until he stilled in her suddenly, rigid in every muscle, straining for greater depth, hot and slick with sweat, and she felt the hot gush of his release at the same moment as he spoke low against her ear.

"Gwendoline," he said and relaxed his full, not inconsiderable weight down upon her.

There was no mattress beneath her back, only the sand beneath the blanket. Who would have guessed sand was so hard and unyielding? But she did not care.

She did not care.

She probably *would*. Perhaps soon.

But not now. Not yet.

He mumbled something after a minute or two and rolled off

her to lie beside her, one arm flung over his eyes, one leg bent at the knee.

"I am sorry," he said. "I must have been crushing you."

She tipped her head to one side to rest against his shoulder. Was it possible that sweat could smell this good? She thought about lifting her dress up over her breasts and pushing down her skirt over her legs, but she made neither concession to modesty.

She slid into a relaxed state halfway between sleeping and waking. The sun shone warmly down on them. The gulls were calling again. Eternally calling. Sounding harsh and mournful. The sound of the sea was there too, as steady and as inescapable as a heartbeat.

She did not believe she would ever be sorry.

But of course she *would*.

The eternal cycle of life. The balance of opposites.

She came back to full consciousness when he got to his feet and, without a word to her, strode the short distance to the water. He waded in a little way and bent to wash himself.

Washing off the sweat?

Washing off *her*?

She sat up and set her dress to rights after reaching beneath it and somehow doing up her laces. She drew her cloak about her shoulders and clasped it at the neck. Suddenly she felt a little chilly.

They drove back to the house in near silence.

The sex had been good. Very good indeed, in fact. And all the more so because he had been starved of it for too long.

But it had been a mistake anyway.

A colossal understatement.

What was one supposed to do when one had bedded a lady? And when it was quite possible that one had impregnated her?

Say thank you and leave her?

Say nothing?

Apologize?

Offer her marriage?

He did not *want* to marry her. Marriage was not about beddings. Not exclusively about them, anyway. And the parts of marriage that were *not* the beddings were every bit as important as those that were. A marriage with Gwendoline was impossible. And, to be fair, that applied to *both* of them.

He wondered if she expected an offer.

And if she would accept were he to make one.

His guess was that the answer to both was a resounding no. Which made it safe to offer, he supposed, and somehow set himself in the right and appease his conscience.

Daft thought.

He took the option of saying nothing.

"How is your ankle?" he asked.

Idiot. Brilliant conversationalist.

"It is coming along slowly but surely," she said. "I shall be careful not to do anything as reckless again."

If she had been more careful a few days ago, she would have climbed safely past his hiding place, unaware that he was there, and he would not have spared her a thought since. Her life would be different. His would be.

And if his father had not died, he thought in some exasperation, he would still be alive.

"Your brother will send a carriage for you soon?" he asked.

It struck him suddenly that he could have offered to take her to Newbury Abbey himself and save her a few days at Penderris.

No. Bad idea.

"If he does not delay in sending it," she said, "and I am sure he will not, then it may arrive the day after tomorrow. Or certainly the day after that."

"You will be happy to be able to recuperate at home with your family about you," he said.

"Oh," she said, "I will."

They were talking like a pair of polite strangers who did not have a whole brain between the two of them.

"You will go to London after Easter?" he asked. "For the Season?"

"I expect so," she said. "My ankle will be healed by then. And you? Will you go to London too?"

"I will," he said. "It is where I grew up, you know. My father's house is there. *My* house now. My sister is there."

"And you will want to look for a wife there," she said.

"Yes."

Good Lord! Had they really been intimate with each other on the beach in the cove less than an hour ago?

He cleared his throat.

"Gwendoline—" he began.

"Please," she said, cutting him off. "Don't say anything. Let us just accept it for what it was. It was . . . pleasant. Oh, what a ridiculous word to choose. It was far more than pleasant. But it is not anything to be commented upon or apologized for or justified or anything else. It just *was*. I am not sorry, and I hope you are not. Let us leave it at that."

"What if you are with child?" he asked her.

She turned her head sharply and looked at him, clearly startled. He kept his eyes on the lane before them, looking steadily between the ears of the horse that trotted along ahead of the gig. Surely she had thought of that? She had the most to lose, after all.

"I am not," she said. "I cannot have children."

"According to a quack," he said.

"I am not with child," she said, sounding stubborn and a little upset.

He looked at her briefly.

"If you are," he said, "you must write to me immediately."

He told her where he lived in London.

She did not answer but merely continued to stare.

George and Ralph and Flavian must have been for a long ride. They were only just stepping out of the stable block as the gig approached. They all turned to watch it come.

"We have been to the cove," Hugo said as he drew the horse to a stop. "It is always at its most picturesque at high tide."

"The fresh air has been lovely," Lady Muir said. "It is sheltered and really quite warm down on that little beach."

Good Lord, even to his own ears they sounded like a pair of coconspirators being so overhearty in their enthusiastic simulation of innocence that they proclaimed themselves as guilty as hell.

"I imagine," Ralph said, "that drawing room conversations today are loud with predictions of the dire suffering we are surely facing as punishment for today's glorious weather."

"No doubt," Flavian said, "it will snow tomorrow. *With* a strong north wind. And we will never again be so foolish as to *think* of enjoying such an unusually lovely day."

They all laughed.

"You do not have your crutches with you, Lady Muir?" George asked.

"Crutches are not much use on cliff paths and pebbles and sand," Hugo said. "I'll drive her up to the doors and carry her inside."

"Off you go, then," George said, giving Hugo a penetrating look. *He* had not been fooled, at least, and it would be nothing short of a miracle if Flavian had. Or Ralph, for that matter. "I daresay Imogen has seen us all arrive and has ordered the tea tray brought up."

Hugo proceeded on his way to the house, a silent Lady Muir beside him.

Chapter 10

The sun was shining just as brightly the following day, though Gwen could see when she stood at the morning room window before Vera arrived that the tree branches were swaying today. It must be windy. And it was a little cooler too, the Duke of Stanbrook had said after an early morning ride.

When Vera arrived, she reported darkly that all her friends agreed with her that they would suffer for this weather by having no summer at all.

"Mark my words," she said. "It is just not natural to have all our good weather this early in the year. I am quite determined not to enjoy it. I will merely become low in spirits when the rain starts, as it inevitably will, bringing the cold with it. And it is not in my nature to feel low, as you very well know, Gwen. I have come to cheer you up. There was no one to greet me when I arrived five minutes ago except the butler. I am not one to complain, but I do think it discourteous of His Grace to neglect the sister-in-law of Sir Roger Parkinson so blatantly. But what is one to expect?"

"Perhaps the carriage returned with you sooner than he anticipated," Gwen said. "He did not neglect to send the carriage, after all, and that is the most important thing. It would have been a long walk for you. And here comes the tray with coffee and biscuits for two. I do thank you for coming, Vera. It is very good of you."

"Well," Vera said as she looked closely at the plate of biscuits on the tray a footman had just set down, "it is not in my nature to neglect my friends, Gwen, as you very well know. I see we are not important enough to be offered the raisin biscuits we had yesterday. It is just plain oatmeal for us today."

"But how tedious it would be," Gwen said, "to be given the same foods day after day. You will be so good as to pour, Vera?"

A little over three hours later, Vera was on her way home despite her suggestion that Gwen must be giving in too readily to low spirits if she *still* needed an afternoon rest as a consequence of her little accident.

Gwen, of course, did *not* need to sleep. She had slept too much last night, or at least she had lain on her bed for too long. She had taken the coward's way out and sent down her excuses when the usual footman had arrived in her room to carry her down to the drawing room at dinnertime. Her outing had left her fatigued, she had claimed, and she begged His Grace to excuse her for the rest of the evening.

She *had* slept. She had had long wakeful spells too, though, during which she had relived the events on the beach and wondered what Lord Trentham would have said if she had allowed him to continue what he had started to say in the gig on the way back to the house.

Gwendoline, he had said after drawing a deep breath.

And she had stopped him.

She would forever wonder what he would have said.

But she had had to stop him. She had been feeling raw with emotion and quite unable to handle any more. She had been desperate for time alone.

She had not seen him since he had carried her up to her room after they took tea in the drawing room with everyone else. He had not spoken a word. Neither had she. He had merely set her down on the bed, stood back and looked at her with those intense dark eyes of his, inclined his head stiffly, and left the room, closing the door quietly behind him.

She opened her book, but it was hopeless to try to read, she realized after a few minutes, during which time her eyes had passed over the same sentence at least a dozen times without once grasping its meaning.

The swelling seemed to have completely disappeared about her ankle today, and most of the pain had gone with it. But when Dr. Jones had called earlier, while Vera was here, he had bound her ankle again and advised her to continue to keep her weight off the foot and to have patience.

It was very hard to be patient.

The carriage from Newbury might possibly arrive tomorrow. More probably it would come the day after tomorrow. It was an endless wait, whichever it turned out to be. She wanted to be gone *now*.

She gave up all pretense of reading and set the book facedown across her waist. She laid her head back against a cushion and closed her eyes. If only she could take a brisk walk outside.

If she had *not* fallen in love with him, she thought, she did not know what words *would* describe the state of her heart. This was more than just lust or the memory of what they had done together down in that cove. It was certainly more than simple attraction and *far* more than just liking. Oh, she was in love. How foolish!

For she was no green girl. She was no hopeless romantic. It was a love that could bring nothing but heartbreak if she tried to cling to it or pursue it. She probably could not pursue it anyway. It took two. She would be leaving here soon. Although both she and Lord Trentham would be in London later in the spring, it was unlikely their paths would cross. They moved in different circles. She would not settle for an affair. She doubted he would. And they were both agreed that marriage was out of the question.

Oh, *why* could Neville's carriage not arrive today?

And then, even as she was thinking it, there was a light tap on the morning room door and it opened quietly. Gwen looked fearfully—and hopefully?—over her shoulder and saw the Duke of Stanbrook standing there.

She was *not* disappointed, she told herself as she smiled at him.

"Ah, you *are* awake," he said, pushing the door wider. "I have brought you a visitor, Lady Muir. *Not* Mrs. Parkinson this time."

He stepped to one side and another gentleman strode past him into the room.

Gwen sat bolt upright on the sofa.

"Neville!" she cried.

"Gwen."

Her eyes did not deceive her. It really *was* her brother, his face all anxious concern as he hurried across the room toward her and bent over her to catch her up in a great bear hug.

"What *have* you been doing to yourself while my back was turned?" he asked her.

"It was a silly accident," she said, hugging him tightly in return. "But it was my bad leg that I twisted, Nev, and I still cannot put any weight on my foot. I feel terribly foolish and really something of a fraud, for it is *only* a sprained ankle, yet it has caused no end of trouble to numerous other people. But what a wonderful surprise this is! I did not expect the carriage until tomorrow at the earliest, and I certainly did not expect you to come with it. Oh, poor Lily and the children, having to do without you for several days all because of me. I will not be very popular with them, I daresay. But oh, dear, it feels like a *year* instead of less than a month since I was at home."

He perched on the edge of the sofa and squeezed her hands in his. He looked very dearly familiar.

"It was Lily who suggested I come," he said. "Indeed, she insisted upon it, and there is no worse tyrant than Lily when she once has an idea stuck in her head. Apparently Devon and Cornwall are overrun with vicious highwaymen, all of whom will relieve you of your jewels and your blood, not necessarily in that order, if I am not with you as you travel, and all of whom will certainly turn tail and run for cover if I am."

He grinned at her.

"Dearest Lily," she said.

"But why are you not at Mrs. Parkinson's?" he asked.

"That is a long story," she said, grimacing. "But, Neville, the Duke of Stanbrook has been extremely kind and hospitable. So have his houseguests."

"It has been our pleasure," the duke said as Neville looked up at him. "My housekeeper will have a room made up for you, Kilbourne, while you and Lady Muir join me in the drawing room for an early tea. Lady Muir has crutches."

Neville held up a staying hand. "I appreciate the offer of hospitality, Stanbrook," he said. "But it is still quite early in the afternoon, and the weather is perfect for travel. If Gwen feels up to traveling with her foot elevated on the carriage seat, then we will leave as soon as her bags have been packed and brought down. Unless it will cause unnecessary inconvenience, that is."

"It will be as you wish," the duke said, inclining his head to Neville and looking inquiringly at Gwen.

"I shall be ready to leave as soon as I have changed into travel clothes," Gwen assured them both.

Where was Lord Trentham?

She was asking the same silent question less than an hour later after she had changed and been brought back downstairs. The footman set her down in the hall, where Lady Barclay waited with her crutches. The Duke of Stanbrook and his other guests were all gathered there too, talking with Neville. Gwen shook them all warmly by the hand and bade them farewell.

But where was Lord Trentham?

It was as if Lady Barclay had heard her thought.

"Hugo came walking along the headland with Vincent and me after luncheon," she said. "But when we turned back, he went down onto the beach. He often spends hours down there before he returns."

All her fellow guests turned their eyes upon Gwen.

"I will not see him again, then," she said. "I am sorry about that. I would have liked to thank him in person for all he has done for me. Perhaps you would say my goodbyes and express my thanks for me, Lady Barclay?"

She was not going to see him again.

Perhaps ever.

Panic threatened. But Gwen smiled politely about her and turned to the door.

Before Lady Barclay could reply, Lord Trentham himself appeared in the doorway, breathing heavily and looking large and flushed and fierce-eyed. He glanced around at them all, and then his eyes focused upon her.

"You are leaving?" he asked.

Relief flooded through her. And she *wished* he had stayed away a little longer.

The old contradictions.

"My brother has come for me," she said. "The Earl of Kilbourne. Neville, this is Lord Trentham, who found me when I hurt myself and carried me all the way here."

The two men looked at each other. Taking each other's measure in that age-old male way.

"Lord Trentham," Neville said. "Gwen mentioned your name in her letter. It sounded familiar then, and now that I see you, I understand why. You were Captain Emes? You led the Forlorn Hope on Badajoz. I am honored. And in your debt. You have been extraordinarily kind to my sister."

He offered his right hand, and Lord Trentham took it.

Gwen turned determinedly to the Duke of Stanbrook.

"You have been kindness and courtesy itself," she said. "Words are not adequate to express my gratitude."

"Our club is to lose its honorary member," he said, smiling in his austere way. "We will miss you, Lady Muir. Perhaps I will see you in town later in the year? I plan to be there for a short while."

And then all the goodbyes were said, and there was nothing left to do but leave. It was something for which she had longed just an hour or so ago. Now her heart was heavy, and she dared not look where she yearned with all her heart to look.

Neville took a step closer to her, clearly intending to carry her out to the carriage, and she turned to hand her crutches to a footman who stood nearby.

But Lord Trentham moved faster than her brother and scooped her up into his own arms without a by-your-leave.

"I carried you in here, ma'am," he said, "and I will carry you out of here."

And he strode out through the doors and half ran down the steps with her, well ahead of Neville or anyone else.

"So this is it," he said.

"Yes."

There were a million things she wanted to say—surely that many. She could not think of a single one. Which was just as well. Really there was nothing at all to say.

The carriage door was open. Lord Trentham leaned inside with her and set her carefully down on the seat facing the horses. He took one of the cushions from the back of the seat opposite, set it flat, and lifted her foot onto it. He looked up into her eyes then, his own dark and blazing. His mouth was set in a grim line. His jaw looked more granitelike than ever. He looked like a hardened, rather dangerous military officer again.

"Have a pleasant journey," he said before withdrawing his head from the carriage and straightening up beside it.

"Thank you," she said.

She smiled. He did not.

At this time yesterday they were making love on the beach, he naked, she as good as.

Neville climbed into the carriage and took the seat beside her, the door was slammed shut, and they were on their way.

Gwen leaned forward and sideways to wave through the window. They were all out there, the duke and his guests, including Lord Trentham, who stood a little apart from the others, his face fiercely expressionless, his hands clasped behind his back.

"I wonder you did not die of fright, Gwen," Neville said, laughing softly. "I daresay it was Captain Emes's face that breached the walls of Badajoz. He deserved all the accolades that followed, though. It is generally agreed that there was no other man in the whole army who could have done what he did that day. He must be justly proud of himself."

Ah, Hugo.

"Yes," she said, resting her head back against the cushions and closing her eyes. "Neville, I am so glad you came. I am *so* glad."

Which did not at all explain why a moment later tears were coursing down her cheeks and she was hiccupping in a vain attempt to silence her sobs and Neville was setting an arm about her shoulders and making soothing sounds and producing a large linen handkerchief from a pocket of his coat.

"Poor Gwen," he said. "You have been through a nasty ordeal. But I will soon have you back home, where Mama can fuss over you to her heart's content—and Lily too, I have no doubt. And the older children have both been asking for Aunt Gwen almost from the moment you left and demanding to know when you will return. They were delighted to see me go when they knew I would be bringing you back with me. The baby, of course, was indifferent to the whole thing. Provided she has Lily close by, she is perfectly content, wise little creature. Oh, and lest you begin to think otherwise, I will be rather glad to have you back home too."

He grinned down at her.

Gwen hiccupped once more and gave him a watery smile.

"And you will soon have plenty more to keep your mind off your ankle," Neville said. "The family will be descending upon us for Easter. Had you remembered?"

"Of course," she said, though in truth it had slipped her mind lately. Lady Phoebe Wyatt, the newest addition to Neville and Lily's family, was to be baptized and a large number of their relatives were coming to the abbey to help celebrate the occasion. They included Gwen's two favorite cousins, Lauren and Joseph.

Oh, it *did* feel good to be going back home. Back to her own familiar world and the people she loved, the people who loved her.

She turned her head to gaze out through the carriage window.

Have a pleasant journey, he had said.

What had she expected? A lover's lament? From *Lord Trentham*?

"We had better stop in the village," she said. "I had better say goodbye to Vera."

Hugo went straight to London after leaving Penderris. He longed to go home to Crosslands, to be quiet there for a while, to see the new lambs and calves, to talk over the spring planting with his steward, to plan his flower garden better than he had done last year, to . . . well, to lick his wounds.

He felt wounded.

But if he went to Crosslands first, he might make excuses to stay there indefinitely, and he might indeed become the recluse some of his friends in the Survivors' Club accused him of being. Not that there was anything wrong with being a recluse if one enjoyed living with oneself for company, as Hugo did, even if his friends insisted that it was not his natural state and he was in danger of exploding somehow one day, like a firecracker waiting for a spark to ignite it.

But there *was* something wrong with being a recluse or even a happy farmer and gardener when one had responsibilities elsewhere. His father had been dead for longer than a year now, and in all that time Hugo had done no more than glance over the meticulously detailed reports William Richardson sent him each month. His father had chosen his manager with care and had trusted him utterly. But, he had told Hugo during those last hours of his life, Richardson was *only* a manager, not a visionary. Hugo's eyes had several times paused upon some detail in the reports, and he had felt an itch to make some change, to force some new direction, to get *involved.* But it was an itch he had stubbornly refused to scratch. He did not *want* to be involved.

It was an attitude he could not continue to hold.

And Constance was getting older by the day. Nineteen was

still very young, of course, even if she sometimes hinted in her letters that it was *ancient.* But he knew that many girls considered they were on the shelf if they were not married before they were twenty. Even regardless of that, though, all girls of eighteen or nineteen ought to be out enjoying themselves with other young people of their own age. They should be looking about them for prospective partners, testing the waters, making choices.

Fiona was too sickly to take Constance anywhere herself, and she was also too sickly to allow anyone else to take Constance away from her. How would she manage without her daughter by her side every second of her waking day?

There was no one more selfish than his stepmother. Only he could stand up to her. And it was something he must do again, for he was Constance's guardian.

He resisted the temptation to go to Crosslands, then, and went straight to London instead. The time had come.

He steeled his nerve.

Constance was more than delighted to see him. She squealed loudly and came dashing across her mother's sitting room when he was announced, and launched herself into his arms.

"Hugo!" she cried. "Oh, Hugo. You have *come. At last.* And without giving us any warning, you wretch. Will you be *staying*? Oh, do say you will. Hugo. Oh, Hugo."

He hugged her tightly to him and let love and guilt wash over him in equal measure. She was youthful and slender and blond and pretty with eager green eyes. She looked remarkably like her mother and made him understand why his sober, steady father had done something as uncharacteristic as marry a milliner's assistant eighteen years his junior after an acquaintance of a mere two weeks.

"I will stay," he said. "I promised I would come this spring, did I not? You are looking remarkably fine, Connie."

He held her at arm's length and looked down at her. There was a sparkle to her eyes and color in her cheeks even though it looked as though she needed to get more sunshine on her skin. He would see that that was put to rights.

His stepmother seemed equally pleased to see him. Not that he often thought of Fiona as his stepmother. She was only five years older than he. He had been a big lad when she had married his father, far bigger than she. She had fawned over him, showered affection upon him, shown pride in him and praised him to his father—and ultimately driven him away. He would not have insisted that his father purchase his commission if it had not been for Fiona. He had not grown up wanting to be a soldier, after all. Strange thought that. How different his life might have been.

It was a thought to add to all the other what-ifs of his existence.

She held out a hand to him now, a handkerchief clutched in it. She was still lovely in a languid, faded sort of way. She was as slender as Constance. There was no gray in her hair and there were no lines on her face. There was an unhealthy pallor to her complexion, though, which might have been caused by real ill-health or by imagined ailments that kept her constantly at home and inactive. She had always had those ailments. She had used them to keep his father attentive, though she had probably not needed to use any wiles to accomplish that goal. His father had adored her to the end, even if his understanding of her character had saddened him.

"Hugo!" she said as he bowed over her hand and carried it to his lips. "You have come home. Your father would have been pleased. He intended that you look after me. And Constance too."

"Fiona." He released her hand and took a step back. "I trust your needs have been fully met during the past year even in my absence. If they have not been, someone will be answering to me."

"Such a masterful man." She smiled wanly. "I always liked that about you. I have lacked for company, Hugo. *We* have lacked for company, have we not, Constance?"

"But you are here now," Constance said happily, linking her

arm through his. "And you are staying. Oh, will you take me to see our cousins? Or invite them here? And *will* you take me—"

"Constance," her mother said plaintively.

Hugo took a seat and set a hand over his sister's soft little one after drawing her down beside him.

He stayed for almost two weeks. He did not invite any of his relatives to his house. Fiona's health would not allow it. He did visit his aunts and uncles and cousins, however, taking Constance with him despite her mother's protests at being left alone. And he realized something very quickly. Most of his relatives were sociable beings and well connected in their middle-class world. They were all delighted to see him and equally happy to see Constance. Some of the younger cousins were in her age group. Any or all of them would be perfectly willing to take Constance about with them. She would make friends in no time. She would probably have a large circle of admirers within days or weeks. She could be married before summer was out.

All she really needed was for someone—*him*—to put his foot down with her mother so that she was no longer incarcerated at home like an unpaid companion. He would not be compelled to marry. Not for Constance's sake, anyway. And he was not eager to rush into marriage for the other reason. He was going to be in London for a while. He could satisfy his needs in other ways than marrying.

It was a bit of a depressing thought, actually, but then so was marriage.

Fulfilling his obligation to his half sister was not to be that easy after all, though. For she had definite ideas of her own about what would make her happy, and they went beyond moving in the world of her cousins, much as she loved them and enjoyed calling upon them.

"You are a *lord,* Hugo," she said when they were strolling in Hyde Park one morning before Fiona was even up from her bed. "And you are a *hero*. It must be possible for you to move in higher circles than Papa ever could. Once people learn that you are in town, they will surely send you invitations. How absolutely *marvelous* it would be to attend a *ton* ball at one of the grand mansions in Mayfair. To dance there. Can you imagine it?"

He looked askance at her. He would really rather not imagine any such thing.

"I am sure you will attract a whole host of admirers from our own world if our cousins take you under their wing," he said. "How can you not, Connie? You are so very pretty."

She smiled up at him and then wrinkled her nose.

"But they are so *dull,* Hugo," she said. "So *staid.*"

"Our cousins, you mean?" he said. "*And* so successful."

"Dull and successful and very dear *as cousins,*" she said. "But all the men they know are bound to be the same way. As husbands they would not be dear at all. I do not want dullness, Hugo. Or even success if stuffy, sober respectability must go with it. I want some . . . oh, some *dash*. Some *adventure*. Is it wrong of me?"

It was not wrong, he thought with an inward sigh. He supposed all girls dreamed of marrying a prince before they actually married someone altogether more ordinary who could support them and care for their daily needs. The difference between Constance and most other girls was that she saw a way of realizing her dream or at least of getting close enough to a prince to gaze upon him.

"And you think upper-class gentlemen will offer you dash and adventure *and* respectability and happiness?" he asked.

She laughed up at him.

"A girl can dream," she said, "and it is *your* job to see that no shocking rake runs off with me for my fortune."

"I would flatten his nose level with the rest of his face if the thought even flitted across his mind," he said.

She laughed merrily, and he joined in.

"You must know some gentlemen," she said. "Even other *titled* gentlemen. Is it possible to wangle an invitation? Oh, it must be.

If you take me to a *ton* ball, Hugo, I will love you forever and ever. Not that I will not do that anyway. *Can* you arrange it?"

It was time to put his foot down quite firmly.

"I daresay it might be possible," he said.

She stopped abruptly on the path, squealed with exuberance, and flung both arms about his neck. It was a good thing there were only trees and dew-wet grass looking on.

"Oh, it *will* be," she cried. "You can do *anything,* Hugo. Oh, thank you, thank you. I *knew* all would be well once you came home. I love you, I love you."

"Sheer cupboard love," he grumbled, patting her back. He wondered what words might have issued from his lips if he had decided *not* to set down a firm foot.

Whatever had he just promised—or as good as promised? As they strolled onward, he felt as though he had broken out in a cold sweat.

And his mind was brought back to the whole gloomy question of marrying. He probably *could* get hold of an invitation if he made a little effort, and he probably could take Constance with him and hope a few gentlemen would offer to partner her on the dance floor. He probably could muddle through an evening, much as he would hate every moment. But would she be satisfied with one ball, or would it merely whet her appetite for more? And what if she met someone who showed more than a passing interest in dancing with her? He would not know what to do about it beyond planting the man a facer, which would not be either a wise or a sensible thing to do.

A wife could help him do it all right.

Not one from the middle classes, though.

He would *not* marry an upper-class wife merely for the sake of a sister who was not yet willing to settle for her rightful place in society.

Would he?

He could feel a headache coming on. Not that he ever suffered from headaches. But this was an exceptional occasion.

He allowed Constance to chatter happily at his side for the rest of their walk. He was vaguely aware of hearing that she had simply *nothing* to wear.

He waited impatiently for the post every morning for those two weeks and shuffled through it all twice as though he thought each day that the letter he looked for had somehow got lost in the pile.

He dreaded seeing it and was disappointed every time he did not.

He had not said anything to her after having sex with her on the beach. And like a gauche schoolboy, he had avoided her the next day and almost missed saying goodbye to her. And when he *had* said goodbye, he had said something truly profound, like *have a good journey* or some such thing.

He *had* started to say something to her in the gig on the way back from the cove, it was true, but she had stopped him and persuaded him that it had all been quite pleasant, thank you very much, but it would be as well to leave it at that.

Had she *meant* it? He had thought so at the time, but really, could women—*ladies*—be so blasé about sexual encounters? Men could. But women? Had he been too ready to take her at her word?

What if she was with child and would not write to him?

And why could he not stop thinking of her day or night, no matter how busy he was with other things and other people? He *was* busy. He was spending part of each day with Richardson, and he was beginning to understand his businesses more fully, and ideas were beginning to pour into his head and even excite him.

But always she was there at the back of his mind—and sometimes not so far back.

Gwendoline.

He would be an idiot to marry her.

But she would save him from idiocy. She would not marry him even if he asked. She had made it very clear that she did not *want* him to ask.

But had she meant it?

He wished he understood women better. It was a well-known fact that they did not mean half of what they said.

But which half did they mean?

He would be an idiot.

Easter was almost upon them. It was rather late this year. After Easter she would be in London for the Season.

He did not want to wait that long.

She had not written, but what if . . .

He would be an idiot. He *was* an idiot.

"I have to go into the country," he announced one morning at breakfast.

Constance set down her toast and gazed at him with open dismay. Fiona was still in bed.

"Just for a few days," he said. "I'll be back within the week. And the Season will not begin until after Easter, you know. There will be no chance of a ball or any other party before then."

She brightened a little.

"You *will* take me, then?" she asked. "To a ball?"

"It is a promise," he said rashly.

By noon he was on his way to Dorsetshire. To Newbury Abbey in Dorsetshire, to be more precise.

Chapter 11

Hugo arrived in the village of Upper Newbury in the middle of a gray, blustery afternoon and took a room at the village inn. He was not sure he was going to need it. It was altogether possible that before dark he would be happy to put as much distance between Newbury and himself as was humanly possible. But he did not want to give the impression that he expected to be offered hospitality at Newbury Abbey.

He walked up to the abbey, expecting at every moment to be rained upon, though the clouds clung on to their moisture long enough to save him from getting wet. Soon after passing through the gates of the park he saw what he assumed was the dower house off to his right among the trees. It was a sizable building, more a small manor than a mere house. He hesitated for a moment, trying to decide whether to go there first. It was where she lived. But he tried to think like a gentleman. A gentleman would go to the main house first in order to have a word with her brother. It was an unnecessary courtesy, of course. She was thirty-two years old. But people of the upper classes set some store by the niceties of courtesy, necessary or not.

It was a decision he regretted soon after he arrived at the abbey itself, as grand and imposing a mansion as Penderris but without the comfort of being owned by one of his closest friends. The butler took his name and headed off upstairs to see if his master was at home—a rather silly affectation in the country.

Hugo was not kept waiting for long. The butler returned to

invite Lord Trentham to follow him, and they made their way up to what turned out to be the drawing room.

And it was—damn it all!—crowded with people, not one of whom happened to be Lady Muir. It was too late to turn tail and run, however. Kilbourne was at the door waiting to greet him, a smile on his face, one hand outstretched. A pretty little lady was at his side, also smiling.

"Trentham," Kilbourne said, shaking him warmly by the hand. "How good of you to call. On your way home from Cornwall, are you?"

Hugo did not disabuse him.

"I thought I would call in," he said, "and see if Lady Muir has recovered fully from her accident."

"She has," Kilbourne said. "Indeed, she is out walking and is likely to get a soaking if she does not get under cover soon. Meet my countess. Lily, my love, this is Lord Trentham, who rescued Gwen in Cornwall."

"Lord Trentham," Lady Kilbourne said, also reaching out a hand for his. "Neville has told us all about you, and I will not embarrass you by gushing. But it is a pleasure to make your acquaintance. Do come in and meet our family. Everyone has come for Easter and for the baptism of our newest baby."

And they took him about the room, the two of them, displaying him like a coveted trophy, introducing him as the man who had rescued their sister from being stranded with a badly sprained ankle above a deserted beach in Cornwall. *And* as the famous hero who had led the Forlorn Hope attack upon Badajoz.

Hugo could cheerfully have died of mortification—if such a mass of contradictions had been possible. He was introduced to the Dowager Countess of Kilbourne, who smiled kindly at him and thanked him for what he had done for her daughter. And he was introduced to the Duke and Duchess of Portfrey—had George not said that the duke had once been his friend?—and to the Duke and Duchess of Anburey; their son, the Marquess of Attingsborough, and his wife; and their daughter, the Countess of Sutton, and her husband. And to Viscount Ravensberg and his wife and Viscount Stern and *his* wife and one or two other persons. Not one of the people gathered there was without a title.

They were an amiable enough lot. The men all shook him heartily by the hand, the women were all delighted that he had been there on that deserted beach when Lady Muir had needed him. They all smiled and nodded graciously and asked about his journey and commented upon the dismal weather they had been having for the past several days and said how pleased they were finally to meet the hero who had seemed to disappear off the face of the earth after his great feat at Badajoz though simply everyone had been waiting to meet him.

Hugo nodded his head, clasped his hands behind his back, and understood the enormity of his presumption in coming here. He was a hero, perhaps—in their eyes. And he had his title—an empty thing, since everyone knew it had come as a trophy of war and had nothing whatsoever to do with birth or heritage. And he had come to suggest to one of their own that perhaps she might consider joining forces with him in matrimony.

His best course of action, he decided, was to take his leave without further delay. He need not wait to see her. He had come supposedly from Cornwall, on his way home from Penderris, and had made a detour out of politeness to inquire whether Lady Muir had recovered from her accident. Having been assured that she *had* recovered, he might now leave without anyone's thinking it peculiar of him not to wait.

Or *would* they think it peculiar?

To the devil with them. Did he care what they thought?

He was not far from the drawing room window, talking to, or rather being talked at by *someone*—he had already forgotten most names—when the Countess of Kilbourne spoke up from nearby.

"*There* she is!" she exclaimed. "And it is raining—*heavily*. Oh, poor Gwen. She will be soaked. I shall hurry down and intercept her and take her up to my dressing room to dry off a bit."

And she turned to hurry away while several of her guests, including Hugo himself, looked out into the driving rain and saw Lady Muir bobbing her way diagonally across the lawn below—her limp really was pronounced—her pelisse flapping about her in the wind and looking as though it was saturated with water, a large umbrella clutched in both hands and tipped sideways to shield as much of her person as was possible.

Hugo inhaled slowly.

Kilbourne was at his shoulder, laughing softly.

"Poor Gwen," he said.

"If this is not an inconvenient time," Hugo said quietly, "I would have a private word with you, Kilbourne."

With which words, he thought, he had just burned a few bridges.

Gwen had recovered fully from her sprained ankle, but the same could not be said of her low spirits.

At first she had told herself that once she was on her feet again, everything in her life would be back to normal. It was mortally tedious to be confined to a sofa for most of the day even though many of her favorite activities were available to her there—reading, embroidering, tatting, writing letters. And she had had her mother for company. Lily and Neville had called every day, sometimes together, sometimes separately. The children, including the baby, often came with them. Neighbors had called.

And then, when she *was* on her feet and her spirits were still low, she had convinced herself that once the family arrived for Easter, all would be well. Lauren was coming as well as Elizabeth and Joseph and . . . oh, and everyone. She had looked forward to their coming with eager impatience.

But now there was no further reasonable explanation for the depression she could not seem to throw off. She was perfectly mobile again, and everyone was at the abbey and had been for the past two days. Even though the weather was dreary and they were all beginning to ask one another if they could remember what the sun looked like, there was plenty of company and activity indoors.

Gwen had discovered with some dismay that she could not enjoy that company as much as she always had. Everyone was part of a couple. Except her mother, of course. And her. And how self-pitying *that* sounded. She was single by choice. No woman who was widowed at the age of twenty-five could be expected to remain a widow for the rest of her life. And she had had numerous chances to remarry.

She had told no one about Hugo.

Not her mother, not Lily—and not Lauren. She had written a long letter to Lauren the day she discovered that she was not with child. She had told her cousin everything, including the fact that she had fallen in love and could not yet persuade herself to fall out again, though she *would*. And including the sordid fact that she had lain with him and had only now discovered that there were to be no disastrous consequences. But she had torn up the letter and written another. She would tell Lauren when she saw her in person, she had decided. There was not long to wait.

But now she had seen Lauren, and she had still said nothing even though Lauren knew there was something to tell and had asked her about it and tried a few times to get her alone so that they could have one of their long heart-to-heart chats. They had always been each other's best friend and confidant. Gwen had resisted each time, and Lauren was looking concerned.

Gwen was walking alone this afternoon instead of accompanying her mother to the abbey for the rest of the day. She would follow later, she had said. Despite the heavy clouds and the blustery wind and the promise of rain at any moment, almost any of her cousins at the abbey would have come walking with her if she had asked. They could have come out in a merry group.

Lauren would be hurt that she had chosen solitude. Joseph would frown slightly and look a little puzzled—rather the way Lily and Neville and her mother had been looking at her lately, in fact.

It was so unlike her not always to be gregarious, cheerful, even sunny natured. She had *tried* to be at least cheerful since coming back home. She had even thought she had succeeded. But obviously she had not.

She had cried the day she knew she was not with child. What

an absurd reaction. She ought to have been over the moon with relief. She *had been* relieved. Just not in an over-the-moon kind of way. Apart from anything else, it had been a further reminder that she could not conceive.

Sometimes—often, in fact—she tried to picture the child she had lost as he or she would have been now at the age of almost eight. Foolish imaginings. The child did not exist. And such imaginings merely left her wretched with grief and guilt.

When was she going to shake herself free of this massive, all-encompassing ennui? She was thoroughly irritated with herself. If she was not careful, she was going to develop into a whiner and would attract only fellow whiners as friends.

She was walking along the secluded woodland path that ran parallel to the perimeter of the park and parallel to the cliffs a short distance away until it reached the steep descent to the grassy valley below and the stone bridge over to the sandy beach beyond. She had always liked this path. She could walk straight onto it from the dower house, and it was overhung with the branches of low trees, which hid the cliffs and the sea. It was quiet and rural. It was not quite muddy today. It was not quite perfect for walking either, and it might yet turn muddy if it rained again—*when* it rained again.

Perhaps her mood would lift once they all moved to London after Easter and all the myriad entertainments of the Season began.

Hugo would be in London too.

Looking for a wife—of his own sort.

Gwen had made a decision in the secrecy of her heart. She was going to give serious consideration to any gentlemen who seemed interested in courting her this year—and there were usually a few. She would at last entertain the thought of marrying again. She would look for a kind, good-natured man, though he would have to be intelligent and sensible too. An older man might be better than a younger. Perhaps a widower who, like her, would be looking for the comfort of quiet companionship more than for anything more exciting. She would *not* look for passion. She had had passion quite recently and she did not want it ever again. It was far too raw and far too painful.

Perhaps by this time next year she would be married again. Perhaps she would even be . . . But, no. She would not think of that only to be horribly disappointed again. And she would *not* seek out the opinion of a physician who might be able to give her an informed opinion on her fertility. If he were to say no, even the faintest of her hopes would be dashed forever. And if he were to say yes, then she would be setting herself up for a worse disappointment if nothing happened after all.

She could live without children of her own. Of course she could. She was doing it now.

She had reached the end of the path and was at the top of the steep descent to the valley. This was the farthest she had walked since returning from Cornwall.

She rarely went down to the valley even though it was very picturesque with the waterfall that fell sheer from the cliffs to the deep, fern-surrounded pool. Her grandfather had built a small cottage beside the pool for her grandmother, who had liked to sketch there. She did not go down today either. She would not have done so even if the rain had not started. But suddenly it *did,* and it was no drizzle, as it had been earlier in the morning and all day yesterday. The heavens opened in a deluge from which even her umbrella was not going to provide much protection.

She turned to flee homeward. But the dower house was quite a distance away, and she knew it would be unwise to dash that far on her weakened ankle along a rain-slick path. The abbey was far closer if she cut diagonally across the sloping lawn to one side of the path. And she had been planning to go there later anyway.

She made her decision quickly and hurried up the grass, her head down, one hand holding up the hems of her dress and pelisse in a vain attempt to save them from becoming soggy and muddy, the other hand holding her umbrella at an angle best designed to keep at least part of herself dry. Before she arrived at the house she needed both hands on the umbrella handle to prevent the wind from blowing it away.

She arrived wet and breathless.

Lily must have seen her through the drawing room window. She was already downstairs in the hall waiting to greet her, and a footman was holding the door wide.

"Gwen!" Lily exclaimed. "You look half drowned, you poor thing. You had better come up to my dressing room and dry off. I will lend you something pretty to wear. Everyone is in the drawing room, and there is a visitor too."

Gwen did not ask who the visitor was. Some neighbor, she supposed. But she followed Lily gratefully up the stairs. She could hardly appear in the drawing room looking as she did.

The drawing room door opened, however, as they reached the top of the first flight of stairs, and Neville stepped out. Gwen half smiled, half grimaced at him and then froze, for another man loomed in the doorway behind him, filling it with his massive presence. His dark eyes burned into hers.

Oh, dear God, the visitor.

"Lady Muir," Lord Trentham said, inclining his head without removing his eyes from hers. He looked fierce and dour and rather like a coiled spring.

Whatever was he doing here?

"Oh," Gwen said foolishly, "I look like a drowned rat."

His eyes moved over her from head to toe and back again.

"You do," he agreed, "though I would have been too polite to say so if you had not said it first."

He was as blunt as ever.

Lily chose to be amused and laughed. Gwen merely stared and licked her lips, surely the only dry part of her person.

Oh, heavens, Hugo was here. At *Newbury*.

"I was about to whisk Gwen upstairs to dry off and change," Lily said, "before she catches her death of cold."

"Do that, my love," Neville said. "Lord Trentham will wait, I do not doubt."

"I will," Hugo said, and Gwen yielded to the pressure of Lily's hand pulling her in the direction of the stairs.

Whatever was he doing here?

Gwen donned a pale blue wool dress of Lily's that was a little too long for her but otherwise fit well enough. Her hair was damp and curled more than it usually did, but it was not quite unmanageable. She was feeling breathless and dazed as she prepared to go back down to the drawing room.

Lily knew why Lord Trentham was here. He was on his way home from Cornwall, and since Newbury Abbey was not far out of his way, he had called to see that Gwen had fully recovered from her mishap.

"It is very obliging of him," Lily said as she took Gwen's soaked garments and set them in a heap close to her dressing room door. "And it is such an honor to meet him. *Everyone* is happy to see him at last. And he does not disappoint, does he? He is so large and . . . *severe*. He looks like a hero."

Poor Hugo, Gwen thought. *How he must be hating every moment.* And he would not have had any idea, poor thing, that large numbers of her family were here. All of them aristocrats. None of them from his world.

Why had he *really* come? Surely he had not been at Penderris all this time? But there was no point in speculation. She would find out.

"And I daresay," Lily said as they were leaving the room, "he has made the detour because he is a little sweet on you, Gwen. It would not be at all surprising, would it? And it would not be surprising if *you* were sweet on *him*. He is severe, but he is also . . . hmm. What is the word? Gorgeous? Yes, he is gorgeous."

"Oh, goodness, Lily," Gwen said as they made their way down the stairs, "you *do* allow your imagination to run away with you at times."

Lily laughed. "It is a pity," she said, "that your mind is set quite irrevocably against remarrying. Or is it?"

Gwen did not reply. Her stomach had tied itself in knots.

A sudden quiet descended upon the drawing room when they

entered it. Neville was over by the window, frowning. Everyone else was present. Except Hugo.

Lily noticed his absence too.

"Oh, has Lord Trentham left?" she asked. "But we were as quick as we could be. Poor Gwen was soaked through to the skin."

He had *left*? After coming all this way to inquire about her ankle?

"He is in the library," Neville said. "I just left him there. He wants a private word with Gwen."

The hush seemed to intensify.

"It really is quite extraordinary," their mother said, breaking it. "Lord Trentham is not at all the sort of man whose attentions you would ever dream of encouraging, Gwen. But he has come to offer for you nevertheless."

"I consider it quite unpardonably presumptuous of him, Gwen," Wilma, Countess of Sutton, said, "even if he did do you a considerable service when you were in Cornwall. I daresay the title and the accolades that followed upon his undoubtedly heroic act have gone to his head and given him ideas above his station."

Wilma had never been Gwen's favorite cousin. Sometimes it was hard to believe that she could possibly be Joseph's sister.

"I did not feel I had the right to speak for you, I am sorry, Gwen," Neville said. "You are thirty-two years old. I do not believe the offer is quite as impertinent as Wilma suggests, though. Trentham does *have* the title, after all, and he has the wealth to go with it. And he certainly is a great hero, perhaps the greatest of the recent wars. He could probably be the darling of polite society if he so chose—as our reaction to meeting him here a while ago would attest. It is perhaps to his credit that he has never sought fame or adulation and that he looked a little uncomfortable with them this afternoon. But his coming here to offer you marriage is a little embarrassing for you. I am sorry I could not merely send him away. I did, however, warn him that you have worn the willow for Muir quite constantly for seven years and are unlikely to give him the answer for which he hopes."

"It is as well you did not try to speak for Gwen, Neville," Joseph, Marquess of Attingsborough, said, grinning at Gwen. "Women do not like that, you know. I have it on Claudia's authority that they are quite capable of speaking up for themselves."

Claudia was his wife.

"That is all very well, Joseph," Wilma said, "when it is a *gentleman* to whom she is to address herself."

"Oh, come now, Wilma," Lauren said. "Lord Trentham seemed a perfect gentleman to me."

"Poor Lord Trentham will be sending down roots into the library carpet," Lily said, "or else wearing a path threadbare across it. We had better let Gwen go and speak to him herself. Go, Gwen."

"I shall do so," Gwen said. "You must not concern yourself, though, Mama. Or you, Nev. Or any of you. I will not be marrying a blunt soldier of the lower classes, even if he *is* a hero."

She was surprised to hear some bitterness in her voice.

No one replied even though Elizabeth, Duchess of Portfrey, her aunt, was smiling at her and Claudia was nodding briskly in her direction. Her mother was gazing down at the hands in her lap. Neville was looking slightly reproachful. Lily was looking troubled. Lauren had an arrested expression on her face.

Gwen left the room and made her way down the stairs, holding up her skirt carefully so that she would not trip over the hem.

She had still not fully tested her reaction to finding Hugo here. She knew now why he had come. But *why*? The fact that they could never marry each other had always been something upon which they were both agreed.

Why had he changed his mind?

She would, of course, say no. Being in love with a man was one thing—even *making* love with him. Marrying him was another thing entirely. Marriage was about far more than just loving and making love.

She nodded to the footman who was waiting to open the library door for her.

Chapter 12

With every mile of his journey to Newbury Abbey, Hugo had asked himself what he thought he was doing. With every mile he had tried to persuade himself to turn back before he made a complete ass of himself.

But what if she was with child?

He had kept on going.

The more fool he. There had been that excruciatingly embarrassing fifteen minutes or so in the drawing room. And that had been followed by an equally embarrassing interview with Kilbourne in the library.

Kilbourne had been perfectly polite, even friendly. But he had clearly thought Hugo daft in the head for coming here and expecting that *Lady Muir* would listen favorably to his marriage offer. He had looked slightly embarrassed and had all but told Hugo that she would not have him. She had loved her first husband dearly, he had explained, and had been inconsolable at his death. She had vowed never to marry again, and she had never yet shown any sign of changing her mind about that. Hugo must not take it personally if she refused. He had almost said *when* she refused. His lips had formed the word and then corrected themselves so that he could say *if* instead.

Hugo was still in the library—alone. Kilbourne had gone back up to the drawing room, promising that he would send his sister down as soon as she appeared there herself.

Perhaps she would not come down. Perhaps she would send

Kilbourne back with her answer. Perhaps he was about to come face to face with the greatest humiliation of his life.

And serve him right too. What the devil was he doing here?

He had done nothing to help his own cause either, he remembered with a grimace. The only thing she had had to say when he had seen her earlier was that she looked like a drowned rat. And he, suave and polished gentleman that he was, had agreed with her. He might have added that she looked gorgeous anyway, but he had not done so and it was too late now.

A drowned rat. A fine thing to say to the woman to whom one had come to offer marriage.

He thought the library door would never open again, but that he would be left to live out the rest of his life rooted to the spot on the library carpet, afraid to move a muscle lest the house fall about his shoulders. He deliberately shrugged them and shuffled his feet just to prove to himself that it could be done.

And then the door *did* open when he was least expecting it, and she stepped inside. An unseen hand closed the door from the other side, but she leaned back against it, her hands behind her, probably gripping the handle. As though she were preparing to flee at the first moment she felt threatened.

Hugo frowned.

Her borrowed dress was too big for her. It completely covered her feet and was a little loose at the waist and hips. But the color suited her, and so did the simplicity of the design. It emphasized the trim perfection of her figure. Her blond hair was curlier than usual. The damp must have got to it despite the bonnet she had worn and the umbrella she had held as she came hurtling up across the lawn. Her cheeks were flushed, her blue eyes wide, her lips slightly parted.

Like a foolish schoolboy, he crossed both sets of fingers on each hand behind his back and even the thumbs of his two hands.

"I came," he said.

Good Lord! If there were an orator-of-the-year award, he would be in dire danger of winning it.

She said nothing, which was hardly surprising.

He cleared his throat.

"You did not write," he said.

"No."

He waited.

"No," she said again. "There was no need. I told you there would not be."

He was ridiculously disappointed.

"Good." He nodded curtly.

And silence descended. Why was it that silence sometimes felt like a physical thing with a weight of its own? Not that there was real silence. He could hear the rain lashing down against the window panes.

"My sister is nineteen," he said. "She has never had much of a social life. My father used to take her to visit our relatives when he was still alive, but since then she has remained essentially at home with her mother, who is always ailing and likes to keep Constance by her side. I am now her guardian—my sister's, that is. And she needs a social life beyond mere family."

"I know," she said. "You explained this to me at Penderris. It is one of your reasons for wanting to marry a woman of your own kind. A practical, capable woman, I believe you said."

"But she—Constance—is not content to meet her own kind," he said. "If she were, all would be well. Our relatives would take her about with them and introduce her to all kinds of eligible men, and I would not need to marry after all. Not for *that* reason, anyway."

"But—?" She made a question of it.

"She has her heart set upon attending at least one *ton* ball," he said. "She believes my title will make it possible. I have promised her that I will make it happen."

"You *are* Lord Trentham," she said, "and the hero of Badajoz. Of course you can make it happen. You have connections."

"All of them men." He grimaced slightly. "What if one ball is not enough? What if she is invited elsewhere after that first? What if she acquires a beau?"

"It is altogether possible that she will," she said. "Your father was very wealthy, you told me. Is she pretty?"

"Yes," he said. He licked his lips. "I need a wife. A woman who is accustomed to the life of the beau monde. A lady."

There was a short silence again, and Hugo wished he had rehearsed what he would say. He had the feeling that he had gone about this all wrong. But it was too late now to start again. He could only plow onward.

"Lady Muir," he said, clutching his crossed fingers almost to the point of pain, "will you marry me?"

Plowing onward when one had not scouted out the territory ahead could be disastrous. He knew that from experience. He knew it now again. All the words he had spoken seemed laid out before him as though printed on a page, and he could see with painful clarity how *wrong* they were.

And even without that imagined page, there was her face.

It looked as it had that very first day, when she had hurt her leg.

Coldly haughty.

"Thank you, Lord Trentham," she said, "but I beg to decline."

Well, there. That was it.

She would have refused him no matter how he had worded his proposal. But he really had not needed to make such a mull of it.

He stared at her, unconsciously hardening his jaw and deepening his frown.

"Of course," he said. "I expected no different."

She gazed at him, that haughty look gradually softening into one of puzzlement.

"Did you really expect me to marry you merely because your sister wishes to attend a *ton* ball?" she asked.

"No," he said.

"Why did you come, then?" she asked.

Because I was hoping you were with child. But that was not strictly true. He had not been *hoping.*

Because I have not been able to get you out of my mind. Pride prevented him from saying any such thing.

Because we had good sex together. No. It was true, but it was not the reason he was here. Not the only reason, anyway.

Why *was* he here, then? It alarmed him that he did not know the answer to his own question.

"There *is* no other reason than that, is there?" she asked softly after a lengthy silence.

He had uncrossed his fingers and dropped his arms to his sides. He flexed his fingers now to rid them of the pins and needles.

"I had sex with you," he said.

"And there were no consequences," she said. "You did not *force* me. I freely consented, and it was very . . . pleasant. But that was all, Hugo. It is forgotten."

She had called him Hugo. His eyes narrowed on her.

"You said at the time," he said, "that it was far more than just pleasant."

Her cheeks flushed.

"I cannot remember," she said. "You are probably right."

She could not possibly have forgotten. He was not conceited about his own prowess, but she had been a widow and celibate for seven years. She would not have forgotten even if his performance had been miserable.

It did not matter, though, did it? She would not marry him even if he groveled on the floor at her feet, weeping and reciting bad poetry. She was Lady Muir and he was an upstart. She had had a bad experience with her first marriage and would be very wary about undertaking another. He was a man with issues. She was well aware of that. He was large and clumsy and ugly. Well, perhaps that was a bit of an exaggeration, but not much.

He bowed abruptly to her.

"I thank you, ma'am," he said, "for granting me a hearing. I will not keep you any longer."

She turned to leave, but she paused with her hand on the knob of the door.

"Lord Trentham," she said without turning around, "*was* your sister your only reason for coming here?"

It would be best not to answer. Or to answer with a lie. It would be best to end this farce as soon as possible so that he could get back out into the fresh air and begin licking his wounds again.

So of course he spoke the truth.

"No," he said.

Gwen had been feeling angry and so sad that she hardly knew how to draw one breath to follow another. She had felt insulted and grieved. She had longed to make her escape from the library and the house, to dash through the rain to the dower house in her overlong dress and on her weak ankle.

But even the dower house would not have been far enough. Even the ends of the world would not have been.

He had looked like a stern, dour military officer when she came into the library. Like a cold, hard stranger who was here against his will. It had been almost impossible to believe that on one glorious afternoon he had also been her lover.

Impossible with her body and her rational mind, anyway.

Her emotions were a different matter.

And then he had announced that he had come—as if she must have been expecting him, longing for him, *pining* for him. As though he were conferring a great favor on her.

And *then*. Well, he had not even made any attempt to hide the motive behind his coming to offer her marriage. It was so that she would use her influence to introduce his precious sister to the *ton* and find a man of gentle birth to marry her.

He must have been hoping that she was with child so that his task would have been made easier.

She stood with her hand on the door after he had dismissed her—*he* had dismissed *her* from Neville's library. She was that close to freedom and to what she knew would be a foolish and terrible heartbreak. For she could no longer like him, and her memories of him would be forever sullied.

And then it occurred to her.

He could not *possibly* have come here with the intention of telling her that his sister needed an invitation to a *ton* ball and that therefore she must marry him. It was just too absurd.

It was altogether possible that he would look back upon this scene and the words he had spoken and cringe. She guessed that if he had rehearsed what he would say, the whole speech had fled from his mind as soon as she stepped into the room. It was altogether possible that his stiff military bearing and hard-set jaw and scowl were hiding embarrassment and insecurity.

It had, she supposed, taken some courage to come here to Newbury.

She could be *entirely* wrong, of course.

"Lord Trentham," she asked the door panel in front of her face, "*was* your sister your only reason for coming here?"

She thought he was not going to answer. She closed her eyes, and her right hand began to turn the knob of the door. The rain pelted against the library window with a particularly vicious burst.

"No," he said, and she relaxed her hold on the doorknob, opened her eyes, drew a slow breath, and turned.

He looked the same as before. If anything, his scowl was even more fierce. He looked dangerous—but she knew he was not. He was not a dangerous man, though there must be hundreds of men, both living and dead, who would disagree with her if they could.

"I had sex with you," he said.

He had said that before, and then they had got distracted by a discussion of whether she had found it pleasant or more than pleasant.

"And that means you ought to marry me?" she said.

"Yes." He gazed steadily at her.

"Is this your middle-class morality speaking?" she asked him. "But you have had other women. You admitted as much to me at Penderris. Did you feel obliged to offer them marriage too?"

"That was different," he said.

"How?"

"Sex with them was a business arrangement," he said. "I paid, they provided."

Oh, goodness. Gwen felt dizzy for a moment. Her brother and her male cousins would have forty fits apiece if they were listening now.

"If you had paid me," she said, "you would not be obliged to offer me marriage?"

"That's daft," he said.

Gwen sighed and looked toward the fireplace. There was a fire burning, but it needed more coal. She shivered slightly. She ought to have asked Lily for a shawl to wrap about her shoulders.

"You are cold," Lord Trentham said, and he too looked at the fireplace before striding over to the hearth and bending to the coal scuttle.

Gwen moved across the room while he was busy and sat on the edge of a leather chair close to the blaze. She held her hands out to it. Lord Trentham stood slightly to one side of the fire, his back to it, and looked down at her.

"I never felt any strong urge to marry," he said. "I felt it even less after my years at Penderris. I wanted—I *needed* to be alone. It is only during the past year that I have come reluctantly to the conclusion that I ought to marry—someone of my own kind, someone who can satisfy my basic needs, someone who can manage my home and help in some way with the farm and garden, someone who can help me with Constance until she is properly settled. Someone to fit in, not to intrude. Someone on whose private life *I* would not intrude. A comfortable companion."

"But a lusty bed partner," she said. She glanced up at him before returning her gaze to the fire.

"And that too," he agreed. "All men need a vigorous and satisfying sex life. I do not apologize for wanting it within a marriage rather than outside it."

Gwen raised her eyebrows. Well, she had started it.

"When I met you," he said, "I wanted to bed you almost from the beginning even though you irritated me no end with your haughty pride and your insistence upon being put down when I was carrying you up from the beach. And I expected to despise you after you told me about that ride with your husband and its consequences. But we all do things in our lives that are against our better judgment and that we regret bitterly forever after. We all suffer. I wanted you, and I had you down in that cove. But there was never any question of marriage. We were both agreed upon that. I could never fit in with your life, and you could never fit in with mine."

"But you changed your mind," she said. "You came here."

"I somehow expected," he said, "that you were with child. Or if I did not exactly *expect* it, I did at least shape my mind in that direction so that I would be prepared. And when I did not hear from you, I thought that perhaps you would withhold the truth from me and bear a bastard child I would never know anything about. It gnawed at me. I wouldn't have come even then, though. If you were so much against marrying me that you would even hide a bastard child from me, then coming here and asking was not going to make any difference. And then Constance told me about her dreams. Youthful dreams are precious things. They ought not to be dashed as foolish and unrealistic just because they are *young* dreams. Innocence ought not to be destroyed from any callous conviction that a realistic sort of cynicism is better."

Is that what happened to you?

She did not ask the question aloud.

"A wife from the middle classes would not be able to help me," he said.

"But I would?"

He hesitated.

"Yes," he said.

"This is not your only reason for wishing to marry me, though?" she asked.

He hesitated again.

"No," he said. "I had sex with you. I put you in danger of conceiving out of wedlock. There is no one else I want to marry—not at present, anyway. There would be passion in our marriage bed. On both our parts."

"And it does not matter that we would be incompatible in every other way?" she said.

Again the hesitation.

"I thought we might give it a try," he said.

She looked up again and met his gaze.

"Oh, Hugo," she said. "One gives *painting* a try when one has never held a brush in one's hand before. Or climbing a steep cliff face when one is afraid of heights or eating an unfamiliar food when one does not really like the look of it. If one likes it, whatever it is, one can keep going. If one does not, one can stop and try something else. One cannot *try* marriage. Once one is in, there is no way out."

"You would know," he said. "You have tried it already. I will take my leave, then, ma'am. I hope you will not take a chill from your soaking and from standing in here in a dress designed for summer rather than early spring."

He bowed stiffly.

He was calling her *ma'am;* she was calling him *Hugo*.

"And one tries courtship," she said and looked down again. She closed her eyes. This was foolish. *More* than foolish. But perhaps he would continue on his way out of her life.

He did not. He straightened up and stayed where he was. There was a silence in which Gwen could hear that there had been no abatement in the force of the rain.

"Courtship?" he said.

"I could indeed help your sister," she said, opening her eyes and examining the backs of her hands as they lay in her lap. "If she is pretty and has genteel manners, as I daresay she does, and is wealthy, then she will take well enough with the *ton* even if not with the very highest echelon. She would take well, that is, if I were to sponsor her."

"You would be willing to do that," he asked her, "when you have not even met her?"

"I would have to meet her first, of course," she said.

Silence descended once more.

"I daresay that if we like each other I will sponsor her," she said, looking at him again. "But it will quickly become known who Miss Emes is, who her brother is. You will probably be surprised to find yourself quite famous, Lord Trentham. Not many military officers, especially those who are not born into the upper classes, are rewarded for military service with titles. And when people learn who Miss Emes is and who you are and who is sponsoring her, it will not be long before word will spread of our meeting in Cornwall earlier this year. Tongues will wag even if there is nothing for them to wag about."

"I would *not* have you the subject of gossip," he said.

"Oh, not gossip, Lord Trentham," she said. "*Speculation.* The *ton* loves nothing more during the Season than to play matchmaker or at least to speculate upon who is paying court to whom and what the outcome is likely to be. Word will soon have it that you are courting me."

"And that I am a presumptuous devil," he said, "who ought to be strung up from the nearest tree by his thumbs."

She smiled.

"There will of course be those who are outraged," she said, "at you for your presumption, at me for encouraging it. And there will be those who are charmed by the romance of it all. There will be wagers made."

Both his jaw and his eyes hardened.

"If you really *wish* to marry me," she said, "you may court me through the coming Season, Lord Trentham. There will be ample opportunity—provided, of course, your sister pleases me and I please her."

"You *will* marry me, then?" he asked, frowning.

"Very probably not," she said. "But a marriage proposal is made after courtship, not before. Court me, then, and persuade me to change my mind if you do not change yours first."

"How the devil," he asked her, "am I to do that? I do not know the first thing about courtship."

She smiled with the first genuine amusement she had felt for a long while.

"You are in your thirties," she said. "It is time you learned."

If he had looked hard-jawed before, he looked positively granite-jawed now. He gazed steadily at her.

Then he bowed again.

"If you would care to inform me after you have arrived in London," he said, "I will wait upon you with my sister, ma'am."

"I shall look forward to it," she said.

And he strode from the room and closed the door behind him.

Gwen sat gazing into the fire, her hands clasped very tightly in her lap.

Whatever had she done?

But she was not sorry, she realized. It would be . . . *fun* to launch a young girl upon the *ton,* especially a girl who was not *of* it. It would brighten the Season for her, make it different from all the rather tedious ones that had gone before it. It would rid her of the low spirits that had been dogging her. It would be a challenge.

And Hugo would be paying court to her.

Perhaps.

Oh, this was a colossal mistake.

But her heart was thumping with something very like excitement. And anticipation. She felt fully alive for the first time in a long, long while.

Chapter 13

Lauren joined Gwen in the library ten minutes later. She closed the door quietly and seated herself on a chair close to Gwen's.

"We saw Lord Trentham stride away from the house in the pouring rain," she said. "We waited for you to come back upstairs, but you did not. You refused him, Gwen?"

"I did, of course," Gwen said, spreading her fingers in her lap. "It is what you all expected, was it not? And wanted?"

There was a slight pause.

"Gwen, this is me," Lauren said.

Gwen looked up at her.

"I am sorry," she said. "Yes, I refused him."

Her cousin searched her eyes.

"There is more," she said. "He has been the reason for your depression of late?"

"I have not been depressed," Gwen protested. But Lauren just continued to look steadily at her. "Oh, I suppose I have been. I have been realizing that life is passing me by. I am thirty-two years old and single in a world where it is not comfortable to be single. Not for a woman, anyway. I have been thinking of looking for a husband in London this year. Or at least of considering anyone who cares to show an interest in me. Everyone in the family will be delighted, will they not?"

"You *know* we all will," Lauren said. "But how would this decision have made you so low in spirits that you do not even want to *talk*?"

She definitely looked hurt, Gwen thought. She sighed.

"I fell in love with Lord Trentham when I was in Cornwall," she said. "There. Is that what you want to hear? I . . . fell in love with him. And I discovered just ten days or so ago that I was not with child by him, and I was hugely relieved and mortally sad. And . . . Oh, Lauren, what am I going to *do*? I cannot seem to get him out of my mind. Or my heart."

Lauren was gazing at her in silent amazement.

"There was a chance," she said, "that you *were* with child? Gwen?"

"Not really," Gwen said. "The physician told me after I miscarried eight years ago that I would never have children. And it happened only once in Cornwall. But that is not really your question, is it? The answer to your real question is yes. I did lie with him."

Lauren leaned forward in her chair and reached out to touch the back of Gwen's hand with her fingertips. She rubbed them back and forth before sitting back again.

"Tell me," she said. "Tell everything. Start at the beginning and end here, with your reason for rejecting his marriage offer."

"I have invited him to court me during the Season," Gwen said, "with no guarantee that I will say yes if he renews his addresses at the end of it. That is not very fair of me, is it?"

Lauren sighed and then laughed.

"How typical of you to start at the end," she said. "Start *at the beginning*."

Gwen laughed too.

"Oh, Lauren," she said, "how could I have resisted love all these years only to fall for an impossibility at the end of it all?"

"If I could fall in love with Kit, considering my frame of mind when I first saw him," Lauren said, "*and* considering the fact that he was behaving most scandalously, stripped to the waist in the middle of Hyde Park for all the world to see while he fought with two laborers simultaneously *and* was using language that shocked me to the core—*if* I could fall in love with him anyway, Gwen, then why would *you* not fall in love with Lord Trentham?"

"But it *is* an impossibility," Gwen said. "He has no real patience with the upper classes even though some of his dearest friends are aristocrats. He thinks us a frivolous, idle lot. He is middle-class and proud of it. And why should he not be? There is nothing inherently superior about us, is there? But I am not sure I could be the wife of a businessman, even a wealthy and successful one. Besides, there is a darkness in his soul, and I do not want to have to live with that again."

"Again?" Lauren repeated softly.

Gwen looked down at her hands once more and said nothing.

"I am not saying another word," Lauren said, "until you start at the beginning and tell me the whole story."

Gwen told her everything.

And, strangely, they ended up convulsed with laughter over the way he had bungled his marriage proposal earlier by giving the impression that his *only* reason for asking her was so that his sister might attend a *ton* ball.

"I suppose," Lauren said, drying her eyes, "you *will* be taking her to a ball?"

"I will," Gwen said.

"It is a good thing I am still firmly in love with Kit," Lauren said. "If I were not, I believe I might be falling a little in love with Lord Trentham myself."

"We had better go back upstairs to the drawing room," Gwen said, getting to her feet. "I suppose everyone had plenty more to say after I left. Wilma, for example."

"Well," Lauren said, following her out of the room, "you know Wilma. Every family has *some* cross to bear."

They laughed again and Lauren linked an arm through Gwen's.

The letter arrived more than two weeks later.

It had been an endless fortnight.

Hugo had thrown himself headlong into work. And he was reminded of how he had never been able to do things by halves.

When he was a boy, he had spent every spare moment with his father, learning everything he possibly could about the businesses and developing ideas of his own, some of which his father had actually implemented. And when he had taken his commission, he had worked tirelessly to achieve his goal of becoming a general—perhaps the youngest in the army. He might have got there too if he had not first gone out of his head.

Now he was owner of the businesses, and he was immersed in the running of them, though part of him longed to be back at Crosslands, where he had lived an entirely different sort of life, not driven either by the demands of work or by the press of ambition.

He took Constance out walking or driving or shopping or to the library almost every day. He continued to take her calling upon their relatives too. He took her to a party at a cousin's home one evening, and she promptly acquired two potential beaux, both of them respectable and personable enough, though Constance on the way home pronounced one to be a prosy bore and the other a *boastful* bore. It was just as well she did not wish to encourage them as Hugo had found his fingers itching all evening to plant them both a facer.

He did not tell her about his visit to Newbury Abbey or its outcome. He did not wish to raise her hopes only to have them dashed again if no letter ever arrived. Though even if Lady Muir did not carry through on her promise, of course, then *he* was going to have to carry through on *his*. He had promised to take his sister to a *ton* ball.

He must know a few ex-officers who had not been hostile to him and who also happened to be in London. And George had said he was coming to town sometime soon. Flavian and Ralph sometimes came during the spring. There must be *some* way of wangling an invitation, even if it was only to one of the less popular *ton* balls of the Season, one to which the hostess would welcome anyone willing to attend short of her chimney sweep.

He kept his distance from Fiona as much as he could during

those two weeks. She was very unhappy to be left alone so often, but she refused to go out with her daughter and stepson. She had long ago broken off all communication with her own family, though Hugo knew that his father had gone to the trouble of raising her parents and her brother and sister out of grinding poverty. He had bought a small house for them and set them up in the grocery shop beneath it. They had managed the shop well and made a decent living out of it. But Fiona would have nothing to do with them. Neither would she consort with her husband's relatives, who looked down upon her and treated her with contempt, she claimed, though Hugo had never seen any evidence of it.

She chose to remain at home now and wallow in her imaginary ailments. Or perhaps some of them were real. It was impossible to know for sure.

She fawned upon him when Constance was present. She whined at him on the few occasions when they were alone. She was lonely and neglected and he hated her, she claimed. It had been a different story when she had been young and beautiful. He had not hated her then.

He had.

But then he had been a boy, clever at his schoolwork and astute in business, but naïve and gauche when it came to more personal matters. Fiona, dissatisfied with the wealthy, hardworking, adoring husband who worked long hours and was many years her senior, had fancied her young stepson as he grew closer to manhood and set out to seduce him. She had almost succeeded too, just before his eighteenth birthday. It had happened on an evening when his father was out and she had sat beside Hugo on the love seat in the sitting room and rubbed her hand over his chest while she told him some tale to which he could not even listen. And the hand had slid lower until it had no lower to go.

He had hardened into full arousal, and she had laughed softly and closed her hand about his erection over his clothing.

He had been upstairs in his room less than one minute later, dealing with the erection for himself and crying at the same time.

The next morning he had been in his father's office early, demanding that his father purchase a commission for him in an infantry regiment. *Nothing* would change his mind, he had declared. It was his lifelong ambition to go into the military, and he could suppress it no longer. If his father refused to make the purchase, then Hugo would go and take the king's shilling and enlist in the ranks.

He had broken his father's heart. His own too, actually.

He was no longer a naïve, gauche boy.

"Of course you are lonely, Fiona," he said. "My father has been gone longer than a year. And of course you feel neglected. He is dead. But your year of mourning is over, you know, and difficult as it may be, you need to get out into the world again. You are still young. You still have your looks. You are wealthy. You can remain here, wallowing in self-pity and making a companion of your pills and your hartshorn. Or you can begin a new life."

She was weeping silently, making no attempt to dry her tears or cover her face.

"You are hard-hearted, Hugo," she said. "You used not to be. You loved me once until your father discovered it and sent you away."

"I went away at my own insistence," he said brutally. "I never loved you, Fiona. You were and are my stepmother. My father's wife. I would have been fond of you if you had allowed it. You did not."

He turned on his heel and left the room.

How different his life would have been if she had been content with his affection after her marriage to his father. But there was no point in such thoughts or in imagining what that other life might have been. It might have been worse. Or better. But it did not exist. That other life had never been lived.

Life was made up of choices, all of which, even the smallest, made all the difference to the rest of one's life.

The letter came a little after two weeks following his return to London from Dorsetshire.

Lady Muir was at Kilbourne House on Grosvenor Square, the letter announced, and would be pleased if Lord Trentham and Miss Emes would call upon her there at two o'clock in the afternoon two days hence.

Hugo foolishly turned the page over to make sure there was nothing else written on the back of it. It was just a formal little note with not a breath of anything personal in it.

What had he expected? A declaration of undying passion?

She had invited him to court her.

That was a thought that needed some examination. *He* was to court *her*. With no guarantee of success. He might try his damnedest all spring and then go down on one knee and offer her a perfect red rose and some flowery proposal of marriage only to be rejected.

Again.

Was he willing to expend that much energy only to end up making an ass of himself? Did he really *want* her to marry him? There was a lot else to marriage and to life than what happened between the sheets. And, as she herself had pointed out, one could not give marriage a try. One either married or one did not. Either way, one lived with the consequences.

It would probably . . . No, it would undoubtedly be better to err on the side of caution and not court her at all. Or ever again offer her marriage. But when had he ever been a cautious man? When had he ever resisted a challenge merely because he might fail? When had he ever entertained the possibility of failure?

He ought not to marry her—even assuming she gave him the chance. And if she helped Constance during the spring and took her to a couple of balls, and if by some miracle his sister met someone with whom she could be happy and secure, then he would not *need* to marry Gwendoline or anyone else. He could go home in the summer with a clear conscience to his three functioning rooms in a large mansion and his barren, spacious park and his own scintillating company.

Except that he had more or less promised his father that when the time came he would pass the business empire on to a son of his own. He needed to marry if that son were ever to be more than a figment of his imagination.

Arrgghh!

Constance had joined him at the breakfast table. She kissed his cheek, bade him a good morning, and sat down at her place.

He set the letter, open, beside his plate.

"I have heard from a friend," he said. "She has just arrived in London and has invited me to call upon her and to bring you with me."

"She?" Constance looked up from her toast, which she was spreading with marmalade, and smiled impishly at him.

"Lady Muir," he said, "sister of the Earl of Kilbourne. I met her earlier in the year when I was staying in Cornwall. She is at Kilbourne House on Grosvenor Square."

She was gazing at him, saucer-eyed.

"*Lady* Muir?" she said. "*Grosvenor Square?* And she wants *me* to call there with you?"

"That is what she says," he said, picking up the letter and handing it to her.

She read it, her toast forgotten, her mouth slightly open, her eyes still wide with amazement. She read it again. And she looked up at him.

"Oh, Hugo," she said, her voice almost a whisper. "Oh, Hugo."

He guessed that she wanted to go.

Lauren was at Kilbourne House on the afternoon when Gwen had invited Lord Trentham to call with his sister. She had begged to be allowed to be there for the occasion. Gwen's mother and Lily were at home too. They had wanted Gwen to accompany them on a visit to Elizabeth, Duchess of Portfrey, and she had felt obliged to admit that she was expecting callers. She could hardly then withhold the names of those visitors.

She would much rather have had only Lauren for company. Oh, and perhaps Lily too—Lily had been absurdly disappointed to hear that Gwen had refused Lord Trentham and that he had gone away without another word. She had seen him as a romantic as well as heroic figure and had hoped he would be *the one* to sweep Gwen off her feet.

Gwen's mother looked puzzled and a little troubled when she learned who the visitors were. Lily, on the other hand, regarded her sister-in-law with bright, speculative eyes but made no comment.

"It was only civil to invite them to call, Mama," Gwen explained. "Lord Trentham *did* save me from what could have been a very nasty fate when I was staying with Vera in Cornwall, after all."

The four of them sat in the drawing room as the appointed hour approached, looking out upon bright sunshine, and Gwen wondered if her visitors would come or not—and whether she *wanted* them to come.

They came, almost exactly upon the dot of two.

"Lord Trentham and Miss Emes," the butler announced, and they stepped into the room.

Miss Emes was as different from her brother as it was possible to be. She was of medium height but very slender. She was blond and fair-complexioned and had light blue eyes, which were as wide as saucers now. Poor girl, it must be a horrid shock to her to find herself confronting four ladies when she had expected one. She stood very close to her brother's side and looked as if she would hide behind him if he had not had her arm very firmly tucked beneath his own.

Gwen's eyes moved unwillingly to him. To Hugo. He was smartly dressed, as usual. But he still looked like a fierce, barbaric warrior masquerading as a gentleman. And he was scowling more than he was frowning. He must be equally shocked to discover that this was not to be a private audience just with her.

Well, she thought, if they wished to move in *ton*nish circles, they must grow accustomed to being in a room with more than one member of the *ton* at a time, and with more than one titled member. Though Hugo had, of course, had a taste of it at Newbury Abbey.

Her heart was thumping uncomfortably.

"Miss Emes," she said, getting to her feet and stepping forward, "how delightful of you to come. I am Lady Muir."

"My lady." The girl slid her arm free of her brother's and sank into a deep curtsy without removing her wide eyes from Gwen's.

"This is my mother, the Dowager Countess of Kilbourne," Gwen said, "and the countess, my sister-in-law. And Lady Ravensberg, my cousin. Lord Trentham, you have met everyone before."

The girl curtsied again, and Lord Trentham inclined his head stiffly.

"Do have a seat," Gwen said. "The tea tray will be here in a moment."

Lord Trentham sat on a sofa, and his sister sat beside him, so close that she leaned against him from shoulder to hip. There was bright color high in her cheeks. If she had been a child, Gwen thought, she would surely have turned her head to hide her face against his sleeve. She had not taken her eyes from Gwen's.

She was passably pretty, Gwen decided, even if not a raving beauty. And she was well enough dressed, though without flair.

Gwen smiled at her.

"I daresay, Miss Emes," she said, "you are happy to have your brother in London."

"I am, my lady," the girl said, and there was a pause during which Gwen thought that making conversation might well prove to be very difficult indeed. How could she help a girl who would not help herself? But she was not finished. "He is a great hero. My papa was fit to bursting with pride before he died last year, and so was I. But more than that, I have adored Hugo all my life. I have been told that I cried for three days straight after he went off to war when I was still very young. I have longed and longed for him to come home ever since. And now at last he has, and he is going to stay at least until the summer."

She had a light, pretty voice. It was slightly breathless, which was understandable under the circumstances. But her words lit up her face and made her several degrees prettier than Gwen had thought at first. And finally the girl looked away from Gwen in order to glance worshipfully at her brother.

He looked back at her with obvious affection.

"Your words do you credit, Miss Emes," Lauren said. "But men will go off to war, you know, and leave their more sensible womenfolk behind to worry."

They all laughed and the tension was somewhat eased. Gwen's mother asked after the health of Mrs. Emes, and Lily told the girl that not *all* women were sensible enough to stay home from war, that *she* had grown up in the train of an army and had even spent a few years in the Peninsula before coming to England.

"It was *England* that was the foreign country to me," she said, "even though I was English by birth."

Trust Lily to talk instead of simply to ask questions. She had set the girl more at her ease, Gwen could see.

The tea tray had been brought in, and Lily was pouring.

This was *not* just a social call, Gwen reminded herself, despite what her mother and Lily must assume. She exchanged a glance with Lauren.

"Miss Emes," she said, "I understand that it is your dream to attend a *ton* ball during the Season."

The girl's eyes went wide again, and she blushed.

"Oh, it is, my lady," she said. "I thought that perhaps Hugo . . . Well, he *is* a lord. But I suppose I am just being silly. Though he *has* promised that he will arrange it before the Season is over, and Hugo always keeps his promises. But . . ."

She stopped talking and darted an apologetic glance at her brother.

He had not told her, then, Gwen thought. Perhaps he did not believe she would keep *her* promise and had not wanted to disappoint his sister.

"Miss Emes," Lauren said, "my husband and I, together with his parents, are to host a ball at Redfield House at the end of next week. It will be early enough in the Season that I daresay everyone will come. It will be a great squeeze, and I shall be flushed with triumph. I would be delighted if you would attend with Lord Trentham."

The girl gaped and then closed her mouth with an audible clicking of her teeth.

Dear Lauren. This had not been arranged in advance. Gwen had thought of taking the girl to a smaller affair, at least for her first appearance. But perhaps a grand squeeze—and Lauren's ball was bound to be that—would be better. There would be larger crowds and therefore less reason for self-consciousness.

"That," Lord Trentham said, speaking for almost the first time since he stepped into the room, "is extremely kind of you, ma'am. But I am not sure—"

"You may come under my sponsorship, Miss Emes," Gwen said, looking at Lord Trentham as she spoke. "But with your brother as an escort, of course. A young lady ought to have a female sponsor instead of just her brother, and I would be delighted to assume that role."

Her mother, she was aware, was very silent.

"Oh," Miss Emes said, her hands clasped so tightly in her lap that Gwen could see the white of her knuckles. "You would do that, my lady? For *me*?"

"I would indeed," Gwen said. "It would be fun."

Fun?

What do you do for fun, Lord Trentham had asked her once at Penderris, and she had wondered at the word addressed to an adult woman.

"Oh, Hugo." The girl turned her head and gazed up at him imploringly. "*May* I?"

His hand came across to cover both of hers in her lap.

"If you wish, Connie," he said. "You can give it a try anyway."

I thought we might give it a try. He had spoken those words at Newbury after he had offered Gwen marriage. He met her eyes briefly now, and she could tell that he was remembering too.

"Thank you," the girl said, looking first at him and then at Lauren and then at Gwen. "Oh, *thank* you. But I have nothing to *wear*."

"We will see to that," Lord Trentham said.

"Neither do I." Gwen laughed. "Which is not strictly true, of course, as I daresay it is not of you, Miss Emes. But this is a new spring and a new Season, and there is all the necessity of having new and fashionable clothes with which to astonish society. Shall we go in search of them together? Tomorrow morning, perhaps?"

"Oh, Hugo," the girl said, looking pleadingly at him again, "*may* I? I still have *all* the pin money you have allowed me in the last year."

"You may go," he said, "and have the bills sent to me, of course." He looked at Gwen. "Carte blanche, Lady Muir. Constance must have everything she will need for the ball."

"And for other occasions too?" Gwen asked. "One ball is not going to satisfy either your sister or me, you know. I am quite certain of that."

"Carte blanche," he said again, holding her gaze.

She smiled back at him. Oh, this Season already felt very different from all the ones that had preceded it. For the first time in many years in town, she felt *alive,* full of optimism and hope. But hope for what? She did not know, and she did not particularly care at this moment. She liked Constance Emes. At least, she thought she would like her when she knew her a little better.

Lord Trentham got to his feet to take his leave as soon as he had drunk his tea, and his sister jumped up too. He surprised Gwen then, before he left the room. He turned at the door and spoke to her, making no attempt to lower his voice.

"It is a sunny day, ma'am," he said, "without any discernible wind. Would you care to come driving in the park with me later?"

Oh. Gwen was very aware of her mother and Lily and Lauren

behind her in the room. Miss Emes looked up at her with bright eyes.

"Thank you, Lord Trentham," Gwen said. "That would be pleasant."

And they were gone. The door closed behind them.

"Gwen," her mother said after a short pause, "that was surely unnecessary. You are showing extraordinary kindness to the sister, but must you be seen to grant favors to the brother? You refused his marriage offer just a few weeks ago."

"He really is rather gorgeous in his own particular way, though, Mother," Lily said, laughing. "Would you not agree, Lauren?"

"He is . . . distinguished," Lauren said. "And clearly he has not been deterred by Gwen's rejection of his offer. That makes him either foolishly obstinate or persistently ardent. Time will tell which it is." And she laughed too.

"Mama," Gwen said, "I invited Lord Trentham to call this afternoon with Miss Emes. I offered to sponsor her at a few *ton* events. I offered to help clothe her suitably and fashionably. If Lord Trentham then invited me to drive in the park with him, is it so surprising that I would accept?"

Her mother gazed at her, frowning and shaking her head slightly.

Lily and Lauren were busy exchanging significant looks.

Chapter 14

Apart from a plain, no-frills traveling carriage, which usually stood in the carriage house at Crosslands for weeks at a time without being brought out for an airing, and a wagon, which was necessary for the farm business, Hugo had never owned a vehicle. A horse had always served most of his needs when the distance he wished to travel was a little too far for his feet to convey him.

But during the past week he had purchased a curricle—a sporting one, no less, with a high, well-sprung seat and yellow painted wheels. He had bought a matched pair of chestnuts to pull it and felt like a dashed dandy. Soon he would be mincing along the pavements of London, using a cane as a prop, inhaling snuff delicately off the back of one kid-gloved hand, and ogling the ladies through a jeweled quizzing glass.

But Flavian, who was in town for a few weeks, had insisted that the yellow-wheeled curricle was vastly superior to the more sensible one Hugo had his eye upon, and that the chestnuts must take precedence over all the other horseflesh Hugo might have preferred. They were *matched,* while no other two were.

"If you must cut a d-dash, Hugo," he had said while they stood together in the yard at Tattersall's, "and why would you be in town looking for a wife if you do *not* intend to cut one, then you must cut it with a flair. You will attract ten prospective brides the first time you tool down the street behind these beauties."

"And then I stop, explain to them that I am titled and rich, and ask if they would care to marry me?" Hugo said, wondering what his father would think of the purchase of two horses that were twice as expensive as any others simply because they were *matched*.

"My dear chap." Flavian shuddered theatrically. "One must hold oneself more dear. It is up to the ladies to discover those facts for themselves once their interest is aroused. And discover them they will, never fear. Ladies are brilliant at such maneuvers."

"I drive down the street, then," Hugo said, "and wait for the ladies to attack me."

"They will doubtless do it with more finesse than your words suggest," Flavian said. "But, yes, Hugo. We will make a fine gentleman of you yet. Are you going to purchase the chestnuts before someone else snaps them up?"

Hugo bought them.

And so he had been able to offer to drive Lady Muir in the park rather than ask her merely to walk there with him.

He still felt like a prize idiot, perched up above the road for all the world to see. And the world was indeed looking, he discovered with some dismay. Although he passed any number of other smart vehicles on the way to Grosvenor Square only a little more than two hours after he had left there with Constance in the plain traveling carriage, his own drew more than its share of admiring glances and even one whistle of appreciation. At least the horses were manageable despite the fact that Flavian had described them rather alarmingly as prime goers.

Lady Muir was ready. Indeed, he did not even have to rattle the door knocker. As he was jumping down to the pavement, the door opened and she stepped outside. Her claim to Constance that she had nothing to wear was clearly a barefaced lie. She was looking very dazzling indeed in a pale green dress and matching pelisse and straw bonnet. The latter was trimmed with primroses and greenery, artificial, he assumed.

She came down the house steps unassisted and approached him across the pavement while he held out a hand to help her up to the high seat. He noticed her limp again. He could hardly *not* notice it, in fact. It was not a slight limp.

"Thank you." She smiled at him as she set her gloved hand in his and mounted to her seat without any inelegant scrambling.

He followed her up and gathered the ribbons in his hands again.

He did not know why the devil he was doing this. She was not actually his favorite person in the world. She had refused his marriage offer, which of course she had had a perfect right to do, and which he was not surprised she had done when he had thought back later to remember exactly with what verbal brilliance he had proposed. But she had not been content with a refusal. She had offered to help Constance anyway, and then she had invited him to court her—with no guarantee that she would look more favorably upon any proposal he cared to make at the end of the Season.

Like a handful of dry seeds tossed to a bird. Like a dry bone cast to a dog.

But here he was anyway even though it was quite unnecessary. She and her cousin, Lady Ravensberg, had already made tidy arrangements for Constance to make some sort of debut into *ton*nish society, and Connie was beyond excited. He had not needed to extend this invitation, then. Neither had he needed to purchase this extravagant and garish toy that he was driving. Had he bought it with her in mind? It was a question whose answer he did not wish to contemplate.

In the meanwhile, he was becoming uncomfortably aware that the seat of a curricle was narrow and really designed to accommodate just one person, especially when that person was large. She was all warm, soft femininity—as, of course, he had discovered on a certain beach in Cornwall. And she was wearing that expensive perfume.

"This is a very smart curricle, Lord Trentham," she said. "Is it new?"

"It is," he said, guiding his horses past a large wagon piled with vegetables, mostly cabbages that looked none too fresh.

A short while later he turned into the park. He must join the fashionable promenade, he supposed, though he had never in his life done so before. It was where the *ton* came in the late afternoons to show off their expensive finery to one another and to exchange gossip and sometimes perhaps even some snippet of real news.

"Lord Trentham," she said, "since leaving Grosvenor Square you have spoken two words. And those were wrung out of you by a question that demanded an affirmative or negative answer. *And* you are scowling."

"Perhaps," he said, looking straight ahead, "you would prefer to be taken home rather than to continue."

He *wished* he had not invited her. It had been an impulsive thing—even though he had bought the curricle for just such an occasion. Good Lord, he was a mess. He felt far out of his depth and in imminent danger of drowning.

Her head was turned toward him. She was studying him closely, he could tell without turning his head to look.

"I would not prefer it," she said quietly. "Your sister is happy, Lord Trentham?"

"Ecstatic," he said. "But I am not convinced I am doing the right thing by her. She does not know what is facing her. She *thinks* she does, but she does not. She will never be one of them—one of *you*."

"If that is so," she said, "and she realizes it early, then no harm will have been done. She will move on with her life and find happiness in a world with which she is more familiar. But you may be wrong. We are a different class, but we are the same species."

"Sometimes," he said, "I have my doubts about that."

"And yet," she said, "some of your closest friends in the world are of my class. And you are one of *their* closest friends."

"That is different," he said.

But there was no time for further conversation. They were upon the masses and must perforce join the promenade of slow-moving vehicles parading about a large empty oval. Most of the vehicles were open so that the occupants could greet acquaintances and converse with ease. Horses moved in and out between them and also stopped frequently for their riders to exchange social niceties. Pedestrians strolled nearby, far enough away not to be trampled but near enough to see and be seen, to hail and be hailed.

Lady Muir knew everyone, and everyone knew her. She smiled and waved and talked with all who paused beside the curricle. Sometimes, if it was a brief exchange, she did not introduce him. Sometimes she did, and Hugo felt eyes upon him, curious, assessing, speculative.

He found himself nodding curtly to people whose names he would never remember, and even whose faces he would forget. If it were not for Constance, he would be consoling himself with the inward promise that he would *never* do anything like this again. But there *was* Constance and his promise to her and the invitation to Lady Ravensberg's ball next week that had already been made and accepted.

He was committed now.

But not to courting Lady Muir, by Jove. He was not a puppet on anyone's string. Just last evening he had dined with the family of one of his cousins, and the only other guest at the table was a youngish woman who had recently lost her widowed mother, with whom she had stayed home dutifully long after her brothers and sisters had married. She was close to him in age, Hugo had guessed, and she was pleasant and sensible and had an attractively full figure even if her face was on the plain side. He had had a good talk with her and had escorted her home. His cousins had been matchmaking for him, of course. But he thought he might be interested. Or at least, he thought he *ought* to be interested.

And then his mind, which had been woolgathering, was snapped back to the present. Two gentlemen on horseback paused beside the curricle and Hugo, looking at the nearer of the two, saw a man he did not know. It was hardly surprising. He knew no one.

It was the other one who spoke to Lady Muir.

"Gwen, my dear girl!" he exclaimed in a voice that was so familiar that Hugo's stomach immediately churned with nausea.

"Jason," she said.

Lieutenant-Colonel Grayson, not in uniform today, looking as coldly handsome as ever and as arrogant and as supercilious. He was one of the few military officers of Hugo's acquaintance whom he had truly hated. Grayson had made his life hell from the first day to the last, and he had had the power to do it in style. Twice he had succeeded in blocking promotions that Hugo had earned both by seniority and by prowess. Climbing the ladder had been a slow business as long as Grayson's eyes had been on him—and they always were—gazing contemptuously along the length of his aristocratic nose.

His eyes were on Hugo now.

"The hero of Badajoz," he said, making his words sound like the grossest of insults. "*Lord* Trentham. Are you sure you know what you are doing, Gwen? Are you sure you have not granted the favor of your company to a mirage?"

"I take it, Jason," Lady Muir said while Hugo looked steadily back at him, his jaw tight, "that you know Lord Trentham? And that he was indeed the commander of the brilliantly successful Forlorn Hope at Badajoz? Have *you* made his acquaintance, Sir Isaac? Sir Isaac Bartlett, Lord Trentham."

She was referring to the other rider. Hugo switched his gaze to him and inclined his head.

"Bartlett," he said.

"I did not know you were in town, Gwen," Grayson said. "I shall do myself the honor of calling upon you at . . . Kilbourne House?"

"Yes," she said.

"It would seem," he said, "that Kilbourne is too indulgent. You need advice and guidance from the head of your late husband's family, since you are not getting it from the head of your own."

And he nodded and rode on. Sir Isaac Bartlett smiled at both of them, tipped his hat to Lady Muir, and followed.

The hatred was pointless, Hugo decided as he moved his curricle onward. What had happened during his years in the military was long in the past and would remain there. But he was too preoccupied with quelling the hatred he felt anyway to concentrate any attention upon Lady Muir beside him as they completed the circuit and she called gaily to a number of acquaintances. He was surprised, then, when he turned his head to ask if she wished to do the circuit one more time, as most people seemed to be doing, and discovered that her face was pale and drawn. Even her lips were white.

"Take me home," she said.

He drew the curricle away from the crowd without delay.

"You are unwell?" he asked.

"Just a little . . . faint," she said. "I will be fine after I have had a cup of tea."

He turned and looked at her again. And he heard the echo of the words she had spoken with Grayson—or, more particularly, the words he had spoken to her.

"Lieutenant-Colonel Grayson upset you?" he asked. Probably the man had an even higher rank by now.

"Viscount Muir?" she said.

He frowned in incomprehension.

"He is Viscount Muir now," she said. "He was Vernon's cousin and heir."

Ah. Small world. But the man's final words to her were now explained.

"He has upset you?" he said.

"He killed Vernon," she said. "He and I together."

And she turned her head to look away from him as his curricle moved out into the street. Only the brim of her bonnet and the primroses and greenery were visible to him.

She did not look back again or say anything else. She offered no explanation.

And Hugo could not think of a blessed thing to say.

Incredibly, Gwen had not seen Jason, Lord Muir, since he succeeded to the title, or at least not since Vernon's funeral.

Or perhaps it was not so very surprising. He had not given up his career when the title became his. He still had not, as far as Gwen knew. He was a general now. He was, presumably, a very important man in the army. He was probably away from England for much of his time or else was in parts of the country remote from London. If he had ever spent time in town, it must have been when she was not here. She had even stopped holding her breath each year for fear that she would see him.

He had been two years Vernon's senior, and had dominated his younger cousin in every imaginable way except possibly in looks—and in social rank. He had been larger, stronger, more successful at school, more athletic, more popular with his peers, more forceful in character. Whenever he had had an extended leave from his regiment, he had spent much of it with them. He had needed to keep an eye on his inheritance, he had always said with a loud laugh, as though he were making a joke. Vernon had always laughed with him in genuine merriment. Gwen's laughter had been more guarded.

Vernon had adored Jason, and Jason had seemed fond of him. He had tried to jolly Vernon out of the dismals whenever he found him in one of his black moods, with admonitions that he had the title to live up to, that he must be more of a *man,* more of a husband for his beautiful wife. He had always been loudly jocular with Gwen, telling her that she must hurry up and produce an heir as well as a spare so that he could relax and concentrate upon his career. He had always laughed loudly at his own joke, and Vernon had laughed with him. He had once or twice set an arm about Gwen's shoulders and hugged her to his side, though he had never made any more overt advances to her. She had always cringed with revulsion anyway. He had apparently been the first to reach her side when she fell from her horse. He had been with them on that occasion, riding a short distance behind her—a very short distance when she had made the jump, almost as though he had felt that he needed to urge her horse to jump high enough.

He had wept inconsolably at Vernon's death and again at his funeral.

Gwen had never known how much was sincerity with him and how much was artifice. She had never known if he loved Vernon or hated him, if he coveted the title or was indifferent to it, if he was really sorrowful at her miscarriage or secretly glad.

And of course he had not *literally* killed Vernon, any more than she had.

She had always hated him with a passion and felt guilty about it, for he never did anything overt to deserve it and she might have been doing him a dreadful injustice. What other military man, after all, would weep publicly over the death of a cousin? He was one of Vernon's few surviving relatives and the only one who had been in any way attentive to him. Vernon's father had died young, and his mother had not lived much longer. Vernon had succeeded to his title at the age of fourteen and had been governed by a pair of competent but humorless guardians until he reached his majority. He had had no brothers or sisters.

Now she had seen Jason again after seven years. And he was threatening to call at Kilbourne House. Neville, he had had the effrontery to say, was too indulgent with her. He must give her advice *as head of her late husband's family*. As though he were head of *her* family. She liked him no better now than she had all those years ago.

She fumed inwardly but said nothing at home.

She called at Lord Trentham's the morning after he had called upon her and was introduced to his languid stepmother, who resembled her daughter to a remarkable degree. Gwen bore Miss Emes off to her own dressmaker.

The shopping trip cheered her up a great deal, long and exhausting though it was. She always enjoyed shopping, and having a pretty young girl to dress from head to toe for any number of upcoming occasions was as much fun as she had expected it to be. Especially as the girl's brother had given them carte blanche to spend as much as they wished.

She had missed a visit from Jason while she was out. So had her mother and Lily, who had gone to spend the day with Claudia, Joseph's wife, who was suffering from the nausea that came with early pregnancy—her second. But Neville had been at home.

"He said something about feeling responsible for you as head of the family," Neville said to Gwen as they sat at a late luncheon. "I was obliged to poker up and stare him down and ask him to which family exactly he was referring. No offense intended, Gwen, but the Graysons have not been scrambling to take care of you since Vernon's passing, have they?"

"I suppose," Gwen said, "he thought it ought to be beneath the dignity of a Grayson, even just the widow of a Grayson, to be seen in Hyde Park with a former military officer whose heroism was so extraordinary that the king himself rewarded him with a title."

"He did hint," Neville said, "that Captain Emes—that is how he referred to Trentham—was perhaps not as heroic on that occasion as the king among others was led to believe. I did not invite him to elaborate. I am sorry, Gwen. Ought I to have? You have never said much about Vernon's cousin and successor. Are you fond of him and inclined to take advice from him?"

"Neither," Gwen said, "and I never did like him, though admittedly he never gave me particular cause. I hope you informed him, Nev, that I reached the age of majority years ago and no longer have a husband to whom I owe obedience. I hope you informed him that I am quite capable of choosing my own friends and escorts."

"It is almost exactly what I told him," Neville said. "I even flirted with the idea of raising a quizzing glass to my eye, but I decided that would be too much of an affectation. Are you regretting that you refused Trentham's offer at Newbury?"

"No." She paused in her eating and looked at him. She was glad her mother was not here. "But I have agreed to introduce his sister to the *ton,* Neville, and therefore I will be seeing him. I like him. Do you disapprove?"

He set his elbows on the table and steepled his fingers against his mouth.

"Because he is not a gentleman?" he said. "No, I do not disapprove, Gwen. I am not Wilma, you will be glad to know. I trust your judgment. I married Lily in the Peninsula, you will remember, when I thought she was my sergeant's daughter. I loved her then, and I loved her when I discovered later that she is actually a duke's daughter. The apparent change in her status made no difference whatsoever to my feelings for her. Trentham just seems . . . morose."

"He is," she said. "Or, rather, moroseness is the mask behind which he feels most comfortable."

Gwen smiled, and no more was said on the subject.

Jason did not call again at Kilbourne House.

Chapter 15

Fiona had succumbed to a mysterious illness, which kept her confined to her bed in a darkened room. No one but Constance was able to bring her any comfort. Her physician, whom Hugo summoned to the house at her request, could not shed any light upon what ailed her beyond saying that his patient was of a delicate constitution and ought to be protected from any major changes in her life. According to him, she still had not recovered her health after the untimely demise of her husband just a little over a year ago.

Constance proclaimed herself willing to devote her time to her mother's care—or to *sacrifice* herself, Hugo thought.

He went to see his stepmother in her room.

"Fiona," he said, seating himself on the chair beside her bed, which his sister had occupied all too frequently in the past few days, "I am sorry you are unwell. Your family is sorry too. Quite deeply concerned, in fact."

She opened her eyes and turned her head on the pillow to look at him.

"I went to their shop to call on them yesterday," he said. "They are prospering and happy. They made me very welcome. The only real blot on their happiness is never seeing you, never knowing how you are. Your mother and your sister and sister-in-law would be very happy to call on you here, to spend time with you, to help nurse you back to health and cheerful spirits."

He did not know if cheerful spirits were even possible for Fiona. He suspected, painful though it was for him since it was his father of whom he thought, that she had sacrificed all real hope for happiness when she had been offered a chance to marry a man who was so wealthy that it was impossible to refuse him.

She stared at him with dull, red-rimmed eyes.

"Shopkeepers!" she said.

"Prosperous and happy shopkeepers," he said. "The business does well enough to support them all, and that includes your two nephews, your brother's sons. Your sister is betrothed to a solicitor, younger son of a gentleman of modest means. They have done well, Fiona. And they love you. They long to meet Constance."

She plucked at the sheet that covered her.

"They would have been *nothing,*" she said, "if I had not married your father and if he had not squandered a small fortune on them."

"They are well aware of that," he said, "and they feel nothing but gratitude to both you and my father. But money is squandered only when it is wasted. The financial assistance he gave them because they were your relatives and he adored you was used wisely and well. They never applied to him for more. They never needed to. Let your mother come to see you. She asked me if you were still as dazzlingly pretty as you used to be, and I told her quite truthfully that you are—or that you will be when you are well again."

She turned her head away from him once more.

"You are the head of the house now, Hugo," she said bitterly. "If you choose to bring my mother here, I cannot stop you."

He opened his mouth to say more but then shut it again. She did not feel she could say yes, he supposed, without somehow losing face. So she had put the responsibility of the decision upon his shoulders. Well, they were broad enough.

"It is time for your medicine," he said, getting to his feet. "I'll send Constance to you."

All people, he thought with a sigh as he left the room, had their own demons to be fought—or not fought. Perhaps that was what life was all about. Perhaps life was a test to see how well we deal with our own particular demons, and how much sympathy we show others as they tread their own particular path through life. As someone had once said—was it in the Bible?—it is easy enough to see the speck of dust in someone else's eye while remaining unaware of the plank in one's own.

"Your mama is ready for her medicine," he told Constance, who was looking pale and wan and rather dull-eyed. He set an arm about her shoulders. "I am going to bring her mother, your grandmother, to see her, Connie. Perhaps tomorrow. It is time. However it is, you *will* be going to Lady Ravensberg's ball and to any other entertainments to which Lady Muir is willing to take you and which you wish to attend. You will have a chance for your own happily-ever-after. I promised you would, and I do not break my promises lightly."

Her eyes had brightened.

"My grandmama?" she asked.

"Did you even know she existed?" He hugged her a little more tightly to his side.

But part of his mind was always elsewhere.

How had Grayson killed Lady Muir's husband?

How had she?

The questions had buzzed about inside his head like bees trapped inside ever since that ride in the park three days ago.

Had she meant the words literally? Well, of course she had not. He knew her better than to believe her capable of cold-blooded murder. But she had not been joking either. One did not joke about such a thing.

So in what sense *had* she killed her husband? Or why did she feel responsible for his death?

And why had she coupled her own name with that of Grayson? He would be quite happy to consider *Grayson* capable of murder.

If he wanted answers, he thought, he was going to have to go about getting them in his usual way. He was going to have to ask.

The evening of the Ravensberg ball inevitably came despite Hugo's attempts to think about it as something comfortably far in the future. Feeling it creep up on him was not unlike knowing a great and bloody battle was in the offing, except that with the battle he could at least look forward to action and the knowledge that once it began he would forget all else, even fear.

He had the horrible feeling that fear would paralyze him when he walked in upon a *ton* ball.

He could get out of going altogether, he supposed, since Lady Muir had agreed to sponsor Constance, and his presence was not strictly necessary. It would not be fair, though, to Lady Muir, who was being kind to Constance only because of him. And it would not be fair to Connie, whom he had promised to take to a ball.

It would help if he could dance. Oh, he could prance about in approximate time to music as well as most other people, he supposed. He had attended a few country assemblies in the last few years and had never quite disgraced himself—except perhaps with the waltz. But dancing at a *ton* ball in London during the Season? It was a three-pronged combination to fill him with terror. He would rather volunteer for another Forlorn Hope.

He was to escort his sister to Redfield House on Hanover Square, the site of the ball. Lady Muir would meet them there. Hugo dressed with care—Connie was not the only one who had new clothes for the occasion—and waited in the downstairs sitting room with Fiona and her mother and sister. The latter two had called for the first time the day before. Hugo had not witnessed their meeting with Fiona in her bedchamber. But as they were leaving, they had informed him that they would return this evening to give her their company while Constance and he were at the ball.

Fiona had come downstairs for the first time in a week and sat, limp and uncommunicative, close to the fire. Her mother, plump, rosy-cheeked, and placid, sat beside her, holding one of her limp hands and patting it. Fiona's sister, twelve years younger than she, sat across from them, working quietly at some crochet she had brought with her. She resembled her mother more than she did her sister though she still had the slimness of youth.

It was a promising situation, Hugo thought.

"I shall go to the kitchen myself, Fee, as soon as Constance and Hugo have gone, and make some soup," Fiona's mother was saying when Hugo came into the room. "There is nothing better to coax an invalid back to health than good, hot soup. Oh, my!"

She had spied Hugo.

He made conversation, but only for a few minutes. Constance was not about to risk being late for her first ball. She burst in upon them, looking as if she were *literally* about to burst, and then stood inside the sitting room door, blushing and self-conscious and biting her lower lip.

"Oh, my!" her grandmother said again.

Like a bride, she had not allowed anyone to see the gown she would wear tonight or even to know anything about it. She was all white from head to toe. But there was nothing bland about her appearance, Hugo decided, despite the fact that even her hair was blond. She *shimmered* in the lamplight. He was no expert on clothing, especially women's, but he could see that there were two layers to her gown, the inside one silky, the outer one lacy. It was high at the waist, low at the bosom, and youthful and pretty and perfect. She had white slippers, white gloves, a silver fan, and white ribbons threaded through her curls.

"You look as pretty as a picture, Connie," he said with no originality at all.

She turned her head to beam at him—and her grandmother wailed and spread a large cotton handkerchief over her eyes.

"Oh," she cried, "you look like your mama all over again, Constance. You look like a princess. Doesn't she, Hilda, my love?"

Her younger daughter, thus appealed to, agreed with a smile after setting down her crochet in her lap.

"Constance." Her mother reached out a pale hand toward her. "Your father would advise you not to forget your roots. *I* would advise you to do whatever will make you *happy*."

It was a remarkable pronouncement coming from Fiona. Constance took her hand and held it to her cheek for a moment.

"You do not mind my going, Mama?" she asked.

"Your grandmother is going to make me soup," Fiona said. "She always made the very best soup in the world."

Five minutes later Hugo and his sister were in his traveling carriage, on their way to Hanover Square.

"Hugo," she said, setting one gloved hand in his, "you are like a rock of stability. I am so frightened that I am sure my chattering teeth will drown out the sound of the orchestra when I get there and everyone will frown at me and Lady Ravensberg will accuse me of ruining her ball. Of course, *you* do not have to be afraid. You are *Lord* Trentham. My grandparents are shopkeepers. Is not Grandmama a dear, though? And Aunt Hilda has eyes that twinkle kindly when she talks. I like her. And I still have my grandpapa and my uncle and aunt and cousins to meet—and Mr. Crane, Aunt Hilda's betrothed. I have a whole other family, as well as Mama and you and all Papa's relatives, even if they *are* only shopkeepers. That does not matter, does it? Papa always used to say that no one, not even the lowliest crossing sweeper, ought to be ashamed of who he is. Or she. I always used to tell him that—*or she, Papa,* I used to say, and he would laugh and say it back to me. I think Mama is happy to see Grandmama, don't you? And I think she is getting better again. Do you think— Oh, I am prattling. I never prattle. But I am *terrified*." She laughed softly.

He squeezed her hand and concentrated upon being like a rock of stability. If she only knew!

They were unable to drive up to the grand, brightly lit mansion on Hanover Square and disappear indoors to find some shadowed corner in which to hide. There was a line of carriages, and they had to await their turn. And when it *was* their turn, they had to allow a grandly liveried footman to open the carriage door, and they had to step down onto a red carpet, which extended from the edge of the pavement all the way up the steps of the house.

And when they stepped into the house at last, they found

themselves in a large, high-ceilinged hall beneath the bright lights of a large candelabrum and in the midst of a chattering throng of gorgeously clad ladies and gentlemen. Hugo, glancing around, discovered without surprise that he did not know a blessed one of them. But at least Grayson was not among them.

"We will go on up, then, Connie," he said to his silent sister, his voice sounding to his own ears remarkably like that of Captain Emes ordering his subordinate officers to form the battle lines.

But the broad staircase, which presumably led up to the ballroom, was no better than the hall. It was just as brightly lit, and it was crowded with chattering, laughing people who were awaiting their turn, Hugo soon realized, to be announced prior to passing along the receiving line.

Oh, good Lord, give him *two* Forlorn Hopes.

"Not too much longer now," he said with hearty jocularity, patting his sister's cold, clinging hand.

"Hugo," she whispered, "I am here. I am really *here*."

And he looked down at her and realized that it was excitement and brimming happiness that she was really feeling. And he had been toying with the ignominious idea of suggesting that they flee.

"I do believe you are right," he said, and smiled at her.

And then they were at the top of the stairs, and a stiffly formal majordomo, who reminded Hugo of Stanbrook's butler, bent an ear to hear their identities, and announced them in loud, firm tones.

"Lord Trentham and Miss Emes."

The receiving line was made up of four persons, Viscount and Viscountess Ravensberg, whom Hugo remembered from the drawing room at Newbury Abbey, and the Earl and Countess of Redford, who must be Ravensberg's parents. He bowed. Constance curtsied. Greetings and pleasantries were exchanged. Lady Ravensberg admired Constance's dress and actually winked at her. She looked assessingly at him and did *not* wink. It was all surprisingly easy. But then the aristocracy were adept at making such occasions easy. They knew how to make small talk, the hardest talk in the world to make in Hugo's experience.

They stepped into the ballroom. Hugo had a quick impression of vast size, of hundreds of candles burning in candelabra overhead and in wall sconces about the perimeter, of banks of flowers and a gleaming wooden floor, of mirrors and pillars, of the flower of the *ton* dressed in all its finery and wearing all its most costly jewels. For Constance the impression was more than momentary. Hugo heard her gasp and saw her turn her head from side to side and up and down as though she could never get enough of a look at her very first *ton* ballroom at her very first *ton* ball.

But it was a very small piece of the scene that soon riveted Hugo's attention. Lady Muir was coming to meet them.

She was dressed in pale spring green again. The fabric of her gown—silk? satin?—gleamed and glittered in the candlelight. It skimmed the curves of her body, revealing a delicious amount of bosom and a tantalizing suggestion of shapely legs—even if one *was* shorter than the other. Her gloves and slippers were a dull gold. She wore a simple gold chain with a small diamond pendant about her neck, and gold and diamonds winked from her earlobes beneath her hair. An ivory fan dangled from one of her wrists.

She was all that was beautiful and desirable—and unattainable. How could he have had the effrontery to make her an offer of marriage not so long ago? Yet he had once possessed that exquisitely gorgeous body. And after refusing his offer, she had invited him to court her.

Did he dare? Did he even want to? And exactly *how* many times had he asked himself those questions?

She was smiling—at his sister.

"Miss Emes—Constance," she said, "you look absolutely delightful. Oh, I would not be at all surprised if you dance every set and even have to turn prospective partners away. Fortunately this is not anyone's come-out ball, so all the focus of attention will not be upon any other young lady in particular. Come." And she held out her arm for Constance to take.

She did glance at Hugo then, after Constance had linked an arm through hers. And Hugo had the satisfaction of seeing the color deepen in her cheeks. She was not quite indifferent to him, then.

"Lord Trentham," she said, "you may mingle with the other guests if you wish or even withdraw to the card room. Your sister will be quite safe with me."

He was being dismissed. To mingle. That simple activity. But with whom, pray? It would be a bit ridiculous to panic, however. She had mentioned a card room. He could go and hide himself in there. But before he went, he wanted to see Constance dance her first set at a *ton* ball. He could trust Lady Muir to see to it that she *did* dance and that it would be with someone respectable.

He spoke before she whisked Constance away into the crowds.

"I hope, Lady Muir," he said, "you will yourself be dancing tonight. And that you will save a set for me."

She did dance despite her limp. She had told him so at Penderris.

"Thank you," she said, and he was interested to note that she sounded almost breathless. "The fourth set is to be a waltz. It is the supper dance."

Oh, Lord. A waltz. The vicar's wife and a few of the other village ladies had undertaken the gargantuan task of teaching him the steps at an assembly eighteen months or so ago, amid much laughter and teasing from them and every other mortal gathered there for the occasion. He had ended up actually dancing it with the apothecary's wife at the end of the assembly, to much applause and more laughter. The best that could be said was that he had not once trodden upon the good lady's toes.

He had promised himself that he would never dance it again.

"I would be obliged, then, ma'am," he said, "if you would reserve it for me."

She nodded, holding his eyes for a moment, and then moved away with Constance.

Hugo was saved from feeling horribly conspicuous and self-conscious, and perhaps from scowling ferociously at a *ton* ball, when the Earl of Kilbourne and the Marquess of Attingsborough joined him and made that small talk with which their kind was so accomplished. Other men joined them for brief spells and were either introduced or reintroduced. Some of them had been in that drawing room at Newbury Abbey. Then Hugo saw Ralph.

He actually *knew* someone.

Constance, glowing visibly with happiness, danced the first set with a ginger-haired young gentleman who looked good-humored and who might or might not be considered handsome by a young girl despite his freckles. He was smiling at her and making conversation and dancing the intricate steps of a vigorous country dance with practiced ease and polish.

Lady Muir was dancing with one of her cousins. Her limp was altogether less noticeable as she danced.

Her eyes met Hugo's and remained on them for a few moments.

He held his breath and heard his heartbeat drumming in his ears.

Chapter 16

Gwen danced the first two sets with her cousins. She was able to relax and make light conversation with them while keeping an eye upon Constance Emes. But there was nothing to worry about there. She was pretty and vivacious enough to attract more than enough partners even if she had nothing else to recommend her. But in fact there was much else. She had *Lady Muir* as her sponsor, and she was the sister of *Lord Trentham,* the famed hero of Badajoz. That fact buzzed quickly about the ballroom after it had been whispered in a few ears, probably, Gwen guessed, by her own relatives. And, perhaps most important of all, Miss Emes was rumored to be as rich as any of the most eagerly courted heiresses of the *ton.*

Gwen's task for the rest of the evening would consist of nothing more onerous than screening the gentlemen who would vie to dance a set with the girl so that no blatant rakes or fortune hunters would be granted the favor. Constance danced the first set with Allan Grattin, youngest son of Sir James Grattin, the second with David Rigby, nephew through his mother of Viscount Cawdor, and the third with Matthew Everly, heir to a decent property and fortune of ancient lineage even though there was no title in the family. They were all perfectly respectable young gentlemen. The Earl of Berwick, one of the members of the Survivors' Club, had bespoken the supper set with Constance though he was aware of the fact that she could not waltz until permitted to do so by one of the patronesses of Almack's. Being seen in his company for that set, though, and during supper could do the girl nothing but good.

Gwen danced the third set with Lord Merlock, with whom

she had been on amiable terms for the past two or three years and whom she had allowed to kiss her at Vauxhall last year. They smiled warmly at each other now, and he complimented her on her looks.

"You are the only lady of my acquaintance," he said, "who actually gets younger each year. It will surely get to the point at which I will be accused of trying to rob the cradle."

"How absurd," Gwen said, laughing as the figures of the set separated them for a few moments.

After kissing her, he had asked her to marry him. She had said no without hesitation, and he had taken her rejection in good part. He had even chuckled at her prediction that he would probably be vastly relieved in the morning.

She wondered now if he *had* been relieved. She might have encouraged him to renew his courtship this year if she had not already invited Lord Trentham to do the same thing. She *wished* she had not done that. Although she did not know Lord Merlock very well, she was quite confident that he would be an agreeable husband. He was well bred and good-natured and mild mannered and—well, uncomplicated. If there were any skeletons in the cupboard of his life, she did not know of them. Though one never really did, did one?

Anyway, she *had* extended that invitation to Lord Trentham, and she was definitely not going to complicate her own life by stringing along two suitors at the same time.

Lord Trentham had left the ballroom ten minutes after the first set began. Gwen had known the moment of his leaving even though she had not been watching him directly. She had wondered if he would return. But of course he would. He had asked her to dance. Besides, he would want to keep an eye upon his sister.

He came back. Of course he did. And he did not even wait until the last moment before the fourth set began. He came to stand beside her as soon as the third set ended, and then he completely ignored her. He spoke instead to his sister, who was eager to give him an exhaustive account of every moment of the ball so far. She fairly bubbled over with excitement as she spoke. The girl knew nothing about fashionable ennui, Gwen thought—thank goodness. There was nothing more ridiculous than a young girl, fresh from the schoolroom and the country, decked out in virginal white, and looking bored and world-weary at yet *another* ball and yet *another* partner.

The Earl of Berwick joined them, and Miss Emes eyed his facial scar.

"You were an officer, my lord?" she asked. "And you knew Hugo in the Peninsula?"

"Alas, not, Miss Emes," he said, "though I did know *of* him. There was not a soldier in the allied armies, from the generals on down to the newest recruit in the ranks, who did not know of Captain Emes, later Major Lord Trentham. He was what we all aspired to be and failed to become. We might all have hated him with a passion had he not been so dashed modest. I met him at Penderris Hall in Cornwall while we were both recovering from our war experiences, and I stood in speechless awe of him until he invited me not to be so daft. He did mention the existence of a sister. I am sure he must have. But he did *not,* the rogue, mention the fact that she was—and is—one of the loveliest ladies in the land."

He had struck just the right tone with her. She gazed worshipfully at her brother for a few moments and then—with blushes—at Lord Berwick. *How wonderful still to be so innocent,* Gwen thought. He had spoken in such a way that the flattery appeared more kindly than flirtatious. His manner was almost avuncular, in fact, though he was surely only in his middle twenties.

He must have left his youth behind on a battleground in Spain or Portugal.

Lord Trentham was a silent member of the group, and he had *still* not even glanced Gwen's way. She might have been exasperated had she not begun to understand him rather well. Ferocious and dour as he looked on the outside—and he looked both at this moment despite the fondness in his eyes when they rested upon his sister—he was very unsure of himself in a social situation. At a *ton* event, anyway. He might protest that he was middle-class and proud of it, and that might even be true. It probably was, in fact. But it was nevertheless true also that he was intimidated by the *ton*.

Even by her.

She had an unbidden memory of him wading out of the sea with unconscious grace in that cove at Penderris, water streaming from his almost naked body, his drawers clinging to his hips and thighs. And of his shedding those drawers later after he had carried her into the sea. He had not been intimidated by her then.

Couples were gathering on the ballroom floor for the waltz, and Lord Berwick bowed to Constance and extended a hand for hers.

"Shall we go in search of a glass of lemonade and a comfortable sofa from which we may observe the dancing?" he suggested. "Though it is probable that I will have eyes only for a certain nondancer."

"Silly," Constance said with a laugh as she set her own hand along the top of his.

Gwen watched them make their way toward the refreshment room and waited. She felt rather amused—and almost breathless with anticipation.

"I have waltzed on one occasion in my life," Lord Trentham said abruptly, his eyes on the departing figure of his sister. "I did not squash my partner's toes, and I did not go prancing off in one direction while she wafted gracefully in another. But my performance *did* incite laughter as well as derisive applause from everyone else present at that particular assembly."

Oh, goodness. Gwen laughed and unfurled her fan.

"They must have been very fond of you," she said.

His eyes snapped to hers and he frowned in incomprehension.

"Polite people," she said, "do not laugh at someone or applaud him derisively unless they know he will understand their affection and join in their laughter. *Did* you laugh?"

He continued to frown at her.

"I believe I did," he said. "Yes, I must have. What else *could* I do?"

She fanned her face and fell a little more deeply in love with him. How she would love to have seen that.

"And so," she said, "you are now brimful of dread."

"If you were to look down," he said, "you would see that my knees are knocking. If there was not so much noise in the room, you would hear them too."

She laughed again.

"I have danced three vigorous sets in a row," she said, "and though my ankle is not aching, it *will* be if I do not use some common sense and rest it. I trust the Earl of Berwick. Do you?"

"With my life," he said. "And with my sister's life and virtue."

"There is a balcony beyond the French windows," she told him, "and a pretty garden below. It is not a *very* chilly evening. Walk out there with me?"

"I am probably depriving you of the pleasure of performing your favorite dance," he said.

He was.

"I believe," she said, "I will enjoy strolling with you more than I would waltzing with someone else, Lord Trentham."

Unwise words indeed. She had not planned them. She was *not* a flirt. Or never had been, anyway. She had spoken the simple truth. But sometimes truths, even simple ones, were best kept to oneself.

He offered his arm and she slipped her hand through it. He led her across the floor and out onto the deserted balcony and down the steep steps to the equally deserted garden below. It was not totally dark, however. Small colored lanterns swung from tree branches and lit the graveled walks that meandered through flower beds bordered by low box hedges.

From the ballroom above came the strains of a lilting waltz.

"I must thank you," he said stiffly, "for what you have done and are doing for Constance. I do not believe she could possibly be happier than she is tonight."

"But I have been at least partly selfish," she said. "Sponsoring her has given me great pleasure. And we have, I am afraid, spent a great deal of your money."

"My father's money," he said. "*Her* father's money. But will she be as unhappy in the near future as she is happy now? She surely cannot expect many more invitations to balls or other events, and she surely cannot expect any of the gentlemen dancing with her tonight to dance with her again. Her mother, Lady Muir, is sitting at home with *her* mother and sister. They make a modest living from a small grocery shop and hardly qualify even as middle-class people."

"And she is the sister of Lord Trentham of Badajoz fame," she said.

He turned his head to look at her in the near darkness.

"You probably have not even noticed that the ballroom is buzzing with your fame," she said. "For years people have waited for some glimpse of you, and suddenly here you are. Some factors transcend class lines, Lord Trentham, and this is one of them. You are a hero of almost mythic proportions, and Constance is your *sister.*"

"That is the daftest thing I have ever heard in my life," he said. "It is that drawing room at Newbury Abbey all over again."

"And for your own part," she said, "I suppose it would be enough to send you scurrying back to the country and your lambs and cabbages. But you cannot scurry, for you have your sister's happiness to consider. And her happiness is of greater importance to you than your own."

"Who says so?" he asked her, scowling.

"*You* have said so by your actions," she said. "You have never needed to put it into words, you know, though you have come close on occasion."

"Damnation," he said. "God damn it all."

Gwen smiled and waited for an apology for the shocking language. None came.

"Besides," she said, "even apart from your fame, rumor is also making the rounds that Miss Emes is quite fabulously wealthy. A pretty and genteel young lady who is properly chaperoned will arouse interest anywhere, Lord Trentham. When she is also richly dowered, she is quite irresistible."

He sighed.

There was a wooden seat at the far end of the garden beneath the shade of an old oak tree. It faced across the flower beds toward the lighted house. They sat down side by side, and for a few moments there was silence again. She would not be the one to break it, Gwen decided.

"I am supposed to be courting you," he said abruptly.

She turned her head to look at him, but his face was in shadow.

"Not *supposed* to," she said, "only invited if you wish to do so. And with no promise that your courtship will be favorably received."

"I am not sure I do wish to," he said.

Well. Blunt speaking as usual. She should be relieved, Gwen thought. But her heart seemed to have sunk down to the soles of her dancing slippers.

"I don't think I want to court a murderess," he said, "if that is what you are. Though why I should object, I do not know, since I could myself be accused of multiple murders without too much of a stretching of the truth. *And* I have entrusted my sister to your care."

Well. So much for romance and light conversation suited to the festive occasion of a ball during the Season.

He had no more to say. There were a few more moments of silence between them. This time *she* was going to have to break it.

"I did not literally kill Vernon," she said. "Neither did Jason. But I *feel* as if we both did. I feel that we caused his death, anyway. Or that I did. And my conscience will always be heavy with guilt. You would indeed do well not to court me, Lord Trentham. You carry around enough guilt of your own without having your soul darkened with mine. We both need someone to lift us free of such heaviness."

"No one can do that for you," he said. "Never marry with that hope. It will be dashed before a fortnight has passed."

Gwen swallowed and smoothed her fan over her lap. She could see the shadows of dancers through the French windows in the distance. She could hear music and laughter. People without a care in the world.

A naïve assumption. *Everyone* had a care in the world.

"Jason was visiting, as he often did when he had leave," she said. "I hated those visits as much as Vernon loved them. I hated *him,* though I could never explain quite why. He seemed fond enough of my husband and concerned about him. Though he *did* go too far at the end. Vernon was in the depths of one of his blackest moods and he had gone to bed early one night. He had excused himself from the dining table, leaving Jason and me together. How we ended up out in the hall talking instead of being still in the dining room I cannot remember, but that is where we were."

It was a marbled hall, cold, hard, echoing, beautiful in a purely architectural sense.

"Jason thought Vernon should be committed to some sort of institution," she said. "He knew of a place where he would get good care and where, with a bit of firm, expert handling, he would learn to pull himself together and get over the loss of a child who had never even been born. Vernon had always been a bit weak emotionally, he said, but he could be toughened up with the proper training. In the meantime, Jason would take a longer leave and manage the estate so that Vernon would be free of worry while he recovered his spirits and learned how to strengthen his mind. The army would have been good for him, he said, but that had always been out of the question because Vernon had succeeded to the title when he was fourteen. Even so, his guardians ought not to have been so soft with him."

Gwen spread her fan across her lap, but in the darkness she could not see the delicate flowers painted there.

"I told him," she said, "that no one was putting my husband in any institution. He was *sick,* but he was not insane. No one was going to *handle* him, firmly or expertly or any other way. And no one was going to *strengthen* his character. He was *sick* and he was sensitive, and I would nurse him and coax him into more cheerful spirits. And if he never got better, then so be it."

She closed the fan with a snap.

"He had not gone to bed," she said. "He was standing up in the gallery, without a light, looking down at us and listening to every word. We only knew he was there when he spoke. I can remember every word. *My God,* he said, *I am not insane, Jason. You cannot believe I am mad.* Jason looked up at him and told him quite bluntly that he was. And Vernon looked at me and said, *I am not sick, Gwen. Or weak. You cannot think that. You cannot think that I need nursing or humoring.* And that was when I killed him."

Her fan was shaking on her lap. She realized that it was her *hands* that were shaking only when a large, warm, steady hand covered them both.

"*Not now, Vernon,* I said to him. *I am weary. I am mortally weary.* And I turned to walk to the library. I needed to be alone. I was very upset at what Jason had suggested, and I was even more upset that Vernon had overheard. I felt that a crisis point had been reached, and I was in no frame of mind to deal with it. I had my hand on the doorknob when he called my name. Ah, the anguish in his voice, the sense of betrayal. All in that one word, my name. I was turning back to him when he threw himself over the balustrade, and so I saw it from start to finish. I suppose it lasted for a second, though it seemed an eternity. Jason had his arms raised toward him as if to catch him, but it could not be done, of course. Vernon was dead before I could open my mouth or Jason could move. I do not believe I even screamed."

There was a rather lengthy silence. Gwen frowned, remembering, something she almost never allowed herself to do of those moments. Remembering that there had been something puzzling, something . . . off. Even at the time her mind had not been able to grasp what it was. It was impossible to do so now.

"You did not kill him," Lord Trentham said. "You know very well you did not. Depressed though Muir was, he nevertheless made the deliberate decision to hurl himself to his death. Even Grayson did not kill him. Yet I understand why you feel guilty, why you always will. I understand."

It felt strangely like a benediction.

"Yes," she said, "you of all people would know how guilt where there is no real blame can be almost worse than guilt where there is. There is no atonement to be made."

"Stanbrook once told me," he said, "that suicide is the worst kind of selfishness, as it is often a plea to specific people who are left stranded in the land of the living, unable for all eternity to answer the plea. Your case is similar in many ways to his. For one moment you were unable to cope with the constant and gargantuan task of caring for your husband's needs, and for that momentary lapse he punished you for all time."

"You put the blame upon him?" she said.

"Hardly," he said. "I believe you that he was sick, that he could not simply pull himself free of his black moods, as Grayson seemed to think he could, especially with a bit of firm handling. I also believe you gave him your all—except when your all had drained you dry and for a moment you decided that you needed a little time to think and recover some strength so that you could give it to him again. I am not surprised that for seven years you have not looked for another marriage."

She had turned one of her hands, she realized, so that it was clasped in his. Their fingers were laced. Her own was dwarfed. She felt curiously safe.

"Say my name," she said almost in a whisper.

"Gwendoline?" he said. "Gwendoline."

She closed her eyes.

"So often," she said, "I hear only that other name, spoken over and over again in his voice. *Gwen, Gwen, Gwen.*"

"Gwendoline," he said again. "Have you told this story to anyone else?"

"No," she said. "And you cannot say this time, can you, that it is the house that has drawn such confidences from me. We are not at Penderris. It must be you."

"You know instinctively," he said, "that I will understand, that I will neither accuse you nor brush off your feelings of guilt as so much daftness. To whom do you feel closer than anyone else in the world?"

You, she almost said. But that could not be true. Her mother? Neville? Lily? Lauren?

"Lauren," she said.

"Has she suffered?" he asked her.

"Oh, more than almost anyone I know," she told him. "She grew up with us because her mother married my uncle and went off on a wedding trip from which they never returned. Her father's people would have nothing to do with her, and her maternal grandfather would not take her. She grew up expecting to marry Neville, and she loved him dearly. But when he went to war, he married Lily secretly, thought the following day that she had been killed in an ambush, and came home without saying a word to any of us about her. His wedding to Lauren was planned. They were at the church in Newbury—it was packed with guests. She was about to walk down the aisle toward him and her happily-ever-after when Lily arrived, looking like a beggar woman. And so all Lauren's dreams, all her sense of security, all her sense of self were destroyed again. It was a sheer miracle that she met Kit. Yes, she has suffered."

"Then she is the ideal person for you," he said. "Tell her."

"About . . . what happened?" She frowned.

"Tell her everything," he said. "Your sense of guilt will linger. It will always be part of you. But sharing it, allowing people to love you anyway, will do you the world of good. Secrets need an outlet if they are not to fester and become an unbearable burden."

"I would not wish to burden her," she said.

"She will not feel burdened." He tightened his fingers about hers. "You *think* she imagines your marriage to have been perfect but blighted by tragedy. She *probably* believes, as others do, that you were the victim of abuse. You *were* a victim, but not exactly of abuse. She will be relieved to know the truth. She will be able to offer the comfort that I daresay you gave her during her far more public suffering."

"The Survivors' Club," she said softly. "That is what they have done for you."

"What we have done for one another," he said. "We all need to be loved, Gwendoline, fully and unconditionally. Even when we bear the burden of guilt and believe ourselves to be wholly unworthy. The point is that *no one* is worthy. I am not a religious man, but I believe that is what religions are all about. No one is deserving, yet we are all somehow worthy of love anyway."

Gwen lifted her gaze to the distant ballroom. Incredibly, everyone was still waltzing. The set had not yet ended.

"I do beg your pardon," she said. "This is a social occasion. I ought to be helping you enjoy yourself, for you did *not* enjoy coming here and would not have done it if it had not been for your sister. I should be making you relax and laugh. I should be—"

She stopped abruptly. His free arm had come about her shoulders, and the hand that had been holding hers was loosely clasping her neck, her chin held firmly in the cleft between his thumb and forefinger. He lifted her chin and turned her head.

She could not see him clearly.

"Sometimes," he said, "you say the daftest things. It must be the aristocrat in you."

And he kissed her, his mouth firm on hers, warm, open. His tongue pressed into her mouth. She clasped his wrist and kissed him back.

It was not a brief embrace. Neither was it lascivious or even particularly ardent. But it was something she felt to the roots of her being. For, physical though it was, it was not *about* the physical. It was about . . . them. He was kissing her because she was Gwendoline, and he cared about her, warts and all. She was kissing him because he was Hugo and she cared about *him*.

After he had finished and had removed his hand from her chin in order to hold her hand in her lap again and she had tipped her head sideways to rest on his shoulder, she felt the soreness of unshed tears in her throat. For she was not, of course, in love with him. Or not *just* in love, anyway.

When had he become the sun and the moon to her, the very air she breathed?

And when had an impossibility become only an improbability?

She must *not* be swayed by romance. And perhaps that was all this was.

And the aftermath of her unburdening.

When had he grown so wise, so understanding, so gentle?

After he had suffered?

Was that what suffering was all about? Was that what it did for a person?

He moved his head and kissed her temple, her cheek.

"Don't cry," he murmured. "The dance must be almost at an end. And look, there is another couple out on the balcony and they are hovering at the top of the steps. We had better go in so that I can sit with Constance and Berwick at supper. So that *we* can sit with them."

She lifted her head, dried her cheeks with the heels of her palms, and got to her feet.

"I still have to decide," he said as she took his arm, "whether I want to court you or not. I'll let you know. I am not sure I can bring myself to court a woman who limps."

They were out from under the tree, and there was lamplight playing across his face when she looked up at him, startled.

He was not looking back at her. But there was a gleam of something in his eyes that might possibly be a smile.

Chapter 17

The damnable thing was that Lady Muir had been right. The ballroom really had been buzzing with the news of his fame. A dozen or more men had wanted to shake his hand during supper, and wherever he looked, he had intercepted nodding heads and plumes and admiring glances. It had been deuced embarrassing and had ended up causing him to look down at his plate more than anywhere else, feeling awkward and very much on display. He had spent the rest of the night dodging from one shadowed corner to another, but it had not seemed to help much. And he had been unable to leave early as Constance danced until the last chord of the final set had been played.

Now this morning there had been a veritable deluge of post, almost all of it invitations to various *ton* entertainments: garden parties, private concerts, soirees, Venetian breakfasts, whatever the devil they were, musical evenings—how were they different from concerts? And how could a *breakfast* be scheduled to begin during the afternoon? Was it not a contradiction in terms? Or did it mean that the *ton* slept all morning during the Season, something that made sense actually, since they obviously caroused all night? Almost all the invitations addressed to him included Constance, a fact that made it difficult either simply to ignore them or to send back a firm refusal.

There were a few invitations addressed just to Constance, as well as three bouquets—from Ralph, young Everly, and someone who had signed his card with such an extravagant flourish that his name was illegible.

Hugo went off to spend the morning with William Richardson, his manager, leaving Constance with her mother and grandmother and the two little boys the latter had brought with her this morning. Strangely, Fiona did not seem unduly distressed by their energy and incessant questions, and Constance was ecstatic at the chance to talk and play with these new cousins. She was to go driving in Hyde Park later in the afternoon with Gregory Hind, one of last night's partners, the one with the loud, braying laugh and the tendency to find everything funny. He had passed Lady Muir's strict scrutiny, however, and Connie liked him. And apparently Hind's sister and her betrothed were to accompany them, so all was perfectly respectable.

Hugo immersed himself in work and longed for the country.

He was not *at all* sure he wanted to court Lady Muir. She limped. Really quite noticeably. But when he chuckled quietly at the memory of saying that to her, he won for himself a puzzled look from Richardson and then an answering laugh as though the man thought he must have missed a joke but would pretend he had not.

No, he was not sure he wanted to court her. He would be no good for her. She needed someone to cherish her and pamper her and make her laugh. She needed someone from her own world. And he needed someone . . . But did he really need anyone at all? He needed someone to bear him a son so that his father could rest in peace. He needed someone for sex. The son could wait, though, and sex could be had elsewhere than in marriage.

A depressing thought.

He did *not* need Gwendoline, Lady Muir. Except that she had taken him with her last night to the very darkest depth of her soul and he had felt curiously gifted. And she had kissed him as if . . . Well, as if he somehow *mattered*. And when he had said that about her limp, she had thrown back her head and laughed with sheer merriment. And except that he had been inside her body in the cove at Penderris and she had welcomed him there. Yes, she had. She *had*, and he, who had only ever had whores before her, had known the difference even though she had lacked most of their expertise.

He had been wanted, cherished, loved.

Loved?

Well, perhaps that was going a bit too far.

But he craved more. *Her?* Was it her he craved? Or *it*. More of *it*.

Or was it *love* he craved?

But he had been wool-gathering for too long and returned his attention determinedly to work.

Later in the afternoon he was rapping the knocker against the door of Kilbourne House on Grosvenor Square and asking the butler if he would find out if Lady Muir was at home and willing to receive him. He fully expected her to be out. It was the time when everyone was out walking or riding or driving in the park and it was a pretty decent day even if the sun was not constantly shining. Hind had been driving off with Constance as Hugo was leaving the house, braying with laughter at something she had said. Perhaps this was why he had come now—because he could be fairly sure that she would not be home.

If he ever grew to understand himself, Hugo decided, it would be a miracle of the first order.

Not only was she at home, and not only would she receive him, but also she came downstairs in person, just ahead of the butler. She was looking pale and listless, a little heavy-eyed.

"Come into the library," she said. "Neville and Lily are out, and my mother is resting."

He followed her into the room and closed the door.

"What is wrong?" he asked.

She turned to look at him and smiled slightly.

"Nothing, actually," she said. "I have just come from spending the afternoon with Lauren."

Her face crumpled and she spread her hands over it.

"I am sorry," she said.

"Was I right?" he asked her.

Good God, what if he had *not* been?

"Yes," she said, lowering her hands, her facial muscles under control again. "Yes, you were right. We have just spent almost a whole afternoon crying like idiots. I am to understand that I am the biggest goose ever born to keep all that bottled up inside for so long."

"No" he said, "you are not a goose. She was wrong there. When we feel like rotten eggs, we would rather no one cracked our shells—for their sake."

"I am a rotten egg, then." She laughed shakily. "Is your sister happy today? I intend to call on her tomorrow morning."

"She is out driving with Hind and his sister," he said. "The sitting room of the house looks and smells like a flower garden. She has received five invitations, not counting the thirteen I received that include her. Yes, she is happy."

"But you are less so?" she asked. "Oh, do come and sit down, Hugo. I will get a crick in my neck from looking up at you."

He sat down on a love seat while she took the old leather chair across from him.

"I would be quite happy to make a bonfire out of the lot of them," he said, "but I have to think of Connie. I came to ask your advice on which invitations to accept."

"Of those?" She nodded at the bundle of papers he held in one hand.

"Yes," he said, holding it out toward her. "Constance's on top, mine below. Which ought we to go to? If any. One *ton* ball was all I promised, after all, and I don't want to raise unreasonable expectations in her."

"She can find happiness only among her own kind, you think?" she asked, taking the pile of invitations from him and setting it on her lap.

"Not necessarily." He could feel his jaw hardening. She was making fun of him. "But *probably*."

She took a few minutes to look through the invitations one by one. He watched her as she did so and was irritated. For he wanted to step over there, scoop her into his arms as he had done at Penderris when he had had every excuse to do so, and carry her back here to cradle on his lap. She was still pale. But he was *not* her keeper. He was not in any way responsible for bringing her comfort or anything else. Her back was ramrod straight. No, that was unfair. It was straight, but her posture was relaxed, graceful. Her spine did not touch the back of the chair, though. Her neck arched like a swan's. She was a lady from the top of her head to her well-manicured fingertips to her daintily shod feet.

And he wanted her something fierce.

"I have received most of these invitations myself," she said. "I would not presume to tell *you* which ones to accept or refuse, Lord Trentham. But there are some it would be wiser for Constance to refuse and a few it would be very advantageous for her to accept. In fact, there are three events to which I was very much hoping she would be invited so that I would not have to go to the effort of securing her an invitation."

She laughed softly and looked up at him.

"You must not feel obliged to come with her," she said. "I shall be delighted to take her with me and to be an attentive chaperon. However, the *ton* will be disappointed if the hero of Badajoz disappears from the face of the earth again after last night, when many of them either did not have a chance to speak with you and shake your hand or else were not even present. The *ton* is a fickle entity, though. After a while the novelty of seeing you at last will be replaced by something else and you will no longer be the focus of attention wherever you go. But everyone is going to have to be offered the chance of seeing you a number of times before that will happen."

He sighed.

"I will accompany Constance to those three events," he said. "Tell me which they are, and I shall send an acceptance."

She set the three on top and handed the bundle back to him.

"How I would love some fresh air," she said. "Will you take me walking, Lord Trentham, or will my limp embarrass you?"

She smiled as she said it, but there was something wistful in her eyes.

He got to his feet and shoved the pile of invitations into his coat pocket, pulling the fashionable garment horribly out of shape.

"You *do* know I was joking last night," he said. "Your limp is part of you, Gwendoline, though I wish for your sake it was not. You are beautiful to me as you are." He held out a hand for hers. "But I still have not decided if I wish to court you. One of those three invitations is to a *garden* party."

She laughed and at last there was a little color in her cheeks.

"It is," she said. "You will acquit yourself well enough, Hugo, if you remember one small thing. When you drink tea, hold the handle of the cup with your thumb and three fingers—but *not* with your little finger."

She shuddered theatrically.

"Go and fetch your bonnet," he told her.

"I have decided not to court you," he said.

They had been walking along the pavement in the direction of Hyde Park, Gwen's arm tucked through his. She had been feeling weary to the marrow of her bones just a short while ago after returning from Lauren's. She probably would have lain on her bed if Hugo had not come. She was glad he had. She was still feeling tired, but she was relaxed too. Almost happy.

They had not been talking. It had seemed unnecessary to do so.

She had been feeling . . . safe.

"Oh?" she said. "Why, this time?"

"I am too important for you," he said. "I am the hero of Badajoz."

She smiled. It was the first time he had spoken voluntarily about that episode in his life. And he had made a *joke* of it.

"Alas," she said, "it is too true. But I draw consolation from the fact that you are too important for *anyone*. You must marry *someone,* however. You are a lusty man but far too important to frequent—"

Oh, dear, she was not made for this kind of banter.

"Brothels?" he said.

"Well," she said, "you *are* too important. And if you must marry, then it follows that you must also court the lady of your choice."

"No," he said. "I am too important for that. I merely have to crook my finger and she will come running."

"Fame has not made you conceited by any chance?" she asked him.

"Not at all," he said. "There is nothing conceited about acknowledging the truth."

She laughed softly, and when she looked up at him, she saw what might be a smile lurking about the corners of his lips. He had been *trying* to make her laugh.

"Do you plan," she asked, "to crook your finger at *me*?"

There was a rather lengthy pause before his answer while they crossed the road and he tossed a coin to the young crossing sweeper who had cleared a pile of steaming manure out of their path.

"I have not decided," he said. "I will let you know."

Gwen smiled again, and they entered the park.

They walked past the fashionable area, where crowds were still driving or riding or walking, though they did not linger there. Even so, their arrival was noticed with far more interest than she alone would have drawn, Gwen thought, and numerous people called out to them or even stopped for a brief exchange of greetings. Both of them were delighted to see the Duke of Stanbrook riding with Viscount Ponsonby. The duke invited them to take tea with him the following afternoon. Constance Emes waved cheerfully from Mr. Hind's barouche some distance away.

But they strolled onward rather than walk the circuit like everyone else, and passed far fewer vehicles and pedestrians.

"Tell me about your stepmother," she said.

"Fiona?" He looked at her in some surprise. "My father married her when I was thirteen. She was working at a milliner's shop at the time. She was extremely beautiful. He married her within a week or two of meeting her—I did not even know about her until he announced abruptly one day that he was getting married the next. It was a nasty shock. I suppose most lads, even thirteen-year-olds, imagine that their widowed fathers loved their mothers so dearly that they could never again even look at another woman with desire. I was fully prepared to hate her."

"And did forever after?" she said, nodding to a trio of gentlemen who passed them and tipped their hats to her and glanced at Hugo in open awe. He seemed unaware of their existence.

"I like to think I would have recovered some common sense," he said. "I had had my father to myself most of my life and I adored him, but I *was* thirteen and already knew that my life did not revolve about him. But it was soon obvious that she was horribly bored. It was obvious *why* she had married him, of course. I suppose there is nothing too terribly wrong in marrying a man for his money. It is done all the time. And I don't think she was ever unfaithful, though she would have been with me a few years later if I had allowed it. I went off to war instead."

"*That* was your reason for going?" She looked up at him, her eyes wide.

"The funny thing was," he said, "that I could never bear to kill even the smallest, ugliest creature. I was forever carrying spiders and earwigs out of the house to set them on the doorstep. I was forever rescuing mice from traps on the rare occasions when they were still alive. I was forever bringing home birds with broken wings and stray dogs and cats. For a while my cousins used to annoy me by calling me the gentle giant. And I ended up killing men."

Much was explained, Gwen thought. Ah, much was.

"Is your stepmother not close to your uncles and aunts and cousins?" she asked.

"She felt inferior to them," he said, "and consequently believed they despised her. I do not believe they did. They would have loved her and welcomed her into the fold if they had been given the opportunity. They all came from humble origins, after all. She cut herself off from her own family in the belief, I suppose, that they would drag her down from the level she had reached by marrying my father. I went to call on them a week ago. They have never stopped loving her and longing for her. Incredibly, they do not seem to resent her. Her mother and her sister have spent some time with her already, and this morning her mother brought her two young grandchildren, Fiona's nephews. There are still her father and brother and sister-in-law to be met, but I am hopeful that it will happen. Perhaps Fiona will get her life back. She is still relatively young, and she still has her looks."

"You do not still hate her?" she asked as he moved her off to the side of the path for an open carriage that was coming toward them.

"It is not easy to hate," he said, "when one has lived long enough to know that everyone has a difficult path to walk through life and does not always make wise or admirable choices. There are very few out-and-out villains, perhaps none. Though there *are* a few who come very close."

They both looked up at the occupants of the carriage, which had slowed to pass them.

It was Viscountess Wragley with her younger son and daughter-in-law. Gwen always felt desperately sorry for Mr. Carstairs, who was thin and pale and apparently consumptive. And for Mrs. Carstairs, who always looked discontented with her lot in life but was always at her husband's side. Gwen did not know either well, since they avoided most of the more vigorous entertainments of the Season.

She smiled up at them and bade them a good afternoon.

The viscountess inclined her head regally. Mrs. Carstairs returned Gwen's greeting in a listless voice. Mr. Carstairs did not speak. Neither did Lord Trentham. But Gwen became suddenly aware that the two men were gazing at each other and that the atmosphere had become inexplicably tense.

And then Mr. Carstairs leaned over the side of the carriage.

"The hero of Badajoz," he wheezed, his voice filled with contempt. And he spat onto the ground, well clear of the two of them.

"Francis!" the viscountess exclaimed, her voice coldly shocked.

"Frank!" Mrs. Carstairs wailed.

"Move on, coachman," Mr. Carstairs said, and the coachman obeyed.

Gwen stood frozen in place.

"The last time I saw him," Lord Trentham said, "he spat directly at me."

She turned her head sharply and looked into his face.

"Mr. *Carstairs* was the lieutenant you told me about?" she asked. "The one who wanted you to abort the attack on the fortress?"

"He was not expected to live," he said. "He obviously had massive internal injuries as well as plenty of outer ones. He was coughing blood and a lot of it. He was sent home to die. But somehow he lived."

"Oh, Hugo," she said.

"His life is ruined," he said. "That is obvious. It must be doubly difficult for him now to know that I am here and that I am being greeted as a great hero. He is as great a hero, *if* that word applies to either of us. He wanted to abort the charge, but he followed when I led onward."

"Oh, Hugo," she said again, and for a moment she rested the side of the bonnet against his sleeve.

He did not move them back onto the path but instead led her across an expanse of grass toward a line of ancient trees and among them along a far narrower path that was quite deserted.

"I am sorry you were exposed to that," he said. "I shall escort you home if you wish and stay away from you in future. You may take Constance to the garden party and those other two places if you will be so good—or not, if you choose. You have already done a great deal for her out of the kindness of your heart."

"Does this mean," she asked him, "that you will never crook your finger at me?"

He turned his head and looked down at her, as grim a soldier as she had ever seen.

"It means that," he said.

"That is a pity," she said. "I had been beginning to think that I might, just *might* look favorably upon your courtship. Though admittedly pride might prevent me from going running toward a crooked finger."

"I cannot *ever* expose you to anything like that again," he said.

"I must be protected from life, then?" she said. "It cannot be done, Hugo."

"I know nothing whatsoever about courtship," he told her after a brief silence. "I have not read the manual."

"You dance with the woman in question," she said. "Or, if it is a waltz and you are afraid of tripping all over your feet or treading all over hers, then you stroll outdoors with her and listen to her pour out all her deepest, darkest secrets without either looking bored or passing judgment. And then you kiss her and make her feel somehow . . . forgiven. You call on her when she is feeling weary to the bone and take her walking. You make sure to lead her along a shady, deserted path so that you may kiss her."

"A kiss each day?" he asked. "That is a requirement?"

"Whenever possible," she said. "It takes ingenuity on some days."

"I can be ingenious," he said.

"I do not doubt it," she told him.

They strolled slowly onward.

"Gwendoline," he said, "I may seem like a big, tough fellow. I am not sure I am."

"Oh," she said softly, "I am quite sure you are not, Hugo. Not in all the ways that matter, anyway."

I am not tough either. Or a tease.

At least she did not *think* she was a tease.

She desperately needed to *think*. She was still very tired. She had slept only in restless fits and starts last night, and today there had been the painfully emotional afternoon with Lauren and now . . . this.

"A kiss a day," he said. "But not necessarily as a signal of courtship on either of our parts. A kiss merely because conditions are favorable and we wish to get physical."

"It sounds like a good enough reason," she said, laughing. "Kiss me, then, Hugo, and rescue today from seeming somehow . . . dismal."

Tree branches laden with their spring coat of light green leaves waved above their heads. The air was fragrant with the smell of them. A chorus of invisible birds was busy with their mysterious, sweet-sounding communications. In the distance a dog barked and a child shrieked with laughter.

He turned her back to a tree trunk and leaned his body against hers. His fingers pushed past the sides of her bonnet into her hair while his palms cupped her cheeks. His eyes, gazing into her own in the shade of the trees, were very dark.

"Every day," he said. "It is a heady thought."

"Yes." She smiled.

"Beddings every night," he said. "Several times a night. And often during the day too. It would be the natural result of courtship."

"Yes," she said.

"*If* I were courting you," he said.

"Yes," she said. "And *if* I looked upon that courtship with favor."

"Gwendoline," he murmured.

"Hugo."

And his lips touched hers, brushed them lightly, and drew back.

"The next time," he said, "*if* there is a next time, I want you naked."

"Yes," she said. "*If* there is a next time."

What *were* all the reasons why all this was an improbability, even if not an impossibility? What was one of those reasons? Even *one*.

He kissed her again, wrapping both arms about her waist and drawing her away from the tree into his body, while her arms twined about his neck.

It was a hard, hot kiss, their open mouths pressed together, their tongues dueling, stroking, in her mouth, in his, back again. They breathed heavily against each other's cheek. And ultimately they kissed softly and warmly and with lips only, murmuring unintelligible words.

"I think," he said when he was finished, "I had better take you home."

"I think so too," she said. "And then you had better pull those invitations out of your pocket before it acquires a permanent bulge."

"It would not do to be walking around looking like an imperfect gentleman," he said.

"No, indeed." She laughed and took his arm.

And she recklessly upgraded her chances of a future with him all the way from improbable to possible.

Though not yet to probable.

She was not *that* reckless.

Chapter 18

Constance, it seemed to Hugo, was having the time of her life. She went shopping with Lady Muir and her cousin and sister-in-law one morning and ended up at a tea shop with an admirer and his mother. She went on a round of visits on another afternoon with the same three ladies and was escorted home by the son of the final household upon which they called, a maid trailing along behind at his grandmother's insistence. She went driving in the park on two afternoons with different escorts. And each morning brought a steady stream of invitations, though so far she had attended only the one ball.

She was well launched upon society, it seemed, and she was happy. Not just for herself, though.

"*All* the gentlemen who have singled me out for attention want to talk about you, Hugo," she told him at breakfast one morning. "It is very gratifying."

"About *me*?" He frowned. "And yet they are courting *you*?"

"Well," she said, "I suppose it is good for their prestige to be seen with the sister of the hero of Badajoz."

Hugo was mortally tired of hearing that ridiculous phrase.

"But they are courting *you,*" he said.

"Oh, you must not worry, Hugo," she said. "I am not going to *marry* any of them."

"You are not?" he asked, his brows drawing together.

"No, of course not," she said. "They are all very sweet and very amusing and very . . . well, very silly. But no, that is cruel. I like them all, and they are very kind. And they are all terribly in awe of you. I doubt any would be able to get his courage up to ask you for my hand even if he wished to do so. You do frown quite ferociously, you know."

Constance was perhaps more sensible than he had realized. She was not pinning her matrimonial hopes upon any of the gentlemen she had met thus far. It was hardly surprising, of course. Her first ball had been less than a week ago. Perhaps he had mistaken her motive in wanting to attend that ball. Perhaps it was not even important to her to move up the social scale by marrying up.

It was an idea that seemed to be corroborated by other things happening in her life.

She went to the grocery shop one afternoon with her grandmother and met her other relatives there. She instantly adored them all and was adored in return. After that first visit she made time every day to go over there to see them—those of them who were not at the house fussing over Fiona, that was. And she spoke of them and of the shop and the neighborhood with as much enthusiasm as she showed when describing her dealings with the *ton*.

There was an ironmonger's next to the grocery shop. The longtime owner had died recently, but his son had promised all his customers that he would keep it open and that he would not change a thing. It was, according to Constance, a veritable Aladdin's den, with narrow aisles that twisted and turned until one was in danger of getting lost. They were *so* narrow that it was sometimes hard to turn around. And he had absolutely *everything* in the shop. There was not a nail or a screw or a rivet or nut or bolt that he did not have. Not only that, though. Just like his father before him, he knew *exactly* where to lay his hand upon even the smallest, most obscure item anyone happened to need. And there were brooms and ladders hanging from the walls, and shovels and pitchforks hanging from the ceiling and . . .

The story went on and on.

And Constance went in there every day, always with one or

other of her relatives, all of whom were particular friends of Mr. Tucker's. Indeed, her grandmother had almost adopted him as an extra son now that his father was gone. He was the same age as Hilda, according to Constance, or maybe a year or two younger. Perhaps three. He was funny. He teased Constance about her refined accent though she did not speak so *very* differently from everyone else and *his* accent was not too broadly cockney. She could understand him perfectly well. He teased her about her pretty bonnets. And he let Colin and Thomas, the two little boys, run about his shop to their hearts' content, though he *did* insist one day when they tipped over two boxes of different nails and got them all mixed up on the floor that they pick them all up and then sit at the counter to sort them out again. It took them almost an hour, and he brought them milk and biscuits to make their fingers more nimble. And then, when they were finished, he ruffled their hair, told them they were good lads, and gave them a penny each on the condition that they leave the shop immediately and not return for at least an hour.

He told Constance funny stories about his customers, though they were never unkind stories. And he insisted on the afternoon it rained upon walking her all the way home while holding over her head a very large black umbrella he had dug out from somewhere at the back of his shop. He would not sleep that night, he had told her, if he had let her walk home without it and thus caused the demise of her bonnet.

Hugo listened to the lengthy, enthusiastic accounts with interest. There was a certain glow about his sister whenever she spoke of the ironmonger that was not there when she talked about any of the gentlemen who danced attendance on her.

All of which suggested to Hugo that he might have avoided all this business with the *ton*. There need not have been the Redfield ball, and there need not be the upcoming garden party. And there need not have been any renewal of his acquaintance with Lady Muir.

His life would have been altogether more peaceful if he had not seen her again after Penderris.

They were starting to fall in love with each other. No, actually they were more than just starting. And it *was* mutual. He had even begun to think that it was all possible between them. So had she. But romance did not last forever. Not that he had any personal experience with romance, but all his observations of life had taught him that. It was what remained to a relationship after the first euphoria of the romance had faded that was important. What would be left to him and Gwendoline, Lady Muir? Two lives that were as different as night and day? A few children, maybe—*if* she could have them? And decisions to make about where they would be educated. She doubtless would want to pack them off to posh schools as soon as they had passed the toddling stage. He would want to keep them at home to enjoy. Would there be anything of love left to them when the romance had dimmed? Or would it all be used up with the energy they would expend upon trying to meld two lives that could not be melded?

"What happens to love when the romance is gone, George?" he asked the Duke of Stanbrook on the afternoon he and Lady Muir had gone to tea, as invited. The Duke and Duchess of Portfrey had been there too, but it was the afternoon it rained unexpectedly—the same afternoon Tucker walked Constance home from the shop. The duke and duchess had taken Lady Muir home in their carriage since Hugo had not brought his.

"It is a good question," his friend said with a wry smile. "As a young man I was taught by all who had authority and influence over me that the two should never be mixed—not by someone of my social stature, anyway. Romance was for mistresses. Love, though it was never defined, was for wives. I loved Miriam, whatever that means. I enjoyed a few romances in the early years of our marriage, though I regret them now. I owed her better. If I were young now, Hugo, I believe I would look for love and romance and marriage all in the same place, and bedamned to any dire warning that the romance would grow thin and the love even thinner. I regret much in my life, but there is no point, is there? At this moment we are both in exactly the spot to which we have brought ourselves through our birth and our life experiences, through the myriad choices we have made along the way. The only thing over which we have any control whatsoever is the very next decision we make. But pardon me. You asked a question. I do not know the answer, I regret to say, and I suspect there *is* none. Each relationship is unique. You are in love with Lady Muir, are you?"

"I suppose so," Hugo said.

"And she is in love with you." It was a statement, not a question.

"It is hopeless," Hugo said. "There is nothing but romance to recommend it."

"That is not so," the duke said. "There is more, Hugo. I know you rather well, and so I know much of what lies beneath the granite, almost morose shell with which you have cloaked yourself to the public view. I do not know Lady Muir well at all, but I sense something . . . Hmm. I find myself stuck for the appropriate word. I sense depths to her character that can match your own. *Substance* is perhaps the word for which my mind is reaching."

"It is still hopeless," Hugo said.

"Perhaps," the duke agreed. "But those who are most obviously in love and well suited to each other often do not withstand the first test life throws their way. And life always does that sooner or later. Think of poor Flavian and his erstwhile betrothed as a case in point. When two people are *not* well suited and know it but are in love anyway, then perhaps they are better prepared to meet any obstacles in their path and to fight them with all the weapons at their disposal. They do not *expect* life to be easy, and of course it never is. They have a chance of making it through anyway. And all this is pure conjecture, Hugo. I really do not *know*."

There was no one else to ask. Hugo knew what Flavian would say, and Ralph had no experience. He was not going to ask any of his cousins. They would want to know why he asked, and then *all* of them would know, and they would all be in raptures because

Hugo was in love at last. And they would want to know who she was, and they would want to meet her, and it did not bear thinking of.

Besides, as George had said, no one could *tell* you about love or romance or what would happen if you married and the romance dwindled away. You could only find out for yourself. Or *not* find out.

You could face the challenge or you could turn away from it.

You could be a hero or a coward.

You could be a wise man or a fool.

A cautious man or a reckless one.

Were there *any* answers to *anything* in life?

Life was a bit like walking a thin, swaying, fraying tightrope over a deep chasm with jagged rocks and a few wild animals waiting at the bottom. It was that dangerous—and that exciting.

Arrgghh!

The day was perfect for a garden party. That was the first thing Hugo realized when he got out of bed in the morning and drew back the curtains at the window of his bedchamber. But for once the sunshine brought him no joy. Perhaps clouds would move in later. Perhaps by afternoon it would rain.

It would be too late by then, though, to cancel the garden party. It would probably be too late anyway, even if it had been raining buckets out there already. No doubt the hosts would have an alternate plan. They probably had a ballroom or two hidden away in their mansion just waiting to accommodate the crème de la crème of English society—as well as Constance and him. And they would all be sumptuously decorated to look like indoor gardens.

No, there was no avoiding it. Besides, Constance was so excited that she had declared last evening she doubted she would get a wink of sleep. And he had not seen Lady Muir for three whole days. Not since she went off home from George's with the Portfreys and he had had to content himself with a mere brushing of his lips over the back of her gloved hand.

So much for a kiss a day. But then he was not really courting her, was he?

The afternoon was as perfect as the morning, and Constance must have slept last night after all since she was looking pretty and bright-eyed and was bouncing with energy today. The whole thing was not to be avoided. Hugo's carriage was at the door five minutes early, and Hilda and Paul Crane, her betrothed, who arrived at almost the same moment, waved them on their way. They had come to take Fiona for a walk, her first outing in a long while.

Constance slipped a hand into Hugo's as they drew near their destination.

"I am not nearly as frightened as I was when we were going to the Ravensberg ball," she said. "I know people now, and they are really quite kind, are they not? And of course, no one will have eyes for me when I am with *you,* so I will not be self-conscious at all. Are you in love with Lady Muir?"

He raised his eyebrows and cleared his throat.

"That would be daft, wouldn't it?" he said.

"No dafter than me falling in love with Mr. Hind or Mr. Rigby or Mr. Everly or any of the others," she said.

"*Are* you in love with them?" he asked her. "Or any one of them?"

"No, of course not," she said. "None of them *do* anything, Hugo. They live on money that is given them. Which is what I do, I suppose, but it is different for a woman, is it not? One expects a man to *work* for a living."

"That is a very middle-class idea," he said, smiling at her.

"It seems more *manly* to work," she said.

He smiled to himself.

"Oh," she said, "I cannot *wait* to see the gardens, and to see how everyone is dressed. Do you like my new bonnet? I know Grandpapa would say it is absurd, but there would be a twinkle in his eye when he said it. And Mr. Tucker would agree with him and shake his head in that way he has when he does not really mean what he says."

"It is a sight to behold," he said. "Quite splendid, in fact."

And then they arrived.

The gardens surrounding the Brittling mansion in Richmond were about one tenth the size of the park at Crosslands. They were about a hundred times less barren. There were mown lawns and lush flower beds and trees that looked as if they had been picked up bodily and placed just so for maximum pictorial effect. There was a rose arbor and an orangery, a bandstand and a summerhouse, a grassy alley lined with trees as straight as soldiers, statuary, a fountain, a three-tiered terrace descending from the house with flowers in stone urns.

It ought to have looked hopelessly cluttered. There ought to have been no room left for people.

But it looked magnificent and made Hugo think with dissatisfaction about his own park. And with longing to be back there. Had the lambs all survived? Were all the crops in the ground? Were there weeds growing in his flower bed? Singular—flower *bed.*

Lady Muir had come with her family and was there before them. She came hurrying toward them as soon as they arrived, her hands outstretched to Constance.

"There you are," she said, "and you did wear the rose bonnet rather than the straw one. I do think you made the right choice. This one has considerably more dash. I am going to introduce you to people you have not met before—at their request in most cases. You have a famous brother, you see, though they will want to pursue an acquaintance with you for your own sake after they have met you."

Her glance moved to Hugo as she mentioned him, and the color deepened in her cheeks.

She matched the sky with her blue dress and yellow bonnet trimmed with cornflowers.

"Do come with us, Lord Trentham," she said as she took Constance by the arm. "Otherwise you will stand here looking like a fish out of water and scowling at everyone who wishes to shake you by the hand."

"Oh," Constance said, looking in surprise from one to the other of them. "Are you not *afraid* to talk to Hugo like that?"

"I have it on the best authority," Lady Muir said, "that he used to carry spiders gently outdoors when he was a boy instead of squashing them underfoot."

"Oh." Constance laughed. "He *still* does that. He did it yesterday when Mama screamed as a huge daddy longlegs scurried across the carpet. She wanted someone to step on it."

Hugo walked about with them, his hands clasped at his back. What a ridiculous thing fame was, he thought as people actually bowed and scraped to him and gazed at him in an awe that often seemed to render them speechless. At *him,* Hugo Emes. There was nobody more ordinary. There was nobody who was more of a nobody.

And then he saw Frank Carstairs sitting in the rose arbor, a blanket about his knees, a cup and saucer in his hands, his discontented-looking wife at his side. And Carstairs saw him and curled his lip and looked pointedly away.

Carstairs had caused him a few disturbed nights in the past week. He had been a brave, earnest, hardworking lieutenant, respected by both his men and his fellow officers. He had been as poor as a church mouse, however, since his grandfather was reputed to have gambled away the family fortune *and* he was merely a younger son. Hence his need to win his promotion rather than purchase it.

Constance was soon borne away by a group of young persons of both genders. They were going to walk down to the river, which could be reached along a private path lined invitingly with flowers and trees.

"The river is at least a quarter of a mile away," Lady Muir said to Hugo. "I think I will remain here. My ankle was a little swollen yesterday, and I had to keep my foot up. I sometimes forget that I am not quite normal."

"Now I know," Hugo said, "what it is about you that has been bothering me. You are abnormal. All is explained."

She laughed.

"I am going to sit in the summerhouse," she said. "But you must not feel obliged to keep me company."

He offered her his arm.

They sat and talked for almost an hour, though they were not alone all that time. A number of her cousins came and went. Ralph put in a brief appearance. The Duke and Duchess of Bewcastle and the Marquess and Marchioness of Hallmere stopped by for an introduction. The marchioness was Bewcastle's sister, and Bewcastle was Ravensberg's neighbor in the country. It was all very dizzying trying to sort out who was who in the *ton*.

"How do you remember who is who?" Hugo asked when he and Lady Muir were alone again.

She laughed.

"The same way you remember who is who in your world, I suppose," she said. "I have had a lifetime of practice. I am hungry—and thirsty. Shall we go up to the terrace?"

Hugo really did not want to go there even though the idea of having some tea was tempting. Carstairs had moved from the rose arbor and was sitting on the second terrace, not far from the food tables. However, staying here was not an option either, he suddenly realized. Grayson, Viscount Muir, had appeared as if from nowhere and was on his way toward them, though he had been stopped for the moment by a large matron beneath what appeared to be an even larger hat.

Hugo got to his feet and offered his arm.

"I shall try to remember," he said, "to extend my little finger when I hold my teacup."

"Ah," she said, "you are an apt pupil. I am proud of you."

And she laughed up at him as they crossed the lawn in the direction of the terraces.

"Gwen," a voice called imperiously as they reached the foot of the lowest terrace.

She turned with eyebrows raised.

"Gwen," Grayson said again. He was standing a short distance away—but far enough that he had to raise his voice slightly and make his words far from private. "I will do myself the honor of walking with you or escorting you to your brother's side. I am surprised he will allow you to let that fellow hang on your sleeve. I will certainly not do so."

They were surrounded suddenly by a little pool of silence—a pool that included a number of listening guests.

She had paled, Hugo saw.

"Thank you, Jason," she said, her voice steady but slightly breathless, "but I choose my own companions."

"Not when you are a member of my family," he said, "even if only by marriage. I have the honor of my late cousin, your husband, to uphold, as well as the name of Grayson, which you still bear. This fellow is a coward and a fraud in addition to being riffraff. He is a disgrace to the British military."

Hugo released her arm and clasped his hands behind him. He set his feet apart and held himself erect and silent as he gazed directly at his adversary, very aware that the pool of silence surrounding them had become more the size of a lake.

"Oh, I say," someone said and was immediately shushed.

"What nonsense you speak," Lady Muir said. "How dare you, Jason? How *dare* you?"

"Ask him how he survived the Forlorn Hope without a scratch," Grayson said, "when almost three hundred men died and the few who did not were grievously wounded. *Ask* him. Not that he would answer truthfully. *This* is the truth. Captain Emes led from behind, *well* behind. He sent his men on the way to their deaths and followed only after they had made the breach that allowed the rest of the forces through. And then he ran up and claimed the victory. There were not many men left to contradict him."

There were gasps to break the silence.

"Shame!" someone said before being shushed. But it was not clear whether he addressed Grayson or Hugo.

Hugo could feel all eyes upon him even though he looked nowhere but back at Grayson.

"It is your word against mine, Grayson," he said. "I do not intend to brawl with you."

From the corner of his eye he could see Constance. Damn it all, she was back from the river already and had moved into the circle of listeners.

He turned to Lady Muir and inclined his head stiffly.

"I will take my leave, ma'am," he said, "and take my sister home."

And then a weak, rather reedy, but perfectly audible voice spoke up from behind him.

"There is one survivor right here to contradict you, Muir," Frank Carstairs said. "I have no reason to love Emes. He took the command that ought to have been mine on that day. And then his bravery showed up my cowardice and has preyed upon my conscience every moment of every day since. I wanted to abort the charge when the men started to die in droves, but he forced us onward. At least, he charged onward himself and did not look back to see if we followed. And he was *right*. We were a *Forlorn Hope,* dash it all. We volunteered for death. We were the cannon fodder that would allow the real attack to break through behind us. Captain Emes led *from the front,* and he earned all the accolades he has received since."

Hugo did not turn. Nor did he move. He felt stranded in the midst of surely the worst moment of his life, worse even than the day he had gone out of his head. Though no, perhaps not worse than that. Nothing could ever be worse than that.

"Dear me," a languid voice said, "I am for my tea. Lady Muir, Trentham, do join Christine and me at our table. It has the advantage of being in the shade."

It was a man he had just met, Hugo saw when he looked away

from Grayson at last—the one with the autocratic air and the silver eyes and the jeweled quizzing glass, which was currently trained upon the suddenly retreating figure of Grayson. The Duke of Bewcastle.

"Thank you." Lady Muir took Hugo's arm. "We will be delighted, Your Grace. And the shade will indeed be welcome. The sun becomes uncomfortably warm when one has been out in it for a while, does it not?"

And suddenly everyone was moving again and talking and laughing again, and the party had resumed as if nothing untoward had happened. Carstairs was not looking his way, Hugo saw when he looked directly at him, but was talking quite pointedly to his wife. It was the *ton*'s way, Hugo realized.

But doubtless polite drawing rooms and club rooms throughout London would buzz with the interchange for days to come.

Chapter 19

"I have decided," Lord Trentham said. "I am not going to court you."

Gwen picked up her embroidery without really realizing she was doing so, and began to stitch. She had been about to say, *Is it for certain this time?* But there was nothing in his face that suggested he might be inviting some verbal sparring from her.

He had arrived at the house just as she was about to leave with Lily and her mother. They were going to make a round of afternoon calls with Lauren. Neville was at the House of Lords.

"Very well," she said.

He was standing in the middle of the drawing room, in his usual military stance, though she had invited him to be seated. He was glowering. She knew he was. She did not have to lift her head to confirm the fact.

"If you would be so good as to escort Constance to the remaining entertainments she has agreed to attend," he said, "I would be grateful to you. But it does not matter if you feel you cannot do it. She has begun to understand that the world of the *ton* is not necessarily the promised land."

"I will certainly do that," she said. "And she may accept more invitations too if she wishes. I will be happy to continue to sponsor her. There is no such place as the promised land, but it would be foolish to reject even an unpromised land as worthless without first inspecting it thoroughly. She has taken well with the *ton* and can expect to make a perfectly respectable match with a gentleman of her choosing if she should so desire."

He stood there looking down at her, and she wished she had not picked up her embroidery. She had to concentrate hard to keep her hand steady. And her green silk thread, she noticed, was filling in the broad petal of a rose instead of the leaf on its stem. The other petals were a deep rose pink.

She decided she would not be the one to break the silence.

"I daresay," he said, "your family had a thing or two to say about your allowing yourself to be caught up in that unseemly scene yesterday."

"Let me see." She held the thread above her work for a moment. "My brother was in favor of slapping a glove across Jason's face and calling him out for the insult he so publicly dealt me—and himself. But Lily persuaded him that it would be a far worse punishment for a man like Jason to be soundly ignored. My cousin Joseph also wanted to call him out, but Neville told him that he must stand in line. Lily suggested that we add Mrs. Carstairs to our list of ladies to be called upon this afternoon, since her husband did something extraordinary yesterday and the lady always looks so desperately lonely anyway. Mama said that she had never been more proud of me than when I told Jason that I chose my own companions—*and* when I took your arm after the Duke of Bewcastle invited us to join him and the duchess for tea. She added that as far as she could see, I chose my companions both wisely and well. Lauren told me that after watching you take that verbal assault with such stoic dignity, she suspected every unmarried lady within hearing range and a few married ones too fell head over ears in love with you. Elizabeth, my aunt, thought it must have been very painful for me to watch Viscount Muir, the man who succeeded to my husband's title, behave so badly in public. At the same time she thought I must be proud of how my chosen companion conducted himself with such dignity and restraint. She considers you a true British hero. The duke her husband believes that rather than tarnishing your fame, Jason's vicious lies and their exposure by Mr. Carstairs have actually enhanced it. Shall I continue?"

She attacked her embroidery with renewed vigor.

"Your name will be on lips all across London today," he said. "It will be coupled with mine. I am sorry about it. But it will not happen again. I shall stay in town awhile longer for Constance's sake, but I will remain in my own proper milieu and among my own people. Society gossip, I have heard, soon dies down when there is nothing new to feed it."

"Yes," she said, "you are quite right about that."

"Your mother will be relieved," he said, "despite what she said to you yesterday. So will the rest of your family."

She had finished embroidering the green rose petal. She did not finish it off. It would be easier to unpick later if she did not. She threaded her needle through the linen cloth and set it aside.

"I suppose that somewhere in the world," she said, "there is someone else with as great a sense of inferiority as you possess, Lord Trentham, though it must surely be impossible that there is anyone with a *greater* sense."

"I do not feel inferior," he said. "Only different and realistic about it."

"Poppycock," she said inelegantly.

She glared up at him. He scowled back.

"If you really wanted me, Hugo," she said, "if you really *loved* me, you would fight for me even if I were the queen of England."

He stared back at her. His jaw line was granite again, his lips a hard, thin line, his eyes dark and fierce. She wondered for a moment how she could possibly love him.

"That would be daft," he said.

Daft. One of his favorite words.

"Yes," she said. "It is daft to believe that you could possibly want me. It is daft to imagine that you could ever love me."

He resembled nothing more than a marble statue.

"Go away, Hugo," she said. "Go, and never come back. I never want to see you again. Go."

He went—as far as the door. He stood with his hand on the knob, his back to her.

She glared at his back, buoyed by hatred and determination. But he must go soon. He must go *now*. Please let him go now.

He did not go.

He lowered his hand from the knob and turned to face her.

"Let me show you what I mean," he said.

She looked back at him, uncomprehending. Her hands were all pins and needles, she realized. She must have been clasping them too tightly.

"This has all been a one-way thing," he said. "Right from the start. At Penderris you were in your own world, even if you did feel awkward at landing there uninvited. At Newbury Abbey you were in your own world and among your own family, not a single one of whom, I noticed, was without a title. Here you have been right in the center of your world—in this house, on the fashionable circuit in Hyde Park, at the Redfield House ball, at the garden party yesterday. I am the one each time who has been expected to step into a world that is not my own and prove myself worthy of it so that I can aspire to your hand. I have done that—repeatedly. And you criticize me for not feeling at home in it."

"For feeling inferior," she said.

"For feeling *different*," he insisted. "Does there not seem something a bit unfair about it all?"

"Unfair?" She sighed. Perhaps he was right. She just wanted him to go and be done with it. He was going to go eventually anyway. It might as well be now. Her heart would be no less broken a week from now or a month.

"Come to *my* world," he said.

"I have been to your house and met your sister and your stepmother," she reminded him.

He looked steadily at her, without any relaxing of his expression.

"Come to my world," he said again.

"How?" She frowned at him.

"If you want me, Gwendoline," he said, "if you imagine that you love me and think you can spend your life with me, come to my world. You will find that wanting, even loving, is not enough."

Her eyes wavered and she looked down at her hands. She stretched her fingers in an effort to rid them of the pins and needles. It was true. He had been the one to do all the adapting so far. And he had done well. Except that he was uncomfortable and unsure of himself and unhappy in a world that was not his own.

She would not ask *how* again. She did not know how. Probably he did not either.

"Very well," she said, looking up again, glaring at him defiantly, almost with dislike. She did not want her comfortable world to be rocked more than it already had been by meeting and loving him.

Their eyes continued to do battle for a few silent moments. Then he bowed abruptly to her, and his hand came to rest on the knob of the door again.

"You will be hearing from me," he said.

And he was gone.

While Gwen and Lily had been on Bond Street this morning, they had met Lord Merlock and had stood talking with him for a while before he offered to take them to a nearby tea shop for refreshments. Lily had been unable to accept. She had promised her children that she would be home in time for an early luncheon before they all went to the Tower of London with Neville. But Gwen had accepted. She had also accepted an invitation to share his box at the theater this evening with his four other guests.

She was still going to go. She was going to do her best to fall in love with him.

Oh, how absolutely absurd. As if one could fall in love at will. And how unfair to Lord Merlock if she were to flirt with him as a sort of balm to her own heartbreak without any regard whatsoever for his feelings. She would go as his guest, and she would smile and be amiable. Just that and no more.

How she wished, wished, *wished* she had not taken that walk along the pebbled beach after her quarrel with Vera. And how she *wished* that having done so, she had chosen to return by the same route. Or that she had climbed the slope with greater care. Or that Hugo had not chosen that morning to go down onto the beach himself and then to sit up on that ledge just waiting for her to come along and sprain her ankle.

But such wishes were as pointless as wishing the sun had not risen this morning or that she had not been born.

Actually, she would hate not to have been born.

Oh, Hugo, she thought as she picked up her embroidery again and looked in despair at the lovely silky green petal of her pink rose.

Oh, Hugo.

Gwen neither saw nor heard from Hugo for a week. It felt like a year even though she filled every moment of every day with busy activity and sparkled and laughed in company more than she had done in years.

She acquired a new beau—Lord Ruffles, who had raked his way through young manhood and early middle age and had arrived at a stage of life perilously close to old age before deciding that it was high time to turn respectable and woo the loveliest lady in the land. That was the story he told Gwen, anyway, when he danced with her at the Rosthorn ball. And when she laughed and told him that he had better not waste any more time, then, in finding that lady, he set one slightly arthritic hand over his heart, gazed soulfully into her eyes, and informed her that it was done. He was her devoted slave.

He was witty and amusing and still bore traces of his youthful good looks—and he had no more interest in settling down, Gwen guessed, than he had in flying to the moon. She allowed him to flirt outrageously with her wherever they met during that week, and she flirted right back, knowing that she would not be taken seriously. She enjoyed herself enormously.

She took Constance Emes with her almost everywhere she went. She genuinely liked the girl, and it was refreshing to watch her enjoy the events of the Season with such open, innocent pleasure. She had acquired a sizable court of admirers, all of whom she treated with courtesy and kindness. She surprised Gwen one day, though.

"Mr. Rigby called this morning," she said at the Rosthorn ball. "He came to offer for me."

"And?" Gwen looked at her with interest and fanned her face against the heat of the ballroom.

"Oh, I refused him," Constance said as if it were a foregone conclusion. "I hope I did not hurt him. I do not believe I did, however, though he *was* understandably disappointed."

She said it without any conceit.

"I believe," the girl added, "his pockets are rather to let, poor gentleman."

"He would have been a very good match for you nevertheless," Gwen said. "His grandfather on his mother's side was a viscount. He is handsome and personable. He would have treated you well, I believe. But if you do not feel any deep affection for him, then none of those things matter and I can only congratulate you for having the courage to refuse your first offer."

"If he had no money," Constance said, "he might have some relative purchase a commission in the military for him or become a clergyman. Both are considered quite unexceptionable careers for the upper classes. He might be someone's steward or secretary with only a little lowering of his pride. Marrying a rich wife is not his only option."

"And that is what he was trying to do with you?" Gwen asked. "Did he admit as much?"

"He did when I pressed him," Constance said. "And he was hardly embarrassed at all. He assured me that we had equal assets to bring to a marriage—money on my part, lineage and social standing on his. And he assured me, I believe truthfully, that he had an affection for me."

"But you were not convinced it *was* an equal exchange?" Gwen asked.

The girl frowned and unfurled her own fan.

"Oh, I suppose it was," she admitted. "But what would he *do* for the rest of his life, Lady Muir? He would have all my money with which to be idle, but . . . *why*? Why would any man *choose* to be idle?"

Gwen laughed.

"Mr. Grattin is coming to claim his set with you," she said.

The girl smiled brightly at her approaching partner.

She had not mentioned Hugo. She did not mention him all week, and Gwen did not ask.

You will be hearing from me, he had said the last time she saw him. And she had expected to hear the next day or the day after.

More fool she.

And then she *did* hear. He sent a letter, which was beside her plate at breakfast one morning with a bundle of invitations.

"Constance's grandparents will be celebrating the fortieth anniversary of their marriage in two weeks' time," he wrote. "These are my stepmother's parents, the grocery shop owners. A cousin on my father's side and his wife will be celebrating their twentieth a few days later. Both sides of the family have agreed to spend five days with me at Crosslands Park in Hampshire in order to celebrate the occasions. If you would care to join us, you may travel in the carriage with my stepmother and sister."

There was no opening greeting, no personal message, no specific dates given, and no assurance at the end that he was her very obedient servant or any such courtesy. Just his signature, boldly scrawled but without any affectation. It was perfectly legible.

"Trentham."

Gwen smiled ruefully down at the single sheet of paper.

Come to my world.

"Is it a joke you are able to share, Gwen?" Neville asked from his place at the head of the table.

"I have been invited to a five-day house party in the country in the middle of the Season," she said.

"Oh, how lovely," Lily said. "Whose?"

"Lord Trentham's," she said. "It is in celebration of two wedding anniversaries, one on his father's side of the family and one on his stepmother's. Both families will be there, at Crosslands Park in Hampshire, that is. And me if I care to go."

They all looked at her in silent inquiry for a few moments as she folded the note carefully and set it back beside her plate.

"He wishes to introduce you to his family," Lily said. "That is significant, Gwen. He *is* serious about you."

"But it is a little strange," Gwen's mother said, "that he has invited *only* Gwen. *Is* he about to renew his addresses to you, Gwen?"

"On the contrary," she said. "When he came here last week, it was to inform me that he had decided not to court me. He was horribly embarrassed by that scene at the Brittling garden party, you know, and feared that he had embarrassed me too."

"Yet he has invited you to a house party?" her mother said. "And you are to be the only guest who is not a member of his family or his sister's? And why would he come here to tell you that he was *not* going to court you?"

"I invited him to court me," Gwen said with a sigh, "when he came to Newbury Abbey."

"There!" Lily exclaimed. "I have been right all along. Admit it, Neville. Gwen and Lord Trentham are head over heels in love with each other."

"Who are Mrs. Emes's people?" Gwen's mother asked.

"They are small shopkeepers," Gwen said with a rueful smile. "His own people are successful businessmen. So is he. He is also a farmer on a small scale. His head, I believe, is with his businesses, but his heart is firmly with his lambs and chicks and other livestock. And with his crops and garden."

"And so," Neville said, "having courted you for the first part of the Season, Trentham is now inviting you to court him for the second part, is he, Gwen? It makes some sense. You ought to know what it is you would be marrying into if you were to wed him."

"There is no question of my marrying him," she said.

"Is there not?" he said. "Then you will refuse his invitation?

Why subject yourself to the company of shopkeepers and businessmen, after all, if there is no serious purpose to it?"

"Gwen must not be pushed, Neville," her mother surprised her by saying. "Clearly she has tender feelings for Lord Trentham just as he has for her. But theirs would be no easy or ordinary match—for either of them. He has acquitted himself well at *ton* gatherings, especially during that sordid episode at the garden party, for which he was *in no way* to blame. But he has never looked quite comfortable despite all his well-deserved fame. Gwen does not yet know how comfortable *she* would be in a gathering of his people, especially one that is destined to last for five days. How clever of him to think of that. Only the most hopeless romantic would be foolish enough to believe that a marriage concerns no one except the two people involved. It concerns a great deal beyond that, not least their families and the society with which they are accustomed to mingle."

"You are quite right, Mother," Lily said, gazing along the table at Neville. "But even so, it is the two people concerned who matter most. I dare not think what my life would be now if Neville had not fought for me when I believed a workable marriage between us was an impossibility."

"There is no question of marriage between Lord Trentham and me," Gwen said again.

Which was a ridiculous thing to say, of course. Why else had he invited her?

If you want me, Gwendoline, if you imagine that you love me and think you can spend your life with me, come to my world. You will find that wanting, even loving, is not enough.

And why was she thinking of accepting? No, she must be honest with herself. Why was she *going* to accept? Because she wanted him? Because she imagined that she loved him? Because she wanted to spend the rest of her life with him? Because she was determined to prove him wrong?

She did not *imagine* that she loved him.

"Then do not go," Neville said.

"Oh, I am going," she said.

Neville shook his head and half smiled. Lily clasped her hands to her bosom and beamed with delight. Gwen's mother reached out and patted her hand though she made no additional comment.

"I am taking Sylvie and Leo to the park this morning while Neville is at the House," Lily said. "Come with us? I can take the baby too if you do. You can do all the running after balls. It seems they will *never* learn how to catch them." She laughed.

"Of course I'll come," Gwen said, getting to her feet. "Perhaps they cannot catch, poor things, because their mother cannot throw. Aunt Gwen to the rescue."

For three years Hugo had jealously guarded his privacy in the country, first at his cottage and then at Crosslands. It was his own domain, his refuge from the tumult of the world. He had never invited anyone to stay, even his fellow members of the Survivors' Club, and he had only rarely invited neighbors for dinner and cards.

But things had changed.

Actually, *everything* had changed.

Come to my world, he had said to Gwendoline. And suddenly he had ached with the need to give her the chance to do just that, not for a mere afternoon of tea and conversation or an evening of tea and cards, but for . . . well, for a long enough spell that she would know what it felt like to be out of her own comfortable domain.

You will find that wanting, even loving, is not enough.

And he felt the desperate hope, the *need* to be proved wrong.

He could and would mingle with her world whenever it was necessary to do so, provided he could keep the reins of his businesses in his own hands and retreat to the country for several months of each year. But could she mingle with *his* world? More important, *would* she? Or, like Fiona, would she ignore them if they were to marry, pretend they did not exist?

He would not be able to bear that.

His family was important to him despite the fact that he had neglected them for years. He had rediscovered them lately, and he was not going to let them go again. Or marry a wife who would ignore them. And he had discovered Fiona's family and liked them even though they were not related to him in any way. They *were* Constance's family, though.

He had known about the upcoming anniversaries for a while. And he had been toying with the idea of inviting both families to Crosslands for a short time during the summer. It could not be for long. These were working people who could not afford to take lengthy holidays.

But why not invite everyone to Crosslands for the actual anniversaries? Why wait until summer? The possibility popped into his mind during the week following his last visit to Gwendoline. When he had told her she would hear from him, he had not known *what* she would hear. And when he had invited her to come to his world, he had not known quite how it was to be done.

But then he *had* known.

And everything had worked out wonderfully well. Despite the short notice, everyone was able to make arrangements to be away from their work for a week. And everyone was excited at the prospect of seeing his large country estate and being together there and celebrating two such grand events.

The only thing that remained to be seen was whether Gwendoline would be able to leave London in the midst of all the activities of the Season. And whether she would wish to. And whether she *would*.

It did not matter anyway, he told himself. He wanted to go for the sake of his family. It was time that he opened the whole of his life to them. And Crosslands and all he had there were a large and significant part of his life.

If Gwendoline could not come or would not, then that would be the end of it. He would not try to see her again, and he would put the pieces of his heart back together and move forward with his life. If she *did* come, on the other hand . . .

But he could not, would not think beyond that. He had told her that wanting, even loving, would not be enough for them. He was not sure he believed that. But he did not *not* believe it either.

And then he had a brief note from her, accepting his invitation.

His house, he remembered then, was like a barn. Although it was fully furnished, he had only ever used three rooms of it. The others were permanently shut up and covered in dust sheets. His servants could easily manage those three rooms and cater to his needs when he was there, but they would be quite overwhelmed by a house party. His stables and carriage house were well managed by a groom and his young helper. They would need more help, though, when a whole cavalcade of carriages and their attendant horses descended upon Crosslands. His park was barren, his flower garden bare soil.

Was there enough bed linen?

Were there enough towels?

Enough dishes and cutlery?

Where would all the extra food come from? And who was going to cook it all?

But Hugo was not his father's son for nothing. He advertised for a butler and chose with care from the seven applicants. After that, everything was taken out of his hands and he was made to understand that any interference on his part was neither necessary nor welcome. His new butler was a man after Hugo's own heart.

Even so, he went into the country several days before his guests were due to arrive. He wanted to see what his house looked like without the dust sheets. He wanted to see what the gardeners the butler had hired had done with the park on such short notice. He wanted to make sure that the guest chamber with the best view had been assigned to Gwendoline.

Everything looked quite respectable, he was relieved and impressed to find, and the butler had turned into a tyrant of efficiency, who demanded hard work and perfection of everyone and got both—as well as total devotion, even from the staff members who had been with Hugo for longer than a year and might have resented the newcomer.

The day when everyone was to arrive was fine though not sunny. And everyone made good time. But that was to be expected of people who were up at dawn every day to work instead of sleeping off the excesses of the night before until noon.

Hugo greeted everyone as they came and turned them over to the care of his housekeeper.

And at last he saw his own carriage approaching the house and felt an uncomfortable lurching of his stomach. What if she had decided after all not to come? Or what if she had so *not* enjoyed the company of Fiona and Constance and Philip Germane, his uncle on his mother's side, that she would insist upon returning to town without further ado?

No, she would not do that. She had the manners of a perfect lady.

The carriage drew to a halt before the house, and he opened the door and set down the steps. Fiona came first, looking far less wan than Hugo had expected. Indeed, she looked considerably younger than she had when he first arrived in London.

Then came Gwendoline, dressed in varying shades of blue, and succeeding in looking as fresh as if she had just stepped out of her boudoir. She looked into his eyes as she set her gloved hand in his.

"Lord Trentham," she said.

"Lady Muir."

She descended the steps. He always forgot about her limp when he was not with her. She did not smile. Neither did she glower.

And then Constance was out of the carriage, helped by his uncle, and was demanding to know if everyone else had arrived and where everyone was.

"We will all be gathering in the drawing room for tea in half an hour or less," Hugo said. "Fiona and Connie, the housekeeper will show you to your rooms. You too, Philip."

He shook his uncle warmly by the hand.

And then he turned back to Gwendoline and extended an arm to her.

"Allow me to show you to your room," he said.

"I merit special treatment?" She raised her eyebrows as she took his arm.

"Yes," he said.

His heart was beating in his chest like a drum.

Chapter 20

Gwen had not known what to expect of Crosslands Park. It must be large, though, she had concluded, if it was to house a sizable number of his family members for almost a week, in addition to her.

It *was* large, even if not quite on the scale of Newbury Abbey or Penderris Hall. The gray stone house was square and Georgian in design. It was not very old. The park surrounding it was square too and must cover several acres. It was possible that the house was in the very center of it. The driveway that led through the park to the house was as straight as an arrow. There were trees, some of them in copses or woods. And there were lawns, which had been freshly mown. There were stables and a carriage house on one side of the main house and a largish square of bare earth on the other side.

There was something potentially magnificent about it all, and yet it all looked curiously . . . barren. Or *undeveloped* was perhaps a better word.

While the other occupants of the carriage gazed their fill and Constance made a few excited comments, Gwen wondered about the original owners. Had they lacked imagination or . . . what? She knew, though, why the property had attracted Hugo. It was large and solid with no nonsense about it, just as he was.

She smiled at the thought—and clasped her hands a little more tightly in her lap.

This was her test—her test in his eyes and her own.

Come to my world.

She did not know how it would work out. But she had rather enjoyed the carriage journey. Constance, who amazingly had never left London before, was exuberant in her enjoyment of the countryside and every inn and tollbooth at which they stopped. Her mother was quiet but reasonably cheerful. Mr. Germane made interesting conversation. He worked for a tea company and had traveled extensively in the Far East. He was Hugo's uncle though he could not be his senior by many years.

What was it going to be like spending several days here? How different would he be in his own world and surrounded by his own people? How well would they receive her? Would she be seen as an outsider? Would she be resented? Would she *feel* like an outsider?

Lily had sat up late with her the night before she left. And she had told Gwen of the struggle she had gone through to transform herself from the wild, illiterate vagabond daughter of an infantry sergeant, wandering about the world in the train of an army at war, to an English lady, under the supervision of Elizabeth, who had still been single at that time.

"There was only one way to make it possible," she had said at one point. "I had to *want* to do it. Not because I needed to prove anything to anybody. Not because I felt I owed Elizabeth anything, though I did. Not to win Neville back—I did not even want to do that after I discovered that we were not legally married after all. He was from an alien world, and I wanted none of it. No, it was only possible, Gwen, because I wanted it *for myself.* Everything else flowed from that. People, especially some religious people, would have us believe that it is wrong, even a sin, to love oneself. It is not. It is the basic, essential love. If you do not love yourself, you cannot possibly love anyone else. Not fully and truly."

Gwen had known of Lily's transformation, of course, and of her ultimate remarriage to Neville. She had not known the inner details of Lily's struggles. She had listened, enthralled. And she had realized why Lily had chosen that particular evening to share her story. She had been telling Gwen that of course it was possible to adjust to a world different from the one with which one had been familiar all one's life, but that there was only one reason that could make the change bearable or worth making.

She had to want it. For herself.

Yet the change in her case would surely not be so very great. Hugo was wealthy. He owned all this. He was titled.

This was just a house party, she told herself as the carriage drew up to the steps before the house. But she was nervous. How odd. She was always confident and brimful of pleasurable anticipation when arriving for a house party. She *loved* house parties.

Hugo was at the bottom of the steps. Master of his own domain. He did not wait for the coachman to jump down from the box and open the carriage door. He did it himself and set down the steps and reached up a hand to assist Mrs. Emes to alight.

And then it was her turn.

His eyes locked with hers as he held out a hand toward her. Dark, inscrutable eyes. Hard jaw. No smile.

Had she expected anything different?

Oh, Hugo.

"Lord Trentham," she said.

"Lady Muir." His hand closed about hers and she stepped down onto the terrace.

Mr. Germane came next, and he turned to help Constance down. The girl was all chatter and excitement.

There was to be tea in the drawing room in half an hour. The housekeeper was to show them to their rooms so that they could freshen up. But no, not quite. Hugo was to show her to her room.

"I merit special treatment?" she said as she took his arm.

"Yes," he said.

And that was all he said. She wondered if he regretted inviting her. He could be relaxing now with his family if he had not. There were two wedding anniversaries to celebrate.

The hall, not unexpectedly, was large and square, the cream walls saved from bareness by several large landscapes of indifferent artistic merit set in matching gilded frames. A wide staircase ahead of them ascended to a landing before doubling back on itself in two branches to reach the upper floor. The housekeeper and her group took the right branch while Hugo and Gwen took the left. And then the others disappeared down a long corridor to the left while Hugo took Gwen to the right.

The architect, Gwen thought, must have had a problem drawing curves. And yet there was a certain splendor about the house. It gleamed with cleanliness and smelled faintly of polish. Paintings similar to those in the hall lined the walls. It was all somehow rather impersonal, like a superior hotel.

The sound of voices, some quiet, a few more animated, came from behind closed doors.

Hugo stopped and opened a door at the end of the corridor. He drew his arm free of hers and stood back for her to step inside. He had not spoken a word the whole way. He had not even inquired about her journey. He looked quite morose too.

"Thank you," she said.

Then he surprised her by stepping into the room behind her and closing the door.

Did he not realize . . . ?

No, probably not.

Besides, his being here with her was not so very improper. Another door, presumably leading into a dressing room, was slightly ajar, and she could hear her maid busy within.

"I hope you will like the room," he said. "I chose it for you because of the view, but then I realized that really the view is quite dismal. There has been no chance to plant the flowers, and last year's were all annuals and have not come up this year. I'll put it right by next year, but that is not going to help while you are staying here. I ought to have put you somewhere else—with a view down over the drive, perhaps."

He had crossed the room while he was speaking and was gazing out through the window.

Even now, Gwen thought as she set her bonnet and her gloves and reticule on the bed, she could be fooled into thinking that

Hugo's morose looks denoted a morose mood. Yet all the time, while the carriage had approached, while she had descended, while he had escorted her up here, he had probably been consumed by anxiety.

She went to stand beside him.

Her window looked down upon that huge square patch of bare earth she had seen from the driveway. From up here she could see that the soil had been turned over and weeded in the past few days. Beyond it there was bare lawn with trees farther out. She might have laughed if she had not feared hurting him.

"I thought you would not come," he said. "I expected to open the carriage door to discover only Fiona and Constance and Philip within."

"But I said I would come," she said.

"I thought you would change your mind."

"If I had done that," she told him, "I would have let you know. I *am* a—"

Lady, she had been about to say. But he would have misinterpreted the word.

"Yes," he said, "you are a lady."

His fingertips were spread over the windowsill. He was looking out, not at her.

"Hugo," she said, setting a hand lightly on his arm, "don't make this a matter of class. If any of your family had changed their minds for some reason, they would have let you know. It is simple courtesy."

"I thought you would not come," he said. "I braced myself not to see you."

What was he saying? Actually, it was pretty obvious what he was saying and Gwen slid her hand from his arm. Her heart seemed to be beating in her throat more than in her chest.

She looked back through the window.

"There is so much potentiality there," she said.

"In the garden?" He turned his head briefly to look at her.

"The park is mainly flat as far as I could see when we were coming up the driveway," she said. "But look, there is quite a dip beyond your flower patch. You could have a small lake down there if you wished. No, that would be too much. A large lily pond would be better, with tall ferns and reeds growing beyond it, between it and the trees. And the flower bed could be reshaped a little to curve down toward it with shrubs and taller flowers to the sides and shorter flowers and ground cover within and a path winding through it and a few seats to capture the view. There could be—"

She stopped abruptly and felt embarrassed.

"I do beg your pardon," she said. "The flowers will be lovely when you have planted them. And the view is really not bad as it is. It is a *country* view. There is no sea in sight and no salt on the air. I far prefer the country inland. This is lovelier than Newbury."

Strangely, she was not either lying or simply being polite.

"A lily pond," he said, resting his elbows on the sill and gazing outward, eyes narrowed. "It *would* look grand. I have always thought of that dip in the land as an inconvenience. I have no imagination, you know. Not for things of the eye, anyway. I can enjoy them or criticize them when I *see* them, but I cannot *imagine* them. I can see all those paintings on the walls, for example, and know they are rubbish, but I cannot imagine the sorts of paintings with which I would replace them if I removed them all and consigned them to the rubbish heap. I would have to wander about galleries for the next ten years picking and choosing, and then perhaps nothing would match anything else, or else they would look all wrong in the rooms where I had decided to set them."

"Sometimes," she said, "having everything matching and symmetrical is no more pleasing to the eye or to the mind than barrenness. Sometimes you have to trust your intuition and go with what you *like*."

"That is easy for you to say," he said. "You can look out that window and see a lily pond and a curving flower garden and plants of different kinds and heights and seats from which to enjoy the view. All I see is a nice square patch of earth just waiting for flowers—if I just knew *what* flowers. And a troublesome dip of lawn beyond it and trees in the distance. I could not even think of a path on my own. Last year when all the flowers were blooming, I had to walk all around the edge of the bed to see them or else come up here to look down on them."

"But what a glorious sight it must have been." She set her hand on his arm again. "And sometimes one brief and glorious splash of color and beauty is enough for the soul, Hugo. Think of a fireworks display. There is nothing more brief and nothing more splendid."

He turned his head at last and looked at her.

It was a long look, which she returned. She could not read his eyes.

"Welcome to my home, Gwendoline," he said softly at last.

She swallowed and blinked several times. She smiled at him.

And wondrously, miraculously, he smiled back.

"I must go down," he said, straightening up, "and meet everyone in the drawing room. You will come down when you are ready?"

"I will," she said. "How will you explain my presence?"

"You have taken Constance under your wing," he said, "and have enabled her to attend a few *ton* entertainments, as befits her status as my sister. My relatives are both amused by and impressed with my title, you know. But they are not unintelligent people. They will soon understand, if rumor has not already reached their ears, that you are here because I am courting you."

"Are you?" she asked him. "The last time I saw you, you said quite definitely that you were not. I thought I was invited here to court you or at least to discover for myself why it is impossible for you to court me."

He hesitated before answering.

"My relatives will conclude that I am courting you," he said. "Everyone loves what appears to be a budding romance, especially when a family member is involved. Whether they are right or whether they are wrong remains to be seen."

But perhaps his relatives would not love this particular budding romance, Gwen thought. They might well resent her. She did not say so aloud, though. She smiled again.

"I will be down soon," she said.

He inclined his head to her and left the room. He closed the door quietly behind him.

Gwen stayed where she was for a short while. She thought back to the day on the beach in Cornwall when she had felt that tidal wave of loneliness. If she had not felt it then, would she have felt it ever? And, if she had not, would she have stayed safely cocooned in grief and guilt that had grown so muted that she had not even realized how they had paralyzed her life? Strangely, it had been a comfortable cocoon. She half wished she were still inside it, or that, if she must have been forced out, she had then proceeded to meet the quiet, comfortable, uncomplicated gentleman she had soon dreamed up—as if any such person really existed.

But she had met Hugo instead.

She shook her head slightly and made her way to the dressing room so that she could wash and change and have her hair freshly brushed before stepping fully into Hugo's world.

Fiona's parents were feeling somewhat overwhelmed, Hugo soon realized, and sat in a sort of huddle with their own family members. Even Fiona's in-laws must seem like grand persons to them, and he knew they looked upon him in some awe.

Too late he realized he should have instructed his ever-resourceful butler to find someone to look after the two boys during the house party. They were sitting on a sofa with their parents, the younger squashed between the two of them, the elder on the other side of his father.

Hugo's own relatives were boisterous, as they usually were in company with one another. But perhaps there was a little self-consciousness added today as they were in a strange place and there were other people present who were virtual strangers.

Fiona sat by the fireplace with Philip. Her mother was gazing wistfully at her.

Constance was flitting about from group to group, her arm through Gwendoline's. She was introducing her to everyone as the lady who had presented her to the *ton,* the lady who was her *sponsor*. It was Hugo who ought to be making the introductions, but he was happy that Constance was doing it for him and unwittingly making it seem that indeed Gwendoline had been invited for her sake.

Ned Tucker stood behind the seated group of his friends from the grocery shop and looked good-humoredly about him. Hugo had wanted to invite him just to discover what, if anything, existed between him and Constance. And her grandmother had made it easy for him. When he had gone to the grocery shop to issue the invitation, Tucker had been with them, and Constance's grandmother had laid a hand on his sleeve and told Hugo he was like one of the family. Hugo had promptly included him in the invitation.

And Hugo, observing the groups around him, realized that he was part of the scene too. He was standing there in the midst of it all, like a soldier on parade. He wished he had some social graces. He should have learned more while he was at Penderris. But he had never needed social graces to mingle with his family. He had never known a moment of self-consciousness or self-doubt when he was growing up among them. And he did not need social graces to mingle with Fiona's family. He merely needed to show them that he was human, that in reality he was no different from them despite his title and wealth. Or perhaps that was what social graces *were*. There was Gwendoline, Constance's arm still through hers, talking with Tucker, and all three of them laughed as Hugo watched them. Gwendoline did not have her nose in the air, as she had with *him* on occasion, and Tucker was not bobbing his head and tugging at his forelock. Hilda and Paul Crane got up from their seats and joined them, and then they were *all* laughing.

Hugo had the feeling he might be scowling. How was he to bring these separate groups together, make a relaxed house party out of it? Really, it had been a mad idea.

He was rescued by the arrival of the tea tray and another,

larger one bearing all kinds of sumptuous looking goodies. He turned to his stepmother.

"Will you be so good as to pour, Fiona?" he asked.

"Of course, Hugo," she said.

And it struck him that she was *enjoying* herself as a person of importance to everyone in the room, since as his stepmother she was in a sense his hostess. It had not occurred to him that he would need one. But of course he did. *Someone* had to pour the tea and sit at the foot of his dining table and stand at his side to greet the guests from the neighborhood when they arrived for the anniversary parties in a few days' time.

"Thank you," he said, and he took it upon himself to circulate among his guests, distributing plates and napkins before he carried around the plate of goodies and persuaded everyone to take one or two.

Meanwhile Cousin Theodora Palmer, recently married to a prosperous banker, carried a cup of tea to everyone as Fiona poured, and her sister-in-law, Bernadine Emes, Cousin Bradley's wife, crossed the room and spoke to the little boys. Her own children, she told them, together with some of their cousins, were having tea in a lovely big room up in the attic. And after they had finished, their nurses were going to take them out to play. Perhaps Colin and Thomas would care to go with them?

Thomas half hid behind his father's sleeve and peeked out with one eye. Colin's face lit up with eagerness, and he looked to his father for permission.

"We do not have holidays often, do we?" Hugo heard Bernadine saying to Mavis and Harold. "Neither do our children. We might as well all enjoy this one to the full while we may. There are two nurses, both thoroughly trustworthy. The children obey them and adore them. Your boys will be quite safe with them."

"I am sure they will," Mavis said. "We do not have a nurse. We like to keep our children with us."

"Oh, so do I," Bernadine said. "They grow up so fast. When I had my first . . ."

Hugo opened the drawing room door, beckoned one of the new servants, who was hovering outside, and told him to inform Mrs. Bradley Emes's nurse that she needed to stop at the drawing room on her way outside with her charges in order to collect two more children.

Gwendoline was talking with Aunt Rose and Uncle Frederick Emes, and Cousin Emily, aged fourteen, was gazing at her in awe. Constance was leading her grandparents toward Aunt Henrietta Lowry, his father's widowed eldest sister, matriarch of the family.

Rome was not built in a day, Hugo thought without any great originality. But it *was* built. And perhaps his house party would not be an unmitigated disaster. He was probably feeling awkward and anxious only because Gwendoline was here and he wanted everything to be perfect. He would not be worrying if she were *not* here, would he?

He went to talk to Philip, who was part of neither larger group but seemed perfectly comfortable anyway as he looked down at Fiona pouring second cups of tea.

They made a handsome couple, Hugo thought in some surprise. Philip and Fiona, that was. Now *there* was a thought. Perhaps he would turn into a matchmaker in his dotage.

They must be pretty close in age too.

And then tea was over and the trays were removed and Hugo explained that everyone was at liberty to remain where they were or to remove to their bedchambers to rest or to wander outdoors for some fresh air.

Most people dispersed. Fiona's mother and father circled the room slowly with Aunt Henrietta, admiring the paintings. Constance went outdoors with a large group of young people that included several of the Emes cousins, Hilda and Paul, and Ned Tucker. Gwendoline was talking with Bernadine and Bradley. Hugo joined them.

"I'll take all the children to see the new lambs and calves and foals tomorrow morning," he said to Bernadine. "There are some chicks and kittens and pups too. I think I would have thought I had died and gone to heaven if someone had done that for me when I was a child."

"We all remember your strays, Hugo," Bradley said, laughing. "Uncle used to sigh when you came home with yet another bedraggled wall-eyed cat or skeletal three-legged dog."

"The children will love it," Bernadine said. "Just do *not,* I beg you, Hugo, allow any one of them—especially one of mine—to persuade you to allow them to take a puppy or a kitten or a lamb or two home with them when they go."

Hugo laughed and caught Gwendoline's eye.

"Perhaps you would all care to come and see the lambs now," he said. "They will still be out in the pasture."

"Oh, Hugo," Bernadine said with a sigh. "The journey was a long one and the country air is killing me—in a thoroughly good way, I hasten to add. And our children are off playing. I am for my bed until it is time to dress for dinner."

"Brad?" Hugo said.

"Another time, perhaps," Bradley said. "I *ought* to walk off that extra cream cake I could not resist, but that bed in our room is beckoning very insistently about now."

"Lady Muir?" Hugo looked politely at her.

"I will come and see the lambs," she said.

"Ah," Bernardine said, "Lady Muir is being polite. You would soon learn to be more selfish if you spent more time with us, Lady Muir."

But she laughed as she took Brad's arm and moved off with him without waiting for an answer.

"Sometimes," Gwendoline said, looking at Hugo, "I think I already am the most selfish of mortals."

"You don't *have* to come," he said.

"Don't *start.*" She laughed and took the arm he had not yet even offered her.

Chapter 21

Walking into the drawing room for tea had taken a surprising amount of courage, Gwen had found. She had not known quite what to expect. She had feared everyone would look at her either with excessive awe or with resentful hostility, either of which would have been isolating and would have made it difficult for her to behave with any degree of ease.

Constance had made it easier, even though she had probably done it quite unconsciously. Although there had been some sign of awe as the girl introduced her, Gwen had detected no hostility. And even some of the awe, she believed, had dissipated during tea. Perhaps after all this was going to be somewhat more doable than she had feared.

She did not care anyway. She was almost fiercely glad she had come. Even open hostility from every single one of his family members would be worth facing just for *this*.

This was the sight of Hugo feeding a lamb, the smallest of the flock. Its mother had died giving birth to it, and the sheep to whom it had been given, though it had lost its own lamb, was not always willing to let it suck. Today was one of those days, and so there was Hugo, sitting cross-legged in the pasture, the lamb half on his lap and sucking greedily from a bottle with some sort of nipple attached to it.

He was talking to it. Gwen could hear his voice, though she could not distinguish the exact words. She stood against the outside of the fence, her arms leaning along the top of it, watching them, though she believed he had forgotten all about her. There was such tenderness in his voice and in his whole manner that she could have wept.

He had *not* forgotten, though. Even as she thought it, he looked up and smiled at her. No, it was not just a smile. It was more of a boyish grin.

"I am so sorry," he said. "I ought to have taken you back to the house first."

"Don't *start,*" she said again.

And he laughed and returned his attention to the lamb, which was finally showing signs of having had enough.

"Or I ought to have had someone else do the feeding," he said a short while later as he let himself out of the meadow. "There *are* a few laborers. I had better not offer my arm. I must smell of sheep."

She took his arm anyway. "I grew up in the country," she reminded him.

He *did* smell faintly of sheep. And he was still wearing the very smart clothes he had worn for tea.

He did not take the path that led directly from the boundary of the park to the stables. Instead, he led her about part of the perimeter of the park, where there were more trees. They were widely enough spaced, though, that it was easy enough to walk among them.

"I can understand," she said, "why you shut yourself up here in the country a number of years ago and wanted nothing more to do with the outside world."

"Can you?" he said. "It cannot be done indefinitely, though. My father's dying dragged me out again. On the whole, I am not sorry."

"Neither am I," she said.

He turned his head to look at her but did not comment.

"I realized something," he said, "when I was feeding that lamb and you were standing there so patiently, watching. I keep my sheep for their wool, not their meat. I keep my cows for their milk and cheese, not for their meat. I keep chickens for their eggs. I have felt very virtuous about it all. But I eat meat. I concur in the killing of other, unknown animals so that I may be fed. And almost all creatures prey upon others for food. It is all very cruel. One could dwell upon it and become massively gloomy. But that is the way life is. It is a continual balance of opposites. There are hatred and violence, for example, and there are kindness and gentleness. And sometimes violence is necessary. I try to imagine Bonaparte having been allowed to reach our shores with his armies. Overrunning our cities and towns and countryside. Pillaging for food and other pleasures. Attacking my family and yours. Attacking *you*. If any of that had happened, I could never have stood by in the name of the sanctity of human life and the tenderness of my conscience."

"You have forgiven yourself, then?" she asked.

He had stopped walking and was standing with his back against a tree, his arms folded across his chest.

"It's funny, isn't it?" he said. "Carstairs has lived with guilt all these years even though he spoke up for retreat at the time and a saving of at least some of the men's lives. And even though he was badly wounded in the attack and has suffered the consequences ever since. He feels guilt because he believes his instinct was cowardly and my actions were *right*. He hates me, but he believes I was right."

"You *were* right," she said. "You have always known that."

He shook his head slowly.

"I do not believe there is right or wrong," he said. "There is only doing what one must do under given circumstances and living with the consequences and weaving every experience, good and bad, into the fabric of one's life so that ultimately one can see the pattern of it all and accept the lessons life has taught. We were never expected to achieve perfection in one lifetime, Gwendoline. Religious people would say that is what heaven is for. I think that would be a shame. It's too easy and too lazy. I would prefer to think that perhaps we are given a second chance—and a third and a thirty-third—to get everything right."

"Reincarnation?" she said.

"Is that what it is called?" He dropped his arms to his sides and looked at her. "I wonder if I would meet the same woman in each life and discover each time that there was a problem. And would the solution that came to mind be foolhardy or brave? To be resisted or embraced? Wrong or right? You see what I mean?"

She stepped forward and stood against him, spread her hands over his chest and rested her forehead between them. She felt his heartbeat and his warmth and inhaled the strangely enticing smells of cologne and man and sheep.

"Oh, Hugo," she said.

The fingers of one hand caressed her neck.

"Yes," he said softly, "I have forgiven myself for being alive."

"I love you," she said into the fabric of his neckcloth.

For a moment she was horrified. Had she really spoken aloud? He did not reply. But he bent his head and kissed her softly and briefly in the hollow between her shoulder and neck.

And so the words had been spoken aloud—by her at least. And really it did not matter. He must know anyway. Just as she knew that he loved her.

Did she know that?

Of course she did. He had just said so in other words. *I wonder if I would meet the same woman in each life . . .*

Love might not be enough. He had said as much in London when he had come to tell her he was not going to court her.

And then again, it might be.

Perhaps love was everything. Perhaps *that* was what they would learn if they had thirty-three lifetimes together.

"Some people have wilderness walks on their estates," he said. "I have thought maybe I ought to have one too. But they usually have hills and masses of trees and views and prospects and all sorts of other attractions. I have none of those things. A wilderness walk here would be just that—a walk through the wilderness. It would be silly."

"Daft?" she said, lifting her head and looking up at him.

He tipped his head to one side.

"That is not a very elegant word for a lady to use," he said.

She laughed.

"A definite path meandering through the woods would be pleasant," she said. "And there is room here for more trees, perhaps some rhododendrons or other flowering trees or bushes. Perhaps a few flowers that would grow well in the shade and not be too gaudy. Bluebells in the spring, for example. Daffodils. There could be some seats, especially in places where there is something to look out upon. I noticed a few moments ago that I could see the spire of the church in the village. I daresay farther along here we will see the house. There could be a little summer pavilion, somewhere to sit even when it is raining. Somewhere to be quiet and relax. Or read. It is what Crosslands is all about, after all, and why you were attracted to it. It is not a place that is spectacular for its picturesque beauty and its prospects, but just a plain statement of something good—of the peace and joy that come with the ordinary, perhaps."

He was gazing down into her eyes.

"It would not need fountains and statues and topiary gardens and rose arbors and boating lakes and alleys and mazes and Lord knows what else?" he said. "The park, I mean."

She shook her head.

"It could do with a few delicate touches here and there," she said, "but not much. It is lovely as it is."

"But a bit on the barren side?" he said.

"Just a bit."

"And the house?" he said.

"The paintings need to go." She smiled at him. "Was the house fully furnished when you purchased it?"

"It was," he said. "It was built by a man who, like my father, made his money in trade. He built it with all the best materials and furnished it with all the best furniture and never actually lived in it. He left it to his son when he died. But his son did not want it. He went off to America, to make his own fortune, I suppose, and left the house for an agent to sell."

Sad, she thought.

"Just as I went off to war and left my own father," he said.

"But you came back," she reminded him, "and saw him before he died. You were able to assure him that you would take over from him and care for his business and his wife and daughter."

"And I have just realized something else," he said. "It would have broken his heart if I had been killed. So I am glad for his sake I did not die."

"And for my sake?" she said.

He framed her face with his great hands and held it tilted up to his.

"I am not sure I am much of a gift," he said. "What do you think of my family and Connie's?"

"They are people," she said. "Strangers who will become acquaintances, even perhaps friends during the coming days. They are not so very different from me, Hugo, and perhaps they will find that I am not so very different from them. I look forward to getting to know them all."

"A diplomatic answer," he said.

And perhaps a little naïve, his expression seemed to say. Perhaps it was. Her life was as different as it could possibly be from that of Mavis Rowlands, for example. But that did not mean they could not enjoy each other's company, find common ground upon which to converse. Or was *that* a naïve belief?

"A truthful answer," she said. "What about Mr. Tucker?"

"What about him?" he asked.

"He is not a relative," she said. "Is there something between Constance and him?"

"I think there may be," he said. "He owns the ironmonger's shop next to her grandparents' grocery. He is sensible and intelligent and amiable."

"I like him," she said. "Constance is going to have a wide variety of choices, is she not?"

"The thing is," he said, "that she thinks your boys, the ones you introduce to her at balls and parties, are sweet, to use her word, but a bit silly. They do not *do* anything with their lives."

"Oh, dear." She laughed. "She has told you that too, has she?"

"But she is enormously grateful to you," he said. "And even if she marries Tucker or someone else not of the *ton,* she will always remember what it felt like to dance at a *ton* ball and to stroll in the garden of an aristocrat. And she will remember that she might have married one of their number but chose love and happiness instead."

"And she could not find either with a gentleman?" she asked him.

"She could." He sighed. "And indeed she may. As you say, she has choices. She is a sensible girl. She will choose, I believe, with both her head and her heart, but not one to the exclusion of the other."

And you? she wanted to ask him. *Will you choose with both your head and your heart?* She said nothing but patted her hands against his chest.

"I am going to have to take you back to the house soon," he said, "if you are to have any sort of rest before dinner. Why are we wasting our time talking?"

She gazed into his eyes.

He bent his head and kissed her openmouthed. She slid her hands to his shoulders and gripped them tightly. A wave of intense yearning, both physical and emotional, washed over her. This was his home. This was where he would spend much of the rest of his life. Would she be here with him? Or would this prove to be just a weeklong episode and nothing else? Not even a week, in fact.

He lifted his head and brushed his nose across hers.

"Shall I tell you my deepest, darkest dream?" he asked her.

"Is it suitable for the ears of a lady?" she asked in return.

"Not in any way whatsoever," he said.

"Then tell me."

"I want to have you in my bedchamber in my own house," he said. "On my bed. I want to unclothe you a stitch at a time and love every inch of you, and make love to you over and over again until we are both too exhausted to do it anymore. I want to sleep with you then until we have our energy back and start all over again."

"Oh, dear," she said, "that really *is* unsuitable for my ears. I feel quite weak at the knees."

"I am going to do it too," he said, "one of these days. *We* are going to do it. Not yet, though. Not in the house, anyway. Not while I have guests. It would not be proper."

Not in the house, anyway.

"It would not," she agreed. "And Hugo? I cannot have children."

Now why had she had to introduce reality into fantasy?

"You don't *know* that," he said.

"I did not conceive in that cove at Penderris," she said.

"I mounted you once," he said. "And I was not even trying."

"But what if—?"

He kissed her again and took his time about it too. She slid her arms about his neck.

"That is the excitement of life," he said when he was finished. "The not knowing. It is often best not to know. We don't *know* that we will ever actually make love all night on my bed at the house here, do we? But we can dream about it. And I *think* it will happen. There will come the time, Gwendoline, when you will be drenched with my seed. And I *think* at least one of them will take root. And if it does not, at least we will have fun trying."

She felt breathless again and considerably weaker about the knees. And she could hear the sound of children's voices approaching from a distance. Typically of children, they all appeared to be talking—or, rather, yelling—at once.

"Explorers," he said, "heading this way."

"Yes," she said and took a step back from him.

He offered his arm and she took it. And the world was the same place.

And forever different.

Hugo had worked hard during his years as a military officer, probably harder than most since he had so much to prove—to them, to himself. He had worked hard during the previous few weeks, learning the businesses again, taking the reins of control into his own hands, making it all his own. Yet it seemed to him during the course of the stay in the country that he had never worked harder than he did now.

Being sociable was hard work. Being sociable when one had all the responsibility of being host was infinitely harder. One had everyone's enjoyment to see to. And it was not always easy.

He doubted he had ever enjoyed any week so much.

Providing entertainment was actually no trouble at all. Even a rather barren park was like a little piece of heaven to people who had lived their lives in London, and a very small piece of London at that, as was the case with Fiona's relatives. And even to his own relatives, most of whom had traveled a little more widely, the chance to wander about in a private park for almost a whole week without the press of work and the continuous noises of a large city was a wonderful thing. And the house delighted everyone, even those who could see its shortcomings. Hugo, who had never been able to explain to himself what exactly was wrong with the house, now knew. His predecessor had furnished and decorated it all-in-one, probably using the services of a professional designer. It was expensive, it was elegant, and it was impersonal. It had never been lived in—not until he moved in last year, that was. Those of his guests who could see the problem amused themselves by wandering about endlessly and making suggestions. His relatives had never been shy.

There was a billiard room that proved popular. There were no musical instruments. There was a library, its walls lined from floor to ceiling with shelves, all of them filled with great blocks of books that Hugo was almost certain no one had read or even opened before him. He had read precious few of them himself, not being particularly partial to books of sermons or books of the laws of ancient Greece or books of poetry by Latin poets he had never heard of—and *in* Latin too. But even those books amused some of his relatives, and all the children loved the moving stairs and darted up and down them and stood together to push them to different locations and made imaginary carriages and hot-air balloons out of them and even a tower from which to screech for rescue from any prince who happened to be passing below.

Fiona's family tended to huddle together for confidence—for the first day or so, at least. But with Hugo's help Mavis and Harold discovered common ground with the other young parents among his cousins, and Hilda and Paul were soon drawn into the company of those of the cousins who were not married or who did not yet have children. Hugo made sure that Mrs. Rowlands met all his aunts face to face, and she developed something of a friendship with Aunt Barbara, five years younger than Aunt Henrietta and rather less of a regal matriarch. Mr. Rowlands fell in with some of the uncles and seemed reasonably comfortable with them.

Fiona did not once mention her health in Hugo's hearing. It must have become clear to her after the first day that the Emes side of the family was not looking upon her with contempt but actually deferred to her as his hostess. And obviously she was the grand, adored one of her own family. She bloomed before Hugo's eyes, restored to health and mature beauty.

And he would be very surprised if a romance was not developing between her and his uncle.

As for Tucker, he was a young man who would be comfortable in almost any social setting, Hugo suspected. He mingled easily with everyone and seemed particularly popular with the younger cousins, both male and female.

Constance flitted everywhere, brimming over with exuberance. If she fancied Tucker, and if he fancied her, they were certainly not clinging to each other and making it obvious. And yet, Hugo would be willing to wager, they *did* fancy each other.

And Gwendoline, with quiet grace, fitted herself in wherever she was able. Aunts who half froze with apprehension at first, soon relaxed in her company. Uncles welcomed her conversation. Cousins soon included her in their invitations to walk or play billiards. Little girls climbed on her lap to admire her dresses, though she dressed with deliberate simplicity during those few days, Hugo suspected. Constance chatted to her and linked arms with her. And she made the deliberate effort to get to know Mrs. Rowlands, who regarded her with almost open terror at first. Hugo found them one morning at the end of an upstairs corridor, their arms linked, discussing one of the paintings.

"We have just spent a pleasant half hour," Gwendoline explained, "going up one side of the corridor and down the other, looking at all the paintings and deciding which one is our particular favorite. I think the one with the cows drinking from the pond is mine."

"Oh," Mrs. Rowlands said, "mine is the one with the village street with the little girl and the puppy yapping at her heels. Begging your pardon, my lady. It looks like heaven, don't it, that village? Not that I would want to live in it, mind. Not really. I would miss my shop. And all the people."

"That is the wonder of paintings," Hugo said. "They offer a window into a world that entices us even if we would not want to step into it if we could."

"How fortunate you are, Hugo," Mrs. Rowlands said with a sigh, "to be able to gaze at these paintings every day of your life. When you are in the country, anyway."

"I *am* fortunate," he said, gazing at Gwendoline.

And he *was*. How could he have foreseen any of this even just a few months ago? He had gone down to Penderris, knowing that his year of mourning was at an end and with it his life in the country as a semirecluse. He had hoped his friends could offer some advice on how he might find a woman to marry, someone who would suit him without interfering too much with his life or in any way ruffling his emotions. Instead, he had met Gwendoline. And later he had gone to London to wrest Constance away from the evil clutches of Fiona and find her a husband as soon as possible, even if it meant his having to marry a woman chosen in haste. And he had found Fiona to be not quite the villain he remembered from his youth, and Constance with firm ideas of her own about what she wanted beyond the doors of her house. And he had proposed marriage to Gwendoline and been rejected—and invited to court her instead.

The rest was all a little dizzying and was proof enough that it was not always a good idea to try to plan one's future. He could never have predicted this.

His house without all the dust covers looked very different. It was elegant but without heart. Yet somehow his visitors made the place cheerful and livable, and he knew that he would spend the next several years adding the heart that was missing. His park looked bare but full of potential and really not too bad as it was. With a lily pond and a curved flower bed and some paths and seats, and with a wilderness walk with more trees and seats and a pavilion, it would be transformed. And perhaps he would plant some tall elms or limes on either side of the driveway. If one must have a straight drive, one might as well accentuate the fact.

His farm was the warmly beating heart of his property.

He was happy, he discovered in some surprise during those days. He had not really thought about happiness with reference to himself since . . . oh, since his father married Fiona.

Now he was happy again. Or at least, he would be happy if . . . Or rather when . . .

I love you, she had said.

It was easy enough to say. No, it was not. It was the hardest thing in the world to say. At least for a man. For him. Was it easier for a woman?

What a daft thought.

She was a woman who had not known real happiness, he suspected, for years and years—probably not since soon after her marriage. And now . . .

Could he make her happy?

No, of course he could not. It was impossible to *make* someone else happy. Happiness had to come from within.

Could she be happy with him?

I love you, she had said.

No, those words would not have come easily to Gwendoline, Lady Muir. Love had let her down in her youth. She had been terrified since then of giving her heart again. But she had given it now.

To him.

If she had meant the words, that was.

She had meant them.

His tongue had stuck to the roof of his mouth or tied itself in a knot or done *something* to make it impossible for him to reply.

That was something he must put right before the end of their stay here. Typically, he had talked quite freely about *making* love to her. He had even enjoyed being quite outrageous. But he had not been able to say what really mattered.

He would.

He offered an arm to both ladies.

"There is a litter of puppies in the loft in the stables about ready to be unleashed upon an unsuspecting world," he said. "Would you like to see them?"

"Oh," Mrs. Rowlands said, "just like the one in the painting, Hugo?"

"Border collies actually," he said. "They will be good with the sheep. Or at least one or two of them will. I will have to find homes for the rest."

"Homes?" she said as they made their way downstairs. "You mean you are willing to *sell* them?"

"I was thinking more in terms of giving them away," he said.

"Oh," she said, "may we have one, Hugo? We have the cat to keep the mice out of the shop, of course, but all my life I have wanted a dog. *May* we have one? Is it very cheeky of me to ask?"

"You had better see them first," he said, laughing and turning his head to look down at Gwendoline.

"Hugo," she said softly, "you really must laugh more often."

"Is that an order?" he asked her.

"It most certainly is," she said severely, and he laughed again.

Chapter 22

The anniversary celebrations had been planned for two days before the return to London. It would be best that way, Hugo had decided, so that everyone would have the day after to relax before the journey. Besides, it was the actual date of Mr. and Mrs. Rowlands's anniversary.

There was to be a family banquet early in the evening. Then neighbors from the village and the surrounding countryside—neighbors of all social classes—were to come for some dancing in the small ballroom, which Hugo had expected never to use. He hired the same musicians who always played for the local assemblies.

"Don't expect too much," he warned Gwendoline when he was showing the ballroom to her and a few of his younger cousins on the morning of the celebrations. "The musicians are renowned more for their enthusiasm than for their musicality. There will be no banks of flowers. And I have invited my steward and his wife. And the butcher and the innkeeper. And a few other ordinary folk, including the people who lived nearby when I had my cottage."

She stood directly in front of him and spoke for his ears only.

"Hugo," she said, "would you find it a trifle annoying if every time you attended a *ton* event I spoke apologetically to you about the fact that there were three duchesses present and enough flowers on display to empty out several greenhouses and an orchestra that had played for European royalty in Vienna just the month before?"

He stared at her and said nothing.

"I believe you *would* be annoyed," she said. "You told me to come to your world. I believe I can remember your exact words: *If you want me, if you imagine that you love me and think you can spend your life with me, come to my world.* I have come, and you do not have to apologize for what I am finding here. If I do not like it, if I cannot live with it, I will tell you so when we return to London. But I have been looking forward to this day, and you must not spoil it for me."

It was a quiet little outburst. All around them cousins were laughing and exclaiming and exploring. Hugo sighed.

"I am just an ordinary man, Gwendoline," he said. "Perhaps that is what I have been trying to say to you all this time."

"You are an *extra*ordinary man," she said. "But I know what you mean. I would never expect you to be more than you are, Hugo. Or less. Don't expect it of me."

"You are perfect," he said.

"Even though I limp?" she asked.

"*Almost* perfect," he said.

He smiled slowly at her, and she smiled back.

He had never had a teasing relationship with any woman—or any sort of relationship, for that matter. It was all new and strange to him. And wonderful.

"Gwen," Cousin Gillian called from a short distance away, "come and see the view from the French windows. Do you not agree that there should be a flower garden out there? Maybe even some formal parterres for ball guests to stroll among? Oh, I could grow accustomed *very easily* to living in the country."

She came and linked her arm through Gwendoline's and bore her away to give her opinion.

"There will be ball guests here maybe once every five years, Gill," Hugo called after them.

She looked saucily back over her shoulder and spoke to him—loudly enough for everyone else to hear.

"I daresay Gwen will have something to say about that, Hugo," she said.

Oh, yes, his family had not been slow to realize that she was here not only because she had introduced Constance to the *ton*.

It was a busy day, though looking back later, Hugo realized that he might just as well have lain back on his bed all day, his ankles crossed, his hands clasped behind his head, examining the design on the canopy over his head. His butler had everything completely under control and actually had the effrontery to look annoyed—in a thoroughly well-bred manner, of course—every time Hugo got under his feet.

He had even produced *flowers* from somewhere to decorate the dining table. And when Hugo glanced into the ballroom again just before dinner to make sure the floor was gleaming again after being walked over during the morning—it was—he was astonished to see that *it* was decorated with flowers too, and lots of them.

How much was he paying his butler? In all good conscience he was going to have to double the amount.

The dinner was excellent, and everyone was in exuberant spirits. There was conversation and laughter. There were speeches and toasts. Mr. Rowlands, who had got to his feet to thank everyone, impulsively bent from the waist and kissed Mrs. Rowlands on the lips, setting up a boisterous cheer around the table. Then, of course, Cousin Sebastian, not to be outdone, had to get to *his* feet to thank everyone for their congratulations on his looming anniversary, and *he* had to bend to kiss *his* wife on the lips and set up another roar of appreciation. Hugo wondered fleetingly if any *ton* dinner would include such raucous displays and put the thought firmly from his mind. Gwendoline was leaning forward in her chair and clapping her hands and smiling warmly at Sebastian and Olga. And then she was turning her head to talk animatedly with Ned Tucker at her right.

Two small, exquisitely decorated cakes were carried in, one for each couple, and the two ladies sliced them, to the applause of everyone else, and the two men handed around pieces for everyone to sample. And everyone seemed agreed when the meal was ended and it was time to remove to the ballroom for the arrival of the outside guests that they would not be able to stuff another morsel of food inside themselves until at least tomorrow.

"I daresay all the supper dainties will have to be consumed by my neighbors, then," Hugo said.

"Let's not be hasty, lad," his Uncle Frederick said. "We are to dance, are we not? *That* will work up a fresh appetite soon enough, especially if the tunes are lively."

And finally it was time to stand in the doorway of the ballroom, greeting the outside guests as they arrived. Hugo had Fiona beside him and Constance beside her and just wished that his father could be here now to see them. He would have been happy.

He glanced about the ballroom, seeing all the familiar faces, knowing that he had done the right thing in bringing everyone here for a few days. The right thing for them, and definitely the right thing for himself. Maybe there would always be a little darkness in his soul when he remembered the brutality of war. He would *far* prefer to nurture life than to take it. But, as he had explained to Gwendoline in different words, life was not made up of neat blacks and whites but of a vast whirlwind of varying shades of gray. He would no longer beat himself to a pulp over what he had done. Perhaps in doing it he had averted a greater evil. And perhaps not. Who was to know? He could only continue his journey through life, hoping that along with experience he was picking up some wisdom.

If there was some darkness in his soul, then there was also a considerable amount of light. One bright ray of it was at the far side of the ballroom, dressed prettily but simply in a pale lemon silky gown with scalloped hem and short, puffed sleeves and modest neckline—and a simple gold chain as her only ornament. Gwendoline. She was talking with Ned Tucker and Philip Germane—and looking back at *him* with a smile on her face.

He winked at her. *Winked.* He could not remember ever winking before in his life.

But his steward was entering the ballroom with his wife, and the vicar and his wife and son and daughter were coming behind them. Hugo turned his attention to his guests.

It was all really quite delightful, Gwen decided during the next hour. She paused to examine the thought, but there was no condescension in it. People were people, and these people were enjoying the occasion with unabashed pleasure. There was none of the restraint and polite ennui one encountered all too often with the *ton,* so many of whose members seemed to believe that it was either naïve or vulgar to enjoy anything with too great an exuberance.

The orchestra made up in enthusiasm what it lacked in skill. Most of the sets were vigorous country dances. Gwen danced them all, having assured the few people who were bold enough to ask that her limp did not deter her from dancing. And in no time at all she was flushed and laughing.

Mrs. Lowry, Hugo's Aunt Henrietta, drew her aside between the second and third sets and asked her without preamble if she was going to marry Hugo.

"I was asked once and said no," Gwen told her. "But that was quite a while ago, and *if* I were to be asked again, I *might* give a different answer."

Mrs. Lowry nodded.

"His father was my favorite brother," she said, "and Hugo has always been my favorite nephew even though I did not set eyes on him for years. He never ought to have gone away, but he did, and he suffered, and now he is back, just as tender-hearted as ever, it seems to me. I don't want to see his heart broken."

Gwen smiled at her.

"Me neither," she said.

Mrs. Lowry nodded again as a few more of the aunts gathered about them.

The next set was to be a waltz. The news was buzzing about the ballroom. Some of Hugo's neighbors had requested it and he had given the order to the orchestra leader and now there was a chorus of laughter from those same neighbors, who were all loudly urging Hugo to dance it.

He, interestingly enough, was laughing too—and then holding up both hands, palm out. For a moment as she watched him, something caught at the edges of Gwen's mind, but it refused to come into focus and she let it go.

"I will waltz," he said, "but only if my chosen partner clearly understands that at worst she may be dealing with squashed toes at the end of it and at best she may have laid herself open to some ridicule."

There were a few cheers, a few jeers, and more laughter—from everyone this time.

"Come on, Hugo," Mark, one of his cousins, called. "Show us how it is done, then."

"Lady Muir," Hugo said, turning and looking fully at her, "will you do me the honor?"

"Yes, go on, Gwen," Bernardine Emes urged. "We won't laugh at you. Only at Hugo."

Gwen stepped forward and walked toward him as he walked toward her. They met in the middle of the gleaming dance floor, smiling at each other.

"Are my eyes deceiving me?" he asked her when they met. "Is no one else stepping onto the floor with us?"

"They are probably all taking heed of your warning about squashed toes," she said.

"Hell and damnation," he muttered—and did not apologize.

Gwen laughed and set her left hand on his shoulder. She held out her other hand for his, and he clasped it. His right hand came to rest at the back of her waist.

And the music began.

It took a few moments for him to get his feet under him and the sound of the music into his ears and the rhythm of the dance into his body, but then he accomplished all three and danced off about the floor with her, holding her firmly at the waist so that it felt as if her feet floated over the floor and there was no discomfort from the fact that her legs were not of equal length.

There was applause from all his family and guests gathered about the perimeter of the room, a few loud comments, a little laughter, one piercing whistle. Gwen smiled up into his face, and he smiled back.

"Don't encourage me to relax," he said. "That is when disaster will strike."

She laughed and suddenly felt a great welling of happiness. It was at least equal to that tidal wave of loneliness she had felt on the beach below Penderris just before she met Hugo.

"I like your world, Hugo," she said. "I *love* it."

"It is not really so very different from your own, is it?" he said.

She shook her head. It was not so *very* different. It was different enough, of course, that moving back and forth between them would not be always easy—*if* that was what was going to happen.

But she was too happy for speculation at this precise moment.

"Ah," he said, and she looked around to see that others were taking the floor and starting to waltz, and the focus of attention was no longer exclusively on them.

He twirled her about a corner of the floor and tightened his hand against the back of her waist. They were not touching, but they were definitely closer than they ought to be.

Ought to be according to *whom*?

"Hugo," she said, looking up into his eyes—his lovely dark, intense, *smiling* eyes. And she forgot what she had been about to say.

They danced in silence for several minutes. Gwen was very consciously aware that they were among the very happiest minutes of her life. And then, before the music ended, he bent his head to murmur in her ear.

"You noticed," he said, "that there is a loft at the far end of the stables? Where the puppies are?"

"I noticed," she said. "I climbed right up there with Mrs. Rowlands, did I not? When she chose her puppy?"

"I cannot have you in my bed here," he said, "while I have family and guests in my house. But after everyone has gone home and to bed, I am going to take you out there. None of the grooms sleep there. I cleaned the loft and spread fresh straw this morning and took out blankets and pillows. I am going to make love to you for what remains of the night."

"Indeed?" she said.

"Unless you say no," he said.

She *ought* to. Just as she ought to have down in that cove at Penderris.

"I'll not say no," she said as the music drew to an end and he waltzed her into one more twirl.

"Later, then," he said.

"Yes. Later."

She felt not a qualm of conscience.

And that little fluttering at the edge of her consciousness that she had felt when he held up his hands earlier to address the pleas that he waltz opened like a curtain from across a window, and she could see what was within.

Gwen did not want the evening to end and yet she did. There was a magnificence to a *ton* ball that she would always enjoy, but there was a warmth to this one that made it at least equally enjoyable. She loved the way all the guests at the house had called her by her first name as soon as she had invited them to do so on the second day here. And she loved the informal, affectionate way in which Hugo's neighbors treated him. He was an angel in disguise, the butcher's wife told Gwen at one point in the evening, forever mending chair legs or clearing blockages in chimneys or sawing off tree branches that were in danger of falling on a roof if the wind ever blew hard enough or working over a garden for someone who was getting too elderly to do it without a great deal of painful effort.

"And him *Lord* Trentham," the woman said. "You could have knocked us all over with a feather when we found that out last year, my lady. But he *still* went on doing it, just as if he was any ordinary man. Not that many ordinary men would do what he does, mind you, but you know what I mean."

Gwen did.

And at last the evening came to an end and all the outside guests drove off or walked in the direction of the village, lanterns held aloft and swaying in the breeze. It seemed forever after that before the last of the houseguests drifted off to bed, though it was only a little after midnight, Gwen discovered when she reached her own room. But of course, all these people worked for a living, and even when they were on holiday they did not stray far from their early mornings and early nights.

Gwen dismissed her maid for the night and changed into different clothes. She set her cloak on the bed—the red one she had been wearing when she sprained her ankle. And she sat on the edge of the bed, waiting.

Waiting for her lover, she thought, closing her eyes and clasping her hands in her lap.

She was not even going to *start* considering whether this was right or wrong, whether she ought or ought not.

She was going to spend the rest of the night with her lover and that was that.

And finally there was a light tap on the door and the handle turned quietly. He too had changed, Gwen saw as she got to her feet and flung her cloak about her shoulders and blew out the candles and left the room to join him in the long, dark corridor. He was holding a single candle in a holder. He took her hand and bent to kiss her on the lips.

They did not speak as they passed along the corridor and down the stairs and across the hall. He handed her the candle while he drew back the bolts on the door and opened it. Then he took the candle back, blew it out, and set it down on a table close to the door. It would be unnecessary outside. The clouds, which had made a dark night of it when the guests were leaving, must have moved off, and an almost full moon and millions of stars made a lamp quite unnecessary.

He took her hand again and turned in the direction of the stables. Still they did not speak. The sound of voices carried far in the night, and some people would not have been in bed for much longer than half an hour.

The stables were in darkness until Hugo took a lantern off a hook just inside the great door and lit it. Horses whinnied sleepily. The familiar smell of them and of hay and leather was not unpleasant. They walked the length of the narrow passageway between stalls, hand in hand, their fingers laced. And then he released her hand to light her way up the steep ladder to the loft before following behind her. Two or three of the puppies were squeaking in their large wooden box, and a quiet woof indicated that their mother was with them.

Hugo hung the lantern on a hook beneath a wooden beam and stooped to spread a blanket over the fresh straw. He tossed a few pillows to one end of it and turned to look at Gwen. He had to stoop slightly so that his head would not bang against the roof.

"I had better say one thing first," he said curtly, "and get it out of the way. Otherwise I won't know a moment's peace."

He was frowning and looking really quite morose.

"I love you," he said.

He glared at her with set jaw and fierce eyes.

It would be absolutely the wrong thing to do to laugh, Gwen decided, quelling the urge to do just that.

"Thank you," she said and stepped forward to set her fingertips against his chest and lift her face for his kiss.

"I didn't do too well with that, did I?" he said—and grinned.

And instead of laughing, she found herself blinking back tears.

"Say it again," she said.

"You would torture me, would you?" he asked her.

"Say it again."

"I love you, Gwendoline," he said. "It is actually a bit easier the second time. I love you, I love you, I love you."

And his arms came about her and he hugged her to him tightly enough to squeeze most of the breath from her body. Gwen laughed with what breath she had left.

He released his hold on her, looked into her eyes, and undid the clasp at the neck of her cloak.

"Time for action instead of just words," he said.

"Yes," she agreed as her cloak fell to the straw at her feet.

Only one thing had kept their lovemaking in the cove at Penderris from being perfect in Hugo's memory. He had had his hands all over her on that occasion, and he had ridden her deep and long, but he had not had her naked. He had not known her flesh to flesh, as a man ought to know the woman he loved. *Know* in the biblical sense, that was.

Tonight they would both be naked, and they would know each other with no barrier, no artifice, no mask.

"No," he murmured when she would have helped him undress her. No, he would not be deprived of this. And there was no real hurry. It must be at least one o'clock already, and the grooms would be here by six. But that still left plenty of time for a few good lovings and maybe a little sleep in between. He had never *slept* with a woman. He wanted to sleep with Gwendoline almost as much as he wanted to have sex with her. Well, maybe not quite as much.

He unclothed her slowly, her dress, her shift—she was wearing no stays—and on down her body until only her silk stockings remained. He stood back to look at her in the lamplight. She was beautifully, perfectly shaped. She had a woman's body rather than a girl's. A woman's body to match his man's body. He ran his hands down lightly over her breasts and in to her waist and over the flare of her hips. She shivered, though not with cold, he guessed.

"I am a little self-conscious," she said. "I have never *done* this before. Without clothes, I mean."

What? What the devil sort of man had Muir been?

"You are wearing clothes," he said. "You still have your stockings on."

She smiled.

"Come," he said, taking her hand. "Lie down on the blanket. I'll take off my own clothes and then cover you with my body and so restore your modesty."

"Oh, Hugo," she said, laughing softly.

She lay down, and he went down on his knees to draw off her stockings, one at a time. He kissed the insides of her thighs, her knees, her calves, her ankles, the arch of her feet as he went. And then, of course, he wanted to release himself and take her then and there. He was ready. She was ready. But he had promised himself that it would be flesh to flesh this time.

He knelt back on his heels and pulled off his coat.

"Do you want me to help?" she asked.

"Another time," he said. "Not now."

She watched him, just as she had watched at the beach when he peeled off his wet drawers.

"I am a great big brute, I am afraid," he said when he was naked. "I wish I could be more elegant for you."

She looked into his eyes as he knelt between her legs again and spread his knees beneath her thighs.

"There cannot be any other man as modest as you, Hugo," she said. "I would not change a thing about your appearance. You are perfectly beautiful."

He laughed softly as he leaned over her, his hands bracing himself on either side of her shoulders, and lowered himself so that he could feel her breasts lightly brushing his chest.

"Even when I scowl?" he said.

"Even then," she said, lifting her hands to cup the sides of his neck. "Your scowl does not deceive me for a moment. Not for a single moment."

He kissed her softly while his loins burned with an urgent heat.

"I wanted *this* to be perfect," he said against her lips. "This first loving tonight. I wanted to play endlessly before taking you to the heights of ecstasy and leaping off into the void with you."

She laughed again.

"I think we can dispense with the play," she said, "and save it for another time."

"Can we?" he asked. "Are you sure?"

She pressed her lips to his and lifted her bosom to press against his chest and twined her legs about his hips, and he forgot that the word *play* even existed. He found her and plunged into her. And if he had feared that she was not fully ready for him, he was soon disabused. She was hot and slick, and her inner muscles clenched about him and invited him deeper.

He withdrew and plunged again and established a rhythm that would bring them to climax within moments. The haste did not matter. This was not about stamina or prowess. And memory came flooding back, *not* a memory that had ever been put into words, but one he had felt at the center of his heart—that Gwendoline was the only woman in his life with whom having sex was subordinate to making love. She was the only woman with whom sex had ever been a shared thing and not just something for his own physical ease and pleasure.

He slowed his rhythm for a moment, raised his head, and gazed down into her eyes. She looked back, her own half closed. She looked almost in pain. Her teeth closed about her bottom lip.

"Gwendoline," he said.

"Hugo."

"My love."

"Yes."

He wondered briefly if either of them would remember the words. Saying nothing and saying everything.

He lowered his forehead to her shoulder and drove them both to the edge of the pinnacle and over it in a glorious descent to nothingness. To everything.

He heard her cry out.

He heard himself cry out.

He heard a puppy squeak and then suckle.

And he sighed aloud against her neck and allowed himself the brief luxury of relaxing all his weight down onto her hot, damp, exquisitely lovely body.

She sighed too, but not in protest. It was a sigh of perfect fulfillment, perfect contentment. He was sure of it.

He moved off her, reached out for the other blanket he had brought this morning—or yesterday morning, he supposed it was—and spread it over them. He lifted her head onto his arm and rested his cheek against the top of her head.

"When I have more energy," he said, "I am going to offer to make an honest woman of you. And when *you* have more energy, you are going to say yes."

"Am I?" she asked. "With a thank you very much, sir?"

"Yes will be sufficient," he said and promptly dozed off.

Chapter 23

"Hugo," she whispered.

He had been sleeping for a while, but he had been making stirring sounds in the last few minutes. She watched the faint light from the lamp flicker across his face.

"Mmm," he said.

"Hugo," she said, "I have remembered something."

"Mmm," he said again and then inhaled loudly. "Me too. I have just this moment remembered, and if you will give me a few moments, I will be ready to create more memories."

"About . . . about the day Vernon died," she said, and his eyes snapped open.

They stared at each other.

"I have always tried hard not to remember those few minutes," she said. "But of course I *have* remembered. Nothing can ever erase the images."

He spread his hand over the side of her face and kissed her.

"I know," he said. "I know."

"And something has always fluttered at me," she said. "Something that did not somehow *fit*. I have never tried too hard to discover what it was because I did not want to remember at all. I still do not. I still wish I could forget altogether."

"You have remembered what did not fit?" he said.

"It happened last evening," she said, "when your neighbors were all trying to persuade you to waltz and everyone was laughing and you held up your hands so that you could give an answer."

His thumb stroked her cheek.

"You held up your hands with your palms out," she said. "It is what people do, is it not, when they want to say something or stop something."

He did not say anything.

"When I—" she began and swallowed convulsively. "When I turned as Vernon fell from the gallery, Jason was turned to him already, and he was holding his hands up above his head to stop him. It was a futile gesture, of course, but an understandable one under the circumstances. Except that—"

She frowned, even now trying to bring the remembered image into focus. But she *was* right.

"His palms were turned inward?" he said. "Beckoning rather than stopping? *Taunting?*"

"Perhaps I have misremembered," she said. Though she knew she had not.

"No," he said. "Memories like that are indelible even if the mind will not admit them for seven years or more."

"He would not have been able to do that," she said, "if I had not turned my back, if I had gone up to Vernon instead of to the library."

"Gwendoline," he said, "if nothing had happened, how long would you have remained in the library?"

She thought about it.

"Not long," she said. "No longer than five minutes. Probably less. He needed me. He had just overheard something very upsetting. I would have understood that as soon as I stepped into the room. I would have drawn a few deep breaths, as I had done on other occasions, and gone to him."

"He took the loss of your child badly?" he asked.

"He blamed himself," she said.

"And he needed comforting," he said. "Did he give *you* comfort?"

"He was *ill,*" she said.

"Yes," he agreed, "he was. And if you had both lived for another fifty years, he would have continued ill and you would have continued to love him and to comfort him."

"I promised for better or worse, in sickness or in health," she said. "But I let him down in the end."

"No," he said. "You were not his jailer, Gwendoline. You could not be standing watch over him for twenty-four hours out of every day. And sick or not, he was not without his wits, was he? You had lost a child as much as he had. More. But he took the burden of guilt upon himself and in the process robbed you of the comfort you so desperately needed. Even in the depths of his despair, he ought to have known that he was placing an unbearable burden upon you and doing nothing to fulfill what *he* had promised *you*. Illness, unless it is total madness, is not an excuse for great selfishness. You needed love as much as he did. He fell. No one pushed him. He was beckoned and taunted. But he was the one who fell—deliberately, it would seem. I understand why you blame yourself. I better than anyone, perhaps, can understand that. But I absolutely absolve you of all blame. Let it go, my love. Grayson cannot really be accused of murder, can he, even though his intent was doubtless murderous. Leave him to his conscience, though I doubt he has one. Leave him to his nastiness. And let yourself be loved. Let *me* love you."

"He was with us when I fell," she said, "when my horse did not clear the hedge. He had never missed a jump before and it was not the highest fence he had jumped. Jason was with us. He was behind me, crowding me, trying to encourage my horse to clear the jump, I have always thought. He could not have . . . Could he?"

She heard him inhale slowly.

"Is it possible," she said, "that I did not kill my own child? Or is it wishful thinking because I have realized that he wanted Vernon out of the way? Even dead? Did he want our child dead too? Did he want *me* dead?"

"Ah, Gwendoline," he said. "Ah, my love."

She closed her eyes, but she could not stop the hot, scalding tears from spilling over onto her cheeks and diagonally across them to drip onto the blanket and pool at the side of her nose.

He gathered her into his arms, spread one great hand behind her head, and kissed her wet cheeks, her eyelids, her temples, her wet lips.

"Hush," he crooned. "Hush now. Let it all go. Let me love you. You have love all wrong, Gwendoline. It is not all give, give, give. It is taking as well. It is allowing the other one the pleasure and joy of giving. Let me love you."

She thought her heart would surely break. All her life, it seemed, or since her marriage, anyway, she had held herself together, tried always to be cheerful, tried not to be negative or bitter. She had tried to love, and she had accepted love in return provided it was the quiet, steady love of her mother or her brother or Lauren or Lily or the rest of her family.

But . . .

"It would be like jumping off the edge of the world," she said.

"Yes," he said. "I'll be there to catch you."

"Will you?" she said.

"And you can catch me when I jump," he told her.

"You will squash me," she said.

And they were both laughing, hugged together in each other's arms, both damp from her tears.

"Gwendoline," he said when they were finally quiet again, "will you marry me?"

She held him, her eyes closed, and inhaled the mingled smells of cologne and sweat and maleness. And the indefinable something wonderful that was Hugo himself.

"Do you think I can have children?" she said. "Do you think I deserve another chance? What if I cannot?"

He clucked his tongue.

"No one ever knows for sure," he said. "We will find out as time goes on. And yes, you deserve to have children of your own body. As for me, don't worry. I would a thousand times rather marry you and have no children than marry any other woman in the world and have a dozen. In fact, I don't think I *will* marry anyone else if you will not have me. I'll have to start going to brothels."

They were snorting with laughter again then.

"Well, in *that* case," she said.

"Yes?" He drew back his head and gazed at her in the lamplight.

"I'll marry you," she said, sobering. "Oh, Hugo, I don't care *how* many different worlds we have to cross in order to find our own little world within. I don't care. I will do what has to be done."

"Me too," he said.

And they smiled at each other until they *both* had tears in their eyes.

He sat up and rummaged around in the heap of his clothing until he found his watch. He held it up to the light of the lamp.

"Half past two," he said. "We had better be out of here by half past five. Three hours. What can we do in three hours? Any suggestions?"

He turned to look down at her.

She opened her arms to him.

"Ah, yes," he said. "An excellent suggestion. And three hours gives plenty of time for play as well as feasting."

"Hugo," she said as his arms closed about her again and he lay down on his back, bringing her over on top of him. "Oh, Hugo, I love you, I love you."

"Mmm," he said against her lips.

Hugo made the announcement at a late breakfast, which everyone attended. He ought perhaps to have spoken with Gwendoline's brother first, but he had already done that once upon a time. And perhaps the announcement ought to have been made to her family first, but . . . why? Her family would be informed as soon as they returned to London.

"Ah," Constance said, looking about the table and sounding wistful, "all the excitement is over, and tomorrow we will be returning to London."

"But every moment of our stay has been *wonderful,* Constance," Fiona said, her voice warm and animated in a way Hugo had never heard before this week. "And there is still today to enjoy."

"And the excitement is not *all* over," Hugo said from the head of the table. "At least, for *me* it is not. And for *Gwendoline* it is not. For we are newly betrothed and intend to spend the day enjoying our new status."

She had told him last night that he might make the announcement today if he wished. She smiled now and bit her lip as the room filled with the sounds of exclamations and squeals and applause and everyone clambering to speak at once and chairs scraping back across the floor. Hugo found his hand being pumped, his back being slapped, his cheeks being kissed. Gwendoline, he saw, was being hugged and kissed too.

He wondered if her family members would react with such unbridled enthusiasm, and it occurred to him that quite possibly they would.

"You owe me ten guineas, I believe, Mark," Cousin Claude called across the table. "I *did* say by the end of the week. And there *were* witnesses."

"You could not have waited another day or two, Hugo?" Mark asked.

"And *when* are the nuptials to be?" Aunt Henrietta asked. "And *where*?"

"In London," Hugo said. "Probably at St. George's on Hanover Square. As soon as the banns have been read. We want to be married and back here for the summer."

They had discussed other possibilities—Newbury Abbey, Crosslands Park, even Penderris Hall—but they wanted both families to attend, and any place outside London seemed impractical, partly because of the number of people who must be accommodated, and partly because his own family members had already just taken a holiday of several days. Besides, the Season would still be in full swing and Parliament still in session. They really did not want to wait until summer.

"St. George's," Aunt Rose said. "Grand! I hope we are all invited."

"We could not possibly hold our nuptials," Gwendoline said rashly, "if you are not *all* there, as well as all *my* family."

"But I have nothing to *wear*," Constance said and laughed merrily. "Oh, I am so happy I could burst."

"Not all over the food, please, Con," Cousin Claude said.

Hugo was tired. He had slept for perhaps an hour after the second, vigorous lovemaking, but he had used up all his renewed energy on a third bout, which had finished perilously close to half past five, the time by which he had decided they must leave the stables. It would have been a ghastly embarrassment to be discovered there by a groom.

Gwendoline had gone to bed when they returned to the house. He had not. He had been too excited—like a schoolboy.

He was tired now, but pleasantly so. His body was sated and relaxed, his mind centered upon happiness. And he would *not* allow entry to any mental warnings about happiness being a precariously temporary state or about romance being even flimsier. He was not just in love with his betrothed. He *loved* her. And he had no illusions about happily-ever-after. He knew that happiness was something that had to be worked for as hard and as diligently as he had worked as a boy at following in his father's footsteps and later at being the best military officer in the British armies.

He was not afraid of failure.

Fiona strolled outdoors with him for a while after breakfast, linking her arm through his. It was a cool, cloudy late morning.

"This is all *so* beautiful, Hugo," she said. "All the time we have been here, people have been telling you what they think you ought to do to develop the park, and you have said yourself that you will be making some changes. Don't make too many. Sometimes nature just *is*."

He looked down at her and was surprised at how much affection he felt for her, this woman whom his father had loved and with whom he had sired a daughter—Constance.

"I am not going to change it a great deal," he said. "I am not going to make a grand, gaudy showpiece of it. Constance and I went to a garden party in Richmond a short while ago, you may recall. The garden was quite breathtaking in its magnificence. But I would not exchange my park here for it for any consideration in the world."

"Good." She walked silently beside him for a while. "Hugo, I know what I did. I know I drove you away to a life for which you were in no way suited despite the fact that you distinguished yourself so brilliantly. If you had died, I—"

He set a hand over hers on his arm.

"Fiona," he said, "no one *drove* me to anything. I *chose* to go. And if I had not done so, you know, I would be a different man today. Perhaps better, perhaps worse, perhaps much the same. However it is, I would not wish to be different. I would not wish to be without the experiences that have brought me to where I am at this moment. If I had not gone, I would never have met Gwendoline. And I did *not* die, did I?"

"You are generous," she said. "You are saying that you forgive me. Thank you. Perhaps I will eventually forgive myself. Your father was a good man. More than good. He deserved someone better than me."

"He chose *you,*" he said. "He chose you because he loved you."

"I wanted to ask you," she said. "The reason I sought you out this morning was to ask you—"

He bent his head toward her.

"Philip—Mr. Germane," she said, "has asked if he may call on me in London. He wants to show me the botanical gardens at Kew and the pagoda there. He wants to take me to the theater because I have not been there in years, and to Vauxhall Gardens because I have *never* been there. Would it . . . *anger* you, Hugo? Would it be disrespectful to your father? Would it be distasteful to you since he is your late mother's brother?"

Hugo had watched the partiality Fiona and Philip had shown for each other all week. He had watched with a certain pleasure.

Philip had married years ago as a very young man, just before Hugo went off to war, but his wife had died in childbed less than a year later. He had remained single since then. And Fiona, despite her recent depression and ill health and selfish clinging to Constance, had suddenly bloomed into a greater maturity. She had borne a heavy burden of unhappiness and guilt, but she appeared to be making a great effort to pull her life back together.

Who knew if a match between the two of them—if it came to that—would bring them lasting happiness? It was a question that was not Hugo's to answer. But he *could* wish them well.

He patted her hand.

"Make sure he takes you to Vauxhall on a night when there are fireworks," he said. "I have heard that those are the best nights."

She sighed deeply.

"I am very happy for you, Hugo," she said. "When Lady Muir first came to the house to take Constance shopping for clothes, I was all prepared to hate her. But I could not quite do it even then. And this week I have seen how completely unaffected her manners are and how she does not condescend to anyone but seems genuinely to enjoy everyone's company—even *Mama's*. And I have seen how much she loves you. You looked so gorgeous together when you were waltzing last evening, despite her limp. Your announcement at breakfast was not *really* a surprise to anyone, you know."

He chuckled, remembering how he had steeled himself up to it.

The first few drops of rain drove them back indoors.

He looked in at the billiards room a short while later and watched a game in progress. When he left, Ned Tucker followed him.

"Are you busy?" he asked. "May I have a word?"

Hugo took him into the library, reminding himself as he did so that he was going to have to find somewhere to donate most of the ghastly blocks of books. Their absence would leave the shelves half empty, but he would rather that than what he faced now every time he walked into the room. He would replace them gradually with books of his own choosing and Gwendoline's. Perhaps she would have some suggestions about what to do with the bare shelves in the meanwhile.

"It was bad of me," Tucker said, "to accept your invitation to come here when you offered only because I was there when you invited Miss Emes's family, and Mrs. Rowlands happened to say that I was like a son to her. You really didn't have a choice, did you? But I ought to have said no. I said yes because I wanted to come, and I have enjoyed myself and thank you."

"I have been more than happy to have you," Hugo said, pouring them each a drink from the decanter on the corner of the desk and indicating two chairs over by the window.

It was still raining, he could see, though it was drizzle rather than out-and-out rain. The roads should not be too badly affected for tomorrow's journey.

"Your sister is enjoying the spring immensely," Tucker said, gazing down into his glass as he slowly swirled his port. "She has been mourning her father for the past year, and before that she was just a girl."

Hugo waited.

"She has been mingling more with her cousins on her father's side and their friends," Tucker said. "With her own kind. And she has been mingling with the *ton* and going walking and riding with a number of gentlemen. I am sure they are all worthy of her, or either you or Lady Muir or both would put a stop to the association. She is too young and too—*new* to life to make any choices yet. Not that that stops a lot of people. But she is unusually sensible for her age, or so it seems to me. And then there is—"

He stopped to take a drink from his glass, his movements a little jerky.

"You?" Hugo suggested.

"I am who I am," Tucker said. "I can read and write and compute. I own my own small house and shop. The shop brings in a steady income though it will never make my fortune. But people will always need hardware. I daresay I will keep the shop all my life and hand it on to my son when I die, just as my father did to me. I dabble in a few things out the back, mostly carpentry and some metalwork. I have made a few dollhouses and kennels and sold them for a nice little profit. I wouldn't mind trying something a bit bigger. A shed, perhaps, though I do like to be able to use some imagination."

"A summerhouse?" Hugo suggested. "A garden pavilion?"

Tucker considered.

"That would be grand," he said, "though I don't know anyone who needs anything like that."

"You are looking at such a person," Hugo said.

Tucker stared at him and then grinned.

"Really?" he said.

"Really," Hugo said. "We'll talk about it sometime."

"Right," Tucker said and returned his attention to the hardly depleted contents of his glass.

"I am not asking for her hand," he said. "Nothing like that. I am not even asking for permission to court her. I don't think she is ready for courtship from *anyone*. What I *am* asking . . ." He paused and drew a deep breath. "If the time should come when she *is* ready, and *if* she seems inclined to like me, knowing full well that she could do oceans better either with her own people or with the upper classes, *would* it be better if I pretended not to be interested, even perhaps if I pretended that there was someone else?"

This was a tricky one.

Or perhaps not so very tricky after all.

"Do you love her?" Hugo asked.

Tucker met his eyes.

"Something dreadful," he said.

"Then I'll trust you to do what is right," Hugo said. "And I'll trust Constance. I already do. The decision must be yours and hers. And her mother's too if the time should come. I wouldn't pretend anything, though, if I were you. It is best to be honest and trust her to make a wise decision."

"Thank you," Tucker said, and he lifted his glass and drained off the port within it. "*Thank you.* Now, *where* did you want that summerhouse to go? And how big were you thinking?"

Hugo glanced at the window. It looked as if the rain had stopped for the moment, though the clouds still hung low.

"Come," he said. "I'll show you. Better yet, I'll go look for Gwendoline and have her come too to show you. Perhaps Constance will want to come with us."

Actually, he could not *wait* to see Gwendoline again, to have an excuse to spend time with her. It was just that as the host of a house party, even if it was only a party of his family members, he felt obliged to spend time with everyone *but* his newly betrothed.

Sometimes life was a foolish business.

And sometimes it was more wonderful than he could ever have dreamed.

Chapter 24

It was raining on the morning of their wedding day. Quite heavily.

Hugo, who did not believe in omens, nevertheless thought that sunshine, or at least fine weather, would have been more convenient for all concerned when there was a wedding to attend. But when the sun *did* come out just as he was leaving the house and the roads and pavements began almost instantly to dry, he thought that perhaps he *did* believe in omens just a little bit after all.

He had asked Flavian to be his best man, hoping as he did so that he was not about to offend at least half a dozen cousins. But Flavian still felt almost as close to him as his own heart. And he had accepted after only a long enough delay to raise his eyebrows and sigh deeply and deliver himself of a short, languid speech.

"Hugo, my dear old chap," he said, "the world would take one look at you and conclude that you must be the very last man on earth to succumb to something as flimsy as romantic love. But any one of the Survivors would have been able to tell the world long ago that if anyone was likely to fall, it was going to be you. And this despite all your very sensible talk earlier in the year about finding a suitable mate. Yes, yes, I will be your best man. And I would wager that you will still be gazing at your bride with the eyes of romance when she is eighty and you are a few years older. And she will be gazing back at you in the same way. You are enough *almost* to restore one's shattered faith in happy endings."

"A simple yes would have sufficed, Flave," Hugo told him.

"Quite so," Flavian agreed.

All of Hugo's family members were to attend the wedding, of course. So were George and Ralph. Imogen had surprised Hugo by accepting his invitation. She would come to London for a few days and stay with George, she had said in her letter. Ben was in the north of England, visiting his sister. Vincent was not at home, and his family did not know where he had gone. But he had taken his clothes and his valet with him, and the man had always proved quite capable of caring for all his needs. No one was worried—yet.

Gwendoline's family had all been invited too as well as a few friends. But it was not to be a typical *ton* wedding of the Season. The church would not be overflowing with the crème-de-la-crème of English society. Large though the guest list inevitably was, they had both wanted an intimate atmosphere with only those closest to them to witness the occasion.

"I think," Hugo said when he arrived at the church and was met by a small crowd of the curious that would inevitably grow larger within the next hour, "I would rather be facing another Forlorn Hope."

"If you had just eaten some breakfast, as I advised," Flavian said, "you would be feeling vastly better, old chap."

"An opinion delivered from the voice of experience?" Hugo asked.

"Not at all," Flavian said. "I never reached the altar or even came within sight of it."

Hugo winced. That had been insensitive of him.

"For which blessing I will be eternally thankful," Flavian said. "It would be a touch deflating, do you not think, to discover *after* one's marriage that when one's bride had said that she would love one for better or for worse, what she had really meant was that she might love one for better but would run like hell if ever confronted with the worse?"

Yes, Hugo thought, it would. And he remembered that when Gwendoline had said those words to her first husband, she had meant them. He reached out and squeezed his friend's arm as they made their way inside the church.

"Do not, I beg you, Hugo," Flavian said with a shudder, "turn sentimental on me. I am beginning to wonder if I would not prefer a Forlorn Hope myself to being best man to a romantic soul."

Hugo chuckled.

By the time his bride arrived sometime later, but not a minute late, he was feeling far more relaxed. And excited. And eager to begin his new life. To live happily ever after. Oh, yes, though he did not believe in it, he sometimes forgot to be skeptical. And surely he could be excused on his wedding day.

She had arrived. The organ had begun to play, and the clergyman had taken his place. Hugo could not decide whether he should stand rigidly facing the altar, or whether he should turn and watch her approach. He had forgotten to ask what was the right thing to do.

He compromised. He turned and stood rigidly watching her come, on the arm of her brother. She was wearing rich rose pink and looked . . . Well, sometimes English was a total, miserable failure of a language. Her eyes were on his, and he could see that behind the light veil that covered her face she was smiling.

He did a mental check of his own expression. His teeth were tightly clamped together. That meant his jaw was hard. His eyebrows were tense. He could almost feel the frown line between them. His hands were clasped at his back. Good Lord, he must look as if he were on parade. Or attending someone's funeral. Why? Was he afraid to smile?

He *was,* he realized. He would not be able to keep all that was within him in place if he smiled. He would feel damned vulnerable, to tell the truth. Vulnerable to what, though? To love?

He had already vaulted off the end of the earth and been caught safely in the arms of love.

What else was there to fear?

That after all she would not come?

She was *here*.

That she would not say *I do* or *I will* or whatever the devil it was supposed to be when the time came?

She would.

That he would not be able to love her forever and ever?

He would, and even longer than that.

He let his hands fall to his sides.

And he smiled as his bride approached him.

Did he imagine a collective sort of sigh from the congregation gathered there?

How strange a thing life was, Gwen thought. If she had not read that letter of her mother's aloud to Vera that day in early March and Vera had not lashed out at her, if she had not gone walking along that rocky beach and stopped to stare out at the distant sea, she might not even have realized how deeply lonely she was. She might have denied reality for a lot longer.

And if she had not climbed that steep slope and sprained her ankle, she would not have met Hugo.

She had never believed in fate. She still did not. It would make nonsense of freedom of will and choice, and it was through such freedom that we worked our way through life and learned what we needed to learn. But sometimes, it seemed to her, there was *something,* some sign, to nudge one along in a certain direction. What one chose to do with that nudge was up to that person.

Her accident, Hugo's presence nearby, both coming so soon after her realization that she was lonely were surely more than just coincidence. And perhaps it really was right that there is no such thing as coincidence.

The chances against her meeting Hugo and knowing him long enough to penetrate his dour military façade until she loved him were massive. But it had happened.

She loved him more than she had known it possible to love.

Her family all approved the match, with the possible exception of Wilma, who unusually offered no opinion at all. They all seemed to understand that what she felt for Hugo was extraordinary, that if she was prepared to love and marry a man so seemingly wrong for her, then he must actually be *right* for her. And of course they were all relieved that at last she had come out of the cocoon in which she had safely resided since Vernon's death and was ready to live again.

Her mother had shed tears over her.

So had Lauren.

Lily had whisked her off to buy bride clothes.

And now it was happening. At last. A month for the banns to be read could sometimes seem more like a year. But the wait was over, and she was inside St. George's on Hanover Square, and she knew that all her family and his were gathered there, though she did not really look to see. She clung to Neville's arm and saw only Hugo.

He was looking very much as he had looked on that slope above the beach, except that then he had been wearing a greatcoat and now he was dressed smartly for a wedding.

He was scowling at her.

She smiled.

And then wonderfully, incredibly, despite the fact that he was on full view with a churchful of people to see, he smiled back at her—a warm smile that lit up his face and made him incredibly handsome.

A murmur throughout the church suggested that everyone else had noticed too.

She took her place beside him, the organ stopped playing, and the wedding service began.

It was as if time slowed. She listened to every word, heard every response, including her own, felt the smooth coldness of the gold as her ring slid onto the finger, sticking for just a moment at her knuckle before he eased it over.

And then, far too soon, but, oh, *at last,* the nuptial service was over and they were man and wife and no man was to put them asunder. He squeezed her hand and smiled at her, looking almost like a little boy brimming over with excitement, and raised her veil and arranged it over the brim of her bonnet.

She gazed back at him.

Her husband.

Her husband.

And then the rest of the service proceeded and the register was signed and they were leaving the church, smiling now to either side of them to make eye contact with as many of their relatives and friends as they could. Her arm was drawn through his and their hands were clasped tightly.

Sunshine greeted them beyond the doors of the church.

And a hearty cheer from the small crowd gathered outside.

Hugo looked down at her.

"Well, wife," he said.

"Well, husband."

"Does it sound good?" he asked her. "Or does it sound great?"

"Umm," she said. "Great, I think."

"Me too, Lady Trentham," he said. "Shall we make a bolt for the carriage before everyone spills out of church behind us?"

"We are too late, I believe," she said.

And sure enough, the open barouche that was to take them back to Kilbourne House for the wedding breakfast was festooned with ribbons and bows and old boots and even an iron kettle. And there were Kit and Joseph and Mark Emes and the Earl of Berwick lying in wait with fistfuls of flower petals that they pelted as Hugo and Gwen made a run for the carriage, laughing.

"I hope," Hugo said as he gave the coachman the signal to start and the barouche lurched into well-sprung motion and rattled out of the square, "no one is intending to use that kettle ever again."

"Everyone will hear us coming from five miles away," Gwen said.

"There are two things we can do, love," Hugo said. "We can cower down on the floor of the vehicle—and that alternative actually has much to be said in its favor. Or we can brazen it out and help take people's minds off the din."

"How?" she asked, laughing.

"Like this," he said, turning to her, cupping her chin in his great hand, and lowering his head to kiss her—openmouthed.

Somewhere someone was cheering. Someone else whistled piercingly enough to be heard above the din of the kettle.

The second alternative, if you please, Gwen would have said if she had had her mouth to herself.

But she did not.

If you enjoy Mary Balogh's sumptuous historical romance novels, you'll love these titles, also published by Piatkus . . .

THE APOTHECARY'S DAUGHTER

Charlotte Betts

1665. Susannah Leyton has grown up behind the counter of her father's apothecary shop in bustling Fleet Street. A skilled student – the resinous scents of lavender, rosemary, liquorice and turpentine run in her blood – her father has granted her the freedom to pursue her considerable talents. But Susannah is dealt a shocking blow when her widowed father marries again, and her new step-mother seems determined to remove her from the apothecary shop for good.

A proposal of marriage from the charming Henry Savage seems to offer Susannah an escape. But as the plague sweeps through London, tragedy strikes, and dark secrets in her husband's past begin to unfold. It will take all of Susannah's courage and passion to save herself from tragedy . . .

978-0-7499-5449-9

MY RUTHLESS PRINCE

Gaelen Foley

To London's aristocracy, the Inferno Club is a scandalous society of men no proper young lady would acknowledge. In private, they are warriors who would do anything to protect their king and country.

In the ultimate battle of good versus evil, the Order's shadow war against the Prometheans reaches a crescendo; Drake Parry, Earl of Westwood, plays out a deadly masquerade to bring down the conspirators' dark cult from the inside. But can the love of an innocent beauty save the tortured agent's soul, or will he be swallowed up by the darkness he came to destroy?

978-0-7499-5741-4

piatkus